THE
SOLDIER'S
RETURN

Also by Alan Monaghan

The Soldier's Song

THE SOLDIER'S RETURN

Alan Monaghan

MACMILLAN

First published 2011 by Macmillan
an imprint of Pan Macmillan, a division of Macmillan Publishers Limited
Pan Macmillan, 20 New Wharf Road, London N1 9RR
Basingstoke and Oxford
Associated companies throughout the world
www.panmacmillan.com

ISBN 978-0-230-74089-1

1 3 5 7 9 8 6 4 2

A CIP catalogue record for this book is available
from the British Library.

Typeset by Ellipsis Books Limited, Glasgow
Printed in the UK by CPI Mackays, Chatham ME5 8TD

Visit **www.panmacmillan.com** to read more about all our books
and to buy them. You will also find features, author interviews and
news of any author events, and you can sign up for e-newsletters
so that you're always first to hear about our new releases.

Part One

Mud

I

He was drowning in the dark. No light, no air, but he could *feel* everything. He could feel the sapping cold of the mud and the slimy wetness against his skin. He could feel it seeping into him, pushing into his nose and mouth, his eyes and ears. He could feel the sullen grip on his arms and legs, and he could feel it growing stronger with every feeble kick and breathless lunge. He could feel himself sinking.

Then he could feel the hands. One gripped his arm and he flinched at the icy touch. Another caught him by the leg, twisting hard and hurting him. He opened his mouth to scream but the mud filled his throat, foul and cold and tasting of sulphur and corruption. More hands fastened onto him. He could see them now; fingers white and writhing like worms, like blind, probing roots sprouting out of the mud. Hundreds of them, thousands, pinching and pulling and wrapping around him, tighter and tighter, until he could feel the life squeezing out of him.

Then he felt another touch, and the dream was shattered. A warm hand had him by the shoulder, shaking him.

'Captain, captain.'

He woke with a gasp. His eyes opened on a grey gloom; a few feet of grimy floorboards, a rickety wardrobe with one door

3

hanging open, and a pot-bellied stove standing cold and black in the corner.

'Captain Ryan, sir.' The shaking continued.

'I'm awake, corporal,' he muttered. But when Carroll took his hand away he didn't move. He felt pinned to the bed. His heart was thumping and his skin was still tingling from the cold slime and the touch of dead fingers. He tried to pull the coarse blanket tighter around himself but he could get little warmth from it. Even though the horror of the dream was fading, the dank reality of the hut wasn't much better. It was so cold he could see his breath misting on the air, and the mattress under him felt damp and lumpy. Then there was the smell – the sharp reek of urine from the chamber pot mingling with the musty odour of cold ash and soot from the stove. It was such an appallingly miserable place that he could feel it sapping his spirit already. Another dreary morning in his dreary hut – dreary, dreary, dreary. He decided he couldn't face it, and closed his eyes again.

'It's seven o'clock, sir,' Carroll told him in a tone that was almost peremptory. 'Time to get up.'

'In a minute, corporal,' he murmured, though the best he could manage was to open his eyes again. He listened to the thump and drag of Carroll's heavy boots as he moved around behind him: first to the window, where the swish of the curtain let in a weak watery light that barely lightened the gloom. Then a quick rustling of papers on the desk, before he shuffled into view, heading for the wonky wardrobe and the cold stove. Lulled by the sound of the familiar routine, Stephen felt his eyelids beginning to droop. He was sinking deeper into the meagre warmth of the blanket when a sudden pain stabbed through his left knee and jolted him awake again. He waited, holding his breath. It was only a twinge, but that was how it always started. Another stab, and he gasped as it finally got its teeth into him. A low, throbbing pain that

4

grew louder, sharper, more excruciating with every beat. It was coming, and he could feel the muscles in his jaw tightening, his spine curving and his hands clenching in fists as he slowly straightened his knee, trying to find that magic spot where the pain would ebb away. But it was never that easy. He knew it well enough by now, and when it hit him like this there was only one thing it wanted – only one thing that would keep it quiet.

But suddenly it was gone. It was as if something had clicked into place and his taut muscles sagged with relief. He let out a long breath and slowly pulled back the blanket so he could look down at his leg. His left knee was tightly wrapped in a clean white bandage, with the livid red tail of a scar snaking under it. The muscle in his calf was twitching, as it often did when the pain started, but otherwise his leg looked completely normal. The wound had been clean, as these things go – a shell splinter in Belgium, four months before – and even though it had been deep, cutting muscle and tendon right to the bone, there had been no infection, no complications except this lingering pain. But the pain was bad. Sometimes it was bad enough to make him wish they'd taken his leg off. It was fading now, but he knew the relief was only temporary. It would be back, grinding at him relentlessly, and the only thing that would save him was the Needle. But Carroll was still there, shuffling towards the stove and hitching up his trousers with one hand. He would have to wait until he was gone. Stephen sat up and tried to cover himself with the blanket again, pulling it all the way up to his chin. But all the warmth was gone out of it and the frigid air felt cold and clammy against his skin.

'The bloody stove's gone out again,' he muttered peevishly.

'Yes, sir, so it has.' Carroll clanked open the top of the stove and peered inside, prodding at the cold ashes with a poker. The sudden clamour set Stephen's teeth on edge and seemed to catch on some damaged nerve in his leg. A sudden jolt of pain made him gasp.

'Leave it, leave it,' he said through gritted teeth. He knew damn well that Carroll had no intention of actually lighting the bloody thing.

'Very good, sir.' Carroll closed the lid with a final clang and shuffled back towards the desk. He was probably the most unmilitary-looking creature Stephen had ever seen. Old, bent, and with a creased and timid face, he seemed incapable of lifting his feet, never mind marching, but he was good at his job. Even though the sun wasn't up yet, there was a mug of tea on the locker and a basin of hot water on the desk, a towel beside it and a stropped razor lying open on top. Stephen's tunic hung on the back of the chair, pressed, brushed and brass buttons gleaming, and his boots glowed deep amber in the meagre light from the window. All these things had been accomplished silently and in the dark, while Stephen had been dreaming of . . . what had he been dreaming of? He had only the impression of it left – nothing but fragments. Hands, fingers, darkness. Suffocating darkness. Nothing else? Nothing more . . . substantial? He looked to the desk beside the door, to the stack of papers that Carroll had tidied up. He'd been at it until the small hours – scribbling and scratching and balling up, until eventually he'd crawled into bed in the hope that sleep would bring a revelation, a breakthrough – something floating up from the depths of his unconscious mind. It had happened before, but not last night. Last night, all he'd got was darkness, suffocation, and death.

Carroll was hovering near the door, watching him as he picked up the mug of tea from the locker and wrapped his hands around it.

'Will there be anything else, sir?'

'No. Thank you, Carroll. That will be all.'

Carroll's gaze wandered across the desk and lingered on the papers beside the basin. He was incurably nosy, and Stephen sometimes wondered what on earth he made of all those complex formulae and Greek letters and Latin phrases jumbled in – not to mention the very German names that were sprinkled through them – names like Leibniz, Euler and Goldbach.

'Will you have anything for the post, sir?'

Stephen yawned and rubbed his forearm across his eyes. He was certain now – last night's dream had all but evaporated from his memory, but it had left nothing behind. Nothing. Another dead end.

'No thank you, Carroll.' He shook his head tiredly. 'Not today, I'm afraid. Perhaps later on.'

'Very good, sir. I'll leave you alone, so.'

Carroll's leaving let in a blast of freezing air that sent Stephen ducking under the blanket, but he didn't wait very long before he threw it off again. His calf was still twitching, but he could hardly feel it. When it was quiet it felt dead, numb, and he had the queer feeling that he was looking at spasms and jerks in somebody else's leg. But the pain was something else. When it came it would be all his, and it would be all through him – as if every nerve, every fibre in his body was connected back to that one hot point hidden under the bandages. And it would come – it always came. He knew it was there, lurking inside him, waiting to pounce.

But for now he could enjoy the peace. He sat quietly for a few moments, sipping the scalding tea and trying to muster the energy to get out of bed. Once again he was struck by the feeling that he was seeing himself as another person; a stranger, a sickly figure slumped crookedly in the bed, barely able to move. What was wrong with him? When he was at the front he'd lived on a few hours sleep, more often than not in a damp dugout that was running with rats and lice, and more often than not interrupted by shellfire or some other alarm. Compared to *that* this was a cushy billet, and yet he couldn't get used to it. He always slept badly now, and usually woke up feeling worse than when he'd gone to bed – hollowed out, half dead. The food here was no worse than the front, and the weather was milder, and yet he felt . . . what was it he felt? Malaise? Was that the word? He felt lethargic and ill and everything around him seemed wrong, faded, broken – all colour and life leeched out of it. Even the tea tasted sour, and when he ran his tongue across the roof of his mouth he found it sticky and foul. There was still that taste – a rancid dryness that had been building up all night. But he knew what would help.

He put down the mug on top of the locker and pulled open the drawer. There was barely a finger's width of liquid left in the brown bottle, but it would be enough to get him through the week. He would be going up to Dublin on Friday and he would have to go and see Figgis about a refill. He didn't relish the thought. *A bit of what you fancy*, was what Figgis would say – and he'd leer at him with his yellow teeth and his little piggy eyes. Still, it would be worth it, for a full bottle. For the heft of it, the security, the comfort.

He dropped the bottle on the bed and pulled out the box. It looked like a jewellery box, but what lay inside was a long cylinder of glass and steel – more like a tool or a weapon. But to him it was the Needle, his only friend – the bringer of comfort and peace. With a practised ease he filled it from the bottle and held it up to the light. Two swift taps of the fingernail and he squirted a few precious drops up into the cold air. Then he turned his leg so he could see the white inner flesh, already dimpled with dozens of little purple marks. But he stopped for a moment. This was the sticking point. For all it promised, he had a horror of the

Needle – the cold stab of it piercing his skin. There was something unnatural about it, something invasive. But as he hesitated the knee gave him an angry twinge and he steeled himself to it. *Hurry up.* He pressed the needle to his skin and felt it sliding all the way into the muscle. A gentle push and he rolled his eyes to the ceiling, letting out all his breath in one long easy sigh. Relief was at hand. Blessed relief.

The Needle enabled him to dress himself. It allowed him to bend his leg enough to pull on his britches and then fasten his boots before he finally stood up and hobbled over to the desk to wash and shave. Shirt and tie and tunic were easy enough, and then there was only his cap and walking stick, which he leaned on as he opened the door of his hut and looked out across the camp.

The sky had lightened about as much as it ever would in November, but still it was dismal. There wasn't much to the place – just a few huts clustered around a flagpole and the concrete hump of the armoury standing a little further away. The firing range was further up the valley, and that was where he would spend his day – limping up and down behind lines of eager recruits fumbling with their first rifles and squirming under the lashing tongues of musketry instructors. The instructors were permanent, but the recruits only temporary. They would arrive soon in lorries, jumping down into the mud and grinning at each other, thinking it was just like going to war. Then the instructors would be on them, and they'd realize that it was just like any other day, except that there was live ammunition, and consequently the risk of death, injury or an almighty bollocking if they didn't do *exactly* as they were told. Still, if they learned anything today it would be that it wasn't as easy as they'd thought. They'd each fire a hundred rounds and miss with most of them, and when they went back to their barracks this evening they would wonder what would happen if they really were at war. What would happen if that was a German soldier charging at them, and they couldn't even put a hole in a bit of paper?

Stephen eased himself out of his hut and onto the little slab of stone that was his doorstep. Beyond that there was mud, ankle deep and churned up fresh every day by the turning lorries, and he looked down uncertainly. The mess was in a hut on the far side of the camp, and he doubted it would be worth the effort. Watery tea and a limp bacon sandwich were all he'd find there, and he wasn't even hungry. He was never hungry after the Needle – though Figgis had warned him about that. It was one of the side effects of the morphine.

He stood on the step and wavered. Go across or go back in? Why was everything so bloody difficult? At the front, he wouldn't have thought twice about it. Straight across and eat whatever they put in front of you – and see if you can scrounge something for later, while you're at it. But then, he wasn't at the front. He was at home, and he couldn't get the front out of his bloody head. What were they doing now, those men he had left behind? They would have rebuilt the battalion, and they were probably back in the line by now. That meant they would already have had the morning stand-to and now they would be changing sentries and relaxing a bit. Another night safely past and the tension easing as breakfast was dished out. Maybe later they would . . . He sighed and stopped himself. He was daydreaming again. All the time he was over there he'd daydreamed about being at home, and now that he was home . . . Well, he should just count his bloody blessings. Three more days up here and then he would be free – for a while at any rate. Three more days and he would be in Dublin – he would see Lillian again, feel the warmth of her, hear her voice. But three days seemed so long. It was so bloody monotonous up here that every day seemed to last forever. Christ, even the front was better than this. At least he'd felt alive there, even though it was so bloody awful – even though it had damn near cost him a leg. But if that was hell then this was limbo, and it just went on and on and on.

He heard the door of the next hut opening and just managed to straighten up and half turn around with his salute at the ready. The knee protested at this sudden movement with a twinge sharp enough to pierce even the thick veil of the morphine and he winced as he saluted Major Redman.

'Good morning, sir.'

'Morning, Ryan.'

Redman waved a limp hand – all he ever did in the way of saluting – and Stephen dropped his hand and watched the major uncertainly. This was a surprise. Redman was the camp commandant, and therefore Stephen's immediate superior, and yet in six weeks they had not spoken to each other more than half a dozen times. Redman rarely ventured out of his hut – and never at this hour of the morning.

'Not a bad morning, sir,' he ventured, trying to gauge Redman's mood from his expression. No easy task, since Redman had a very red and veiny face, puffy and with heavy bags under his pale eyes. An inscrutable face, in its way, and Stephen sometimes wondered how he had ended up here. Had he been through the fire in France? Or had he simply been put out of the way, quietly labelled as good for nothing else? It was impossible to tell. Redman rocked back on his heels, then forward again. He seemed to be considering Stephen's statement.

'Hmm, not bad,' he agreed at last, and after a considerable pause he added: 'Everything all right, Ryan?'

'Yes, sir, perfectly all right.'

Another pause. Stephen could hear him thoughtfully working his jaws as if he were sucking a toffee.

'General Yorke is coming up on Friday, you know.'

'Really, sir? Well, that's something to look forward to,' Stephen said, although it wasn't anything to look forward to. Yorke was what they called a *dug-out* – an old soldier dug out of retirement when war broke out. Only Yorke was far too old and decrepit to be much use for anything, so he sat in a dusty office all week, and sent himself on day trips whenever he got bored. Officially, he would be carrying out an inspection on Friday, but in reality all he wanted was a whiff of gun smoke, a decent lunch, and somebody to listen to the adventures of a younger, slimmer Yorke in Matabeleland. Since Redman always vanished into his hut after formally welcoming the general, this task would fall to Stephen, and he was beginning to think he knew the stories better than Yorke did.

Redman now seemed on the point of vanishing into his hut again, but something was detaining him.

'Everything in hand, Ryan?'

'Yes, sir, no problems to report.'

'Good, good. Well, carry on.' Redman nodded, and managed to get one foot in the door of his hut before he stopped again. He turned to Stephen with a quizzical look, as if trying to remember something.

'Got your medical board next week, haven't you, Ryan?'

'Yes, sir, Monday morning.'

Redman gave his leg, and the stick, a long and significant look. Then his face cleared, as if whatever he had been trying to remember had suddenly come to him.

'Yes, Monday. Of course. I had a message about it.'

Stephen's heart sank. Monday was the ideal day because it

meant a long weekend in Dublin – he could hitch a lift back to camp with the recruits on Tuesday morning. But if they'd postponed it . . .

'About my medical board, sir?' he enquired.

'No, no, not that.' Redman's veiny jowls quivered as he shook his head. 'Afterwards, you see. A Captain Maunsell called on the telephone.'

Redman stopped and frowned, as if he thoroughly disapproved of the telephone.

'Captain Maunsell, sir?' Stephen prompted.

'Yes. He wants to see you. He's got an office in the Royal Barracks and you're to drop in after your medical board. Didn't mention a time – whenever the medicos are finished with you, was all he said.'

It was Stephen's turn to frown.

'But . . . but did he say . . . ?' he began, but Redman had already stepped into his hut, closing the door behind him. Stephen looked at the door for a few moments, then shrugged and looked back towards the mess. There was a thin twist of smoke rising from the chimney – it would be warmer than his hut. But then he thought of the papers neatly stacked on his desk. He had a good half-hour before the lorries came, and he might see something in the cold light of day. In his mind he was already at it, already picking his way through the convoluted logic. Something in Lillian's last letter was niggling at him, drawing him back to it, and almost before he realized it he had his free hand on the doorframe and was steadying himself with the stick as he lifted his good leg inside. There was something in one of those special cases she had worked out, he thought, and as he pulled himself through the doorway he felt a glimmer of elation. That was the key, he was sure of it – the solution was right there in front of him. As he propped his stick against the desk and gently pushed the basin aside, his mind started racing ahead, and he hardly felt any pain at all as he sat down to work.

24 Percy Place
Dublin

21 November 1917

Dear Stephen,

I was so thrilled to get your last letter that I could hardly wait to open it. I can't believe it's only a month since we started working on the problem – but what a month, and how far we've come! These days I can think of nothing else – not my own work, nor my students, and every time I see Prof Barrett I must resist the urge to blurt it out to him. But we must tell him soon – we must! I haven't breathed a word to him, but I'm sure he knows I'm up to something. You will remember that he has a nose like a bloodhound for these things and I fear I am as transparent as a piece of glass.

But I agree that we should have our proof as near complete as we can make it before we reveal anything. After your last letter I think we are finally in reach, and I believe the two special cases I have worked out on the back put the final touches to your transcendental method, which, of course, will lend itself to a whole host of applications. It will have to be thoroughly checked, of course, but (I'm touching wood as I write this) I think it could be the biggest thing in mathematics for the last five years – and it will certainly be of enormous help in solving some of the great problems on Professor Hilbert's famous list. It's so exciting! If we tell anybody, it must be Professor Barrett, because he has been such a good teacher and friend to both of us, and

I can think of nobody better to check our work before we show it to the world at large.

Please write by return of post to let me know what you think. If you are agreeable, I will tell him on Thursday and perhaps even show him some of our workings. Then you can talk to him about it at the Lady Registrar's birthday party on Friday night. Now, I'm sure I can see your knuckles whitening when you read that last sentence, but I promise it won't be as excruciating as you think. Vivienne is really a nice old girl, if a little bit dotty, and she has been nothing but a friend to me ever since I started working at the college. I have already told Prof Barrett that you will be there and his face fairly lit up at the prospect of seeing you again.

So there, you can't say you will have no one to talk to! I'm sure you'll find it very stimulating, and if all goes well, then we'll have plenty to keep us busy on Saturday and Sunday.

Oh! Writing this has brought you so close to mind I can't believe it is only Tuesday. I'm not sure I can wait three more days before I see you again, but I will do my very best.

With love and kisses,

Yours ever,

> *Lillie*

A bit of what you fancy. Stephen pulled the door behind him and rubbed his palm on his tunic, trying to rid himself of the lingering traces of Figgis's oily handshake. He picked his way down the garden path – cracked, mossy and dangerously slippery to a man with a stick – and breathed a silent sigh of relief when he was safely on the pavement. Despite the rubbing, his hand still tingled with the memory of Figgis's limp hand and the smell of the surgery was still on him – the dry, dusty stink of formaldehyde mingled with sweat, and with undertones of something rotten, something that not even the aseptic tang of ether could cover. He looked at the tarnished brass plate that hung beside the squealing black iron gate. *Joshua Figgis, Physician.* Physician? He smiled bitterly to himself. How long was it since Figgis had healed the sick? But then he felt the bulge of the bottle in his tunic pocket and his spirits lifted. Another month's salvation. Figgis might not have been much of a healer, but it was in his power to dispense one very powerful cure – one that could be had for a small consideration.

'Now then, captain,' he'd said, after they'd gone through the charade of introductions and how-do-you-dos, 'let's have a look, shall we?'

Stephen had to steel himself for this examination. He was used to being poked and prodded by doctors – six weeks in a London hospital had seen to that – but there was something about Figgis, with his sallow skin and long, greenish fingernails, that made his skin crawl. Nevertheless, he dropped his breeches and sat on the threadbare couch while Figgis laboriously knelt down to examine his knee. To take his mind off it he let his gaze wander around the room. Everything in it was old, dirty, cracked or creaking. The high ceiling was cobwebbed and yellow with age, while the ancient linoleum on the floor was cracked and curling at the edges. The walls were lined with tall wooden cabinets with grimy glass doors and filled with dusty bottles of God-knew-what. A *surgery*? Surely it was far too filthy to be called that.

Figgis wasn't down for long. Two or three brushes of his cold, claw-like fingers and he was getting to his feet again.

'A serious wound, captain,' Figgis had told him, dusting his hands before returning to his chair. 'I dare say it gives you a fair amount of pain.'

'It does,' Stephen admitted, and Figgis showed him a mouthful of yellow teeth and gave him a conspiratorial look over his half-moon spectacles. They both knew what he was here for, after all. Nevertheless, he tried to keep his face stern, impassive. Don't let him see you're keen. Don't let him think you need it.

'Indeed, indeed.' Figgis was the one who betrayed himself, sliding open the drawer for the prescription book. A little too quick.

Well then, captain. How about a bit of what you fancy?

He really relished the rank, and used it again as he laboriously wrote out the prescription. '*Captain* Ryan . . . Shall we say a thousand drops?' Another grin, his reptilian eyes gleaming in their slits. 'That should keep you going for a while.'

Stephen just nodded, feeling his mouth go dry as he watched Figgis write out the arcane marks of the prescription. If it was for a thousand drops he would get five hundred. That was their bargain: the rest was for Figgis. A little of what *he* fancied – and there could be no doubt that he fancied it. He had the parchment skin, the bony hands and sunken cheeks of a confirmed addict. Watching him sign the prescription with a flourish, Stephen realized that he couldn't tell how old he was. His dried-up scaly features gave him the look of a lizard, and it was difficult to say whether the years of his habit had preserved him or aged him prematurely.

Then came the pouring. Figgis stood up and opened one of the cabinets, using a key he kept on his watch chain. Out came the squat brown bottle, a tiny funnel, and he was suddenly all business. Remarkably dextrous, considering, Stephen thought, as his bottle was placed on the desk in front of him. He'd looked at it deliberately for a few moments, resisting the urge to snatch it up and get out of there as fast as he could.

'There's the usual fee, of course,' Figgis reminded him, still holding two bony fingers on top of the bottle He was grinning again, a death's head, but Stephen wouldn't meet his gaze. He took out his wallet and paid, throwing the notes on the desk. Figgis released the bottle and delicately picked up the money.

'A pleasure doing business with you, captain.'

Stephen took his stick and pushed himself upright, picking up the bottle with his free hand. *That's what you bloody think.*

Safely outside, he went a few steps up the street and looked back at the house he'd just left. It was early evening and the tall Georgian façade loomed up over him in the gathering dark. In this prosperous street, it stood out like a sore thumb. Grey and dirty, with grimy windows and an overgrown garden. Christ, how had he ever come to this? Small comfort that he'd been driven to it. The supply of drugs they'd given him at the hospital had lasted barely a week after he got home. He'd gone to the MO for more, but received instead a lecture on the perils of addiction. *Grin and bear it, my boy. It'll get better.*

But it didn't get better. It was eating him alive. He couldn't sleep and could hardly walk. But he wasn't alone. The barracks had its share of wounded men – released from hospital but temporarily unemployed while the army tried to decide what to do with them. The mess was full of limps and tics and scars – and whispers about Figgis. He was the man to help if the MO knocked you back. Figgis could ease your pain, and he was only a stone's throw from the barracks gate.

The turn of a corner, and Stephen could see the barracks gate. He limped slowly towards it, the bottle in his pocket but no spring in his step. Figgis could ease your pain, but at what price? He was going back to a bare room and another go with the Needle. He could see himself sitting on the bed, trousers down again, the Needle piercing his flesh. So sordid that even the thought of it now turned his stomach. He felt dirty, false. He should give it up. He should tell the MO what he was at, or perhaps the medical board on Monday. But he knew he wouldn't.

He was through the gate and halfway across the square before he realized he had started to hurry. He knew he would be late at Lillian's, but that wasn't what was driving him. His hand was in his pocket, clutching the heavy bottle, and his stick clattered on the cobbles as he made for the staircase. Up two flights with hardly a pause – even though stairs were always the worst – and then he was in his little cell-like room, unbuckling, flopping down on the bed, rooting in his valise for the Needle. A few minutes later he was floating. No pain, no sensation but the warmth of his own blood coursing through his veins and a feeling of vague happiness. It was Friday night and he had a long weekend to look forward to. Three full days before he had to report back to the mud and the tedium of Kilbride. When he went back down and crossed the square again, he hardly had to use the stick. Just a tap-tap on the pavement, and then a tip of his hat to the saluting sentry as he passed out into the street, free again.

II

It was twenty past seven and Lillian was still at her dressing table. She was starting to fret. She had never known Stephen to be late for anything and yet here it was; twenty minutes past the hour and no sign of him. She picked up the hairbrush from the dressing table but quickly put it down again. *Stop fidgeting*, she told herself. Her hair had been brushed and pinned this last half-hour. She always liked to be ready early, unlike her sister, who would have said it was so *unfashionable* to be early. But Lillian had never bothered much with fashion. She liked having a few minutes to relax, to look forward to the evening, instead of all that breathless rushing around that some people went on with.

But those few minutes were long gone and now they would be late. Had something happened? Had there been an accident – a misfire or a carelessly pointed rifle? Ever since he'd been wounded, she found it hard not to fear the worst. Perhaps that was because he hadn't just been wounded – at least not as far as she knew. The first she'd learned of it was when she saw his name on that dreadful list in the newspaper – missing, presumed killed in action. Even the thought of it now sent a chill down her spine. She remembered the despair, the sheer desolation she'd felt when she read his name and how it had almost overwhelmed her. Missing, presumed killed. It had seemed so final, with no room for hope – and yet he had survived. He had come back from the dead, but even that blessed telegram from Belgium had not quite dispelled her despair. She had been scarred, and it made her fearful. She felt as if death had seen him, had marked him, and would reclaim him at the first chance.

Growing agitated, she got up and went to the window. The street was dark and empty – not even the lamps lit because of the gas shortages. The only light was the silvery strip of the moon reflected in the canal across the road. It was sure to be nothing, she told herself. Probably some silly hold-up at the rifle range. God knew he practically ran the place by himself, even though they had no business sending him up there with his leg as bad as it was . . .

She stopped herself and went back to the dressing table. It was no good mooning around, fretting. She should do something useful. She sat down, opened the drawer, and took his last letter from the sheaf she kept tied up with a ribbon. She made herself read it slowly, word by word, and then turned over to the mathematics written on the back. Now she read even more slowly, carefully tracing every line, following each step with a growing sense of excitement until she finally reached the end and found herself smiling, clasping her hands together, as if she were afraid to touch the page. She must have read it a dozen times already, but still it amazed her – the more so when she remembered how bad he'd been in the hospital. He'd been so very nearly destroyed when she found him. Not his leg – though that was bad enough – but his mind, the thing she'd thought was stronger than any other. The doctors were concerned that he couldn't speak – not an unusual occurrence, they said, though they had rarely known it to persist for so long – but she was more worried that he had lost his connection with numbers. That ability had run so deep in him that to lose it was almost to lose himself and it was this

– more than the bandaged leg, more than the wheelchair and the haunted look behind the silence – that had drained his spirit. He'd put on a brave face, of course, and he tried his very best to get past it, but she'd come to dread those long afternoons of silence, showing him the simplest equations, coaxing him, cajoling him, and hoping only for the faintest glimmer of recognition.

But if ever she needed proof that he was back in the land of the living then this was it. She knew she would never really comprehend the horrors that had caused the break, but the sudden restoration was even more of a mystery. It had started with the return of his voice. It had been tentative at first, but she could feel it going on inside him – a raw energy, gathering force, gathering momentum. On the train home from London he'd sat up all through the night, scribbling furiously in a notebook. It was very basic stuff – old theorems, proofs of Euclid – but it had poured out of him. And now this, his masterwork. The intricacy of it and yet the simplicity of it; the pure beauty of the logic almost took her breath away. Here on the page in front of her was the old Stephen Ryan – or rather the new Stephen Ryan, for the old Stephen would never have been this audacious. He was the most naturally gifted mathematician she had ever met, and yet he had always been slightly wary of his own talent. It was as if he had been struggling with his gift, trying to rein in its power. But now, ever since the hiatus, he'd been letting it run: run so far and so fast that she was struggling to keep up.

But when she turned the page over and read the postscript again, she wondered if he'd overreached himself at last. *Do not show this to Professor Barrett.* Why not? Was he not certain of it? She'd wondered if there was a flaw, a mistake, a weakness in the logic, but she'd checked twice and found nothing. He'd had no problem with Professor Barrett seeing all the earlier letters, so why keep this one a secret? The only thing she could think of – and she thrilled at the mere thought of it – was not that he'd overreached himself, but that he *wasn't finished*. If the earlier letters had laid down the foundations, this was the one that tied them all together, that gave them direction. But the direction he had chosen – what this letter so clearly pointed to – was so ambitious that she could hardly believe it. It was one of the most famous problems in mathematics, and still unsolved after two hundred years. But did he really think he could do it? Could he really be thinking of a proof of Goldbach's Conjecture?

The garden gate creaked open and she jumped up and ran to the window. She'd been so absorbed in the letter that she hadn't even heard his footsteps coming down the street. But there was no mistaking the tap of his stick on the path. At last! Carefully putting the letter back with the others, she gave her hair one last look in the mirror, closed the drawer and ran out onto the landing as the sitting-room door opened downstairs. She smiled to herself. Her mother had been watching for him as well – she would have to be quick. She darted to the top of the stairs and then down, giggling like a girl. There he was, the khaki shadow of his greatcoat looming in the glass of the hall door. She heard the grind of the knocker as he lifted it and then the sharp double-thump, and almost crashed into her mother as she came out of the sitting room.

'I'll get it, Mam,' she called over her shoulder, and flew down the hall to open the door.

When Stephen was in college, the Provost's house had been a place of minor dread. As a *sizar*, he had been expected to attend functions there once or twice a year, to wear a starched collar with his best suit, and to speak knowledgeably when spoken to. He was not one of the usual run of students, being both working class and Catholic, and the distinction never felt as strong as it had on these evenings. He remembered many surprised looks, often followed by a patronizing smile and the observation that his parents must be *awfully* proud. He remembered, too, gulping down the tiny glasses of sherry, and constantly watching the mantel clock to see if he could safely excuse himself and leave.

After three years away, the entrance hall seemed much more colourful than he remembered. Perhaps it was the austerity of the war – the shortages, the gloom, the feeling that they were living through hard times – but it seemed like the inside of a jewelled casket. The great crystal chandelier glittered and cast a warm yellow light down into the marble hall, illuminating the heavy oil paintings, the winding scarlet staircase, and the ornate plaster ceiling high above. He found himself gaping at it, twisting his neck to take it all in, until he was startled by a smiling porter in a velvet uniform asking for his coat. Lillian held his stick and helped him balance while he shrugged it off, and then they both looked at the broad stairs. Stairs were the worst. His knee was starting to throb already, and it was barely an hour since he'd had the Needle.

'Put your arm around me, sweetheart, and I'll help you,' Lillian whispered, and they climbed up slowly, Stephen's other hand on the curving banister, his stick clacking noisily against the oak panelling until she reached across and gently took it from him. He let her take it without protest. He could feel his face glowing red and his hand was beginning to shake. Up they went again, and when they reached the top he swayed unsteadily, one hand on the wall for balance. His whole leg was on fire, the throbbing pain so great it took his breath away.

'Are you all right, Stephen?' Lillian asked, with a pang of guilt. She should have remembered the stairs – she knew he found them very hard.

'I'm fine, I'm fine,' Stephen said through gritted teeth, forcing a smile and absently straightening his uniform. 'Let's go in, shall we?'

She pressed the stick into his hand but kept her arm around him as he took a step towards the double doors of the salon. The party was well under way, and the loud hum of conversation carried out onto the landing – but not loud enough to mask the gasp from Stephen as he put his weight onto his injured leg.

'We must find you a chair when we get inside,' Lillian said.

'Don't be worrying about me,' he told her, though he'd had exactly the same thought. He had to get the weight off that knee or he would faint with the pain.

'Lillian dear! How good of you to come!' The Lady Registrar must have been watching the door, for she came straight at them in a blaze of green silk and pearls. Stephen remembered her as a rather severe, hawk-like woman who had sometimes chaperoned Lillian at tutorials – sitting in a corner with her knitting on her lap and a stern eye on her charge – but she was bubbling with good humour on her birthday, and kissed Lillian on both cheeks.

'And Mr Ryan, too. Stephen, isn't it?' she said, shaking his hand. 'Or would you prefer captain? How lovely to see you again. Lillian's told me all about your adventures in the war.' Her eye darted to the stick. 'Is your leg very bad? I dare say you should sit down. I wonder if we can find you a chair?' Her name was called and she looked around distractedly, 'Oh Lord, there's Margaret Robinson. Lillian dear, I really must introduce you. She's on the board of Girton, you know, and she's terribly keen to meet you.' She gave Stephen an apologetic look. 'Do you mind awfully if I steal her away from you for a minute?'

'Not at all,' he said lightly, though Lillian was still holding his waist – more for his support than hers. He bent his head a little so he could whisper in her ear. 'Go on. You should meet these people. I can look after myself for a few minutes. Come and find me later.'

She let him go reluctantly and allowed herself to be led away, smiling uncertainly over her shoulder. Stephen rested on his stick and looked around for a seat, but the room was crowded and the few little gilded chairs he could see had already been taken. Then, out of the corner of his eye, he saw a familiar figure perched on an ottoman at the far end of the room, furiously waving at him and brandishing a walking stick.

The room was long and his knee was still throbbing after the ordeal of the stairs. On top of that, he had to negotiate the numerous knots of people who stood in his way, step aside for a stout woman who came barging past him, and stop sharply as an unthinking arm shot out to snatch a drink from a passing waiter. Consequently, he was red-faced and quite out of breath by the time he fetched up in front of Professor Barrett, who sat in the centre of the ottoman with both his hands clasped on top of his walking stick. The professor gazed up at his former student, his grey eyes peeping over his spectacles with something approaching admiration. They had not spoken, Stephen realized with a start, in over three years.

'My dear boy,' Barrett said warmly, 'how good it is to see you again. How is the . . . ?'

He was jarred into silence by an elbow bumping against his arm. Stephen saw that it belonged to another young man in uniform – a lieutenant with gleaming cavalry boots and red staff-tabs on his collar, who was sitting on the end of the ottoman, enjoying an animated conversation with his neighbour. Barrett turned in that direction, scowling.

'You, sir!' he barked. 'Are you wounded?'

The young man allowed Barrett a glance, a shrug, and then

returned to his conversation. Stephen suppressed a grin as he saw the colour rise in the professor's face.

'Speak up, sir. I say, are you wounded?' Barrett rapped the man's leather-clad shins with the end of his walking stick.

'I beg your pardon!' The lieutenant turned sharply, ready to let fly, but in turning he caught sight of Stephen, a superior officer, and the steam went out of him. He went on in a strangled voice, 'No, sir, I am not wounded.'

Barrett glared at him.

'Then kindly get up off your bony arse and let this gentleman sit down. Can't you see that he *is* wounded?'

The lieutenant grimaced, but stood up and bowed faintly to Stephen as he gestured at the empty seat. 'I beg your pardon, sir,' he murmured. 'I didn't see you there. Please, take my seat.'

It was both gracious and grudging at the same time, but Stephen let it pass. His knuckles were white on the handle of his stick and there was a cold sweat forming on the back of his neck. As the young man edged away, he sat down awkwardly and straightened his leg with his hands, sighing with relief. Barrett watched him with considerable interest.

'I was about to ask you how was the leg, but I see it troubles you,' he observed. 'Is it very bad?'

'Sometimes,' Stephen admitted. 'But at least it's still there.'

'There's that to be thankful for, I suppose,' Barrett agreed, and looked down at his feet. 'I'm sure it puts my own troubles in the ha'penny place.'

Stephen followed his gaze to the floor and saw the professor was wearing carpet slippers with his evening suit. Now that he thought of it, the walking stick was a new addition too. Barrett had always seemed old to him – he must have been approaching sixty when Stephen had first become his student – but it was as if he had always been old, as if he was ageless, somehow eternal.

Now it looked like age was catching up with him.

'What's the matter?'

'Gout,' Barrett admitted, clasping his hands on top of his cane. 'I am, as my housekeeper would say, a martyr to it. Not the gout itself, mind – though that's bad enough. No, it's this bloody diet the doctor has me on – it'd make a stoic weep. No red wine, and very little meat, and that's just the start of it. I came damned close to telling him to just put me out of my misery, I can tell you. Sackcloth and ashes is what it amounts to. Still, a glass of sherry is allowed, on special occasions . . .' With a practised wave, Barrett caught the attention of a waiter and plucked two glasses of amber sherry from his tray. 'What shall we drink to?' he asked, handing one to Stephen. 'To your safe return, or to the Goldbach Conjecture?'

Stephen considered his sherry for a moment, doing his best to keep his face straight. Barrett had never been one to beat around the bush.

'To my safe return,' he said deliberately, and raised his glass.

'To your safe return.' Barrett touched his glass lightly, took a sip, and then chuckled quietly.

'I know very well what you're up to, my boy.'

'What *we're* up to, professor. Whatever it is, it's a joint effort.'

'Joint effort, my aching foot!' Barrett dismissed him with a wave of his glass. 'I know Lillian Bryce and I know you, dear boy. I taught you both, don't forget. Lillian is an outstanding mathematician, but her real talent lies in other areas, as you well know. As a matter of fact, she's doing some very interesting work with Professor Lorentz's transformations, but that's beside the point. This work she showed me is number theory, which was always your particular speciality. Besides, the dear girl told me it was all your work. She said she was only checking your calculations.'

28

Stephen smiled to himself. She *would* say that.

'The lady doth protest too much,' he said, and, after considering for a moment, he added, 'the work on the partitions is almost entirely hers, and the rest stands on that, as you know.'

'Hmm, hmm.' Barrett grunted, nodding to himself with his eyes narrowed, deep in thought. 'Well, if that's the case, then her ability runs even deeper – or rather broader – than I suspected. But to return to the work, there is more, is there not? You have developed this transcendental method to incorporate the prime partitions, haven't you?'

Stephen opened his mouth to protest, but closed it again. How did he know about that? He knew Lillian wouldn't have shown him the letter, but had she let it slip somehow? Barrett's face crinkled with amusement at his obvious consternation.

'Oh come along, my boy. Surely you didn't think you could keep it hidden? Any fool with an ounce of common sense could tell that's where you were going. And if you were successful in that attempt, then the Goldbach naturally follows.'

Stephen felt his mouth twist into a wry grin. He should have known he couldn't show so much to Barrett and think he wouldn't guess the rest. Lillian had guessed it too, early on. Was he really that transparent? He knew it made no difference to the work, but he wished they wouldn't bandy that name about quite so easily. *The Goldbach*. It was one of the most famous problems in mathematics and many famous mathematicians had failed to prove it. Others had wrecked their careers on it – either by claiming a solution that was proved wrong, or by spending years and years, whole lives even, fruitlessly chasing an elusive proof. It was a monumental piece of mathematics and, for the first time in his life, he wondered if it was bigger than him.

'I don't know whether it does,' he began, and hesitated, tapping his glass with his finger. 'It's so big . . . such a leap. I don't know if I should make the attempt. I'm not sure if I have the energy for it. I'm not even sure if I want to.'

'Indeed?' Barrett turned and looked him up and down, then nodded slowly – apparently neither surprised nor disappointed. 'I suppose it seems rather trivial compared to what you've seen in the war. Still, at least you have considered it; the idea is planted and it will bloom when the time is right. After all, the war will end someday, but mathematics is infinite.' He paused and seemed to consider this statement for a moment before he went on. 'In the meantime, have you thought of publishing what you have so far? It would make a very fine paper in itself.'

'Publishing it?' Stephen laughed. 'Hardly! I'm a soldier, and one without an undergraduate degree at that. I doubt the journals would look at anything I sent them.'

'Now who's protesting too much?' Barrett demanded. 'You know very well that papers are published purely on merit. And, as you said, it's a joint effort. The fact is, I ask not for your sake, but for hers.'

There was something in the professor's tone that made Stephen frown. He half turned in his seat and looked at him directly.

'What do you mean?' he asked. 'Is something wrong?'

Barrett met his gaze and held it steadily for a few moments. He was considering how much Stephen already knew – almost nothing, by the look of it – and how much he could safely say.

'Do you remember Hypatia?' he asked.

'Of course.' Stephen nodded. Among the great Greek mathematicians of antiquity, Hypatia had stood out as the only woman. In her day, she had been a brilliant and innovative astronomer and a teacher at the library in Alexandria.

'Then you will recall that Hypatia, while she was a great mathematician and an excellent teacher, suffered from two faults that eventually led to her demise. First, she was a woman in a man's world – and, to be honest, neither you nor I will ever really understand that difficulty. Second, she couldn't keep a moderate tongue in her head. She felt compelled to speak her mind regardless of the consequences – and you know how that ended up.'

Stephen grimaced. For all her brilliance, posterity had remembered Hypatia only for the manner of her death; flayed alive with oyster shells by an angry Christian mob.

'Is she in trouble?' he asked. He had glimpsed Lillian again, far down the room and locked in conversation with the Lady Registrar and a shorter woman whose iron-grey hair gleamed in heavy, marcelled waves.

'Not yet,' Barrett answered with a sigh. 'But it's coming, as sure as there's carts to horses. There is a sense that the war must end soon – for better or worse – and there are already wounded men coming home. These men must have work, and some people who tolerated having women on the staff as one of the exigencies of the war now feel they should make way for them.'

'That's hardly fair,' Stephen said, although he had caught the surreptitious glance at his leg when Barrett had mentioned the wounded men coming home.

'No, it is not fair, and if all things were equal I would think that our Hypatia was safe in her job. She is not without supporters.' Barrett jerked his chin in the direction of the Lady Registrar, who had come closer now, and stood with her head bowed, listening intently to Lillian. 'And her abilities are beyond reproach. Unfortunately, ability is not the issue. It's more to do with reputation and the company she keeps. Which is why, if her name were to appear in a prestigious academic journal—'

'What do you mean by the company she keeps?' Stephen cut across him, and Barrett clenched his mouth shut and shot him an uneasy glance. The ice was getting thin.

31

'Well,' his voice dropped to a whisper, 'to put it bluntly, the dear girl has fallen in with the anti-war crowd.'

'The anti-war crowd?' Stephen frowned again. 'What anti-war crowd? She's not said a word to me. Do you mean to tell me she's become a pacifist?' He looked towards Lillian. She was even closer now, though still trapped in conversation. She looked at him directly, gave him a secret smile and a little wave.

'Not as such, no, and certainly not to the same degree as Bertie Russell. You have heard what happened to him, I take it?'

Stephen nodded uneasily. Russell's dismissal from Cambridge had shaken him, the more so as it had followed a prosecution under the Defence of the Realm Act. Russell had been an eminent man – a peer, an established author, and a fellow of his college – and he had been all but ruined for writing a leaflet that criticized the jailing of a conscientious objector. If that could happen to *him*, Stephen reflected grimly, then it wouldn't take much to lay low an unknown assistant lecturer – and a woman in a man's world, as Barrett had pointed out.

'What has she done, precisely?' he asked. He was watching her now. The knot of women was breaking up; they were laughing, parting with smiles and clasping hands.

'Precious little, on the face of it.' Barrett sniffed. 'She's been to a few meetings and made her views known to some people. But you must remember that what she's done doesn't matter so much as how it looks. This college has sent dozens of men off to fight – yourself among them – but many of them have not come back, and shouting the odds against the war looks a lot like speaking ill of the dead . . .'

'But,' Stephen broke in, but Barrett held up his hand.

'I said that's what it *looks* like, my boy. I'm sure it's not what she intends, but you can see how it might be made to appear by those who weren't kindly disposed to her in the first place. That's why I was especially happy to see you here tonight. Just by walking into this room on your arm – on the arm of a serving officer – she's managed to wipe a few eyes. But that will only last so long, Stephen, and she is in deep water. Do remember what I said about that journal.'

This last came out in a hurried whisper because Lillian was coming towards them. The sway of her hips, the way her head was held and the way she smiled at him made something stir deep inside Stephen. Another side of her had been revealed to him and, far from shocking or offending him, it made his chest swell with pride and affection. He understood the risk she was taking and he knew very well why she was doing it. He felt his heart bound when she bent down and kissed his cheek.

'Lillian, my dear,' Barrett said, in a gayer voice, turning his face to accept his own kiss, 'you look simply radiant tonight.'

'Why thank you, professor,' she laughed, though her cheeks flushed bright red. 'I see you two are thick as thieves already. Were you catching up on old times?'

'Oh, of course, my dear,' the professor declared, and his face was as happy and innocent as a child's. 'As a matter of fact, on very old times. We were just discussing the ancient Greeks and the perils they faced. It appears my gallant friend here has managed to retain at least a little of what I taught him. Isn't that right, my dear boy?' And he gave Stephen a sidelong look that spoke a thousand words.

The taxi ran quickly along empty streets. Right around College Green and down Brunswick Street, there was no sound but the hum of the engine and the hiss of tyres on the wet cobbles. Lillian pulled her coat tightly around her. The car was cold after the heat of the party, and she could see her own breath misting the air as they passed the gaslights outside the police station. She caught a glimpse of the pale blur of Stephen's face in the opposite corner. In the passing flicker of light he looked gaunt, his skin stretched over hollow cheeks. He sat lost in himself – silent, staring out of the other window. He'd been like that all evening and she again regretted dragging him to the party. He'd put a brave face on it, of course, but she'd soon given up pointing out familiar faces and old acquaintances and telling him what they were up to. It was as if he was sitting in their midst but he was removed from them, withdrawn into the uniform that encased him like a suit of armour.

'Did you enjoy the party, Stephen?' she asked tentatively. She didn't like these silences of his. It wasn't that he was quiet – he'd always been quiet – it was the *quality* of the silence. There was a tension to it, an air of things not being said.

'It was a lovely evening,' he answered, and she thought she saw the glimmer of a smile. But again, she felt like he was speaking to her from a distance and her heart sank as she realized that it wasn't just the party. Five years they had known each other, first as students together, then as friends. And yet, as close as they had grown, particularly in these last few months, there was still this . . . this gap between them. This close and no closer, she thought, aware that even in this tiny space they sat apart, staring out of different windows. It was as if they were frozen in place, and the lack of intimacy was suddenly unsettling to her. It was not natural. They hardly ever touched, and when they did – as when she was helping him up the stairs – there was this dreadful cold utility about it. It was a necessity – and worse, he resented it. He resented it because he was ashamed of needing help, and he resented her for helping him.

On an impulse, she reached across and put her hand on his. Even through two pairs of gloves she could feel the life in it.

'Professor Barrett was delighted to see you again,' she went on. 'I don't think I've seen him as happy in months.'

Perhaps it was the touch of her hand, but she thought she detected some warmth coming back into him. He didn't answer, but he took her hand in his and squeezed it gently. She felt his shadow turning towards her and she was encouraged to slide closer to him.

'Did he ask you about the Goldbach Conjecture?'

Another squeeze, and he laughed.

'I hadn't thought it was so obvious,' he admitted. 'Though I'm pleased he was impressed with it.'

'He said we might send it to Hardy or Littlewood. They'd be very interested to read it and—' She stopped herself. Was she being too forward here? She took a breath and plunged on. 'Well, it might help you to get a better job – in the army, I mean. Hardy is still in Cambridge, but Professor Barrett tells me Littlewood is a soldier now – one that does mathematics instead of fighting. They made him an artillery captain and put him in an office in Woolwich arsenal, where he does the calculations for ballistics tables.'

'Did he now?' There was a humorous note in his voice, but it didn't quite conceal his distaste.

'I know it sounds boring,' she admitted, 'but it would be better than that old rifle range, and much safer than—' Again, she stopped herself. Much safer than the trenches? Of course it was, but she couldn't just say it out straight like that. They'd never spoken about him going back and, even though she was half sure that he wouldn't be able to go with his leg so bad, there was no telling what might happen with the army so short of men. They were even talking about conscription again, about bringing it in to Ireland . . .

'He told me we should think about publishing it,' Stephen said suddenly.

'Oh? Well, that would be just as good, wouldn't it? I'm sure it would help with the war office, if you wanted to get a job like Littlewood's.'

'Actually, he thinks it would be of more benefit to *you*. He says the knives are out for you in the college, and having your name in an academic journal might help secure your position. Is that true?'

Lillian didn't answer straight away. She felt a pang of . . . it wasn't guilt, more like indignation. He was bound to find out about that eventually, but it wasn't his problem. He shouldn't have to worry about it – he shouldn't have to worry about *her*. God only knew he had enough on his plate. She looked out of the window for a few moments. Even though it was dark she knew this area. They were near the bakery and she could smell the warm, yeasty scent of tomorrow's bread.

'Don't worry about me, sweetheart,' she said, and squeezed his hand. 'I'm well able to look after myself.'

'But I do worry about you – especially if you're doing it on my account.'

'Not *just* on your account, Stephen,' she countered. 'You know as well as I do that this war has gone on too long. And you know better than anybody the real cost of it. If nobody speaks up, then there'll never be an end to it, so I'll speak my mind and be damned to those old fools in the college. For the love of God! The way they carry on about it, you'd think I was running naked through the place!'

'Some of them might prefer it if you did,' he said with a grin, and she laughed, feeling some of the heat go out of her. But as he went on, his tone grew more serious. 'What I mean to say is, you've got enough of a fight on your hands without giving them another stick to beat you with. And it's a big stick. You could be prosecuted for just going to a meeting against the war or for handing out a leaflet – and even if you weren't thrown in jail, the college would be perfectly within its rights to sack you. Remember what happened to Bertrand Russell.'

'I know perfectly well what happened to Russell and I think it's disgraceful. But this is Ireland, Stephen. Things are different over here.'

'They're different, all right. They're different to the extent that the only political party that opposes the war is Sinn Fein, and you'll get even shorter shrift from the college if they hear you've been knocking about with *them.*'

'Well,' she began, but she saw they were nearly home, 'we'll see about that.'

The cab was climbing over the canal bridge, and in a moment it would turn and then stop outside her house, and she would kiss him goodnight and then get out and watch him drive away towards the barracks. She knew all these things would happen, but she wished they wouldn't – not so quickly. Why was it that they had been together all evening, but it was only in these last few minutes that she'd felt close to him? She wished the car would go on and on and on through the night, and they could sit close together like this, and talk until the sun came up.

But then he reached up and tapped the glass and the brakes squealed and the cab shuddered to a halt. He still held her hand and she wished he wouldn't let go, but she could feel the gap already growing between them. There was a solitary gaslight burning on the canal bank, and the glare of it etched the lines into his face. He looked fragile in the light – worn and hurt, as if the wound was visible in his face.

'Shall I come around tomorrow?' he asked.

'Yes, do,' she answered, though tomorrow felt such a long way off. She was already preparing herself for the coming ritual: dressing for bed, brushing her hair, lying in the dark. It seemed so lonely. She leaned across and kissed him, trying to imprint on herself the warmth of his lips, the firm feel of his hand on her waist. Something to take to bed with her.

'Come early – come for breakfast,' she told him, and then she got out quickly and watched as the cab drove off towards the barracks.

There was a motor car parked in the darkened street, its windows fogged a pearly white. Joe Ryan was watching it through a gap in the curtains. He knew there were two men inside and though he didn't know their names he knew what they looked like, and he smiled at the thought of them in the cramped car: tired, hungry, yawning. Serves them right, he thought, and took another sup of his tea.

'Are they still out there, Joe?' Garvey asked from the table, speaking through a mouthful of his dinner. Joe rolled his eyes but didn't reply. Garvey talked too much. He was an excitable little man and he'd been chattering away all day. Tired, wet and cold by the time he came in for his dinner, Joe had been in no humour to listen to him any more. It had been a relief when Garvey was called away by his brother – at least he'd been able to eat his dinner in peace. But now he was back, Garvey was making up for lost time and jabbering away fourteen to the dozen.

'Are they asleep, are they?' Garvey's words tumbled out in a rush as he hurried his dinner. They had a meeting to go to in a few minutes.

'I doubt it,' Joe murmured, and as he spoke he saw a thin plume of cigarette smoke rising up on the far side of the car. They probably hadn't had much sleep these past three days. It seemed like every time he'd turned around they'd been there –

either the car or the two men in it. They never came too close but they watched everything, scribbling it all down in their note-books like reporters. They were attentive, he had to give them that – but that made him all the more wary of them, and he mended his words when they were around. They were harmless enough as long as they were only watching, but one slip and they might pounce. It wasn't long since Ashe had been arrested for making a seditious speech in Longford, and even Collins was on the run from a warrant for the same crime. These days, you had to be careful what you said, and who was listening.

'Maybe we should sneak out and roll a bomb under them. That'd wake them up, wouldn't it? That'd wake the feckers up all right!'

Garvey cackled over the remains of his dinner but Joe still said nothing. He didn't like Garvey, but it wouldn't do to antagonize him. Garvey was the candidate's brother, while he was just a blow-in sent down from Dublin to help with the canvassing. They'd put Garvey with him as a sort of local guide and, while there was no denying that he knew his way around the parish, there was something not right about him. The runt of the litter, Joe thought, as he stood up and walked back to the table. From a distance he looked as small and frail as a child, but he had an old man's face, sharp and narrow, quick eyes, and a pinched, shrewish expression. Then there was the leg. He'd never said anything about it, but he had an obvious limp and one of his shoes was built up. A club foot? He could get around on it easily enough, but sometimes Joe had the feeling he was playing it up for all it was worth. Other times he was a cocky little bastard – too cocky by half – and Joe had noticed the wary looks on the faces of farmers when they came calling. They knew him, all right, but they neither liked him nor trusted him. And it was a sorry pass if his own people didn't trust him.

Joe went to the fireplace and tried his hand on the overcoat that hung on the back of a chair, steaming gently in front of the fire. It had been a wet and blustery day out in the fields, and by the time they turned back towards town he had been soaked to the skin. The only things on his mind had been a warm fire and a hot meal, but as they had tramped along a muddy lane, his eye had caught the pale blur of a thatched roof behind the bare branches of some spidery ash trees.

'Whose place is that?' he asked, stopping so suddenly that Garvey went a few yards without him. Maybe he was cold, but he seemed to be hurrying – not talking for once, head down and shoulders weaving over that heavy limp. He turned and scowled at the cottage.

'That's the Clancy place,' he said. 'You'll get nothing out of them. They were Parnellites in me father's time, and followed Redmond after that. Their boy signed up for the army and got blown to bits last year.' He cocked his head up and looked around the iron sky, where the pale pinpricks of stars were just starting to show. 'There's no sense in wasting your time. It's near dark already and we've another three miles to walk.'

But Joe considered the cottage for a moment. There was a slim pillar of smoke spiralling out of the chimney, and the smell of burning turf drifted down to him. He was enticed not so much by the prospect of a vote as the fact that Garvey seemed to be afraid of the place. Even as they stood there in the lane, he was shifting uneasily, anxious to get moving again.

'Sure we're here now. Where's the harm in showing our faces? At least they can't say they were never asked.'

He started towards the rickety iron gate, but Garvey didn't budge.

'I'm telling you; there's no point. They won't even give us the time of day.'

'Then you wait here, so. It won't take them long to say no.'

Joe was through the gate and off up the stony path to the cottage before Garvey could say anything else. It was a steep climb to the muddy yard, scattered with hay, and then he caught the sharp, sour scent of pigs and heard something snuffling loudly behind a crooked door as he walked past the outhouse. The cottage was low and long, whitewashed and huddled against the hillside, and it reminded him a bit of his grandfather's place in Mayo. A white-haired old woman was outside, bent over and picking sods of turf from under a tattered tarpaulin.

'Can I give you a hand there, missus?' he asked, and when she straightened and turned around, he took off his cap, the better to show his face in the weak yellow light that spilled out of the kitchen window.

'Are you that Ryan fella?' the old woman asked, after a long stare.

Joe carefully folded his cap and slipped it into his pocket.

'I am indeed. But how do you know that?'

'News travels fast in these parts,' she told him sternly. 'And what do you mean by calling here at this hour of the night?'

'Well, I was on my way back into town, missus,' Joe started to explain, but before he could get much further, she cut him off.

'You'll not get a vote out of himself. He stuck with Parnell even after the split, and he wouldn't vote for Sinn Fein if his life depended on it.'

Joe smiled. 'Sure since I'm here, I thought I'd do him the honour of asking him myself. Is he in, at all?'

The old woman studied him for a few seconds – for so long that he wondered if he'd gone too far. But at last she shook the turf deeper into the belly of her apron and jerked her head over her shoulder.

'He's not, but he's only above in the top field and he'll be down

41

now it's getting dark. You can come in and wait for him, if you like.'

The kitchen of the cottage was like any of the dozens he'd been in over the last two days: small and low-ceilinged, but clean, warm, and welcoming. Again, he was reminded of his grandfather's place, but he couldn't remember how many years it was since he'd been there.

'Sit down by the fire and warm yourself,' the old woman commanded, and she went to the nook and emptied the contents of her apron into a tall basket. Joe eased himself down on the settle and felt his face and hands begin to glow in the heat of the fire. The room was very plain, and everything in it was worn with use. The only decorations were two pictures on the mantelpiece – one a painting of Parnell, and the other a photograph of a young man in an army uniform, standing with his hand on the back of a chair. The uniform made him think of his brother, but he dismissed that thought instantly. It wouldn't be right to bring him up and, besides, they'd probably think he was having them on. His brother in the army and him in Sinn Fein? Sure who'd believe that? He smiled at the thought of it, and then the door opened again and a squat man in a grey overcoat and woollen cap came in, stamping his feet on the step and blowing into his hands to warm them.

'There you are, Paddy,' the old woman called over her shoulder. 'We have a visitor. This is Mr Ryan from the Sinn Fein, he's after coming over to see if you'll vote for them.'

'I will not.' The old man shrugged off his coat and hung it on a peg, then nodded at Joe as he pulled off his cap. 'But sure we'll give him a cup of tea anyway. This is no kind of weather to be out looking for votes.'

Joe stood up and offered his hand. 'Sure a cup of tea will be grand. It's been a hard old day.'

'It has that,' Mr Clancy agreed, and he warmed his hands at the fire for a few moments before sitting down and watching his wife hang the kettle on a hook over the glowing embers. 'I hear you came down from Dublin to do the canvassing.'

Joe smiled self-consciously. It wasn't the first time he'd heard that line, and despite the friendly intentions it always came out with a slightly hostile undertone.

'I did,' he admitted, 'and what else did you hear about me, then?'

The old man looked him up and down for a few moments, narrowing his eyes. 'I heard you were out in the Easter Rebellion, and you went to jail for it.'

'I did that too – and I wasn't the only one.'

'Indeed and you were not.' The old man grinned, showing the gaps in his teeth. 'But still and all, you'll not be getting my vote.'

'Why not?'

'You know very well why not.' Mr Clancy nodded towards the mantelpiece, though Joe couldn't be sure if he meant his dead son or Parnell. 'But there's another reason, and I'll tell it to you, if you'll listen.'

Picking his moment, Joe pulled out a packet of cigarettes and offered one.

'Go on, so.'

'Is that fella Garvey with you?' Mrs Clancy asked, peering out through the small window into the blackness of the farmyard.

'Sure of course he's not, woman,' her husband answered gruffly, before Joe could get a word in. 'They know better than to send that little sleeveen out here – and aren't they after bringing this fella all the way from Dublin to do the canvassing?'

'Mrs Dempsey said he was with him this morning,' Mrs Clancy said with a sniff, 'and I thought I heard something outside.'

'He was only showing me where to go,' Joe answered defensively.

'Was he now?' Mr Clancy lit his cigarette with a spill of paper from the fire and gave him a knowing look through the smoke. 'Was he doing that, or was he keeping an eye on you? You wouldn't know, would you? What?' He cackled with laughter while Joe shifted uncomfortably in his seat.

'See, *that's* why you'll not get my vote,' Mr Clancy went on. 'Them Garveys is no good and never was neither. I don't mind a fella who comes and says what he's at out straight like – even if I don't agree with him. But that fella you've got standing for you is a two-faced liar and a bully, and his brother is worse.'

'Vicious,' Mrs Clancy remarked, still looking out of the window.

'Aye, a vicious little pup that should have been put in the mad house years ago. There's some say his leg made him like that, but that's only nonsense. Them Garveys was always bad, going right back to the famine . . .'

It was almost an hour later that Joe walked back out into the yard, still without a vote but feeling warm and fuzzy and filled with tea and poteen. When he got back down to the gate he was dismayed to see Garvey wasn't there. It wasn't that he minded the three-mile walk back to town, it was finding his way. After a moment's thought, he turned around to go back in and ask for directions, but there was a rustling and a scraping and Garvey emerged from the ditch, slightly breathless.

'Where did you get to?' Joe demanded, a little sharply. His sudden appearance had given him a fright.

'Sure wasn't I sheltering in the ditch?' Garvey answered, but he sounded shifty. Then he went on the offensive. 'What kept you?' he asked in a wounded tone. 'You said you wouldn't be long, and here's me after nearly freezing to death waiting for you. This wind would skin you, so it would.'

'Them two could talk the hind leg off a donkey,' Joe told him, though he had a feeling Garvey knew that already. He would have liked to be able to see his face, but it was fully dark now, and all he could make out was a blur in the light of the waning moon. He turned and took a few steps up the road. 'Come on, we'd best be getting back. We've got a meeting tonight with your brother and I don't want to be late.'

He let this meeting be his excuse for stretching his legs and walking the three miles at top speed. It cost him some discomfort – the old wound he'd got in the rebellion still pained him a bit if he exerted himself – but it cost Garvey more to keep up with his gammy leg. Joe knew it was cruel, listening to him puffing and scraping behind him, but he didn't care. At least it kept him quiet.

It was an hour since they'd got back and the overcoat was still damp, but Joe picked it up, shook it, and then shrugged it on. The meeting was in Kehoe's, a pub belonging to one of Garvey's cousins.

'Is there a back way?' Joe asked, jerking his head towards the window. 'We don't want to tip off the boys in the car.'

Garvey gulped down the last of his tea, then grinned and gave him a conspiratorial wink.

'Ah, now, don't you be worrying about them,' he said, and led him down a narrow passage to the back door of the house. They stepped out into the cold air, swirling with a light drizzle, and went down a damp slippery path that soon turned into a sort of ditch, lined with privies and turf sheds. They turned again, and passed crates of empty bottles, the smell of stale beer wafting up from the damp ground. Garvey tapped on the window, and the small back door opened beside them, letting out a narrow wedge of yellow light.

'There you are now, Vincent,' said the face that appeared, a woman's face, young and strong. She opened the door and let them in. 'Good evening to you, Joe,' she said with a smile as he ducked in out of the cold.

'Good evening, Mrs Kehoe. How are things?'

'Oh, fine, thank you, Joe. The boys are waiting for you upstairs.'

'I'd best be going up, so.' He put his hand on the banister, and Garvey made as if to follow him.

'You wait down here, Vincent,' Mrs Kehoe said, putting her hand on his arm. 'Come along into the bar and I'll get you a drink.'

The angry look on Garvey's face wasn't lost on Joe, but he put it from his mind as he went up the stairs and into the long room above the bar. There was a knot of men standing at the far end, and he recognized Garvey's brother among them, but his eye was drawn to a man sitting apart from them – in a chair by the window, watching the street just as he himself had been doing. He was so pleased to see a familiar face that he went straight up to him, ignoring the stares from the locals.

'Jesus, Mick. I didn't think I'd see you here.'

Collins let go of the curtain and jumped up with that quick, sudden movement that Joe remembered well. He caught Joe's hand in a strong grip and clapped him on the shoulder.

'It's good to see you Joe,' he said. 'But I'm not stopping long. I'm on my way down to Cork for a few days and I only called in to see how you were getting on. Sit down there for a minute.'

He sat down, and Collins waved to the others. 'We'll be with ye in a minute, boys.'

Joe suppressed a smile as Collins flopped back into his chair. He hadn't been here five minutes and already he had them eating out of his hand. He'd been just like that when they were interned together in Frongoch – no rank or authority to speak of, but he could impose himself by the sheer force of his personality.

'I see our friends are keeping you company,' Collins said, nodding to the window. 'Have they been giving you any trouble?'

'Not much – the usual stuff. If I stopped to piss against a wall I'd probably wet their trousers.'

'Well, you be careful of them, now,' Collins warned. 'It's a hard enough life without having a warrant around your neck – trust me, I know.' His eyes darted to the men at the end of the room. They were growing restive now, and Joe heard chairs scraping as they sat down around the table. 'What about them? How are they treating you?'

'Well enough, I suppose,' Joe admitted. He couldn't complain on that front – not with a warm bed down the street, and hot food served up to him. But he leaned closer to Collins and dropped his voice to a whisper. 'We're not going to win this one, Mick.'

He was surprised when Collins nodded as if he knew this much already.

'Sure we can't win them all, and we always knew the Parliamentary Party man was popular here. His father had the seat back in Parnell's time. The thing is to show them we're not afraid of a fight.'

'If we wanted to show them that, we would have picked a decent candidate,' Joe said, nodding over Collins's shoulder. Garvey's brother was sitting at the head of the table – a much bigger man, stern-looking, but somehow just as dangerous. 'That fella's no good.'

'Yeah, but he's powerful,' Collins said, his eyes narrowing. 'He's got connections, friends and money.'

'That doesn't make him a good candidate. The people don't like him, and that's why we're not going to win.'

'The people?' Collins's face cracked into a grin. 'By Jesus, Joe. You're still a socialist at heart, aren't you?'

'Maybe I am,' Joe said seriously. 'But what is any of this worth

47

without the people? They need somebody to stand up for them, Mick, but what are we doing? It's getting on for two years since the rebellion and what have we got to show for it? Nothing, only three seats in Westminster that we refuse to fill. All we're doing is manoeuvring. What good does that do the people who voted for us?'

Collins looked exasperated. He threw out his hands.

'Well, what would you have us do, Joe? Do you want another rebellion, with half our people still in jail and hardly any guns between us? You know as well as I do that the Easter Rebellion failed because it went off half-cocked. Yes, we're manoeuvring now, but that's what we have to do to build up support. We need people on our side – even people like Garvey, there. We need his money and we need his friends and when we have enough of that, then our day will come. Then the people will get their turn.' Collins stood up and clapped him on the shoulder. 'But you mark my words, Joe, there will be blood. You'll be sick of fighting by the time we're finished. Sick to death of it.' A squeeze of his powerful hand and Joe heard him laugh, 'Patience, Joe. That's all it takes. Now let's get a tint of that whiskey before all the talking starts.'

III

This close to Christmas there was no colour in the gardens. The flowerbeds were nothing but mounds of bald brown earth and the rain-sodden lawns looked drab and lifeless under the ashen sky. The tall trees were bare and black, their branches whipping in the wind that rattled the grimy windows with fitful blasts of rain.

Inside the waiting room the mood that morning had not been much brighter. A fire had been lit in the grate, but the turf was wet and it had produced much smoke and little heat before finally sputtering out. Only the musty smell lingered, amplifying the feeling of damp in the air.

Stephen sat in his greatcoat and gloves, idly knocking the handle of his stick against the arm of his chair. When the clock high above the hospital courtyard clanged out for noon he stopped and listened, but then he started knocking again. He didn't have to worry about annoying the others because there were none left. Roberts had gone in half an hour ago, and he'd been left alone ever since. He should have known they'd leave him until last. They were doing all the Rs today, and they were being doggedly alphabetical about it. Rafferty had been first in, and he'd been back out in five minutes, his B certificate clear from the big grin on his face – a lopsided grin, pulled down by the livid scar that curved from his temple to his chin. But still, he was safe. He'd got his ticket – another three months at home.

There was less hope for poor bloody Roberts. Not much wrong with him – not that you could see, at any rate. When his name was called he had stood up and marched into the examining room. Back straight, arms swinging – he might have been on the parade ground. But Stephen knew he only went in like that so they wouldn't see how terrified he was. The shaking in his hands would do for him if they were sharp-eyed, but he'd probably sit on them and let the sweat soak into his breeches. What would he do if they told him they were sending him back? Probably smile and thank them. That was the usual thing. That was what was expected, so that was what you did. But he didn't like the look of Roberts. He'd seen a few that far gone before. He looked like he might go back to barracks, put his revolver on the bed, and try to work up the courage to use it.

The door opened and Roberts came out. He looked shrunken, broken. No arms swinging now, no marching. He had his cap in his hands and looked like he might tear it to shreds. Only when he saw Stephen still sitting there did he straighten up a bit. The brave face came back and he forced a ghastly smile.

'Well, cheerio, then.'

'Cheerio,' Stephen answered absently, and when Roberts was gone his eyes rested once more on the door to the meeting room. What were they up to? Probably going over his file, turning over pages, passing them along. He imagined it was quite thick by now. Malaria and dysentery, souvenirs of Turkey, then the leg wound, of course, a right nasty one, and finally his *episode*. What would they make of that? No doubt it had been described in detail by Hardcastle and Rivers; nightmares, hallucinations, and six weeks of utter implacable silence. What was the name that Rivers had given it? Aphasia – the loss of words. But what name would the men in *there* pin on it? Would they call it shell shock, or neurasthenia, or just bloody malingering? Would they think he was putting on the limp?

The door opened and a trim lieutenant smiled out at him.

'Captain Ryan? If you please?'

The lieutenant held the door open as he got up and stumped across the waiting room, trying to keep the stick in time with his injured leg, trying to walk as straight as he could, trying not to lean on it too hard. Trying not to look a cripple, he thought. The other room was large and the doctors were ranged behind a long table in front of the window, with a single chair facing them from the middle of the floor. He felt their eyes on him as he walked to the chair but he didn't look at them until he'd taken off his cap and sat down with his hands clasped on top of the stick. When he did, he found them equally split: two were reading, frowning at the table in deep concentration, and the other two were smiling at him indulgently.

The senior doctor was Addis, a lugubrious old man with puffy jowls and a bushy grey moustache. He had examined Stephen's leg earlier that morning and had shaken his head in wonder at it.

'You're a lucky man, captain,' he'd said. 'Another inch and they would have had to have taken your leg off. Another inch again and you would have saved them the bother.'

Intrigued by his remark, Stephen had looked down at his own scar. He did not know it very well because he kept it bandaged – and even when he was bathing he kept it covered with a face-cloth, as if not seeing it would somehow block the pain. It was a livid red and twisted upwards from the outside of his calf to the top of his kneecap. At its widest it was thicker than his finger, and such a vivid colour, such a hard lump of tortured flesh, that it was clearly the embodiment of the sharp ache that kept him awake at night. Even the sight of it made him crave the Needle.

Addis motioned him to get dressed and flipped through a few pages in the file. 'Give you much pain?'

Stephen paused in buttoning his breeches.

'A little, going up stairs or if I turn around sharply.'

Liar. But he'd already made up his mind to give them that much. If he said it didn't hurt, they'd be suspicious, and he didn't want them to think he was being dishonest. He didn't want them looking up the leg of his drawers, where they'd see the marks all over his thigh. He didn't want them to know he'd stumped out to the bathroom five minutes after they called Roberts in and made sure the knee wouldn't trouble him during the interview.

Addis went first, giving him a friendly look over the top of his spectacles.

'And how are you feeling today, captain?'

Stephen shifted in the chair and straightened his leg a little and thought for a few moments before answering. It was a straightforward enough question – but perhaps less so if a panel of doctors put it to him. Even the most innocent answer might be turned on its head, might reveal something.

'I'm fine, thank you.'

'Good, excellent.' Addis nodded as if this answer had cleared something up. Then he turned towards the young lieutenant who had called Stephen in and whispered something. The lieutenant nodded, turned a page and cleared his throat.

'Good afternoon to you, captain. My name is Nugent and I am a psychiatrist. I see you were treated in London by Doctor Hardcastle and Doctor Rivers for a . . . for a speech impediment.'

A *speech impediment*. Well, that was a new one.

'Yes,' he answered in a strong voice, to make it clear he no longer suffered from any impediment.

'You suffered from aphasia. You were completely mute for a period of several weeks. Is that correct?'

'Yes.' Even louder.

'Well, I must congratulate you on your recovery.' Nugent smiled. 'Your speech seems perfectly normal to me. But I wonder if you would tell us how your condition arose? Can you remember how it happened?'

Now Stephen was struck dumb again. Of course he could remember. Once Rivers had dragged it out of him he could remember all too clearly, but just thinking about it made his skin crawl, and he could already feel that familiar metallic taste creeping up his tongue. But he cleared his throat and blinked and answered: 'I had temporary command of a tunnelling company in the Messines Ridge operation. The enemy blew in our tunnel and I was buried for a short time. Doctor Rivers identified this as the . . .' As the what? What were the words Rivers had used? Trauma? Was that it? '. . . As the cause of my trouble,' he got out, and then clamped his mouth shut again. He could feel sweat on the back of his neck.

'So it had nothing to do with your leg wound?'

He had to blink again. He could smell the earth, taste it, feel it on his skin.

'No.'

'I see. And what about your other symptoms? Doctor Hardcastle mentions nightmares. Do you have any trouble sleeping?'

Nugent was smiling at him. Obviously trying to be as kind as he could. Stephen smiled back.

'Sometimes, yes. But I usually sleep very well.'

A short whispered conference followed, after which Addis returned his attention to Stephen and asked, almost sheepishly: 'Captain, would you be kind enough to walk about for us? Just up and down a few times, if you please.'

Walk about? He got uncertainly to his feet, trying not to grimace, but at the same time trying not to use the stick. It was impossible. Even through the morphine, a sharp stab of pain came up his leg, and it gave him such a jolt that he almost toppled over. Steady, steady, he told himself, and he tried to find his balance, leaning as lightly as he could on the stick. He felt a band of sweat break out under his collar, a chill run down his spine. His knee was trembling by the time he reached the end of the room, and he was aware of the awkward clumping and scraping noise he was making on the polished oak floor. Turning took all his concentration. *A right bloody fool you'll look if you fall on your arse.* But then he found his stride, lopsided though it was, and made decent speed back across the room. He kept his eyes on the wall, not looking at them, not wanting to see their faces. He felt like a performing dog.

'That will do, captain. You may sit down again,' Addis interrupted him when he reached the chair again, and he sank into it gratefully. His whole leg was tingling and there was a queasy feeling in the pit of his stomach. The doctors huddled together and had another whispered conference.

'Your leg troubles us, captain,' Addis said at last. 'The wound is rather severe and your movement appears to be somewhat restricted. How difficult do you find it to get around?'

'Not too bad, sir,' Stephen answered lightly, though he could feel his knee trembling.

'Hmm.' Addis grunted ominously and gave him a piercing stare. 'Earlier in the war, captain, we would have discharged you with a wound like that. However, considering the current manpower shortage, we are of a mind to certify you for home service. What do you think about that?'

For a moment Stephen thought of Roberts. This is what they should have offered him. They couldn't do this; they couldn't send him back to Kilbride to stew in his own juices until the whole thing was over and they could safely boot him out. Not after all *that*, not when it was still bloody haunting him. Not before it was finished. He gripped the top of his stick with both hands and looked Addis straight in the eye.

'Well, sir. I think I can get around pretty well, and I'm improving all the time. I think if you would give me a few more weeks—'

'Do you mean to say,' Addis cut across him, taking off his spectacles the better to glare at him, 'do you mean to say, captain, that you wish to return to active duty?'

'Yes, sir.'

'And do you really think you could command men under combat conditions? I can see from your record that I don't have to tell you what that would entail.'

'Yes, sir, I believe I can.'

Addis turned his head to gauge the reaction of the others. Stephen kept his eyes fixed straight ahead. A small voice inside his head was screaming: *What the hell are you doing?* But he knew it was right. He knew it was what he had to do. He was holding his breath. The others were smiling – Nugent was looking at him with something like admiration. Addis put his spectacles back on and turned back to face him.

'Very well, captain. We will see you again after Christmas. This board will convene again in January. If you would care to present yourself then, we will see if you are fit for active duty.'

Stephen let his mask crack into a smile, but a wave of nausea caught him. The pain was starting to throb in his leg and he knew the Needle was wearing off. So soon? It must have been all that walking. Then a monstrous cramp twisted in his stomach and he clamped his mouth tight shut. Wouldn't do to be sick in front of them. Wouldn't do at all. No. He had to show them he was strong. He had to show them he was still able. His hands gripped the top of the stick with all the strength he could muster and he propelled himself upright in one swift, painful bound. Swaying on his feet, he freed his right hand and threw up his most impressive salute.

'Thank you very much, sir.'

Addis wasn't smiling. He lowered his eyes to the file and made a note.

'Thank you, Captain Ryan.'

The walk from the Royal Hospital to the Royal Barracks should have taken him ten minutes but it took almost an hour. By the time he passed the sentry at the barracks gate, his leg was one pulsing shard of pain and he was bathed in sweat and wheezing, barely able to return the sentry's salute. He slumped against the wall under the archway to catch his breath and looked out across the barracks square. Was it really three years since he'd stood there with his men, proud and erect, with his sword held up straight? More than a thousand of them had paraded there, inspected and applauded before they marched off to war. How many were dead now? he wondered. How many maimed, wounded, broken?

He couldn't linger. The pain was eating at him and he knew what he had to do. He pushed himself off the wall and stumbled along the colonnade. Even after three years he still knew his way around the place, and he quickly found the NCO's latrine, pushing inside and flopping back against the door as he pulled the Needle from his tunic pocket.

A few minutes later he walked out upright, refreshed, thinking clearly. He strode across the square and into the long corridor of offices – the Pay Corps, Transport, Intelligence. He found a corporal clerk hunched behind a narrow desk.

'Captain Maunsell, sir? Up the stairs, second door on the right.'

The clerk beamed at him helpfully. Stephen scowled at the stairs, but turned towards them with hardly a pause.

'Thank you, corporal,' he said and started to pull himself up. By the time he reached the top he was sweating again, but he hardly paused to straighten his cap before he stumped along the corridor. The second door on the right was dirty, nondescript and stood slightly ajar. He knocked, waited for the grunt, and pushed the door open. Inside was a space not much bigger than a broom cupboard, with a desk forming a barrier across it and a rickety chair for visitors. The man behind the desk was small, grey-haired and trim. Stephen couldn't see his face at first as his head was bent over a piece of paper, upon which he was scribbling furiously.

'Yes?' he asked, with a slow intake of breath, but without looking up. He continued writing, and when he reached the end of the page, he turned it over and continued.

'My name is Ryan,' Stephen said, uncertain how to address him. They were of equal rank, after all. 'I had a message to see you today.'

Maunsell stopped writing, seemed to consider for a moment, and then looked up with a singularly false smile. He was an older man, perhaps fifty or so, and he had a deeply lined face that was unusually pale, as if he'd rarely seen sunlight. His eyes were small and hooded and his cheeks were already grey with stubble.

'And so you did. Thank you for coming.' He gestured at the chair that stood just inside the door. 'Please, sit down. I won't be a minute. All right?'

He finished writing to the end of the page, blew on it to dry the ink, and then opened a drawer and slipped it inside. After screwing the top back on his pen, he set it carefully on the desk and leaned back to regard Stephen for a moment with his hands clasped across his belly. Then he opened another drawer and took from it a slim manila file. He laid this in the centre of his desk and looked across it at Stephen, as if daring him to guess what was inside.

'Captain Stephen Ryan. Royal Dublin Fusiliers. All right?'

Stephen frowned. The man had a very peculiar way of speaking.

'Yes, that's correct.'

'Formerly a student at Trinity College. Took a temporary commission at the outbreak of war and saw action in Turkey and France. Military Cross for rescuing wounded men under fire and mentioned in dispatches for taking care of a particularly troublesome sniper. All right so far?'

He had delivered this in a steady monologue, without taking his eyes off Stephen's face and without lifting his small, slightly pudgy hand from the file that lay on his desk. Stephen nodded.

'Quite correct, yes.'

'You're currently home on sick leave.' Maunsell leaned forward and looked down at Stephen's legs for a few moments. 'A wounded leg, I see. But this isn't the first time you've had sick leave. Between your postings in Turkey and France you were laid up for several months. Spent the time here in Dublin. Is that right?'

Stephen could see where this was going. He felt his jaw become tighter and his answers became shorter, more clipped.

'Yes.'

'You were here for the Easter Rebellion.'

'Yes.'

'And your brother, where was he during the rebellion?'

Despite himself, he fell into the trap. The moment he opened his mouth he knew he should have simply told the truth, but he couldn't help prevaricating.

'My brother?'

'Yes. Joseph Ryan.' Maunsell opened the file, pulled up a page, and read aloud: 'Formerly Sergeant Joseph Ryan, of the Irish Citizen Army. However, since his repatriation, he's changed his allegiances somewhat and is currently a lieutenant in the Irish Volunteers and a known associate of one Michael Collins and the late Thomas Ashe, among others. He is your brother, is he not?'

Stephen felt himself stiffen in his chair and involuntarily glanced at the file. He might have known it would be something like this. He might have known they would come back to him eventually. He managed to regain control of himself and looked Maunsell straight in the eye.

'Yes, he is.'

'And how is he these days?'

'I don't know. I haven't seen him for a while.'

'How long is a while?'

'A few weeks. We met just after I came home from England and I haven't seen him since.' Was he going too fast? Was he saying more than he meant to? Maunsell's eyes were boring into him.

'That long? Really?' Maunsell nodded to himself. 'Has he been away?'

Stephen's jaw tightened. He stared at his interrogator for a few seconds before answering. 'I don't know. As I said, I haven't seen him.'

'No, you haven't. Not for several weeks.' It was a statement more than a question and it hung in the air between them for several seconds. Stephen began to wonder how much he already knew – and what it was he wanted to know.

'We were never very close.'

'He was wounded during the rebellion, wasn't he?'

'Yes, he was.'

'And when he was interned in Wales you went to visit him there – had to pull a few strings to do it, too.'

'Yes.'

'That's quite a lot of trouble to go to if you were never very close.'

'I'd just been posted to France and I wasn't sure if I'd be coming back. Under the circumstances, I thought I should see him before I went.'

Maunsell seemed to consider this for a moment, lightly drumming his fingers on top of the desk. He looked like he had something on his mind, and Stephen felt a tiny dart of joy that, somehow, he was winning. Maunsell wasn't getting this all his own way, and he didn't like it.

'We have him under observation,' he said at last. 'He's quite the golden boy, is your brother, and we've taken an interest in him.'

There was menace in those words, but Stephen didn't answer. He kept his eyes fixed on Maunsell's until he looked away, pulled open a third drawer, and produced a battered cigarette tin.

'Smoke?'

'No, thank you.'

Maunsell helped himself to a cigarette and lit it with a match, which he let burn down almost to his fingers before shaking it out and dropping it into an ashtray at the end of the desk. Smoke came spilling out through his nostrils as he leaned back in his chair and regarded Stephen through half-hooded eyes.

'You come from a fairly humble background, don't you, Ryan?' Maunsell said, and the sudden change of direction threw him off his guard, so that he felt his cheeks begin to burn. There was a derisory, slightly supercilious note in his voice that Stephen found annoying. He counted a couple of breaths and refused to answer.

'Your dad was a boilermaker, wasn't he? You went to university on a scholarship.'

'Actually, he was a blacksmith,' Stephen answered, trying to sound polite and disinterested, but grinding out the words. He felt the hate growing in him.

'A blacksmith, indeed?' Maunsell gave him another false smile. 'Well, I'm glad you cleared that up. Anything else you want to add?'

'No.'

'No?' Maunsell suddenly shot forward in his chair, stubbed the cigarette out in the ashtray, and planted his elbows firmly on the desk. His face had changed, had hardened around his eyes and somehow turned even paler. 'Are you sure, Captain Ryan?'

'Quite sure.'

'You're quite sure, and yet you've been sitting here for ten minutes listening to me tell you your entire life's history, and you don't even know why you're here. It hasn't even crossed your mind to *ask* why you're here.'

'I'm sure you're about to tell me,' Stephen answered, with just the right amount of impertinence. Maunsell's face grew paler still, and his eyes narrowed. *Fuck you*, Stephen thought. But he met Maunsell's gaze without a flicker, without the slightest hint of resentment.

'All right, I'll tell you why you're here. You're here because you're Irish. You're here because you're working class and, despite your best efforts, you can't really hide it. Oh, you make a pretty passable gentleman, Ryan, but I bet you can still bring on the accent when you need to. I bet you could blend right in.'

'I don't see what that has to do with anything.'

'Oh, come along, Ryan, stop playing stupid. I've read your file. I know you better than you think. You know exactly why you're here and you know exactly what I want you to do.'

'You want me to spy for you.'

'There it is.' Maunsell smiled and, for the first time, Stephen thought it might be genuine. 'Of course *spying* is a bit melodramatic. We leave that to the chaps in the penny novels. No, what I want you to do is intelligence gathering. Nothing very high level. Just go to a few meetings, look out for a few faces, listen to what they're saying. Most of our chaps would stick out like a sore thumb, but you, on the other hand . . .'

Maunsell sounded jovial now but Stephen found him even more repulsive.

'You can't order me to do that.'

'Oh, can't I?' Maunsell leaned back in his chair again and clasped his hands together over his meagre pot belly. 'Well, perhaps not directly, but I know several people who could – though that's beside the point. You see, I always find that it's no use getting a chap to do work like this unless you provide him with some sort of incentive. More often than not it's money, but I'm sure that would be repulsive to an upstanding chap like you. No, I've got something else to offer you. As I said, we have your brother under close observation, and I can assure you that he's knocking around with some . . . shall we say unsavoury? Yes, that's it, some very unsavoury characters. The sort of people who can get you arrested just for talking to them. One telephone call is all I need, captain. Just one telephone call, and your little brother will be banged up in Mountjoy before teatime. And your brother wouldn't like it in there, not one little bit. So he'll go on hunger strike like they always do, and then they'll have to feed him with the hose and the stomach pump. And you saw what happened to that poor bugger Ashe, didn't you? Bloody awful way to go, if you ask me, but he did insist on not eating his victuals.'

Smug, sure and reptilian. Stephen knew he was looking at the real Maunsell now. He felt the blood draining from his face, but he still managed to get out the question: 'Are you threatening me, Captain Maunsell?'

'Oh, spare me the indignation, Ryan. I know you boys fighting at the front think you're all very honourable and brave. But every one of you would shoot a chap as soon as look at him, and I'm no different in the job that I have to do. Yes, of course I'm bloody threatening you. If that's what it takes to get what I want, then that's what I'll do. You see, you might think you're cleverer than me, and you certainly think you're better than me. But I don't care what you think.' He reached forward and tapped the desk with two fingers, to emphasize his point. 'I simply don't care. I only want one thing from you, and that is cooperation. Do you understand?' He cocked his head to one side, watched Stephen for a few moments, and then gave him yet another false smile. 'Good, I knew you would. Now let's get down to business, shall we?'

IV

A stormy Thursday night and the rain was blowing in sheets down darkened streets, gushing in the gutters and rattling like gunfire against the window panes. Despite the weather, it was standing room only in the big ballroom of Vaughn's Hotel. The air was warm and moist and smelled of damp raincoats. He'd been there half an hour and thought he'd seen the place filled, but still they trickled in by twos and threes, shaking their umbrellas and removing rain-soaked hats, nodding to people they knew or just stepping quietly to some vacant spot and standing expectantly, looking at the stage.

It was, Stephen thought to himself, a lot like a late Mass. There was the same buzz of whispered conversation, hurried along in case the priest appeared and they would have to stop talking – the same air of hushed reverence, of anticipation. The same slightly formal feeling, as if they would soon be in the presence of greatness.

He stretched out his leg and gently rubbed his knee. The man sitting beside him glanced down at it, but looked away quickly. Then, as if to cover his curiosity, he offered him a peppermint from a paper bag.

'Sure it's a filthy auld night, isn't it?'

'Oh, terrible altogether,' Stephen agreed, wincing inwardly at the automatic inflection in his own voice. He hated to prove Maunsell right. 'But there's a big crowd out all the same.'

'Sure that's Dev for you. They'll come up from Kildare and Wicklow to hear him speak – and the weather won't put them off. Hail or rain, they'll come out to hear him. He's a great man, so he is.'

Before Stephen could reply, he felt a sharp jab in his ribs. His friend Billy Standing was sitting on his other side, as excited as a schoolboy.

'There's Andrew Freeman,' he whispered out of the corner of his mouth, watching a solemn, grey-faced man shuffling towards an empty chair. 'He's a judge on the Leinster circuit. Blimey, Stephen, this is starting to feel like a works outing. That's three judges I've seen, and God knows how many barristers.'

'It's a proper nest of vipers,' Stephen observed dryly, but Billy didn't hear him. He was off again, craning his neck and standing half out of his seat. What he hadn't let on to Stephen was that many of the faces were familiar to him from other meetings like this one. But for all those he recognized, he still hadn't spotted the one he wanted to see. This was Oliver Creedon – he of the tawny mane and narrow loins – an absurdly handsome young man who worked in his chambers. It was he who had first enticed Billy to hear Arthur Griffith speak – but as Billy's interest in Sinn Fein had grown over the intervening weeks, Creedon's had faded, and he had hardly seen him since.

For his part, Stephen was glad he'd brought Billy along. Maunsell had warned him not to tell anybody what he was doing, but after three years in the army, and most of that overseas, he needed a guide. He needed somebody who could put faces to names he knew only from the newspapers and Billy could certainly do that. He also provided some useful cover, since Stephen was sure that spies didn't go around in pairs – and certainly not one as outwardly mismatched as them. While Billy was the picture of elegance in his pinstripe suit and astrakhan coat, Stephen felt shabby by comparison. He'd been in uniform for so long that his old suit was moth-eaten and still creased from the trunk where he'd stored it. His boots pinched his toes and his cap felt so strange that, in spite of the rain, he'd taken it off and carried it folded in the pocket of his jacket.

The knee throbbed again, and he straightened it as much as he could, trying not to make it so obvious that he attracted the attention of the man with the peppermints. He needed the Needle again, and wished he hadn't taken his dose as early as he had. It worried him that it seemed to be wearing off more quickly every time, but he hardly had a moment to think about it. The lights were going down, and a small man in a loud check suit appeared at the side of the stage.

'Ladies and gentlemen, thank you very much for coming out this evening. I know many of you have come a long way, and on an evening like this I'm sure it was an arduous journey even for those of you who live more locally.' He paused and pulled a handkerchief from his trouser pocket before continuing. 'Before we come to the main business of the evening, I would like to say a few words to you about the predicament of our brave brothers in arms who have been once more imprisoned . . .'

'Who's he?' Stephen whispered, but Billy shrugged.

'How the devil should I know? He's only the warm-up act.'

'. . . I want you to spare a thought for those fine men who sit not far from here, in a cold prison cell in Mountjoy. Many of them are on hunger strike, and subjected to barbaric treatment such as that which did for our fine comrade, Thomas Ashe. They run the risk of murder at the hands of the Government, ladies and gentlemen. They run it right now, as we sit here, and on our behalf, on the behalf of Ireland, and freedom for Ireland.'

Applause erupted even before he finished speaking, but Stephen did not join in. He was reminded of Maunsell's threat to put his brother in Mountjoy, and the idea of a hunger strike was repulsive to him. He'd seen men do many strange things in battle – some might say they were brave, some foolhardy. But to coldly starve oneself to death? That seemed like something else. It was like slowly smothering the will to live. Even thinking about it gave him a chill.

'Oh, get on with it!' he heard Billy mutter under his breath. The man on the stage was going red in the face as he warmed to his subject, prowling up and down and pausing to face the audience with his hands planted provocatively on his hips.

'And what about the heroes of Easter?' he demanded. 'What about them? What would they say if they could see the goings-on now? What would they say if they could see British troops still occupying our great country? What would they say if they could see fine Irish boys going off to fight Britain's war for her? What would they say if they could see Irish food, the produce of our fertile land, going to feed British mouths while the poor folk of Ireland go hungry?'

'He isn't half laying it on, is he?' Billy whispered. 'He missed his vocation. He should have gone into the music hall.'

But Stephen hardly heard him. His eyes were fixed on the stage and he was absorbed in the atmosphere, the shouts of agreement and the continuous applause. It wasn't lost on him that *he* was one of those Irish boys fighting Britain's war for her. And yet he remembered when it was different. He remembered the very *day* when it was different – the day he marched through the city with his battalion before they sailed for Turkey. Then the streets had been thronged with well-wishers. The parade had been held up more than once by the sheer weight of citizens pressing in on all sides, clapping them, touching them, kissing them. And it only felt like yesterday. How had everything changed so quickly?

'Well, I have one of them here,' the man on stage continued, 'the last of the heroes, you might say. He's travelled a long way to talk to you tonight, so I'm sure you'll give him your full attention. Ladies and gentlemen, please welcome Mr Eamon de Valera!'

With a flourish, the man pointed to the side of the stage, then ran towards it to shake hands with a tall, bony-looking figure as he emerged from the wings. The whole room leapt to its feet and Stephen, caught unawares, lumbered painfully after them, leaning heavily on his stick and the back of a chair as his knee complained sharply. He stared at the stage, thinking this didn't look much like a hero, being a thin, sallow man with a narrow face and thick, round spectacles. And yet there was something about the way he moved, the way he came to the centre of the stage and stood there, quite erect, waiting for the rapturous applause to die down.

'Sit down, please,' he said, motioning them with his hands. His voice was harsh and reedy, but it carried well, and there was undeniable strength in it. The crowd obeyed, slowly sinking back into their seats, and an expectant hush once more filled the room.

'First of all, thank you for coming out tonight. I'm here to talk to you about two things. The first concerns those Irish men who have been deceived by the propaganda of Mr Redmond and his colleagues and who still flock to the colours to continue this terrible war that has already claimed so many lives.'

Stephen shifted uncomfortably in his chair – but it wasn't the leg this time. He felt as if de Valera was speaking to him directly, as if he was staring straight at him through those thick spectacles. Not a sound came from the room as de Valera paused to take a breath. He seemed to have grown even taller, towering over them all, and Stephen realized that there was something about his voice – harsh and croaking though it sounded – there was something piercing about it, something that gave it the ring of authority.

He risked a sideways glance at Billy and was surprised to see his brow furrowed in concentration, as if he were hanging on de Valera's every word. What had happened to the fervent Home Ruler he'd known? Where was the supporter of that same John Redmond who de Valera had just called a deceiver?

'I feel sorry,' de Valera went on, 'I feel sorry for those men who believed the lies of John Redmond. I feel sorry for those poor Irish men who are fighting and dying in the fields of northern France for a country and a cause that would have nothing to do with them if it didn't need soldiers to fight its battles.'

Suddenly the spell was broken. Stephen felt the hairs rise on the back of his neck as anger mounted inside him. Who was this man to be offering his sympathy? Who did he think he was to be passing judgement on him? What right did he have to feel sorry for those men in France? What did he know about it? Stephen stared at him so intensely that his eyes began to water.

'Good man yourself!' the man with the peppermints exclaimed, and Stephen shot him a furious look. De Valera had paused again as the cheers and applause rose to a crescendo. Stephen's leg was starting to throb and he moved it a little to ease the ache. For the first time he realized he was the odd man out. They all loved this. It wasn't him that de Valera was speaking to, it was *them* – and they hung on his every word. But what did they know? How many of them had been over there? He studied a few he could see: the man in front of him with his tweed cap and pocked neck, the man beside him with the peppermints, standing there in his good suit and spats and the handle of his umbrella hooked over his arm. A bootmaker and a bank manager, by the looks of them. What the hell did they know about the trenches in northern France?

'We need those men,' de Valera went on, now with his hands in fists on his hips, 'Ireland needs all her young men. She needs all of her young people, because they are the future of this country. So we say bring all of them home. Let all of the sons and daughters of Erin come home to her, to help her in her hour of need.'

'Stirring stuff indeed,' Billy whispered when the applause rose to another peak. 'Don't you think? You can see why they're becoming so popular.'

But de Valera wasn't finished. Calming the crowd with his hands, he cleared his throat and waited a few moments until it was quiet enough for him to speak. Stephen noticed that he was sweating now; behind the spectacles, his face looked red and flushed, and there was palpable electricity in the atmosphere.

'This brings me to my next point,' he went on at last, 'some would say this is *not* our hour of need. Some would say that we should be happy with our lot. We are not Belgium, whose land has been invaded, dug up and torn apart by warring armies. We are not Servia, whose king and government is in exile, cast out by an overwhelming imperial force. But are we in any better state? Are we any better off when military rule is imposed on our country, when the army prowls our streets, arresting innocent people and throwing them in jail – where they run the risk of wilful murder by the state? Are we any better off when the very food that we produce – the basic means of sustenance for men and women and children up and down the country – is taken from us to feed British mouths, is—'

'Oh, now hold on a minute,' Billy muttered, standing up out of his chair like a jack-in-the-box. 'Excuse me!' he said, in a loud voice. There was an audible gasp from every corner of the room and all eyes turned to him. Including Stephen's. He craned his neck to look up at his friend, feeling the intensity of all those stares.

'Oh my God!' he murmured to himself, rolling his eyes.

'Excuse me, Mr de Valera, but if I might clarify a point. That food is not being taken from us, it is being sold by the farmers who produce it, and in return for a very fair price, if I'm not mistaken.'

This seemed to nonplus the audience. There was a low murmur of discontent and Billy sat down again. De Valera fiddled with his glasses for a moment, then his face cracked into a sort of grimace that Stephen took to be a smile.

'Well . . .' he began, then squinted in their direction, as if trying to see where Billy had disappeared to.

'What the bloody hell do you think you're doing?' Stephen demanded out of the side of his mouth, and then, to cover himself, he added, 'I thought you agreed with what he was saying.'

'I do agree with him, by and large. But I couldn't let him get away with that thing about the food. That's just propaganda.'

Stephen didn't answer. Out of the corner of his eye he could see the man with the peppermints looking past him, frowning at Billy.

'Well,' de Valera began again, 'my young friend is quite correct. The food is not being taken from us in the sense that it is being seized by force. Instead, it is being stolen in a much more subtle fashion. I would draw a parallel with those young Irish men I mentioned a few minutes ago – the ones who have joined, and continue to join the Crown forces. Now, we do not have the terror of conscription in this country – not yet, at any rate, though I fear Mr Lloyd George and his henchmen are determined to force it on us – but we do have something much more insidious, which some people call economic conscription. To understand this you must ask yourself why these young men are taking up arms under the British colours. Is it because of their love for the Crown?' De Valera paused to let the laughter subside, and grinned at his audience, confident that he had them in the palm of his hand once more. 'No, of course it is not. Is it out of desire to fight for the rights of small countries like Belgium and Servia? No, of course it is not that either. That was the excuse three years ago, when they all said this war would be over in a few weeks, with hardly a drop of blood spilled, but that won't wash any more. No, the reason they are still joining up – despite the deaths, despite the losses we read about every day – is money. I wish I could say there was a more noble cause than that, ladies and gentlemen, but there is not. The King's shilling is all it is. And they are not mercenaries – no, we cannot call them that. They are not mere adventurers, in it only for the money. They are doing it out of need, to feed their families, to put bread on the table and keep their family homes. They are doing it because they have no choice, because the British government has stripped this country of its resources, has allowed landlordism to run rampant, the soil to be destroyed and what native industry we have to go fallow. They have done this because it suits them, ladies and gentlemen; it suits them to have us in need. It suits them to keep us in check, to make us rely on grants and handouts and the poor houses. It is nothing more than slavery, ladies and gentlemen, slavery in this day and age.'

A cheer went up, a roar of applause that took over a minute to die down. Whatever doubts Billy had sown had been well and truly exploded, and de Valera smiled once again, clearly pleased with his work.

'Those farmers must feed their families. That is not to be denied, and we will not stop them from selling their produce. But when famine stalks this land – yes, famine, once again; and we all know the dread that word strikes in every Irish heart – when famine stalks this land of ours we will not stand by and see the very stuff we need to stay alive sold to the highest bidder. We all know that when the potato crop failed in the great famine, when it failed and failed again – and still the British landlords demanded their rent – then the other crops were all exported. The grain that could have kept millions alive, that could have kept them on the land instead of taking the coffin ships to America – that grain was pouring out of this country to bake bread for British mouths. Well, we will not stand by and see that happen again. You all know the meaning of the words Sinn Fein: they mean *we ourselves*. And you all know what they stand for: they stand for self-reliance, for self-sufficiency. And so I am happy to report to you that our local men, our network of good and willing men and women, in villages and towns the length and breadth of the country, have taken it upon themselves to do everything in their power to make sure that Irish foodstuffs stay in Ireland. We can but ask these men to put the Irish people before profit, and that is what we are doing. Asking them to sell to Irish merchants instead of English, to keep the food here where it is needed. It is a small and simple act, but a necessary one, a very necessary one, and one that not a single town or county council in this country has thought to undertake. So where the local government neglects the people we will not. We, Sinn Fein, are from the people and are for the people and we will do everything that is humanly possible to make sure that no Irish child goes to bed hungry, or that the diseases and ill-effects of starvation do not once again bring this fine country to its knees. We will look after the people of this land and we will show the British invader that we, ourselves, can stand alone, that we can be counted among the nations of this earth, and that we will no more lie down under their boots!'

The applause was deafening, and Stephen found himself clapping too. Billy was out of his seat again, applauding and cheering, and Stephen automatically climbed to his feet when everybody else stood up, filling the hall with a deafening cheer until de Valera had left the stage, waving as he went.

'Blimey, that man can't half talk up a crowd!' Billy exclaimed, looking about him as the cheering finally gave way to the scraping of chairs and tramping of feet as people started making their way out of the room. 'What did you think, yourself? I mean, I know some of it might have been a bit close to the bone, but still, you've got to admit he made some sense, and he can certainly hold an audience.'

A stab of pain caught Stephen before he could answer. He caught the back of a chair and leaned heavily on his stick, but still it ground at him.

'Are you all right, Stephen?' Billy's look changed to one of concern, and he caught Stephen by the arm, afraid he might fall over.

'I'm fine, I'm fine.' Stephen gently shook off his hand. 'I just need the toilet is all.' And as he turned and limped away, he added, 'Wait for me in the lobby, will you?'

Billy was leaning on his umbrella when Stephen found him in the lobby. He wore a mischievous grin that broadened into laughter as he came closer.

'I just shook Mr de Valera's hand.'

'Congratulations,' Stephen said, without much enthusiasm.

'Oh come on, Stephen. You might not have agreed with what he said, but you must admit he puts on a good show. And he's perfectly charming to talk to. He and his friends even invited us along for a drink.'

'Well, at least that's one good idea he's had,' Stephen admitted, though he didn't like the look of the windswept street. The rain had abated but the wind was rattling the glass doors and chasing papers and other bits of detritus along the still-wet cobbles. 'Where have they gone? Is it far?'

'Kirwan's. It's just down the road.'

'Well, it would be churlish to refuse an invitation, wouldn't it?' He grinned as he took his cap from his pocket and set it carefully on his head. The Needle had taken effect and he could do it easily, tucking the stick under his arm as he did. 'I suppose a quick one before we go home wouldn't be such a bad idea.'

'My thought exactly,' Billy agreed, and crammed his bowler firmly on top of his head before stepping out into the wind.

They walked in silence for a few moments, buffeted by unruly gusts that seemed to push them towards their destination. Then Billy picked up the thread of the conversation they'd been having before they reached the hotel. Stephen had already told him about his medical board, and the fact that he hadn't yet mentioned it to Lillian.

'So, you don't think she'll be in favour of you going back, then?'

'Hardly.' Stephen grimaced. 'She thinks I was lucky to get out alive after I was wounded. As far as she's concerned, going back would be sorely tempting fate.'

'She might have a point,' Billy observed. He had seen for himself the corrosive effect that the war had had on his friend, even before he was wounded. He remembered the tics and the tremors and the nightmares, and he knew that those things concerned Lillian as much as any physical injury.

'I'm not saying she doesn't,' Stephen said, with a wry smile. 'And, bless her, she means well. She's already suggested that I should use my mathematical credentials to try to get a job doing . . . well, I'm not sure what exactly. Something safe, at any rate.'

'Well, it's an idea – ' Billy nodded at the stick ' – and it might suit you, what with your leg and all. Do you think it could be done?'

'Oh yes, quite easily. Professor Littlewood from Cambridge has already done it. Of course, I don't have a degree yet, but with the work I've been doing recently and a letter from Professor Barrett, I'm sure something could be arranged.'

'And yet, you don't sound very enthusiastic.'

'I'm not.'

'Why on earth not? Surely . . .' Billy stuttered, throwing up his hands, momentarily lost for words. 'Surely, after everything you've been through, after all you've given – surely you've done enough?'

'That depends,' Stephen began, but something caught his eye. A motor car parked across the street. Nothing unusual about it except that there was a man sitting inside. He felt a sudden prickle of fear and was instantly on the alert, scanning every shadow, every corner, as they walked down the street. A shop doorway, twenty yards past the car; deep shadow inside, but was there something darker still?

'Depends on what?' Billy asked, shouting over a gust of wind.

'It's complicated.'

'How complicated can it . . . oh, here we are.'

They had reached a drab-looking place with green curtains in the windows and the smell of stale porter wafting out through the door. A tiny sign was nailed over the lintel: 'Jas. Kirwan. Licensed to sell ales and tobacco.'

They stepped inside, half pushed by another gust of wind, and found themselves in a dingy low-ceilinged room with a rickety wooden counter and sawdust on the floor. It was packed to the door with men in overcoats, but he just had a glimpse of de Valera's lanky form near the end of the bar. He was bent down and shaking the hand of a wizened old woman with snow-white hair. There was laughter, the hum of talk, and some good-natured jostling as men tried to make their way to the bar.

'God bless you, missus,' de Valera was saying, but then Stephen felt Billy take him by the arm.

'In here, Stephen,' he said, nodding to a partition of smoke-stained frosted glass with a rickety door that opened into a tiny snug with a turf fire. They had it all to themselves, and Billy went and stood before the fire, lifting up the tails of his overcoat to warm himself, while Stephen went to the bar. The partition was paper-thin and the bar was so small that he could hear the rumble of talk from the other side. De Valera was clearly as popular here as he had been back in the hotel.

'Eamon, will you come here and say hello to this gentleman. He came all the way from Athlone . . .'

'That was a fine speech, Mr de Valera . . .'

'Eamon, what will you have?'

'Oh, just a small one for me, Michael.' Stephen recognized de Valera's creaking voice even as he switched to Irish, '*Tá mé ar an mbóthar arís ar maidin.*'

A thickset man with grey hair and a closed, hard face came down the bar and nodded at Stephen. His arms were so brawny that they hung from his shoulders like heavy muscular ropes and he had the looming, vaguely threatening air of a prizefighter.

'What can I get you, sir?' he asked in a voice that was strangely soft and musical, although his eyes were sharp and cool.

'Two pints of Guinness, please,' Stephen said, and coughed uncertainly, unsure if that had come out right. Once again he recalled what Maunsell had said to him and wondered if he was right. Perhaps the army had dulled his accent – or perhaps it had even given him one? When he had first joined he had always felt like he sounded different from the other officers, but he hadn't noticed it as much after a while. He couldn't even remember the last time he'd tried to sound like them. Had it become second nature? How much had seeped in? How much did he sound like a captain in the British Army?

'Two pints of porter. Very good, sir.' The barman nodded with a sly smile, and Stephen's eyes narrowed. Very good, sir? What sort of thing was that to say to a customer in a place like this?

But the drinks were delivered without another word, and Stephen took them back to where Billy was steaming gently in front of the fire.

'Why did you want to come to this meeting?' Billy asked, watching him lower himself stiffly into a chair. 'You obviously don't agree with what the man said – and I can hardly blame you, given that he just called you a dupe of the imperial power.'

Stephen's eyes flickered upwards and for an instant he thought of telling Billy the truth. But he just shrugged. 'It was something I had to do,' he said. 'Anyway, I wouldn't say I disagreed with everything he said. There was a certain amount of truth in it – even about going off to fight for the Crown.'

Billy's eyes widened.

'Well,' he began, but he had to pause to gather his thoughts. 'If that's the case, why are you having to think so hard about getting out? I would have thought you'd jump at the chance.'

'I don't know.' Stephen stared into the fire for a few moments, feeling the heat stretching the skin on his face. 'I mean I really don't know. Some days I wake up and I think I should do it. But other days, I just can't get it out of my head. The things I've seen, that I've done . . . and the men. The men I know, who are still there, and who died there. They'll haunt me for the rest of my life if I give up now.'

'Maybe they will anyway,' Billy said gently. 'Maybe it would be better to be haunted by them than to join them, don't you think?'

Stephen shrugged again, as if trying to shake off these thoughts.

'Well, I have a few weeks to think about it. And it's not all bad – at least I'm closer to Lillian now. I can see her every evening.'

This much was true. Maunsell had arranged to have him posted to Beggar's Bush Barracks, which was only a few minutes walk from Lillian's house. Officially, he had a job, but it didn't amount to much more than a few hours of paperwork every day. This was the first evening he hadn't been to see her, and he felt guilty that he'd lied to her. On the other hand, if he'd learned anything about her, it was how much of a closed book she was. There were hidden depths there – and no telling how much she really knew about him.

'Well, while I admire your willingness to lie in the bed that you made,' Billy said thoughtfully, 'I do think the situation has changed. Going off to fight in the war might have looked like a good idea at the time, but it can hardly seem so now. And, politically speaking, the one thing that has become clear is that the Unionists will not back down – not for the sacrifice you and your comrades have made, nor for any other. They still won't even accept Home Rule, and wild horses wouldn't drag them into an independent Ireland.'

Stephen didn't answer. He was tired of politics, tired of the infighting, the backbiting, the endless bickering that went on. What did any of it mean? How was it related to the real fighting that was going on, to what he had seen with his own eyes? What use was it to the men who were enduring the front line, another winter upon them, a new enemy to add to the shells and gas and guns? What he had said to Billy was the truth but not the whole truth. Every day he thought about going back. The medical board and then the meeting with Maunsell had focused his mind on it. Did he want to? That was the first question. The thought of it filled him with dread, but part of him relished the idea, too. It was cleaner over there. Everything was simpler. It was just about you and the man next to you, and living through the day. No, even simpler than that. Surviving the next hour, the next few minutes. It was the purest kind of living because it was so completely in the moment. Minute to minute. He dreamed of going back because he would be truly alive then. Even if it meant risking death, there would be one hot moment that came before.

He knew everybody would think he was mad – and perhaps they were right. But they wouldn't understand. They didn't know what it was like. Anyway, it was by no means assured that he would even be allowed to go back. The medical board had to be convinced that he could still do his job – that he was still capable of fighting – and that was no small task. With Russia out of the war the army needed men more than they ever had, but they didn't need a cripple . . .

The door opened and a young man came striding in, smiling at them and with his hands thrust into his trouser pockets. His familiar bulk almost filled the doorway, and Stephen found himself automatically starting up out of his seat, surprise showing plain on his face.

'God bless all here,' Joe said, and stopped in the middle of the small space, feet planted wide apart, as if he owned it. 'There you are now, Stephen – and Billy, isn't it Billy? What has the pair of you out on a night like this?'

'We . . . we were at the meeting in Vaughn's,' Stephen admitted warily. What was the point of saying otherwise? His brother clearly wasn't the least bit surprised to see him, and if he knew he was here then it was damn sure he knew where he'd been. Then he remembered the two men he'd seen across the street and wondered if he was in more dangerous territory than he'd imagined.

'Go on out of that! You went to see Dev? Sure I never thought I'd see the day.'

'It was my idea,' Billy spoke up, his eyes darting from one to the other. He knew something of the history between them, but he detected an oddly defensive look from Stephen that betrayed something much deeper than embarrassment. 'I'm becoming quite enamoured of Sinn Fein, and I thought a bit of political talk would do him a power of good, help bring him back to normal, you know.'

'Were you there?' Stephen asked on an impulse. 'I didn't see you.'

'No, no, I wasn't there. I had business to take care of here sure. I'm staying upstairs for a little while. Will you have a drink?'

'Oh no,' Stephen and Billy said almost together. 'We'll have to be getting home soon. We only came in for one.'

'Ah, you'll have one for the road. You'll need it going home on a night like this.' He stepped up to the bar and leaned over. 'Shay? Three Jamesons when you're ready.'

Now that he was standing up, Stephen felt drawn to stand near his brother. Despite his embarrassment and confusion, he was thinking clearly. He had a feeling that everything was not as it seemed. This was confirmed when Joe took him by the arm and pulled him close enough to whisper in his ear.

'What the hell do you think you're doing?'

'What are you talking about?'

'Jesus Christ, Stephen. You're supposed to be the clever one. You should know better than this.'

'Better than what? Better than going to that meeting? It was a public meeting, anybody could go.'

'You didn't just go. You were sent.'

'I don't know what you're talking about,' Stephen said, but he had a sinking feeling in his chest. He felt his brother's grip tighten on his arm.

'You were sent by Maunsell, weren't you?'

'Maunsell? Who's Maunsell?' Stephen winced as he said it. He knew he was a terrible liar.

'He's the fella you went to see in the Royal Barracks last Monday afternoon,' Joe said in a clipped, precise voice, breaking off as the barman brought the three whiskies. 'Good man yourself, Jim. Are the boys gone upstairs?'

'They're heading up now.'

'Sure I'll be up myself in a few minutes.'

'Right you are, so, Joe. Sure there's no rush.'

There was no missing the deference the barman showed to his brother, and Stephen knew he was in it now. He was in it right up to his neck. His cover was blown. He knew this even before Joe picked up two of the glasses and handed him one.

'Maunsell is the Chief of Military Intelligence for the Dublin district,' he murmured. 'You'd be a fool to think we don't have his office watched, and you'd be a fool to think we can't put two and two together. The boys told me you'd been in to see him the minute I came back up from the country. They were watching for you at the meeting, and they were watching for you here. Maunsell's got two of his boys outside watching us right now, but we're watching them as well. It's all about watching, Stephen.'

Joe turned and raised his glass in Billy's direction. 'I can't stay, I've got a meeting to go to. Here's to the pair of you.' And he downed half the glass in one gulp, before leaning closer to Stephen and whispering, 'I know you're in the army, and orders is orders, but don't keep going the way you are. They're letting me warn you off as a favour, but the last fella wasn't so lucky. Finish your drinks, and then go back to your barracks and we'll say no more about it.'

Stephen felt a flush of anger. To be caught out so completely was embarrassing, but to hear this was something else.

'The last fella? What last fella?'

'His name was Carpenter. Why don't you ask Maunsell about him when you go back to see him?' He emptied his glass and clapped his brother on the shoulder. 'Maybe we'll meet up for a drink over Christmas – somewhere else, though, eh?' He raised his hand in farewell to Billy, 'Goodnight to you now, Billy. I'll be seeing you.' And without another word he was gone. Billy stayed by the fire for a few moments longer and then slowly walked over to the bar. Stephen was staring into the bottom of his glass of whiskey, leaning heavily on the counter to take the weight off his leg.

'What was that all about?' he asked in a low voice, and they looked at the ceiling as a pair of heavy boots thundered up the stairs and tramped steadily over their heads.

Stephen didn't answer at first. He considered his whiskey for a few moments, swirling it slowly around the glass.

'Family stuff,' he said at last.

'Well,' said Billy. 'You know what they say. You can choose your friends . . .'

'Only sometimes,' Stephen countered, and raised his glass with a smile. 'Let's drink to families instead.'

'All right. Here's to families,' Billy agreed, and they clinked their glasses together.

Stephen went clean across the barracks square and up the stairs without a pause. Down the corridor and past the startled clerk he went, stone-faced, furious, and determined. The leg didn't bother him now, and he carried his stick in his fist, brandishing it like a weapon. Figgis had been right – the vein was far more effective. It worked much faster, and was more soothing while it lasted. He felt fit and energetic after it – almost elated. But still, it hadn't taken the edge off his anger – not after he'd seen Carpenter's battered face.

It hadn't been hard to find him – two afternoons visiting hospitals and nursing homes, until he'd finally tracked him down to the officers' hospital in Dublin Castle. The weather had turned snowy by then, the cobbles in the courtyard were icy, and he'd picked his way across carefully, still wary of the leg, and not fully trusting the new injection to protect him if he fell. The matron had eyed him uncertainly, glancing at the sign that listed the visiting hours. It was almost teatime. But he was a captain, he was wounded himself, and he pleaded an imminent departure to England. All he wanted was the chance to say goodbye to his old comrade Carpenter who, if it hadn't been for his unfortunate . . .

'Riding accident?' the matron asked looking up from her ledger.

'Yes,' Stephen agreed. 'He was never much of a hand with a horse.'

'You can say that again,' the matron said, leading him down a gloomy corridor that smelled of boiled food and laundry starch. 'He really should choose a more docile mount. I'm afraid the animal gave him quite a nasty kick.'

'I'm sure it did,' Stephen agreed, but he was distracted now. Every open door reminded him of his own stay in hospital, and he shuddered at the thought of it. But at least he'd got out before the winter set in and confined him. These men looked like prisoners; grey-faced and sullen, dozing in their pyjamas, sitting in wheelchairs, wrestling awkwardly with crutches. He caught the eye of one of them and saw envy there, before he looked away quickly. Then the matron stopped at a door that stood closed, knocked once and swept in brightly.

'Lieutenant Carpenter, your friend is here to see you,' she said, as Carpenter looked up. He was sitting on his bed, holding one side of a newspaper up with one hand. His other arm was in a plaster cast, and slung across his chest in a spotted scarf. Fortunately for Stephen, his face was so badly bruised, with one eye blackly swollen, that the matron didn't notice the suspicious frown that came on when he saw Stephen. Also, there was something wrong with his mouth, for when he tried to speak all he could manage was a metallic clucking sound.

'His jaw is fractured, so you'll have to be patient with him,' the matron whispered to Stephen.

'Thank you, Matron,' Stephen said, ushering her out with a pleasant smile. 'I'll try not to tire him out.'

He shut the door and stood with his back against it, looking at Carpenter, whose one good eye was fixed on him, beady and frightened. He was clucking again, working his throat furiously as he tried to speak.

'Well, well,' Stephen said, before he could get a word out. 'You have been in the wars, haven't you?'

'W-who are you?' Carpenter managed eventually, although it came out more like a protracted groan.

'My name is Ryan. You don't know me, but we have a mutual acquaintance – a Captain Maunsell.'

Captain Maunsell. He remembered how Carpenter's good eye had widened at that name. He remembered, too, how Carpenter had talked and talked, though it had obviously caused him pain, and when they finally shook hands and Stephen left the hospital, he had been fuming.

Maunsell's door was closed, but Stephen burst in without knocking. Maunsell was hunched over his desk, reading something under the yellow light of an electric lamp. There was a thin ribbon of smoke rising from the cigarette tilted into the ashtray, and this was blown into thin air by the sudden commotion.

'What the devil do you mean by this?' he demanded, starting out of his chair. Despite the shock, his face looked hard and dangerous, but Stephen towered over him, feeling ten foot tall in his wrath.

'I might ask you the same bloody thing,' he said, and kicked the door shut behind him. The noise of it was loud enough to make Maunsell jump, and Stephen hid a triumphant smile. He thought he had him on the back foot, although there was still that hard, shifty belligerence. He knew he had to keep the pressure on.

'You bloody knew, didn't you?' he said, with hardly a pause.

'I knew what?' There was a shrill note in Maunsell's voice, and his jowls wobbled. 'Now, look here—'

'Don't you bloody "look here" me. You knew they'd see me coming, didn't you? You knew, but you sent me anyway. That was the whole idea, wasn't it?'

'No,' Maunsell answered, a little too quickly.

'No? Then why haven't you asked for my report? Why haven't you sent for me to see what I found out? Because you don't bloody care what I found out, do you? That wasn't the point. The point was to bloody provoke them, wasn't it? You saw what they did to Carpenter, so you sent me along to see if they'd do it again.' Stephen had his hands planted firmly on the desk and his face close to Maunsell's. Close enough to see him wince when he mentioned Carpenter's name. 'That's why you had me followed, isn't it? That's why you had those men sitting in the car outside the hotel. You were hoping I'd bring some of their hard men out into the open, so you could grab them. I was the bloody goat tied to the stake.'

He knew he was right, but Maunsell's affronted look turned into a sneer.

'Why, what's the matter?' he asked, sinking into his chair. 'Haven't you ever taken part in a diversion before? A feint? Didn't you learn anything over in France? Or did you just keep shooting until you bloody well hit something?'

'A feint?' Stephen laughed, though his hackles were still up. 'Oh, please, don't come the strategist with me. Your plan was half-arsed and you know it. No wonder they're running bloody rings around you. If you were any good at your job, you would have known they had me pegged the minute I walked out of this office. When I showed up at that meeting they knew who I was, who sent me, and who you had sitting outside. They're the ones who are watching you, you bloody half-wit.'

Maunsell clasped his hands across his meagre paunch and looked like he'd swallowed something disagreeable.

'It's easy for you to talk,' he said, though his eyes wouldn't meet Stephen's. 'You don't know what it's like. You don't know how hard it is to fight this sort of war. And it *is* a war . . .'

'Balls,' Stephen said shortly, annoyed as much by Maunsell's whining tone as by the fact that he was making excuses. 'It's not a war – not yet, anyway. It's a game, and your side is losing because you're making the same mistake you always make. You think you're better than they are. But you're not – you're just bigger. For Christ's sake, you didn't even know my brother was going to be there – and it's just as well for me that he was, otherwise I'd be in the hospital beside Carpenter and you'd be beating the living daylights out of a couple of thugs who know nothing and would tell you less.'

Maunsell eyed him coldly, a look of pure hatred on his glabrous face.

'Spy, my arse,' Stephen threw at him, jerking the door open. 'You couldn't keep an eye on your own grandmother.'

'If you think I'm bothered by insults, you can think again,' Maunsell said, with a quiet vehemence. 'I haven't finished with you yet.'

'Yes, you have.' Still with his hand on the door, Stephen turned on him. 'You have, and you know it. I'm bugger all use to you now.'

'Well, then, we'll just have to send you back to where we found you,' Maunsell retorted, with spite in his voice. 'See how you like that.'

'Do what you like,' Stephen called back from the corridor. He felt light-headed now, and the knee bit him sharply as he turned, making him wince. So soon? He hadn't thought it would wear off so quickly. But it quietened again as he walked away, though he suddenly felt drained. 'Do what you like,' he repeated in a quieter voice. 'I don't bloody care.'

24 December 1917

Still in barracks and slowly going around the bend. What little work I once officially had to do is long since finished, and now they don't know quite what to do with me. Every day I report to the orderly room, and every day I get some dull little piece of work that rarely stretches out to lunchtime. On the other hand, this leaves the afternoons free for my exercise regime, or for my self-flagellation – I'm not sure which describes it best.

I managed to walk four miles yesterday but when I came back the pain was so bad that I couldn't do anything – not even record the distance in my diary. It was paralysing – and, what was worse, I could feel it coming. It starts off as just a throb, a twinge as the morphine starts to wear off, and then it gets its teeth into me. It won't be ignored, and when it really bites I am good for nothing: neither reading nor writing, and certainly not for mathematics.

It got so bad last night that I almost gave myself another injection. The only thing that stopped me was Figgis's warning about the dosage. I know he's worse than a quack and a charlatan, but if anybody knows about the risks of an overdose, he does. Besides, I've seen for myself how

88

dangerous it is. At the front, it's not unknown for doctors to give an overdose to badly wounded men when they are beyond hope. It's a mercy in those cases, but it's so easily done that I must be careful.

Nevertheless, I think it's worth the risk. For about an hour after the injection, it feels like there is nothing wrong with my leg. I can climb stairs, walk, run and jump. It's as if the nerves have been disconnected, and I wonder if this might be part of the problem. Perhaps I'm overdoing it a bit, and paying the price when the morphine wears off. Still, I only need to last an hour or so – long enough to get past the medical board in a few weeks.

Since it's Christmas Eve, I have even less work to do than usual. I knocked off at lunchtime and went shopping. On my way out the gate, I met Lieutenant Carpenter, who is billeted here now. His bruises have gone down a bit, but his jaw is still wired and his arm is still in a cast. He doesn't say much, for obvious reasons, but as far as I know he is still sticking to his story about a riding accident. I'm not going to say any different because it's none of my business now. It's a week since I saw Maunsell and I haven't heard a word from him. I only hope he leaves me alone long enough to sit the next board and get out of here.

Anyway, I got Lillian a necklace for Christmas, which I think she'll like – I hope so, because she's still upset since I told her I intended going back to the front. I don't think she's angry at me as such – she understands it's something I need to do – but she doesn't like it, and I can't say I blame her. I hope to find her in better form tonight, and I'm looking forward to spending Christmas with her. However it goes, I'll be happy just to have her near. It's just started to snow and that's really put me in the mood. When I *think of last Christmas, when the snow and the bloody bone-numbing cold made us all miserable, I realize the difference it makes to be home, to be safe and warm.*

Sometimes I wonder what the hell I think I'm doing.

Christmas day was snowy and cold. By late afternoon the sky was dark and the flakes that fluttered down seemed unnaturally white in the gloom. It was very quiet, and even the soft thump of the front door closing sounded loud in the snow-muffled street. While Lillian pinned her hat, Stephen drew in a few breaths of the frigid air and found it refreshing after the heavy warmth of the house.

Lillian tightened her scarf, then took his arm and reached up and kissed his cheek.

'Thank you for putting up with all that – I know you don't like to be fussed over.'

To say he had been fussed over was putting it mildly. He had been fed almost to the point of bursting, had drunk port and brandy and mulled wine until he felt dizzy whenever he stood up, and had been sat near a fire of sea coals that burned so hot he could still feel the glow on one side of his face.

'Oh, I don't mind.' He smiled. 'It's nice to be fussed over now and again.'

He was in a high good humour, having excused himself to the bathroom before he put on his coat for the walk. Now he felt numb and a little bit euphoric, as if he were floating above the snow. Lillian gave him her arm to help him down the steps, but he hardly needed it. He held his stick in the crook of his arm and slid his hand down the cold iron railing, sending a little flurry of snow tumbling into the garden.

'Well, thank you, anyway. It was a wonderful day – and such a treat to have you here.'

He smiled, but a little uneasily. He knew what she was driving at – that it was such a treat to have him here when he seemed so hell bent on going away.

'It was my pleasure,' he said, as they walked arm in arm down the garden path, the snow crisping and creaking under their shoes. The familiar street, with the canal and tall trees, looked much different in its coat of winter white. The reeds in the canal – that he'd often heard whispering as he walked along here – were frozen in place, and the whole surface of the canal was black and solid, dusted with snow and starred with cracks. The rooftops were uniformly white, and every chimney trailed a thin tendril of smoke against the chilly evening air. Shortages be damned. It was Christmas.

They didn't speak for a while, but they were comfortable in their silence. After crossing the icy street they turned along the canal bank and Stephen felt a sense of enormous satisfaction welling up inside him. This was the most perfect end to a perfect day. He knew Lillian felt the same – he could feel that she was happy just to hold him by the arm, and he was just as happy to have her there. To be connected to her was enough. They didn't need words.

Three ducks came whirring down between the trees, wings flapping and feet outstretched to land. But at the last moment they saw the canal surface was frozen and their wings beat even harder as they rose up and wheeled away again.

'Disappointed ducks,' Lillian said, and they laughed together as they watched the ducks disappear over the rooftops. They walked on, and the path gradually rose up towards the bridge. It was one of the oldest bridges on the canal, and very steeply arched. Their feet slipped and skidded in the snow as they climbed up, giggling and pulling one another, until at last they stood at the top and could see the broad black reach of the canal running arrow-straight away from them. Stephen leaned on the parapet and eased the weight off his leg. Lillian stood beside him, close enough for him to smell the dry, light fragrance of her hair. He put his arm across her shoulders and pulled her closer.

'Are you happy, sweetheart?' she asked, struggling against him.

He nodded. 'I'm happy. This is the best Christmas I've had in years.'

'But – ' she began, and broke off, afraid to spoil the mood. What was the point? She already knew the answer to the question that was on her lips. But she had to hear it from him. 'If you're happy here, I don't see why you feel so compelled to go back. Why would you leave all this behind when you've already done enough? You know you have. You've done more than most, and you've been wounded. There would be no shame in saying you're not fit to go back – none at all.'

'I know that,' he answered softly, though he knew there was every chance that he wouldn't even be allowed to return to France. There was still the board to face in January, and if they turned him down then it would all have been for nothing – the deception, the morphine, everything. But the more he thought about it, the more he was convinced that he had to go back. He had to make it all mean something.

'You're right,' he said after a pause, making a fist with his free hand and pounding it lightly on the snow-dusted parapet of the bridge. This wasn't the day for this conversation. But it was in the air: he couldn't hold back now. 'You're absolutely right. People wouldn't think any less of me if I didn't go back, but it's not them I'm worried about.'

'Then why are you so . . . so anxious to go back?'

'I think you know why,' he answered with a wry smile. 'It's the same reason why you protest against the war. You could lose your job for doing that – but still you do it. Why? Because you're a decent person and your conscience won't let you just sit back and do nothing.'

'Your conscience?' She gave him a questioning look. 'You'll have to explain your conscience to me, Stephen, because you know as well as I do that the war has gone on too long. You don't agree with the war, you don't agree with conscription, and yet you're going back to fight for the third time. Is it really your conscience, Stephen? What about that man Sassoon? He has a conscience, too, but it's telling him not to go back so he's not letting them send him back. What about him, Stephen?'

'He's not well,' Stephen answered uneasily. He knew all about Sassoon, and he'd seen the name of Rivers mentioned in the papers alongside it. 'He's worn out, most likely. He's in hospital.'

'They put him in hospital. They put him there to keep him quiet and to make his protest look like the ravings of a madman. He's not mad, Stephen, and you know it. Maybe he's the only sane one in this whole mess.'

'Maybe he is, but if he's half the officer everybody says he is, then he'll go back. He'll go back eventually.'

'Why?' She stepped away from him and looked him up and down. 'Because it's his duty? Because he took some stupid oath?'

'Because it is his duty – but not to the King, or even to God. It's his duty to his men. His duty not to leave them out there getting killed and maimed while he swans around in Blighty telling everybody how terrible it is. It's his duty to go back and stand next to them and do what he can for them. And that's my duty too, that's what I have to do as long as the war lasts and as long as there's breath in my body. That's what I have to do so I don't wake up every day for the rest of my life wondering if I could have done more.'

It was only when he stopped talking that he realized his voice had grown stronger, more forcible. In the muffled stillness of the afternoon, it was almost as if he had been shouting, gesticulating, waving his arms. Lillian was looking at him strangely, her head tilted to one side, her hands clasped together, almost as if she was praying.

'I'm sorry,' he began, but she stepped closer, put her arms around him and hugged him tight, resting her head on his shoulder.

'Don't be sorry. You have a good heart, Stephen Ryan,' she whispered, and he could feel the warmth of her breath in his ear, smell the scent of her hair. 'Just you make sure you damn well come back again.'

V

Étaples, 20 January 1918

My dearest Lillie,

You will be happy to hear that I have finally made it as far as France. The crossing to Boulogne was a bit rough, but I'm thankful for small mercies, since rough weather keeps the German submarines in port. On the other hand, the weather hasn't improved since I got here. I'm in the base depot at Étaples and, even as I write, the sleet is rattling on the tent, and there is a wind blowing in off the sea that is sharp enough to cut you. Not only is it freezing cold, but it carries with it clouds of sand from the beach. This salty grit covers everything, and manages to make the place look even greyer than usual. In their customary mangling of French names, the men call this place 'Eat Apples', but right now it couldn't be further from apples and the thoughts of summer they conjure up.

At least my leg appears to be behaving itself. I'm getting about quite easily without the stick, and although the limp is noticeable, it doesn't slow me down very much. We had our first route march today and I went most of the way on horseback – which I wouldn't have done before – but

I made a point of dismounting and marching the last couple of miles with the men, just to show I could do it.

My domestic arrangements are much the same as they were the last time I was in one of these camps, in as much as I share my tent with another officer. This time, however, I'm the old hand and my tent-mate, Lieutenant Rowan, is the novice. He is in many respects the ideal companion, since he is quiet and considerate, keeps his kit tidy and doesn't snore. His one fault is his endless praying. He is very religious in the way that some Protestants are – much given to personal prayer and quoting scripture. I rarely find him without a Bible in his hand, and he is up before me every morning, kneeling by his cot and saying his prayers. I don't know why I find it so unsettling. I suppose I keep thinking of what he and I will be doing a few weeks from now. It's hard to square his devotion to God with the idea of him putting murder in his heart and doing in his fellow man. I only wonder if he will have the stomach for it.

On the other hand, I have no such doubts about the Americans. There are a few hundred of them here – sent by General Pershing's staff to learn how us old hands get things done – and they are as keen as mustard. They attend all the lectures and demonstrations with the avidity of schoolboys and if there is a drill to be done, they will do it better, faster and harder than anybody else, just to show that they can. But for all their ardour, they have yet to see action and they are in awe of anybody who has. They are not the least bit shy either, and I can't walk from here to the mess without being buttonholed by a couple of them. They are always exceptionally polite, but sooner or later one of them will always ask the question they all want answered: how many Germans have I killed?

Remarkably, Rowan has fallen in with a few of them and went off drinking with them last night. On the face of it, you really could not look for a worse match, because Rowan is so shy and reserved, while the Yanks (they don't seem to mind that we call them that) are a pretty raucous bunch, much given to knocking each other's hats off and wrestling with one another. Nevertheless, they get on like a house on fire, and all went to an estaminet in the town last night. Rowan came home rather late and rather drunk – drunk enough, at any rate, to trip over the wonky duckboard at the door of the tent, before picking himself up and crawling into bed without saying his prayers. I suspect the Almighty was wroth over missing his nightly bulletin, because he visited upon poor Rowan a morning head of biblical proportions!

But for all their peculiarities, I'm glad the Americans are here. They liven up the place, and while I'm sometimes afraid that the fizz will be knocked out of them when they finally go into battle, I am heartened by their energy and their optimism. Everybody else is fairly miserable about our hopes come the spring. With Russia out of the war, the Germans now have thousands and thousands of extra men to fight in the west, and it's widely assumed that as soon as the weather turns half decent they will fall on us like a ton of bricks. The one hope against that is the Americans. With their inexhaustible numbers, they may be the only chance we've got against the onslaught.

Well, I must be going now. Rowan is at his evening prayers and will soon turn out the light. I think of you now, as I always do, and I look forward to seeing you again soon.

With all my love,

Stephen

It was getting dark at last. Stephen lay on his cot and watched the air grow dim above his head. He'd spent the whole day watching that little patch of canvas, listening to the rain drumming on it, waiting, waiting, waiting. Thank Christ it was over at last. Another night to endure, but that didn't seem so bad. The darkness was comforting, and there was a slim chance of sleep. He scratched himself and twisted irritably within his clothes. The sound of the rain was getting loud again, beating on his ears, hurting him. It was so familiar that he should have found it soothing, but he wouldn't be soothed. He was cold and sore and his skin itched. He could feel his shirt rubbing on it like sandpaper, and smell the rank sweat oozing out of his pores. He reached up and scratched his neck again, hard enough to hurt, but it did no good. *Everything* itched, and it was deeper than the skin, it was all over, all through him. His whole body prickled and stung. It was maddening.

It wasn't lice either. He'd checked for the little buggers and found none – it was too early for them. He knew it was the Needle – he missed the Needle. Twenty hours since he used up the last of his morphine, and that stretched out to such a small dose that his hands had shaken as he tried to draw it out of the bottle. It had been just enough to get him to sleep last night, but the pain had woken him in the small hours. He'd fumbled on his clothes and gone out into the dark, through a freezing gale of salty sleet blowing in off the North Sea. The hospital lay half a mile away, in a series of tall marquees that ranged along the shore like circus tents, and it was slow going without the comforting mask of the drug. By the time he got there it was already growing light, but inside the tents were gloomy and crowded – rows and rows of cots, all full, and men lying on mattresses in the spaces between them. He felt the heat of fever in the air, thick and mephitic, and was appalled at the sight of grey faces, writing

98

limbs and sweaty chests. He'd been expecting the usual collection of sprains, hernias and hopeless syphilitics, but this . . . this was a charnel house. Doctors and nurses hurried about, all wearing cotton masks, and the warm, stale air was filled with the sound of coughing, of groaning, of harsh, laboured breathing.

'And darkness lay upon the face of the deep.' Rowan's voice came suddenly from across the tent, loud enough to make Stephen jump and send a bolt of pain jabbing up his leg. He looked across in irritation, but what he saw reminded him of the hospital that morning. Rowan's face was almost as pale as his pillow, and his breath was sawing in his throat. He'd been in bed all day – sometimes asleep, sometimes awake, but usually somewhere in between – twitching weakly in his delirium and quoting chapter and verse. Christ! He felt bad enough without Rowan putting the willies up him like that. Another racking shiver and he pulled the blanket up to his chin. The gale was still blowing outside, and now and then the steady drumming of the rain was interrupted by the harsher rattle of sleet, hurled at the bucking tent in a gust of wind that blew in through the laces and sent icy draughts scurrying through the dark.

The hospital had been so full that he'd been embarrassed to ask for a doctor. But a nurse had seen him limping in and, after asking about his leg, had directed him to the row of clapboard huts that ran beside the big hospital tent. He might find a doctor in one of those, she'd told him, and he'd gritted his teeth and limped across.

The first two huts were empty, though he saw a dentist's chair in one and in the other assorted straps and tools that must have belonged to a veterinarian. In the third he found a man slumped over a desk with his head pillowed on his arms. He was snoring loudly, but he was wearing a doctor's coat. Stephen knocked politely on the half-open door, but to no effect. Leaning against the door jamb, he rapped with the top of his cane and the head jerked up suddenly.

'What?' The face was that of an older man, intelligent but severe. His deeply creased cheeks were covered with grey stubble and he clearly didn't like being woken up. 'What the hell do you want?'

'I'm looking for a doctor.'

'Aren't we all?' the man muttered absently, patting his pockets. Then he frowned and his eyes suddenly came into focus, pale blue and as sharp as knives. He glared suspiciously at Stephen. 'Why? Have you got the fucking flu?'

Stephen was taken aback – the more so as the doctor suddenly pulled open a drawer and started rooting in it.

'Not that I'm aware of, no.'

'You're from Dublin, aren't you?'

'Yes, I am.'

Stephen found himself suddenly transfixed by the eyes again, this time accompanied by a singularly false grin.

'Me too, as it happens. Now, since we're such good chums, perhaps you'd like to offer me a smoke.'

'I beg your pardon?'

'A cigarette, you idiot, have you got a . . . hah!' He pulled a pack of Woodbines from the back of the drawer, put one to his lips and lit it. 'Christ!' He sat back, pinching the bridge of his nose, and exhaled a cloud of white smoke. 'What time is it?'

Stephen looked at his watch.

'It's half past six.'

'Already? Damn, it feels like I only went to sleep five minutes ago.' He looked Stephen up and down, narrowing his eyes. 'Well, don't just stand there, man. You were looking for a doctor and you've found one. Dunbar is my name. Come in, sit down. Tell me what brought you out at this ungodly fucking hour.'

'It's my leg,' Stephen told him, and negotiated the two steps into the hut with some difficulty.

'So I see.' Dunbar pointed to the low, ramshackle bed that almost filled one side of the tiny hut. 'What did you do? Pull a muscle on a route march? Fall out of one of the estaminets? Well, anything's better than another case of the fucking flu. Drop your drawers and let's have a shufti.'

Stephen did as he was told, and shuddered as the freezing air washed around his bare legs. He lowered himself on to the rough mattress and looked straight ahead at the bare boards of the far wall.

'Christ almighty!' Dunbar exclaimed when he saw the scar. 'Where on earth did you get that?'

'Ypres, last August.'

'And they sent you back? With that?' Dunbar was still standing up, staring at the wound with his hands planted on his hips, 'No offence, captain, but I didn't think we were that stuck for men.'

'I asked to be sent back,' Stephen answered defensively, 'I can still walk and move about. I just need something for the pain.'

'I'll bet you do.' Dunbar got down on one knee and seized him by the leg. He ran his long fingers up and down the length of the scar, then pressed down hard.

'That hurt?'

Stephen shook his head. 'Not particularly.'

The fingers moved higher. 'What about that?'

'No.'

'There?'

Stephen couldn't answer because his jaw was clamped shut with the pain. He saw white spots in front of his eyes and the top of his head tingled as his whole body went rigid.

'Jesus Christ!' he panted when Dunbar let go, but the doctor wasn't finished. He slid his fingers along the edge of the kneecap and pressed again. This time Stephen screamed.

'Interesting,' Dunbar said to himself. Then he got up and sat on the cot beside Stephen. He seized his wrist and held it for a few moments.

'Your pulse is racing, captain.'

'Why do you think that is?' Stephen retorted. His hands were still shaking and he could taste blood at the back of his throat.

'What do you take for the pain?'

'Morphine.'

'How often?'

'Now and again – whenever I need it.' He kept his eyes fixed on the far wall, feeling Dunbar glaring at him.

'I see.' Dunbar changed his grip, holding his wrist firmly in one hand while he deftly opened his shirt cuff with the other. Before Stephen could get free, he pulled the sleeve up, revealing the livid chain of needle marks up the inside of his forearm. 'Now and again, eh?'

Stephen didn't answer. He turned his face away again and kept his mouth shut tight until Dunbar let go of his arm and stood up.

'How long since your last injection?' he asked, walking back to the desk.

'Last night. It wasn't enough. The pain woke me.'

'And how long have you been injecting intravenously?' Dunbar flopped into his chair and picked up his Woodbine from the ash-tray.

Stephen first pulled up his trousers, then carefully pulled down and buttoned his sleeve, slowly restoring his dignity.

'About a month,' he said at last, meeting Dunbar's eyes.

'Which would have been just when you went in front of a medical board, right? I bet you were walking on air for them, weren't you? I bet you could have danced a jig with brother Morpheus coursing through your veins.'

Stephen nodded, feeling ashamed. Somehow, the fact that he'd done it to get back in the fight was lost on him now. What was the point? He was a wreck. He could hardly walk, never mind march or run, and he felt like he hadn't just fooled the medical board, but fooled himself as well.

'Morphine is highly addictive, captain,' Dunbar began in a lecturing tone, but he smiled and took a long drag on his cigarette. 'But then, you've guessed that already, haven't you? You've noticed that it always takes a little bit more to give you comfort. A little bit more and a little bit more, until there is nothing else left. You don't need me to tell you where it ends.'

'I only want a prescription,' Stephen said doggedly, buttoning his breeches.

'Well, you're not going to get one,' Dunbar said, stubbing out his cigarette. 'Not from me, at any rate.'

Stephen felt something sink in his chest. He suddenly felt the cold grip of fear. 'But . . . I only want—' he began, but stopped himself. He stared sullenly at Dunbar.

'Don't get me wrong – I'll help you, but not like that,' Dunbar told him. 'But first I need to see if you want to be helped. I want you to go back to your tent and stay there. Come back here tomorrow and I'll see what I can do about that knee.'

Stephen shook his head and laboriously pushed himself upright, his arm wobbling on top of the stick. No help – they were all the bloody same!

But Dunbar had followed him up and came around the desk to shake his free hand.

'I don't believe I caught your name, captain.'

'It's Ryan, Stephen Ryan. Royal Dublin Fusiliers.'

'Well, Stephen Ryan.' Dunbar kept his hand in a tight grip.

'Let me tell you about today. Today will be a very important day for you. It won't be the easiest day you've ever had, but it will end in time, I assure you. Now I know what you're thinking. I know *exactly* what you're thinking. You're thinking you'll limp into the village and find some clap doctor or an abortionist – some grubby little civilian who'll take your money and give you a taste of what you need. But don't bother, because I'll know if you do. You come back and see me tomorrow morning and I'll help you – I'll help you in any way that I can. But if you do anything else, I'll have you sectioned, and before I send you back for a dishonourable discharge, I'll make sure you know exactly how bad withdrawal can be. Is that clear, captain?'

Is that clear, captain? Stephen's eyes opened and he drew a deep breath. The tent was completely dark now, and he could only hear the canvas above him, drummed softly by the wind. He must have slept. He felt better – or at least different. The itching had stopped, but he was cold and his body felt stiff and sore. His stomach was sore too, and stiff as a board. But at least the cramps had eased. Had he really felt them, or had they been part of a dream? He'd felt the rippling and writhing inside his body, as if his intestines had turned into snakes. He slipped his hand under the blanket, touching his own flesh, feeling the clamminess, the sticky heat. He shivered again and pulled the blanket tighter. It was very quiet now. The wind had died down, and he could smell the salt in the air, the deeper reek of rotting seaweed and mud, the stink of low tide.

'Oh God!' Rowan whispered from across the tent. 'Behold . . . behold . . . Joy cometh in the morning!'

In his dream he saw Lillian standing in a field of flowers. She was wearing a white summer dress and a broad straw hat. The sky was deep and flawless blue and the sun warmed his shoulders as he walked towards her. The air was heavy with the scent of flowers, and he felt their long stalks brushing his legs as he passed. She looked up at him and smiled . . .

'Ryan, Ryan!'

Stephen opened his eyes. The tent was filled with a grey gloom, but it was no longer night. The voice came in such a low, hoarse whisper that he didn't recognize it, but then he felt fingers plucking weakly at his sleeve. He looked down and saw Rowan's face looking up at him. It was not the face he remembered. The eyes were sunk deep in sockets that were the colour of bruises and his skin had a waxy pallor with a faint tint of blue. As he struggled to draw another breath, it rattled in his throat.

It took him a moment to realize that Rowan must have dragged himself out of bed and across the tent to try and wake him. He was lying on the boards between their beds and his legs were twisted in a blanket. The top of his pyjamas was soaked in blood and God-knew-what.

'I'm not well,' he groaned.

Stephen was already trying to sit up. As he did, a wave of nausea swept his body, something like a protracted shiver that started at his feet and rolled slowly upwards. He gagged as it moved up his throat, thinking he might be sick. His body was covered in sweat, and his arms and legs felt like lead.

Rowan's head had sunk on to the edge of mattress. 'Would you mind fetching a doctor?' he asked, in a feathery voice.

Stephen winced at the sharp, inevitable pain that stabbed him when he tried to move his legs.

'Christ Almighty!' He groaned, throwing off the blankets. He felt groggy and weak and as the nausea passed it left behind a pounding headache that thumped at the back of his eyes. He managed to get his feet on the floor before he had to pause to catch his breath. He still had on his boots and breeches, which was something – but, when he tried to sit up, a monstrous cramp knotted in his stomach and he had to roll to one side, retching. There was nothing there, though. Nothing to eat and nothing to drink all day, and all he got was his own hot breath scorching his throat and the taste of bile in his mouth. He lay on his side for a few moments, panting.

Rowan didn't seem to notice. His eyes were closed and he wasn't moving. He looked so pale and waxy that Stephen thought he was dead, but then he groaned and caught a ragged breath, drawing it in with a long gasp, as if he were suffocating.

With hands as weak as a newborn's, Stephen reached for the tent pole. One, two, three, and he was up, swaying unsteadily on his feet. The floor looked like it was miles away and his legs were like jelly. A deep breath, and then he had to wait for a bolt of nausea to pass. His guts were turning to water, and yet there was something alive inside them. He could feel his own stomach rippling and knotting and cramping. When he tried to put some weight on his bad leg, a shaft of pain stabbed up through his thigh and his knee crumpled under the shock. He let out a scream and clung to the pole for dear life, shuddering as the pain clawed its way up his spine and finally died away.

The stick stood upright at the end of his bed, just out of reach, but with a turn and a lurch he had it, supporting himself on the bed frame. Next, the door nearly did for him; all hooks and eyes and laces, with the canvas shrunk drumhead tight from all the rain during the night. When the flap finally fell open, the cold air washed over him in a wave. He stumbled outside.

There was a thick fog lying over the camp. It had rolled in from the sea and he could taste the salt in it. Even though the tent was right behind him, he suddenly felt very cold and isolated. Everything was muffled and dim and it took him a few moments to get his bearings, to figure out which way was the hospital. A long way, he remembered, feeling the fog settle on his skin – ice cold, each crystal sharp and stinging. It was only a few hundred yards, but it might as well be bloody miles.

'Help!' he shouted, but it came out as a croak. There was no sound, nothing came through the fog. He tried to turn around on the stick but stumbled, barely managing to stay upright. He would never make it. Whatever about his legs, his arms were weak and wobbling with the effort of keeping him upright. He had to grit his teeth before he took another painful step along the duckboards.

'Help!' He tried again. 'Is anybody there?'

Only the wind, cold on the back of his neck. He shivered, but kept going; one step, lift the stick, plant it again. One step, lift the stick . . . Another wave of nausea hit him, rising up from his feet, and he felt himself go light-headed, as if he was fading into the mist. He could see nothing, feel nothing, only the cold fog as he fell through it, tripping over the stick, and landing hard in the freezing mud.

He couldn't feel his leg. It took him a while to notice, because he couldn't feel anything at first. His whole body was numb. He was floating in a grey void that stretched away into deepening gloom. Eventually, he realized he was in a tent – only it was much bigger than he remembered. He could hear the rain drumming on canvas, but it was further away. It didn't matter. He was tired. He felt himself drifting back into sleep. Soft sleep, easy sleep – free from pain.

When he woke again the numbness was gone, but he still couldn't feel his leg. His body was racked by cold, and he shivered so hard his teeth chattered. Then heat washed over him in waves – dry, intense, febrile heat. But he still couldn't feel his leg. He tried to look at it, but he didn't have the strength to sit up that far. The effort sent his head spinning, and he sank back against the pillows gasping, anxious. At some point a face floated into his field of vision. It was a woman's face, but not Lillian's. He smiled at the woman anyway, but then she went away. He closed his eyes and went back to sleep.

The next time he woke he could hear noises. There was coughing and talking and the thump of feet hurrying by. There were rough curtains hung around his bed, but one had been drawn aside so that he could see another bed with somebody lying in it; a fringe of black hair beyond the bulge in the blankets. The rain had stopped drumming, but now he could hear dripping. Loud dripping, with a very metallic *plink*, directly behind him. He was wide awake now – but almost too awake. He felt light-headed and edgy, slightly giddy. There was a strange taste in the back of his throat, and his skin itched all over again.

He heard footsteps approaching and then a nurse appeared in the gap in the curtains. She was carrying a basin full of bandages, but she stopped and smiled at him.

'Good afternoon, captain,' she said brightly. 'Glad to see you're awake. How are you feeling today?'

'My leg,' he gasped.

'Oh?' She set down the basin before pulling up the blankets at the end of his bed. 'Is it giving you pain? Let's have a look now, shall we?'

'I can't feel it,' he began, but when he raised his head again, he saw two feet sticking up from under the blankets. 'Oh, thank Christ!'

'Colonel Dunbar gave you a local anaesthetic for the operation. It will probably take a while to wear off. Don't worry, you'll be as right as rain in no time.'

It took him a moment to take all this in. Then he frowned.

'*Colonel* Dunbar?'

'Yes. You're very lucky that he insisted on treating you himself. He's very busy, you know – particularly with this fever that's going around. But he'll be doing his rounds this evening and I'm sure he'll see you then. In the meantime, you should drink. You mustn't become dehydrated. I'll pour you some water, shall I?'

She poured a glass of water from the pitcher beside the bed and he drank greedily, feeling the cool water flowing down his throat and relieving the parched, shrivelled feeling. It restored his voice, and when he spoke again he sounded stronger to his own ears. 'What about Rowan? Lieutenant Rowan. He was in my tent. He was very sick.'

'Yes, he was. And we'd never have found him if it wasn't for you. You did insist rather strongly that we fetch him first. But he was already very far gone, I'm afraid.' She smiled sadly. 'I'm sure Colonel Dunbar will talk to you about him too, when he comes to see you.'

Picking up her basin of bandages, she went back about her business and Stephen let his head fall against the pillow. He closed his eyes for a few moments, and when he opened them again it had grown darker. All the curtains had been drawn from around his bed, and he could see the full extent of the cavernous tent – bed after bed stretching away in a long line lit by paraffin lanterns.

After a while, a curious figure appeared in one of the pools of light. As it came closer, he realized it was Dunbar – but it was Dunbar as he had not seen him before. He was wearing his mess-dress uniform, and his scarlet tunic with all its gold braid and brass buttons sparkled and glowed every time he passed under one of the lanterns.

'Evening, Ryan,' he said curtly and pulled up a chair beside the bed. 'They told me you were awake. How do you feel?'

'A bit strange,' Stephen answered, surveying Dunbar's tunic in all its glory. He was indeed a colonel as the nurse had said, but

Stephen's eyes widened when he saw the small red ribbon on top of the many others that adorned his left breast. 'Where on earth did you get that?'

'South Africa, in the last war.' Dunbar dipped his head self-consciously towards the Victoria Cross, then shrugged. 'I, too, was a Dublin Fusilier, once upon a time. I did something idiotic but brave, so they gave me this trinket – and now they won't let me within ten miles of the front, and everybody thinks I must have got it out of a pawnshop. Now, what about that leg of yours? Giving you any pain?'

'Hardly any. It's still a bit numb.'

'Well, it'll take a while for the anaesthetic to wear off. Anything else bothering you?'

'Itching, cramps, fever. A generally . . . odd feeling.'

Dunbar chuckled. 'Like ants under the skin, isn't it? That'll be the withdrawal from the morphine.'

'You sound like you're speaking from experience.'

'I am.' Dunbar said, matter of factly, and pulled out a pocket watch and flipped it open. 'Let's just say it came with the medal. Three Boer bullets made me take the dictum "Physician, heal thyself" a bit too far. Bloody stuff damn near did what the Dutchmen couldn't. Anyway – ' he held up the watch for a moment before slipping it back in his pocket ' – time heals all, and you've been off it for nearly two days now, so I think it's safe to say the worst is over. You should consider yourself lucky.'

'But I've got hardly any pain in my leg. And this anaesthetic everybody talks about, what did you do?'

'Ah, yes. Well, since you were delivered to me in a conveniently unconscious form, the first thing I did was take an X-ray photograph of your leg, which confirmed what I suspected when I examined you the other day. So, I gave you a hefty shot of novocaine and cut open your knee.' He pulled a small glass vial from his trouser pocket and tossed it to Stephen. 'Here's what I took out.'

Stephen held the vial up to the light. It contained a small fragment of metal about the size of a sewing needle, but much thicker, and more jagged.

'That's a shell splinter.'

'You're damn right it's a shell splinter. It's probably the little brother of the one that gave you that big scar. Only where the big one kept going, that one got stuck in your knee. It was embedded in the cartilage and moved about whenever you bent your leg. I'd imagine the pain would be comparable to having a nail driven into your kneecap.'

Stephen stared at the splinter with a mixture of wonder and revulsion. His mouth was dry at the memory. So much pain from something so very small.

'Of course, if those fucking horse-doctors at the clearing station had bothered to look before they sewed you up, they would have saved us both a lot of bother,' Dunbar went on. 'It wasn't really hard to get out – or it wouldn't have been at the time. Bit harder now, what with all the old scar tissue.'

'So that's it?' Stephen asked, still not sure that he could believe it. 'My leg is fixed?'

'Alas, no. Miracles are more the purview of your friend Rowan. I can only work within the bounds of medicine. Your leg was damn near cut off and there was extensive damage to tendon and muscle. So, you *will* walk with a limp for the rest of your life, and there's nothing I can do about that. But it will give you less pain, which should keep you from needing the morphine.'

'Thank you.' Stephen nodded, almost overwhelmed. On his best days with the morphine, the pain had been worse than it was now, with nothing. He could put up with this; he could *live* with it. 'You mentioned Rowan. How is he?'

'Well, to put it in a nutshell, he's buggered.' Dunbar stood up and straightened his tunic. 'He's got what our American chums call the Three-Day Fever. Only, in his case, I'm afraid his three days are nearly up.'

'Three-Day Fever?' Stephen asked. 'What's that?'

'It's the flu to you and me,' Dunbar said, though he knew he'd have the devil of a time convincing the brass hats that the epidemic that was raging through the rear areas was anything so simple. That was the reason for his dress uniform. He had been summoned to Army HQ to render an opinion, and he suspected his was the latest in a series of opinions they'd already had, each one more ludicrous than the last. He'd heard most of them whispered back as rumours; germ warfare, some sort of long-range poison gas, even poisoned aspirin specially cooked up at the Bayer factory and slipped into their supplies. After all that, the brass were bound to be disappointed if he told them it was only the bloody flu.

'The flu?' Stephen looked uncertainly around him. There had been a lot of coughs and wheezes coming from those other beds. 'Is it dangerous?'

'Generally, no. It's debilitating, but no worse than any other sort of flu. Most people get better after a few days – hence the name – but some don't, and I'm afraid your God-bothering friend is one of those. It's gone deep into his lungs, you see. There is pneumonia, and I suspect some sort of bacterial infection as well.' Dunbar smiled grimly and turned to leave. 'I'll come back to see you after dinner, but I should be surprised if Lieutenant Rowan lasts that long.'

VI

He must have fallen asleep on the train. When he woke, the window was misted over and the compartment was empty. Closing his eyes, he settled himself deeper into the warmth of his greatcoat and listened to the steady clack of the rails as the train rolled on into the dark.

This was the final stretch, and he knew he would be at the front by the time the sun came up. His leg was still stiff, as Dunbar had warned, but the pain was gone, and that in itself was hard to get used to. He still expected it to spring on him when he climbed a step or bent his knee, still tensed himself for it – but it never came. He felt its absence like a missing tooth. Now and then he even probed it, bending his leg or gingerly feeling along his kneecap, but it was gone for good.

He didn't miss the pain, but he thought he would miss Dunbar. He'd grown to like him over the past few weeks and, for all his gruff exterior and his foul language, he had a feeling that Dunbar would miss him too. He'd made a point of coming to see Stephen every day in hospital, often sitting to chat until late in the night, as the nurses whispered up and down the aisle, and the other patients groaned in their sleep. Then, after Stephen was discharged from the hospital and placed on light duties, Dunbar had invited him to dine as his guest in the doctors' mess. At first, Stephen suspected Dunbar was keeping an eye on him; making sure he didn't relapse into his old habit. But as time passed, he realized that Dunbar was bored and lonely in his post, and pleased to have somebody to talk to. They had parted as firm friends.

He hoped to find other friends when he reached his battalion, but for this night he was alone and, as he sat in the empty railway carriage, things started to crowd in on him with almost physical force. To begin with, he could feel the war looming closer. It was out there in the dark, waiting for him, and he regarded it with a mixture of dread and excitement, hating the thought of going back, but anxious to get it over with. And the closer he got to the front, the more he thought of Lillian. Faraway fields are greener, he told himself, but the mere memory of her moved him in ways he would never have dreamed. When he thought of her he felt as if he'd been cleaved in half, as if there was an enormous hole somewhere in the centre of himself. So much was missing, so much he'd left behind . . . When he opened his eyes he saw his own reflection in the window, his face a white blur in pitch black. He could have been afloat on a vast dark sea, alone, drifting.

Dozing again, he let the rocking carriage take him back to that last Sunday they'd had together. They had taken the train to Greystones and walked hand in hand along the beach. It was freezing. The surf thundered and hissed on the shingle and the wind roared in from the sea, whipping strands of hair from under Lillian's hat. She stood gazing out at the horizon, her eyes as grey as the sky. She loved the sea. There was salt in her blood, she said; her father and grandfather had been sailors. As Stephen stood near her he thought he could feel their strength in her; calm and immovable against the rolling of the waves. He was drawn to her stillness, and was surprised at the quickness of her touch when their hands met and he felt the spring of life in her fingers. Then again at the heat in her lips when they kissed.

In the evening they had taken the train back around the lightless curve of Dublin Bay. Lillian fell asleep with her head resting on his shoulder and as he felt the touch of her hair and breathed its scent, warm contentment flooded his chest. Everything was good in that moment, even the rain rattling against the windows as the train chivvied around the bay. He wished it would never arrive at its destination. The war was a million miles away and he could happily have sat there for ever with her hair brushing his cheek and the warmth of her hand in his.

With a screeching of brakes the train jolted, stopped and bumped him awake. He was alone again.

'Amiens! Last stop! Amiens!' a Scottish voice shouted in the corridor. As the locomotive gave out its last steamy breath he heard soldiers passing under the window and the distant rumbling of guns in the east.

Nightingale sat at his desk in Ronssoy schoolhouse, scribbling furiously. It was the teacher's desk, but he still felt like a schoolboy, with his inky fingers and the smell of chalk in the air. He was under the same sort of pressure too; had to finish this report for division, had to hand it in by five o'clock, or else . . . He paused, his pen almost touching the paper and smiled grimly to himself. Or else what? Would they keep him back after school? He doubted it somehow. He was writing a readiness report, and there were only so many ways he could say that they were not ready.

Half ready, those were the words he would use. They had just the right flavour of a muddle, of one leg in the britches. The brass wouldn't like it, but that was their hard luck. Perhaps they would even call him up there to dispute it. He knew what they'd say – that the front lines were well manned. But how could he make them understand that the front lines weren't the problem? The idea was defence in depth, a trick they'd picked up from the

Germans – and picked up the hard way in that bloody awful mess around Ypres – but at some level they still had a great deal to learn. *Defence in depth*. It had a nice ring to it, but they always looked only at the front lines, at the tip of the iceberg. And they were right in that respect. The outposts were strong enough, and the front line too, but the second and third lines were still only half dug, and no matter how forcefully he put it in his report, they would still be only half dug when the Germans marched across them.

But he couldn't just write it down like that. The staff liked numbers, statistics, quantifiable amounts. The fact that the Germans were plainly massing just over the ridge meant nothing to them. All they were interested in was man-hours, yardage, sandbags filled. Of course they knew there was a big attack coming – everybody knew that – but what infuriated Nightingale most of all was their eternal bloody optimism. The hole in the heart of their plan was that they didn't really think they would need it. When the shortfalls became obvious, when it was clear that the gaps were just too large, they would tell themselves that the German attack, when it came, would surely fall somewhere else. Fools! With them it was always going to be somewhere bloody else.

As Nightingale turned over the page and continued his dull, prosy, but factually correct list on the other side, there was a polite knock on the door.

'What is it?' He sighed, scribbling, scribbling, but without any heart. It never came out the way he wanted – he was too good a soldier for that. He might hint at a few problems, but he'd leave them decently hidden by more palatable facts and statistics. He'd go along with their charade.

'Captain Ryan reporting for duty,' said a familiar voice from the doorway. A broad grin spread across Nightingale's face, and he jumped up, screwing the top back on his pen.

'Stephen!' he cried, looking his friend up and down. 'I wasn't expecting you to . . . well, it's been so long, I thought you'd been attached to another regiment. But, my God, look at you. You're back! It's so good to see you.' Pumping Stephen's hand, Nightingale had already forgotten his report and the oafs who would read it.

'It's good to be back,' Stephen said uncertainly, taking off his cap and looking at the papers spread across the desk. 'What happened? Have they made you adjutant?'

'I'm afraid so,' Nightingale admitted. 'In a strictly acting temporary capacity, of course – though it's already been a month. I'm sorry to say I'm starting to get used to it. I should think I list off reports and readiness figures in my sleep. Please, sit, sit.' He pulled up one of the tiny chairs. 'Excuse the furniture. Needs must, and all that.'

Stephen eased his weight on to the chair, carefully straightening his leg as he did so. Nightingale watched him with considerable interest.

'How is it?' he asked. 'Does it hurt much?'

'Not any more, no.' Stephen grinned and patted his knee. 'And it's still there, at any rate. How about you? Are you well? How do you find being the battalion chit-wallah?'

'Please! Don't remind me!' Nightingale made a face, but grinned again as he pulled a bottle of apple brandy from his desk drawer. Evening was drawing in, and dusk turned to dark while they sat close together, chatting amiably. Five o'clock came and went but Nightingale paid it no attention. He was so delighted to see a familiar face – a fit and healthy face – that he had no qualms in neglecting his duties. The last time he saw Stephen he'd been nearly dead – covered in mud and blood and with the white bone showing through the wound in his leg. But there he sat, a million miles from the gaunt and shattered creature he had seen at Ypres.

Yet there was still something of it there, he thought, hidden behind the smile. There was the grimace when he moved his leg a certain way, and the hesitancy – was it apprehension?

After a while Nightingale got up and lit a lamp. The light fell on the map pinned to the blackboard and Stephen simply nodded towards it. He didn't even need to ask.

'It's not a pretty picture, is it?' Nightingale said, looking at the dozens of pins that represented the German divisions and battalions and regiments that were ranged against them. Then it was *his* turn to be apprehensive. Telling it to the staff was one thing, but Stephen would be one of the ones at the sharp end and he knew the implications. Nevertheless, he laid it out for him as plainly as he could, just as he saw it, just as he expected it to be. More than once he paused and tried to take stock of what he had just said. Surely he was exaggerating? Surely those numbers were too high? But no, he told himself, this is the army that fought the Russians to a standstill. This is the entire German Eastern Front moving west, coming down on top of us. In the dark stillness of the classroom, his words sounded appalling to his own ears.

When he was finished, Stephen sat quietly with his hands folded in his lap, staring at the map for more than a minute. Then he nodded slowly, his face grave.

'So, it's coming soon,' he said at last.

'It certainly is, old man,' Nightingale agreed. 'And we're for the chop, no doubt about it.'

The dugout was buried just below the crest of the ridge that overlooked Ronssoy on one side and Epehy on the other. It was the deepest dugout he'd ever been in – twenty steps down from the fire-trench – but although it was roomy and comfortable, he never slept down there. He'd been buried alive once, and it took an effort to ignore the tightness in his chest, to convince himself that the walls weren't closing in. Instead, he visited his outposts every night – there were two of them, Yak and Zebra, each commanded by a subaltern with a telephone line to his command post – and the men thought it was very conscientious of him, not realizing that he was only waiting out the night. When morning came, after stand-to, he would snatch a couple of hours' sleep on the fire step with the empty sky over his head and the watery sun for a blanket.

But there were still the grey hours at the end of the night, when everybody else was asleep, and to while these away he sat in his chair and read the book Lillian had given him when they parted at the North Wall. It was *The Principles of Mathematics* by Bertrand Russell, and she had handed it to him as they stood together for the last time, with the rain drumming and dribbling off her umbrella and the slick side of the Holyhead packet towering over them. The book had jarred with him at first. Russell was all over the newspapers again with his anti-war activities, and for a moment he wondered if she was making some sort of statement, but one look at her face told him it meant much more to her than that.

'My father gave me this for my birthday,' she said, biting her lip. 'It was the last thing he ever gave me and it's very precious.' She forced a smile. 'You have to promise me you'll bring it back yourself. With your own hand, Stephen – I don't want it back in a parcel with condolences. Promise me you'll give it back to me with your own hand.'

'I promise,' he answered, the words catching in his throat, and they kissed for the last time before she gently pushed herself away and he walked unsteadily up the gangplank, feeling her eyes on him all the way. They stood looking at one another while the gangplank was trundled in and the mooring ropes splashed into the inky water. The deck trembled and hummed under his feet and with an ear-piercing shriek the ship nosed out into the stream and gathered way. The last living thing he had seen on the shore was the pale blur of her face.

He hadn't opened the book in Étaples. He'd kept it safe in the bottom of his valise, saving it for just such a time as this. Reading it by candlelight, with half his men snoring behind the curtain, he could feel her very strongly. She had made notes in the margins: curt little phrases and exclamations in a neat hand. When he whispered them to himself he could picture her asleep in a silent room, far away from all this. He smiled when he turned to the dedication at the front of the book. It was written in a bold copperplate hand:

April 1912
To Lillie, my First Mate. With best wishes
and all my love on your birthday.
Quod erat demonstrandum.
Daddy

Quod erat demonstrandum. Stephen traced the words with his finger. Which was to be proved. He was dismayed to remember how he had left her standing on the quay in the rain. Although she put a brave face on it, he knew he was breaking her heart by going back. That leaving her also broke his own heart was no comfort, and when he looked back at her standing alone on the quay he felt more desolate than he had ever done. He knew he was doing it out of necessity, but still it galled him. It was no longer simply a question of his personal honour or peace of mind, of his being judged purely within the trammels of the war. Suddenly, unexpectedly, there was the future to think of, and the magnitude of it oppressed him.

'I'll be back!' he'd shouted, as the gap opened between them, but in the wind and the rain and the churning of water against the quay wall, he wasn't sure if she'd heard. Now he could only smile bitterly to himself. That assertion was still to be proved, as Professor Barrett would have said – what sort of guarantee had he left her with? Nothing more than a kiss and a promise to return that was hardly his to make. No other sign or word, nothing to mark the change she had wrought in him. Why hadn't he been able to tell her that she was the first thing he thought of when he woke in the morning, or the way his heart leapt when he set eyes on her?

The telephone at his elbow jangled into life, like breaking glass in the stillness of the dugout. It rang for a few seconds and then died abruptly. Automatically, he looked up to the ceiling.

Near Ronssoy,
21 March 1918

My dearest Lillie,

The Germans have opened their attack with the heaviest barrage I have ever seen. It has been going on since four o'clock this morning and it is falling right on top of us. Our dugout is holding up very well, although the roof is groaning and thumping like it is fit to fall in. It is impossible to go outside and all we can do is sit with our gas masks and rifles at the ready, waiting until the shelling stops.

There are a few things I wish I had said to you before and I'm ashamed that I wasn't able to say them to you instead of writing them down. But at this moment even the act of writing to you is a comfort and if the worst should happen I would rather you knew by any means.

It is hard to keep my concentration with all the noise.

*I don't know if you can smell fear, but you can certainly sense
it and it is all around me in this dugout. I know these words
are coming out the wrong way – they are certainly not what
I intended, but I want you to be absolutely certain that I am
not writing this now because I am afraid. To say it plainly,
I love you, Lillian. I have known it for a long time and,
waking or sleeping, I think of you always. I don't know why
it took so long for me to see it. It is like a proof that you
rack your brain to find, only to discover it is so beautifully
simple that it has been looking at you all the time. And
proof is the right word. Do you remember Professor Barrett's
definition of proof from our first year? He said there can be
no possible doubt that it is right, that there is no other
solution possible. Well, that is how I feel about you. You are
everything to me and I look forward to the day when I give
you this letter to read and see that I am right.*

*Be in no doubt that I fully intend to keep my promise to
you; I will live through this, and I will come back to you.
As long as there is breath in my body I will never stop
trying. Life was never as precious to me as it is now. If the
worst should happen, then you will know that I fought as
hard as I could to prevent it. I will fight like a madman to
get back from here and see you again.*

*Well, I must go. The barrage is lifting and I must go
outside to see what is coming after it.*

With all my love,

> *Stephen*

Smoke. The smell of burned earth and cordite. The trench was
wrecked, blown in; a mess of splintered timber and sandbags
underfoot. Above them, the sky was shrieking with German shells
travelling over, falling to the rear.

'Ten rounds rapid, FIRE!' Kinsella bellowed, and the ragged volley crackled again. The thick fog was clearing at last, shredded by the morning breeze, and they could see the mass of grey figures swarming towards them. It seemed impossible that there were so many – and so close! Yak and Zebra were gone, that was for certain. The Germans were almost on top of them now. Stephen could see them loping up the shattered ground, dodging and darting like rabbits. He had a rifle and he worked it methodically, picking his targets at long range, firing, opening and closing the bolt with steady deliberation. Every shot must count. The intense bombardment had smashed all their lines of communication and supply and it didn't need a mathematician to work out that they would quickly run out of ammunition.

But it was touch and go as to whether they would run out of ammunition or be overrun first. The Germans had already broken in once – a little knot of them rushing up from a deep crater in the direction of Ronssoy – and they had met them hand to hand. One of them ran on to Stephen's bayonet, knocking him over backwards with the rushing weight on the point of his rifle, and screaming, gurgling hot in his face. As Stephen had struggled to get up he saw Kinsella charging into them, swinging a shovel right and left. He was screeching unintelligibly as the steel edge of the shovel bit into flesh, his furious face sprayed with blood.

They had knocked them back that time, but it would be harder to keep them out the next time. The trench was taking fire from every side and this was eating into the dwindling knot of men. If they didn't pull back soon they would be overwhelmed. He could feel the tide coming in around them, slowly rising to cut them off, and even if they retreated now, they'd have a fight on their hands just to get out.

'Well, Stephen, what news on the Rialto?' a voice called up to him, and he glanced down to see Nightingale crouched on the floor of the trench, grinning from under a bloodstained bandage around his head. Father Doran was with him and between them they were carrying a crate of ammunition, which the priest dragged towards Kinsella's firing line as Stephen slithered down from his post and nodded to the bandage around his friend's head.

'What happened to you?'

'Shell blew the roof off Battalion HQ,' Nightingale explained. 'We had to clear out in a bit of a hurry, as you can imagine. How are you holding up?'

Speaking over the thunder of shells and the angry snap of bullets whipping across the trench, Stephen told him about the first break-in and the likelihood of another. Nightingale listened closely with his unbandaged ear. What Stephen said supported what he already knew from the surviving posts along the line: Ronssoy was in German hands and they were reinforcing up the Epehy road. The whole battalion was in danger of being overrun.

'Well,' he said, and ducked as a mortar landed just beyond the parapet and made the ground thump under them, showering them both with dirt, 'I don't need to tell you we're in a bloody tight spot. It looks like the Lancashire division on our right has broken, which leaves that flank in the air and the Germans moving around behind us. Our artillery's been blasted to hell, by the way, so don't expect any help there. Major Wheeler has taken command of the brigade, and he said we should get ready to pull back to Ridge Reserve, consolidate, then make a dash for the Brown Line.'

Stephen nodded his agreement. The Brown Line was their incomplete third defensive position, weaving around the village of St Emilie, about half a mile behind them. It would offer hardly any shelter from an attack of this magnitude, but if they pulled back that far it might give them some time to reorganize – and it would certainly ease the pressure on their flanks. He pulled the tattered map from his pocket, with red, yellow, brown and green lines traced across the landscape. They were standing on the red. Getting back to the brown looked straightforward enough on paper, but not with the Germans pressing them as hard as this in broad daylight. It would be bloody murder.

'You know, it's funny. We've never had to retreat before. I'm not sure if I remember how it's done,' he said, with a grin.

Nightingale laughed grimly.

'First time for everything, isn't there? But if this keeps up, I think we're going to have to bloody well get the hang of it.'

A few minutes later, it started. Back they went; back and back again. Harassed and harried, they gave ground slowly, pausing every few yards to beat back the Germans as they tried to engage them on the run. The cost was high – they lost men at every stop – but Stephen shuddered to think what it must have cost the enemy to come after them.

As it got dark they pulled out of the Brown Line and fell back through St Emilie itself. They stopped in a railway cutting to the west of the village, to gather their wits and count heads. Even with the stragglers trickling in all afternoon the battalion numbered less than a hundred, from a fighting strength of over six hundred. Exhausted, they flopped down along the tracks and tried to sleep. There was little talk, just the thundering of the artillery falling on the Brown Line. Flares and shell flashes lit the night, and the acrid stench of cordite from their clothes was suddenly nauseating.

Stephen felt the knot in his stomach finally start to loosen, and the first hunger pangs came on. He rummaged in his haversack for a bar of chocolate, but felt the angular bulk of Lillian's book wrapped in its oilskin cloth. He had folded his letter inside for safekeeping and, after thinking for a moment, took the book out and weighed it thoughtfully in his hand. Nightingale trudged up and sat beside him on the steel track.

'We're off again in a few minutes. Back to Tincourt this time,' he said wearily, and in the flash of a flare he saw the book. His grimy face split into a broad grin. 'This is hardly the time for reading, Stephen.'

'I want you to keep this for me,' Stephen told him, solemnly handing him the book. 'Make sure it gets to Lillian if anything happens to me.'

Nightingale took it reluctantly. The odds were far from good for either of them, but as the flare sank slowly to earth he could see the sombre look on Stephen's face, and he knew it was no time to argue.

'Right-oh,' was all he said, and he slipped the book into his haversack. Then he looked hungrily into Stephen's. 'I say, you wouldn't happen to have anything to eat, would you? I'm starving.'

25 March 1918

I don't know how long we can go on like this. Four days and I doubt I've slept four hours. Back and forth, dodging through the country, turning, fighting. The Germans are all over the place, but still we fight, we stab at them; one thrust, and we run. It cannot last; every minute it feels like my luck is running out. This afternoon we came to Cappy for the second time in as many days. Yesterday we passed through the same village as we fell back across the Somme. But no sooner had we reached the other bank than we were turned around and sent back to this side to hold the bridgehead. God help us! Things must be in a right state if we're all they can spare to hold such an important river crossing. Our numbers are so low that we have formed a ragtag unit with the Munster Fusiliers and whatever stragglers we can hold on to, but even at that we are barely two hundred strong.

We are bloody and battered, but at least we have stopped giving ground for the time being, and the men are cheerful. They talk about reinforcements being rushed over from England and they are sure the Americans must arrive at any moment. It keeps their spirits up and they make me proud when I think what we saw at Doingt: men rushing past unarmed, literally running away. They shouted for us to run for it too, but they got short shrift from our lads. Kinsella sent a string of oaths after them and told them he'd see them in hell. Then he cackled with laughter, which wasn't a pleasant sight, since he managed to lose his false teeth a couple of days ago. The other men rib him about it constantly, and one even offered him a pair he found in a wrecked house, but Kinsella didn't bite, as it were. He takes it all in good heart, however, and I think he even plays up to it a bit because he knows it is good for morale. God knows there's precious little else to laugh about.

Still, we must keep going. We are exhausted, outnumbered and encircled, but we have come so far that we are determined to hold on, no matter how hopeless the situation. Rank and ceremony have gone by the board and we are all in this together; eating and sleeping on top of each other in hastily dug holes. The spirit is still strong and the Germans can push us all the way to Calais if they want, but they will never get past us.

They watched Nightingale darting along the moonlit road, doubled over as he ran, until he slid breathless into the ditch between them. Then they listened to his breathless report. There wasn't much to say: the bridge was in German hands. He'd seen two sentries with a machine gun on this side, and there was no telling how many across the river.

'Just our rotten bloody luck!' Major Wheeler hissed. 'A couple of hours earlier and we'd probably have beaten them to it.'

Stephen knew he was right, and whatever luck had taken them this far was starting to run out. They were so close they could smell the river from here; that earthy stink of weed and slime was the Somme itself, and salvation lay just on the other side if the noise of the guns was anything to go by. But the river was deep and broad, and without a bridge they were hemmed in against it. Darkness was their only cover, and if they were still on this side when the sun came up, then the Germans would have them.

Slowly, they wormed their way back under cover and struck a match to look at the map. Their men lay scattered through the trees, where most of them had fallen asleep the instant they lay down. It had been a long week since the attack began, with little sleep and no food except what they could pick up from the deserted houses and farms they passed. Stephen had long since given up trying to understand how they kept going, but they did; stripping the dead of ammunition and drinking water from what canals, rivers or wells fell in their path.

But a look at the map only confirmed that they couldn't go on much longer – they were running out of space. That evening they had abandoned the line of old French trenches between Morcourt and Chuignolles after skirmishing with the Germans all day. The Germans were in no rush, and had spent the day probing and prodding and softening them up for the attack. As the evening drew on they'd brought up their field guns, and when Stephen saw those he knew the game was up. Wheeler knew it too, and he'd ordered the withdrawal. Their orders had been to stand as long as possible to let the other brigades pull back across the river, and now that they had done so, they were alone on the wrong side. It was time to shift for themselves. Slipping out of their trenches, they had crept back towards the Somme under cover of the early dark. They'd passed by Cerisy, which was the closest bridge, because they assumed the Germans had already taken it. But now that they'd reached Ecluse, four miles further upstream, they'd found the village in flames and sentries on the bridge, as Nightingale had just reported.

'Looks like it's back to Cerisy, gentlemen,' Wheeler said softly. In the flickering light of the match, he looked ancient. 'Unless either of you has a better idea?'

They looked at him dully and shook their heads. Cerisy was four miles back the way they had come, every step of it through German territory, but they had no better ideas.

'All right then.' Wheeler nodded. 'I'll tell the men myself. Let's say another ten minutes' rest before we go.'

Ten minutes! The time weighed heavily on Stephen because he knew if he fell asleep he wouldn't wake up for hours. He yawned, every fibre of his body urging him to sleep.

'Christ! I'm so bloody tired!' he said aloud, but Nightingale had already nodded off where he sat.

Presently, they formed up in the road and started to march. There were no orders, no bawling, no singing – nothing but the regular clump of boots and the creak and clank of webbing. Stephen kept his eyes forward, straining them into the darkness for the first sign of a German patrol. Sometimes he stumbled heavily, his eyelids gumming up with fatigue. Time lost all meaning, and it soon seemed as if they had been marching for ever. But they marched on unmolested. They passed through Morcourt for the second time and the flames from the burning village lit their way, the crackling heat warming tired faces. Then it was back into the darkness and cold, shoulders drooping, feet aching, and only the rhythm of the march keeping them going. Eventually, more buildings loomed out of the darkness, gaping windows and broken brickwork, and he realized that they were creeping through the smashed outskirts of Cerisy. They marched on through the village, eerily quiet but for the sound of their boots, and when they saw the hump of the bridge they took to the ditches again and Nightingale went forward. He was hardly gone before Stephen started to fret. A minute passed, two minutes. What the hell was keeping him? He could see the bloody bridge from here. He glanced at the blurred shape of Wheeler, opened his mouth to speak, but then he heard voices and held his breath. He couldn't make out words, or even language; they were dulled by distance, indistinct.

Then silence. He strained his eyes through the darkness, squeezing, squeezing on the grip of his revolver. Any moment now there would be a flash, a shot, and the game would be up. But then a dark shape flitted across the road, there was a rustling of leaves, and Nightingale was there, the steam of his breath a pearly cloud in the moonlight. 'Germans,' he whispered. 'But only two of them, and they haven't had time to dig in. They're just standing in the middle of the bridge. I think we could rush it.'

'Well, I bloody well hope so because it's a bit cold for swimming,' Wheeler shot back, with a flash of his teeth. But then, after he had considered a moment, he added, 'Very well, but we'll bluff it as far as we can. Have the men take their helmets off so they won't know who we are until we're on the bridge. Then we can take a run at 'em.'

Stephen looked from one to the other. They all understood the risk, but he knew they didn't have any choice. In a couple of hours it would be light, and if they were still on this side of the river, they wouldn't last another two hours after that. Forming the men up in fours on the road, they started to march, officers in front. Stephen walked with one hand on his revolver, hearing only the steady, even tread of Kinsella marching close behind him. Before he realized it, they were on the bridge and he felt acutely aware of the column of men following him. He glanced across at Nightingale who was marching on the other side of Wheeler, just a shadow. He could hear the water gurgling underneath the bridge now, and still they tramped on. The far bank was looming out of the darkness. Two figures detached themselves from the shadows in front of them.

'*Guten abend!*' Nightingale shouted cheerfully, raising his hand.

'*Guten abend!*' one of them called back, laughing. '*Wo fahren sie?*'

'Chipilly.'

'*Ach . . .*' One of them switched on an electric torch and in that instant he was finished. Kinsella darted forward before Stephen had even pulled out his revolver and he heard the thud of his bayonet going home, then the crack of a revolver to his left as Wheeler shot the other German.

'Double time, lads!' Nightingale shouted over his shoulder, and they broke into a run down the other side of the bridge and clear across the river.

VII

*I still can't really believe we are here. It is springtime
and the hedges are bursting with life – the fields are
green and the sky is blue. What a change has come over us!
A fortnight ago we were fighting for our lives and all I can
remember about it is darkness, fear and sudden death. I
recall saying something to a man as he moved past me and
then seeing him fall down dead right before my eyes. What
was his name? I can't even remember that much, nor his
face, nor anything except that he died and I was only glad
that it wasn't me.*

*Coming here was like waking from a dream, albeit a very
bad dream. The losses we suffered are enough to make the
mind boggle. Nightingale and I are the only two officers
who survived unscathed, and when we took our battalion
out of the line we could muster barely a hundred men.
Backs to the wall indeed. The German advance seems to
have stopped for the moment, and every day that passes
gives us time to reorganize and regroup, but I think history
will record that first German attack on the Somme as the
nearest damn thing of the whole war.*

But, on the other hand, we are near the sea, and even though I can't see it, I can smell it on the breeze. It reminds me of Lillian, and when I go to bed at night it's not all the fighting I'm thinking about, but her. I miss her so much it hurts. But I mustn't mope. The food is good and plentiful here and the weather is getting warmer. The sense of having survived an ordeal is very powerful.

Of course, it isn't all idyllic. Now that the tension has eased, everybody can find something to complain about. Petty arguments that were put aside in the heat of battle have reared up again with even greater force, and it's sad to see men who were prepared to die together now at each other's throats. It is even worse for the replacements that arrive every day to make up our woefully small numbers. It's not their fault but, since they were not in the last battle, they are looked down on by those who were, and there is a considerable amount of bad blood building up between the two factions. I'm afraid the only way to bring them together will be to send them into battle. Since the Germans appear to be getting ready to launch another offensive around Armentiéres, I'm sorry to say that could happen much sooner than I'd like.

PROCEEDINGS OF

THE LONDON MATHEMATICAL SOCIETY

SOME PROBLEMS OF 'PARTITIO NUMERORUM': ON THE EXPRESSION OF A NUMBER AS A SUM OF PRIMES

By

L. E. BRYCE   and   S. J. RYAN
Trinity College,   Trinity College,
DUBLIN

Introduction

I.I. It was asserted by GOLDBACH, in a letter to EULER dated 1 June 1742, that *every even number 2m is the sum of two odd primes*, and this proposition has generally been described as 'Goldbach's Conjecture'. There is no reasonable doubt that this conjecture is correct, and that the number of representations is large when m is large; but all attempts to obtain a proof have been completely unsuccessful. Indeed it has never been shown that every number (or every large number, any number, that is to say, from a certain point onwards) is the sum of 10 primes, or of 1,000,000; and the problem was quite recently classified as among those that are unsolvable in the present state of mathematics.

In this memoir we attack the problem with the aid of our new transcendental method. We do not solve it, but we do hope to open some new avenues which may well lead to an eventual solution.

Anti Conscription Pledge

Denying the right of the British Government to enforce compulsory service in this country, we pledge ourselves solemnly to one another to resist conscription by the most effective means at our disposal.

---

24 Percy Place
Dublin

21 April 1918

Dear Stephen,

I was so happy to receive your letter that I can hardly find the words to describe it. Thank God you are safe! The last time I heard from you, you were moving up to the line, and when I heard about the German offensive

I knew – I just knew – that you were in the thick of it. Now I am so glad that you are out of it. I hope you are safe and well and I am counting the days until you come home for good.

I have enclosed a copy of the Proceedings of the London Soc. Isn't it wonderful? I think it came out very well. Prof Barrett is as pleased as punch and I've lost count of the number of people who have congratulated me on it. Of course, every single one of them asked after you as well and they all said it was such a pity that you were not here to enjoy your new-found fame.

I have no doubt you've heard all about this conscription business. It's such a scandal I don't know what to say. The whole country is in a fine taking about it and it would do you good to see how united we all are. The Parliamentary Party has walked out of Westminster en bloc to come home and stand alongside Sinn Fein (before he left, John Dillon told the House that forcing conscription on Ireland would be tantamount to recruiting Germans, which is probably the cleverest thing he's ever said). Labour is organizing a general strike against it, and even the bishops of the Catholic Church are putting their oar in. There are rallies and demonstrations every other day, and today an Anti-Conscription Pledge was displayed in every Catholic church in the country for people to sign when they came out of Sunday Mass.

I'm ashamed to say that the Church of Ireland is more lukewarm about it. There was no pledge at my own church, so I had to walk over to the Catholic one on Haddington Road to sign it. As I was going home, I happened to bump into our vicar, who is a terribly nice young chap and he wished me a good afternoon. Well, I'm afraid I savaged him rather badly over not having the pledge, and I doubt he'll be coming to tea at our house any time soon.

But of course, from a purely personal point of view, the best thing about it is the vindication. Now that the world and his wife is against conscription, those fellows of the college who frowned and tut-tutted at me before for being so radical can only congratulate me on my foresight and moral courage. Stephen, how I wish you were here, if only to see the looks on their faces!

Having said that, I'm afraid all these shenanigans might give some of your comrades the wrong impression. Some of them – particularly those who were conscripted themselves – might reckon this is a funny way to be going on, and might even accuse Ireland of stabbing them in the back again. But surely they can understand that we have nothing against them and would say not a word against any man who volunteers to fight – as so many Irishmen have already done. But when it comes to a pass like this, when young boys and old men must be taken up as cannon fodder, then surely it is plain to everybody that this war has gone on too long.

Too long by far. I wish, I wish, I wish that you were here with me. Please write to me soon and let me know how things stand with you. I want to know every little detail of your life, spare me nothing. Then, at least if you can't be here with me I can, in some sense, be there with you.

I love you and I miss you every day, and I remain,

Yours truly,

Lillie

24 April 1918

A day of mixed blessings. On one hand, I was delighted to get Lillian's letter, particularly as she enclosed a copy of the proceedings with our paper in it. On the other hand, I've managed to have an almighty row with Nightingale.

The sad thing is, it was Lillie's letter that started the whole thing off. That, and the copy of the proceedings, put me in mind of her book, which I had entrusted to Nightingale in case I got knocked over during the German offensive. So, feeling rather pleased with myself, and with my copy of the proceedings tucked under my arm, I went and asked him for it back. He gave me a long, uncomfortable look, and then admitted that he'd lost it.

To be fair, it wasn't as if he put it down somewhere and forgot about it. It was in his haversack, which was blown up by a German shell somewhere near Cappy. I suppose he was damn lucky that he wasn't wearing it at the time, and in all the confusion I never even noticed that he'd lost it. Given the circumstances, I should have been more understanding, but all I could think of was how much that book had meant to Lillie, and I'm afraid I rather lost my rag.

Of course, once we got started, it was rather hard to stop. I suppose our nerves are a bit frayed after our recent experience and, despite being in a rest camp, we are both working very hard to rebuild the battalion. We had a right old ding-dong and, although most of it was just hot air, we soon got down to something that turned out to be a very sore point – conscription.

Neither of us was conscripted, though I suspect that Nightingale might have been if he hadn't volunteered. I suppose this explains his views on the subject. He bloody hates the idea of conscription, but he thinks that if it has to be done, it should be done fairly, and clean across the board. This is probably reasonable enough, only he said it in such a way that he managed to get my Irish hackles right up. The *only part of the British Isles that doesn't have conscription is Ireland, and he knows it. I started to protest, but he went on to say that he thought it was the height of hypocrisy for me to sit here, having seen with my own eyes the massive losses we suffered in the German Spring Offensive, and tell him that Britain has no right to take men from Ireland. I told him that Britain has no right to take anything from Ireland (my brother would have been proud of me!) and, furthermore, that if the British people had stood up against conscription as the Irish are doing, then we might have had an armistice a year ago. (Lillie would have been just as proud of me!)*

Well, that was like a red rag to a bull, and from there on the argument got very bitter indeed. I stood my ground manfully, but now that we've cooled off a bit, I'm starting to feel guilty. It occurs to me that if the enlistment age in England is raised to fifty, then Nightingale's father (who I believe is forty-eight) could be conscripted. Under these circumstances, who can blame him for complaining about Ireland, which has yet to see conscription in any form?

However, at the time it got so heated that I took myself off for a walk before one of us said something we would later regret. The evenings are getting longer and it's not too cold, so I took a wander away from our camp, eventually reaching a little sort of bluff from which I could see the sea. There was a lighthouse winking at me from somewhere just up the coast, and it reminded me that we are not very far from Étaples. I was surprised to realize that it's only six weeks since I left that vile place. Nevertheless, it has occurred to me that Dunbar might still be beached there, and if I can wangle the transport, I might take a spin over to see him.

PROCLAMATION

BY HIS EXCELLENCY
FIELD-MARSHAL VISCOUNT FRENCH,

Lord Lieutenant-General and General Governor of Ireland.

WHEREAS it has come to our knowledge that certain subjects of His Majesty, the King, domiciled in Ireland, have conspired to enter, and have entered into treasonable communication with the German enemy:

AND WHEREAS such treachery is a menace to the fair fame of Ireland and its glorious military record, a record which is a source of intense pride to a country whose sons have always distinguished themselves and fought with such heroic valour in the past, in the same way as thousands of them are now fighting in this war:

AND WHEREAS drastic measures must be taken to put down this German plot, which measures will be solely directed against that plot:

NOW, THEREFORE, WE, THE LORD LIEUTENANT OF IRELAND AND GENERAL GOVERNOR OF IRELAND, have thought fit to issue this OUR PROCLAMATION declaring, and it is hereby declared as follows:—

That it is the duty of all loyal subjects of His Majesty to assist in every way His Majesty's Government in Ireland to suppress this treasonable conspiracy and to defeat the treacherous attempt of the Germans to defame the honour of Irishmen for their own ends.

That WE hereby call upon all loyal subjects of His Majesty in Ireland to aid in crushing said conspiracy, and, so far as in them lies, to assist in securing an effective prosecution of the war and the welfare and safety of the Empire.

That as a means to this end we shall cause still further steps to be taken to facilitate and encourage Voluntary Enlistment in Ireland in His Majesty's Forces, in the hope that, without resort to Compulsion, the contribution of Ireland to these forces may be brought up to its proper strength and made to correspond to the contribution of the other parts of the Empire.

Given at His Majesty's Castle of Dublin this 16th day of May, one thousand nine hundred and eighteen.

EDWARD SHORTT

Joe heard the rumble of the lorry behind him before he saw it. A squeal of brakes and he turned his head a little to see it slewing across the street. Then it stopped, nose to the kerb, and boots scraped and thumped in the back. Men jumped down with rifles, helmets – bootnails ringing on the cobbles. Joe lengthened his stride; hurrying, but trying not to look like it.

He went past the grocer's shop and up the steps to the broad green door. It opened easily under his hand, and he stepped inside and locked it behind him. The hallway was dark and quiet, with only the dim glow of a light filtering down from upstairs. That's where they'd be. He started up, two steps at a time, but before he'd got halfway a door opened below and Dick Mulcahy came up from the kitchen, carrying a mug of tea.

'Is he here?' Joe called down over the banisters.

'He's above in the office. Broy is in with him. Why?'

'They're setting up a roadblock down the street.'

'Ah, shite!' Mulcahy put the mug down on a side table and ran up the stairs after him. There was a small window on the top landing, and Mulcahy went to it and looked out while Joe knocked once on the door and pushed into the office. Collins was leaning back in his chair, hands clasped behind his head, talking to another man leaning against a filing cabinet with his hands in his pockets. Collins turned lazily in his chair to look at him, but the other man looked startled, straightening his narrow frame and looking like he might bolt out the door given half a chance.

'They're putting up a roadblock down the street, Mick,' Joe said, darting a glance at Broy. He knew little about him, except that he was a policeman, and he'd watched him coming and going from Dublin Castle a few times. Far from looking surprised, Collins just grinned and popped his hat on his head. He was already wearing his overcoat.

'Looks like you were right, Ned,' he told Broy. 'Well, I suppose we'd better be going. There's no sense in waiting for them to kick the door in.'

'You knew they'd be coming?' Joe asked, looking from Collins to Broy.

'Yeah, but I didn't think they'd be this quick,' Broy answered, looking uncomfortably towards the window as he took his hat from on top of the filing cabinet.

Collins was scooping papers into a battered briefcase.

'See how General French fights us on conscription?' he asked. 'He tells people we're against it because we're in league with the Germans. And if he can throw the lot of us in jail as well, that's all to the better.' He cast a quick glance towards Broy. 'They've probably got Dev already. He's letting them take him because they'll only look foolish when they have to let him go for lack of evidence – but they're not getting me. I think I'll take me chances on the run.'

'Well, you'll have to run out the back way,' Mulcahy warned, walking into the office and taking his coat from a peg. 'They have both ends of the street blocked now. They'll be here any minute.'

'You'd better come with us, Ned,' Collins told Broy, jerking his head towards the back of the house. 'You'll have a bit of explaining to do if they find you here and us gone.'

Joe felt the excitement building in his chest. The last few weeks had been hectic, but strangely mundane. Meeting after meeting, rallies, conferences, hurrying up and down the country to speak against conscription. But it had been nothing but preparation and politics. Talk, hot air. At least he'd had the sense that people were listening this time, that the threat of conscription had woken them up. And yet there was something missing. The British were wary. He'd been afraid they might try to negotiate, offer a carrot with the stick. They needed the men for France, and could afford none to fight in Ireland if the country rose up. But then they'd put Lord French in charge, an army man, and it was back to the old ways. Whatever chance the British had had of luring the people away with more promises were blown now. If Dev went to jail for standing up to conscription, he'd be a hero. And if Collins went on the run, he'd be a hero too. They couldn't lose.

'Have we got everything, now?' Collins asked, closing the briefcase.

'It's as clean as a whistle.' Mulcahy nodded. Joe knew that the filing cabinets were mostly empty. All the important papers were well hidden, or kept on the move.

'And neither of you is carrying a gun?'

They both shook their heads. If they were stopped, a gun would get them all arrested.

'Grand, let's be off, so.'

Collins led the way into the back room. It was a clerk's office, with writing desks and typewriters. But there was a window that overlooked the back garden. Mulcahy parted the heavy curtains and pulled up the sash. Cool air blew in the scent of the apple tree just starting to flower in the garden.

Collins went out first, followed by Broy and then Mulcahy. Joe stood with his back to the door, listening. He heard their shoes scraping on the wall, then the thump as they landed on the kitchen roof below. But then he heard another sound and thrilled at it. Running footsteps out the front, the thud of rifle butts against the locked door. More pounding and, finally, a crash as they kicked the door in. It was starting. Feeling light and strangely happy, he went to the window. Boots rumbled downstairs, harsh voices shouting orders. He slid out under the sash and perched awkwardly on the edge of the windowsill while he pushed the window closed. With a final shove, all was quiet. There was only the quiet tread of the others creeping across the roof, clambering down to the privy next door. Barely balanced against the glass, he looked around at the darkened houses. This was the other side of the immaculate Georgian façade that faced the street. Even in the dark he could make out downpipes and outhouses and sheds, vegetable gardens and compost heaps. And despite the precariousness of his position, he felt at home. This was the real city, where he belonged.

Inside, the door of the office crashed open and the light came on. They were so close now – just beyond the curtain.

'Joe!' Mulcahy hissed, hanging half off the kitchen roof. 'Joe! Will you ever come on?'

Joe nodded, twisted round and got his hands on the cold granite of the windowsill. Footsteps thumped about inside, a chair crashed to the floor. But he was not afraid. He smiled secretly as he lowered himself into the darkness.

It was the guns that woke him. But as he lay in the dark and listened he thought it must have been something else. All he could hear was the whisper of the breeze through the trees. Now and then the canvas tarpaulin stretched overhead thumped and flapped, but that wasn't it either. Then the breeze died away and he heard it quite clearly, though it was intermittent. It swelled and faded like distant music, but there was no mistaking that familiar tune – the rumble of the guns.

After a while he sat up and listened, trying to gauge how far away it really was. It had got inside his head now, so there was no point in trying to go back to sleep. Distant though it was, it was like an echo from the past. Five months since he'd heard it, and now it had touched some nerve inside him. He looked up through a gap in the tarpaulin and saw the faint, pulsing luminescence of it, like faraway lightning to distant thunder, and suddenly realized that he had missed it. He had missed that sound and those sights; he had missed it all these last few months.

This troubled him, and after a few moments he stood up and looked around at the humped blankets scattered in the patches of moonlight between the trees. Was this what he had missed? No, this was only something to be endured. This was what he had to go through so he could get back to what he really missed. But the crisis was coming, the real test. That was what the sound of guns really meant. He pulled his blanket around his shoulders and, picking his way carefully through the sleeping men, he walked down to the narrow road.

'As you were, corporal,' he murmured, when the sentry stood up to challenge him. He walked out until he had a clear view of the sky, and pulled up the collar of his greatcoat. It was cold now. Autumn was definitely upon them and winter wouldn't be far behind. When he looked up he could see a milky swathe of stars splashed across the clear black sky. The moon was three-quarters full but riding low, down near the notch in the trees, as bright as a new shilling. But when he turned his back to it he could clearly see the flickering white light on the northern horizon. Pulsing, throbbing, dancing to the beat of the distant gunfire.

He stood and watched for a while, entranced, until he heard a step behind him and turned to see Nightingale stepping out of the trees, his face a pale blur in the moonlight.

'Couldn't sleep?' he asked, and Stephen nodded and thrust his hands deeper into his pockets. He could see his own breath streaming out on the frigid air.

'It was the guns,' he said, nodding at the flickering light. 'It's a while since I've heard them.'

'Feeling nostalgic, eh?' Nightingale asked, and they both laughed because they knew it was true; they both felt the same mixture of pleasure and dread. 'Well, looking on the bright side, at least they're probably ours. Doing a spot of softening up for us, I should think.'

Stephen knew what that meant but he didn't say anything. The next day would see them back in the fighting. This was new territory for them: far, far past the old lines, and with the Germans well and truly on the run. He still could hardly believe it. They'd spent the summer rebuilding the battalion after their disastrous losses in the spring, but every week they'd expected to be called forward to try and stem the latest catastrophe. In April the Germans had launched a series of attacks around Ypres, in May and June they had pushed hard along the river Aisne. Then, in July, they had struck south for Paris, and almost had it in their grip before they were stopped, for the second time, at the Marne. Watching all this from afar, Stephen had felt like the Germans were probing the line for weaknesses, trying to find the one chink that would let them through – and once they were through, there would be no stopping them.

But they didn't get through. Their high-water mark was at the Marne, and it was there that the allies struck back for the first time, then again at Amiens, and again on the Somme. The German armies that had seemed almost invincible just a few months before had started to crumble, and now they were falling back every day, slowly but surely retreating towards Germany. They had already crossed the Hindenburg line and lost their old elaborate defences, so that now they were being forced to improvise: fortifying farms and villages, digging in behind rivers and canals. But always fighting, nowhere running, nowhere routed. It seemed like the closer they came to their homeland, the more the German resistance hardened. He'd heard rumours of mutinies, of food shortages and riots in Germany, but that didn't mean they had given up – not by a long chalk. Stephen remembered the Spring Offensive, when the Germans had had *them* on the run; how hard they had fought, and how desperation and the fear of defeat had sustained them well past the limits of human endurance. No, he thought, the bitterest part was yet to come. The war would end soon – there could be little doubt of that. But there was still a price to be paid, and it would be high.

'I have a bad feeling,' he said suddenly, without taking his eyes off the flashes. 'Did you ever get it? The sense that you've gone on too long. The feeling that you can't keep beating the odds much longer.'

Nightingale nodded, but he didn't say anything. Stephen shivered and pulled his collar closed.

'I feel things more ever since I came back; the cold, the . . .' He stumbled into silence and looked to see if Nightingale was still listening. How to explain it? He hadn't noticed it when they were still in their rest camp, but it had been growing in him ever since they started to move up towards the front line. It felt like they had left the summer behind and were marching into winter, but the weather had held good and the journey had been long. After a few days of marching and rattling bus rides, he'd had the notion that maybe they would never get there. He'd fooled himself into thinking that maybe the front was receding too quickly, the Germans were falling back too fast, and if they ever caught up with them the war would be over. But, gradually, a vague sense of unease had hardened to a certainty. They had arrived. They could hear the guns, and see them. And this would not end happily.

'I shouldn't worry about it.' Nightingale's teeth flashed in the moonlight as he smiled. 'It's just nerves.'

A few seconds later, the shelling stopped. The thunder of the guns died without an echo and the sky went black, as if somebody had thrown a switch.

'We'll be all right,' Nightingale said out of the sudden darkness, and he clapped Stephen on the shoulder. 'Don't you worry, old man. We've made it this far. We'll see it through now.'

Part Two

Blood

VIII

The war is over. The war is over. The words followed him like a shadow, whispering in his ear. *Something* was following him. He could feel it between his shoulder blades. He stopped suddenly and listened, but there was no sound except the lapping of water against the canal bank. It was a foggy night – so thick he could see nothing, but he could smell the city in it. Soot and grime and boiled dinners. No gun smoke, no sulphur, but still he listened. No sound, nothing.

He hitched the haversack up on his shoulder and started walking again. Down to the lock and across the canal and he would be home. But his mind was drifting. He remembered there had been fog one morning – the day they had crossed the Selle. Christ, that had been a year ago – how the time had flown! But that morning the fog had been so thick he could hardly see the men in front of him, and it had been cold, too, the damp worming its way into his bones. And yet he'd felt alive, alert, his skin tingling in the mist as it swirled past, leaving tiny beads of dew in his eyebrows. He'd felt the soft ground through the soles of his feet and the heft of the rifle in his hand. He'd had the most intense sense of himself that morning, crouched in the fog.

'The war is over.'

He heard the words so clearly that he stopped again and looked over his shoulder. He was nearly at the lock, and he could hear the water gushing into the void, the echo thundering around the walls and under the bridge. That was all. He was hearing things.

Or remembering things. Professor Barrett had said those words to him. An hour ago, in his rooms. Had brought him in and sat him down in the chintz chair and poured the little glasses of sherry. *The academic sacrament*, Stephen had thought, and he took his glass and held it between his fingers – but he would not drink it. Barrett had sat in the chair opposite, leaned forward with his elbows on his knees.

'The war is over, Stephen,' he'd said, gently, but Stephen had felt resentment hardening inside him. For Barrett, the end of the war was all about church bells and bunting and people kissing in the street. What the hell did he know about it? What had he seen from his ivory tower? Distant smoke, an inconvenience? Stephen's gaze had wandered to the chessboard near the fireplace – a game in progress and a small stack of letters lying beside it. Well, that about summed it up. He'd never liked that bloody game.

A breath of wind blew a hole in the fog and he saw black water, then the thick wooden limb of the lock gate drawing him on. He walked towards it, averting his eyes from the water. Why did he always come this way? Why did he walk the tow-path and cross by the lock? It would be just as easy to walk on the road and cross the bridge. At least he wouldn't have to worry about ghosts in the bloody water. But then again, maybe it was the ghosts that he missed. At least they understood.

Barrett didn't understand. He hadn't been there. He didn't realize that you couldn't just say 'the war is over' and draw a line under it, like one of his axioms. Unfortunately, the rest of his little talk had been based on this assumption. He'd gone on about the need to focus, to concentrate, to do well in his exams. There had been a hint of steel in Barrett's voice – a touch of disappointment. It was clear that Stephen wasn't living up to his expectations. He'd dangled the prize again – if he got a good degree then a studentship next year would be his for the taking. The money would not be much, but it would be enough to live on, and there were so many soldiers out of work. Barrett made it sound almost therapeutic. A little teaching and a lot of time to work on whatever interested him. Then the flattery; with a talent such as his, a fellowship would surely follow – no question there. But Stephen had turned the little glass between his fingers and let the words wash over him. They had no meaning. Barrett just didn't understand.

Stephen put his hand on the wooden arm of the lock gate. How solid it felt in the swirling fog. He looked down into the void of the lock, where a stream of water plunged through the clouds. He could see slimy walls and the foamy surface of water far below. He sometimes wondered what it would be like if he went in there. A long drop and then the cold shock of the water. His feet would never find the bottom and there would be no grip on the slick stone walls. He'd thrash and splash for a while, but eventually his strength would go and the haversack and heavy coat would drag him down. But he shivered at the thought of it. That was no way to go.

He went across the lock gate, holding tight to the rail. It was impossible not to look into the water lapping a few inches below his feet – just as it had been on the Selle that morning. They'd been directed to a bridge, but it was hardly worthy of the name. Two planks wide and bobbing gently on floating barrels, stiffened by a rickety handrail that ran along one side. Stephen had watched his men go across one by one and then followed, placing his feet carefully on the wet wood, until a machine gun barked out and sent him sprawling. False alarm: the gun was miles away, but as he lay flat on the planks he looked down at his own reflection in the dark water. Then he saw the first corpse: an officer, floating face down, with his helmet still on and the cross-strap of his Sam Browne glistening wetly. Then another, blue-faced and black-eyed, his arms out and his pale hands floating like dead fish, and another, bumping gently against the bank, and another . . .

Panicking, he'd scrambled across the last few feet and thrown himself on to the far bank, appalled. Christ almighty! He was glad his men couldn't see him – they were spread out along the bank, facing into the impenetrable fog. Then one of them loomed closer and Kinsella's voice grumbled out, unnaturally loud.

'All right, sir?'

'Yes, sergeant,' he'd gulped, glancing uneasily behind him. 'Carry on.'

He hauled himself up to the towpath and around the curve of the bridge abutment to the granite flags and the kerb. Then there was the *putt-putt-putt* of a motorcar, and two yellow eyes pierced the fog, creeping slowly over the hump of the bridge and rolling past him, squealing its brakes before the gears clashed and the car disappeared once more into the fog. He followed it down the deserted street – no lights, no sounds, no signs of life at all. When he found his turn he felt like he was disappearing into a maze – a claustrophobic feeling, as if the fog was closing in behind him, barring his way back. But he walked on steadily, feeling the terraced houses closing in against him as the street narrowed. Signs of life at last – a square of yellow light in an upper window, then the boom of a door slamming and the wail of a baby. Another turn took him down a lane – his shortcut through the hidden insides of the slums. Here, the cobbles turned to rutted, hard-packed earth and the smell of horseshit wafted out of makeshift stables. He caught another smell – the tang of urine and stale beer from a clapboard shebeen – and then stopped in his tracks as a shape detached itself from the shadows and stepped out in front of him.

'You're late tonight, soldier boy,' the shape said, though Stephen could only make out a squat figure, standing a few feet away with his legs braced apart and his arms folded. Close as he was, Stephen couldn't see his face – but his voice was guttural, hard and menacing.

'I'm not a soldier.'

'You're wearing a soldier's coat,' said another voice, and Stephen's head jerked towards it. A second man, to his right and slightly behind, moving closer.

'It's an officer's coat,' the first man observed. 'You must've been a big shot in the war. I bet the King was real proud of you – his little Irish lap dog. Maybe we should be saluting you. Would you like that, mister officer, sir?'

'Look, I don't want . . .' Stephen began, but he heard a step directly behind him. Three of them – and they had him penned in. He knew what was coming, but he felt strangely relaxed. 'The war is over,' he said, in a strong voice.

'That's what you fucking think,' the man in front of him said, and then he felt something hit him hard between his shoulder blades.

There was nothing remarkable about the waiting room. It was rather on the large side, and the plaster ceiling was more ornate than he might have expected, but otherwise it was shabby and musty and in need of a coat of paint. Three mismatched chairs were placed along one wall, and a man in a Jacobean wig watched over everything from the dusty oil painting above the fireplace, where a small fire crackled in the grate.

Billy Standing looked down at his gleaming shoes and wondered if he was overdressed. But then, he wasn't very sure what he was here for. True, he had known Frank Mercer since they were at school together, but last week was the first time he had seen him in years – and the circumstances of that encounter had hardly been fortuitous. All the more reason to dress up, he'd decided, so he'd put on his best suit and polished his shoes and taken great pains over brushing both his overcoat and his black homburg. Even if his surroundings were shabbier than he'd expected, it was best to be on the safe side, he reflected. Then he looked up sharply as the door opened and a young man stuck his head into the waiting room.

'Mr Standing? Will you follow me please?'

Folding his overcoat over one arm and picking up his hat, Billy followed the young man out into the corridor. Again, it was unremarkable; rather dim, dusty and well worn. He had to remind himself that he was in Dublin Castle, the very heart of the British Administration in Ireland. The Heart of Darkness, as he'd heard one wit call it. To get inside, he'd passed an armed sentry at the gate and another at the door, but the place seemed so ordinary, so quiet, that he could hardly believe he was here.

They passed an open door to the clacking of a solitary typewriter, and as Billy glanced inside he saw a man looking up from his work on a high table. The next door was closed and forbidding, but the young man opened it without a pause and led him into a small office with a large desk and lots of files, maps and other documents stacked all over. Billy smelled ink and old paper and he knew they were getting close. The next door was small and dark and cracked down the middle, but the young man knocked politely, waited a moment, and then stepped inside.

'Mr Mercer, sir? Mr Standing to see you.'

There was a muffled cry from within, the creak of a chair, and

Billy walked past the young man to see Frank Mercer striding towards him, hand outstretched.

'William Standing! How are you? By God, it's been years, hasn't it? But you prefer Billy, don't you? D'you mind if I call you Billy?'

'Not at all,' Billy said agreeably, but he was on his guard. It's been years? What was that supposed to mean? It wasn't likely that Mercer would have forgotten last week's encounter so quickly. Nevertheless, he made a show of sizing him up and telling him the years had been kind, even though they had not. At school, Mercer had been whip thin and as handsome as a Greek god – but now a pot belly hung over his skinny legs and his face was pudgy and yellow. Perhaps the years were most unkind to the most beautiful people, for Mercer looked far older than was right for a man still in his early twenties.

'Thanks for coming, Billy. I'm sure you're a very busy man,' he said, gesturing to the couch under the window. Again, Billy was on his guard. He'd been fairly drunk the other evening, but he distinctly remembered letting self-pity get the better of him and crying into his cups about how work was so scarce. It was his own bloody fault, of course. He had thought things would pick up once the war was over – to the extent that he'd told his old gaffer he must look for another junior – but how wrong he'd been. Now that he was out on his own, he was learning how lonely his profession really was, and he was sure he'd poured out his woes to Mercer, his old schoolmate, when he'd bumped into him in their private club. Their *very* private club, he thought, his eyes narrowing as he caught the flash of a wedding ring on Mercer's finger. He hadn't been wearing *that* the other night. But then he hadn't been wearing very much else, either. Billy wondered about the little note Mercer had sent the next day – casual, but official at the same time, written on Castle notepaper. Indeed, about this meeting, about passing the sentries, about the long wait in that dusty room and about being summoned to his presence by the young acolyte. Was Mercer trying to frighten him?

'I'm sorry my note was rather cryptic,' Mercer was saying, easing his bony shanks on to the other end of the sofa. For the first time, he looked rather uncomfortable – crossing his legs, and then uncrossing them again. He forced a smile. 'Well, you know how things are.'

'Of course.' Billy nodded, though his idea of how things were was probably miles from Mercer's. Still, if Mercer could pretend that nothing had happened, then so could he. He decided to get straight down to business. 'You mentioned a job, some work you wanted carried out?'

'Yes, yes I did.' The discomfort dropped from Mercer's face and his relief was palpable. He smiled broadly this time – a genuine smile. 'Well, then, let's get down to business, shall we? Your name was mentioned in connection with a case last year – a fellow called Dwyer, a confidence man. You helped prosecute the blighter, if I'm not mistaken.'

Billy tried to mask his surprise. What on earth could Mercer have to do with that case? True, there had been considerable sums involved – Dwyer had managed to fleece some very wealthy people with his particular line of patter – but it was hardly worthy of the attention of a . . . well, whatever Mercer was. But then . . . was it possible that the man had taken him for some money too?

'Yes, I did,' he answered with a guarded smile. 'Though I wasn't the senior counsel. That was—'

'Mr Barton, yes, I know. But I understand you were the one who tracked the money down. In order to build your case, you had to find out where the bugger had hidden it and I'm led to believe there were several bank accounts – dozens of them, in fact. Most of them under false names, even bogus companies that he'd set up.'

'Yes, but I believe we got most of it back, in the end.'

'I believe you did too.' Mercer grinned, looking even more relieved, and Billy relaxed a little. Whatever all this circumlocution was about, Mercer was clearly going out of his way to be agreeable.

'Yes, I believe you did,' Mercer said again, half to himself. 'Now, tell me, what do you know about Sinn Fein?'

Billy felt his mouth clench shut involuntarily. What he knew about Sinn Fein and what he was prepared to admit to Mercer were not the same. He'd never actually joined the party but he was a regular at their meetings, he was at least on nodding terms with some of the higher-ups, and he'd done his fair share of work during all that conscription business. He swallowed nervously. Perhaps he'd been spotted. Perhaps this was the pinch Mercer had been working towards. Being connected with Sinn Fein would not do his career much good – certainly not if he was hoping to pick up some government work. Was Mercer looking to make a trade – silence for silence? But then he saw the look on his face, the half-hidden indulgent smile, and he realized with a swell of relief that Mercer didn't suspect a thing.

'Well, I know a little bit about them. What I read in the newspapers, and so forth,' he answered tentatively.

'Well, I'm happy to say we know a little bit more than *that*.' Mercer smiled and tapped the side of his nose. 'But sadly, not as much as we'd like. What we do know is that this chap de Valera – he's their president, I believe – is in America at the moment, raising funds for the cause. You may recall we had him in Lincoln Jail, but his friends broke him out and spirited him away to the States.'

'You don't say?'

'The remarkable thing is, the money he's raising over there isn't a patch on what they're taking in over here. They're selling bonds, don't you know – like the war bonds the Government used to sell – and people are simply throwing money at them. They're taking in thousands and thousands of pounds at this racket, and it's really getting to be a problem for us. You know they've set up this alternative government – this *Dail*, as they call it – and they're using the money to finance it. You'd scarcely believe the things they're getting up to, with all their authorities and ministries, and even courts of law in towns and parishes up and down the country. It's all pretty ludicrous, really.'

'I'm sure it is,' Billy agreed, although he knew very well that the Sinn Fein organization was far from ludicrous. He'd never made any secret of the fact that he was a barrister, and consequently he had not only been asked to draw up several briefs but had actually taken the bench in a Sinn Fein court.

'But ludicrous or not, Billy, it is fiendishly complicated – at least on the financial side. One of their top men is a chap called Collins, and he's quite the wizard. He used to work for the Post Office Bank in London, and then for a firm of stockbrokers. He's their minister for finance, and he's not only good at getting money in, he's devilishly good at hiding it. False bank accounts, stocks, bonds, shares – you name it, he's got money in them.'

The penny dropped, and Billy's mind raced. It was very clear to him what Mercer was working up to – and equally clear that it would put him on the spot. He smelled an offer, a *proposition*, and he was uneasy about it, to say the least. His political beliefs had changed, but instead of mellowing with age, as he'd thought they might, they had hardened. He might have settled for Home Rule once, but not any more. Independence was the only thing, even if independence meant overthrowing the Castle Administration. And here they were, about to offer him a job. The irony of it was not lost on Billy, but he didn't see that he had much choice. He wasn't on his uppers just yet, but how much longer could he last? Work was work, and he could hardly afford to sniff at it. Then again, he knew it wouldn't do to look too eager.

'I'm sure you have some very good people who can help you find it,' he said modestly.

'We do, we do. But strictly in an official capacity, as it were. They can subpoena the bank accounts and go through them, but that will only start the fox, if you know what I mean. The minute they get an inkling we're on to them, they'll shift all their money somewhere else and we'll be back to square one. No, what we need is somebody with experience in this sort of thing and, above all, somebody who can be discreet.'

Billy gave him a knowing smile.

'I think I know what you mean.'

'Of course you do, Billy. And I know very well how discreet you can be.' Mercer reached across and put his hand on his leg. 'I knew I could rely on you.'

The barrier went up with a squeal and Maggie Clancy walked out of Portobello Barracks with her collar pulled up around her ears and her hat held down with one hand against the quickening breeze.

'Goodnight, Maggie,' the sentry called out, and she dimly saw his hand move through the shadows. No getting him out of his box on a night like this, she thought, and she put her head down and walked through the rain towards Rathmines village, where she could get a tram to take her back into town. She was weary now, after such a long day. They'd asked her to work late again, but she could hardly say no. Three of the other typists were out with this flu that was going around, but there was still the same amount of work to be done, still all those orders to be copied. Anyway, she was glad of the overtime.

She was halfway to the main street when she heard the foot-steps behind her. They started so suddenly that she knew it wasn't a soldier following her out of the barracks. She quickened her pace and kept her eye on the yellow glow of the street lamps along the main street. They were close – close enough for her to see the tramlines glistening and swaying in the wind. Another minute and she would be safely there. *Faster, girl.*

But the footsteps quickened to keep up with her and she felt a cold shiver of fear down her spine. She risked a glance over her shoulder, but in the dark and the wind all she got was a glimpse of an overcoat and a flat cap bowed down against the wind. He was so close she was sorry she had looked, and she tried to go faster. Faster, faster – she was almost running, but she could hear the footsteps quickening to keep up. Then she heard the rush of his heavy boots and felt a hand on her arm. She squealed in fright.

'Got you!' a familiar voice exclaimed, and laughed heartily. Maggie's heart was still in her mouth and she lashed out at him, hitting him a heavy thump in the arm.

'Jesus, Mary and Joseph!' she cried. 'Joe Ryan! You frightened the life out of me.'

He gave her an indignant look. 'And how do you think I feel? I've been waiting out here for hours. I'm soaked to the skin and frozen half to death. What kept you?'

'I had to work late. We're short-handed with this flu that's going around, and Captain Parry asked me to stay and finish the orders for the Southern Division.'

'Oh, it's Captain Parry, is it?' Joe grinned as he gave her his arm and they walked together towards the tram. 'And what's he like, then, this Captain Parry?'

'He's very nice, if you must know,' Maggie told him. 'A perfect gentleman. At least he doesn't go around sneaking up on girls and scaring them half to death.'

'That's because his wife wouldn't let him,' Joe said smugly, and she frowned at him.

'How do you know he's married?'

'I know lots of things, Maggie,' he answered with a wink. 'I have my sources.'

'Oh? And am I one of them sources?' She asked this half in jest, but felt him stiffen. She had touched a nerve.

'Ah, Maggie, of course you're not!'

'Is that right? Then how come you only come down here to meet me when you're looking for something?'

'You know it's more than that, Maggie. You know I come and see you when I can,' he answered, but that was all he said, and they walked on in silence until they reached the tram stop, where she was able to see his face in the flickering gaslight. He looked drawn and tense, and she regretted teasing him like that. She knew what he was doing was hard and dangerous, and she knew, too, that he couldn't talk to her about it. She tightened her grip on his arm and bumped his hip with hers, and they huddled together against the drizzle for a few minutes. She was trying to make it up to him, but she knew she'd put him off his stride. He was dying to ask her – he *had* to ask her – but then she wasn't going to make it that easy for him. She wasn't going to *offer*. It was a grubby business they were about, and dangerous for her too. If that sentry at the gate had decided to stop her, then God knows what would have happened . . .

'Did you get anything for us?' he blurted out, and then clamped his mouth shut and looked like he'd swallowed something nasty.

For us? Who was this us? Oh, she had an idea, all right, but she'd never met any of them except Joe – although she'd some-times seen a skinny little whippet of a man with a bad leg who sometimes came with him. She didn't like him, but she knew who was in charge. It was Lily Mernin who had recruited her, and her cousin was the big man – the man with his name in all the newspapers.

'I did, of course. I got copies of everything they gave me. Sure don't I slip in an extra carbon just for you.'

'Good girl yourself! Where are they?'

She gave him a shocked look. 'Well, aren't you terrible impatient?'

He grinned, and she knew he was better now it was all out in the open – or almost. 'Business is business, Maggie dear. I have me orders just the same as yourself.'

'Well, you know very well where I've hidden them,' she told him primly. 'You'll just have to wait until you get me home.'

The knocker rapped out three times, echoing down the hallway, and Dunbar looked up from his ledger. His eyes darted to the ormolu clock on the mantle. It was half past nine at night and he had been up since six that morning, making house calls, taking temperatures and writing death certificates. Too many death certificates.

'Bugger off,' he muttered, and he let his eye run down the ledger in front of him. It used to be that this book kept track of his patients' accounts and all he'd had to worry about was outstanding fees and the odd disputed payment. But now it was turning into the book of the dead. Three more crossed out this week and it was only Wednesday. This disturbed him because his was a wealthy practice with wealthy patients. Most of the people he saw were middle class, comfortable and well fed. They didn't suffer from rickets or malnourishment or TB or any of the other things that afflicted the poor. Their illnesses tended to be more uncomfortable than life-threatening: gout, sciatica and dyspepsia. When they did go, they were taken by cancer, strokes and congestive heart failure – and usually only after they'd had their full three score and ten. But not this winter. This winter they were going well before they were ready.

It was the influenza again, but he couldn't make up his mind if it was the same strain he'd seen in the war, or something much more virulent. Whichever it was, it was killing his patients, and bloody quickly too. By the time he got to them it was usually too late. He'd got to the stage where he could tell even before he turned on the light in the darkened bedroom. He could hear the rattling breath, smell it, sense death in the room. And he had to pause now before he went in, to gather his strength. For the first time in his life he felt afraid of death. He'd always thought of it as a natural thing, a biological imperative just like any other. If the organism could no longer sustain life then death naturally followed – and it would always come eventually. But now it had assumed a personality – it was vindictive, and he could feel it stalking him, mocking him. Because it wasn't the old ones it was taking this time, it was the young. The young once again, just like in the bloody war.

He put down his glasses and rubbed his tired eyes. Now he was getting bloody superstitious – a sure sign of old age. But when he looked down at the ledger he saw the last name he'd crossed off. Annabel O'Brien, aged thirty, wife of Matthew O'Brien, aged thirty-three. Both young, both healthy, and both dead within days of each other – cut down in the prime of their lives. Thank Christ there were no children.

Still listening for the door, he put on his glasses and picked up his pen. If it was urgent they would knock again. Or they would telephone. Most of his patients had telephones, even if they no longer had servants. He wrote down the cause of death as secondary bacterial infection. That was how a lot of the fittest ones went. They were strong enough to survive the initial attack but, just when they thought they were over the worst of it, some invisible bug in their lungs would finish them off when they were at their weakest. It was a right little bugger that way.

The knocker rapped out again, three more knocks that seemed to echo for even longer in the empty hallway.

'Oh, for fuck's sake,' he muttered irritably, getting up and tightening the knot on his dressing gown. 'All right, I'm coming, I'm coming.'

He stopped when he turned on the light in the hallway and saw the figure through the frosted glass of the door. It wasn't clear enough to see a face, but he recognized the khaki overcoat. He frowned. What the hell did the army want with him now?

He opened the door and blinked in surprise at his visitor. Then he sneezed; once, twice, again.

'Are you all right?' Stephen asked, concerned.

'I should ask you the same,' Dunbar answered, frowning at the large bruise on Stephen's cheek, just starting to turn yellow at the edges. 'What the bloody hell happened to you?'

'Some people didn't like the colour of my coat.' Stephen spread his arms, and Dunbar saw the torn sleeve, the faint spots of blood on the lapel.

'There's a lot of it about,' Dunbar muttered, stepping aside and motioning him to come in. 'How did you know where to find me?'

'Well, you told me you lived on Northumberland Road, and that brass plate beside the gate has your name on it.'

'Hmm. So it does.' Dunbar closed the door and looked his visitor up and down. Apart from the bruise on his cheek, there was a smear of blood under one ear and, from the way he carried his arm, it looked like there was more damage under the coat. 'My, you have been in the wars, haven't you?' he observed, and then sneezed again, twice, and pulled a handkerchief from the pocket of his dressing gown.

'Are you sure you're all right?' Stephen asked. Dunbar looked smaller than he remembered – and older. Quite domesticated in his quilted dressing gown and carpet slippers.

'Cats.' Dunbar blew his nose. 'I'm allergic. I had a lodger in the basement, you see. A Miss Kennedy, up from the country. A nice girl, or so it seemed. Butter wouldn't melt and all that. But she had a cat, and the blasted thing used to sleep on the doormat.'

'Used to?'

'I had to give them both their marching orders. I'm afraid I was very specific about pets. Anyway, come on through. I've got a fire. You can warm yourself while you tell me how you've been. What are you doing with yourself now?'

'I'm back in college,' Stephen began, walking down the tiled hallway. He suddenly felt very shabby, walking through this big house with its polished wood and heavy curtains. The front room was fitted out as a surgery, with a desk, a couch and walls lined with glass-fronted cabinets. The sitting room was much larger. It was the width of the house – elegant and warm and dominated by a broad fireplace flanked by a pair of gleaming Chesterfield armchairs.

'I'll be with you in a tick,' Dunbar called after him. 'Make yourself at home.'

Stephen went and warmed his hands at the fire. In its way, this room reminded him of Lillian's house. Despite its size it was comfortable and friendly – and a long way from his grubby little flat with damp walls and grimy windows. Just thinking of it made his heart sink, and thinking of Lillian made him feel ashamed. He hadn't wandered down Northumberland Road by accident. Her house was only around the corner from here, and that had been his destination – until the last moment, when he lost his nerve. He hadn't been to college since the attack, nor had he seen her or spoken to her. He knew she'd called at the flat – had listened to her knocking – but he hadn't answered. He didn't want her to see the bruises. He didn't want any fuss.

Dunbar came in with a black medical bag but Stephen shook his head when he saw it.

'Look, there's no need. I'm fine,' he said. 'I didn't come here looking for—'

'Nonsense. You're not fine. You look like you got a right kicking.' Dunbar dropped the bag on one of the armchairs. 'Come on, let's be having you. You know the drill.'

Stephen slipped off his coat, feeling the weight of the bayonet he now carried in the inside pocket, and started to undress. Dunbar watched him closely, not surprised by the stiffness across the shoulders as much as the obvious emaciation. His arms were thin and bony, and his ribs were clearly visible – though partly hidden under a set of spectacular bruises that stretched halfway across his back.

'When did you get out of the army?' he asked, taking Stephen's wrist and feeling his pulse. It was weak, but steady.

'March.'

'Gor blimey,' Dunbar grimaced, 'they must have liked you.'

Stephen shrugged. 'Students didn't come very high up the list of important occupations, so I ended up with a low number.'

'You must have been nearly the last one home.'

'Pretty much.'

Another shrug and Dunbar felt the ribs move under his fingers. He gently probed around the kidneys, then quickly warmed the bell of his stethoscope and listened to Stephen's chest. Again, his breathing was a little shallow, but regular and clear.

'And when did this happen?'

'Three days ago.'

'How many of them were there?'

'Three or four. I'm not sure – it was dark.'

Dunbar shook his head sadly. With every week that passed, the level of violence in Ireland was getting higher. Ambushes, shootings, raids on farms – the newspapers were chock-full of them every day. While he might not agree with it, at least he could understand it. Sinn Fein had tried to achieve their ends by peaceful means – they had even sent a delegation to the Peace Conference after the war – but they had been rebuffed, and now they were starting their own war. Unfortunately, the most hapless victims of that war were not the army or the police, who were armed and could at least defend themselves, but the poor bastards who'd thought they were finished with fighting. Some of them maimed, some of them wounded in ways that weren't as easy to see – none of them expecting to be called traitors, to be despised by the people who'd cheered them off to war. He'd seen a few of them jeered at in the street, even spat at, but he'd never seen anything this bad.

'This is no country for heroes, is it?' he asked with a wry smile. 'Well, there's nothing broken, anyway. You can get dressed. Want me to give you something for the pain?'

'What about some morphine?'

Dunbar's mouth was already open before he caught the half-smile as Stephen pulled his vest back on over his head.

'Oh, very fucking droll,' he said, but chuckled as he went to the sideboard. 'Perhaps we'll just stick to the port, eh? How is the leg, by the way? Giving you any gyp?'

'It's about the only part of me that doesn't hurt,' Stephen admitted, taking a glass of port and easing himself stiffly into one of the armchairs. Dunbar flopped into the other and raised his glass.

'Well, here's to civvy street – and all her disappointments.'

'To civvy street.' Stephen raised his own glass, drank the toast, and then added, 'I thought it was only me.'

Dunbar shook his head.

'I've been through two wars, and coming home is always the same. You've spent so long dreaming about it that the reality is always a bloody let-down. But don't worry, you come to terms with it eventually. At some point you realize that, no matter how bad or boring life is, it's better than being bloody shot at.'

'I don't know,' Stephen began, but he broke off and stared into the fireplace for a few moments, feeling the heat on his face and the knots in his muscles starting to unwind. For the first time he felt he might just nod off to sleep, right there in the chair. It took an effort to continue. 'I don't know. Sometimes I feel like everything is falling apart. Not just me, everything. The world. Nothing makes sense any more. It's all meaningless, chaotic.'

'War is really very simple,' Dunbar told him. 'Friend or enemy, live or die – kill or be killed, even. It all boils down to these ridiculous choices, but it's not real life. Real life is much harder to manage. Of course, it helps if you have a purpose, a routine.' He waved his hand around the room. 'It was easy for me, I suppose. All I had to do was take off my uniform, tell the locum to bugger off, and, hey presto, business as usual. What about you? How does university suit you?'

'Not very well. My heart's not in it. I'm supposed to finish my degree next year but I can't be bothered, to tell you the truth. I just can't see the bloody point.'

'No ambitions? No plans for the future?'

Stephen gave him a bitter smile.

'If I learned anything in the war, it's that there is no future. There's only now.'

'Oh?' Dunbar chuckled. 'You have got it bad, haven't you?

And what about that girl you had? Your long-haired chum. She still on the scene?'

'She is.' Stephen's lips compressed into a thin line. 'For the moment, anyhow. I think she's running out of patience.'

'What makes you say that?'

'Well, I bloody well would have by now.'

Dunbar didn't reply. Once again, he was struck by the similarity to his own experience. He'd had a wife once, but she had left him. And not because of the war or because of his wounds, or even because of the morphine. She'd left him because he'd pushed her away. She'd been a good and kind and loving woman, but he'd been so determined to wallow in his own pain that he'd locked her out. And he'd been so absorbed by it, so bloody self-obsessed, that he hadn't even noticed what he was doing, until one day she was gone.

'Well . . .' he began, but then the telephone jangled in the hall. 'Oh, bugger it!' he groaned, and hauled himself out of the chair. 'Excuse me, I won't be a moment.'

Stephen took a mouthful of port from his glass and turned his feet closer to the log fire. The port was sweet and warm and tasted sticky, but it was nicer than whiskey. He'd been drinking a lot of whiskey, even though he didn't really like it. Never had. And cheap whiskey, too. Port was much nicer, he thought, and sagged back in the armchair. At least he was starting to feel warm now, and he could feel the tension sliding out of his muscles like water. Christ, he'd have to find somewhere decent to live. Somewhere with a real fire.

'Sorry about this,' Dunbar said, and Stephen blinked awake. Had he been dozing? Dunbar had shed the dressing gown and slippers and he was buttoning up his overcoat. 'I have to make an emergency house call, I'm afraid. One of my patients has taken a turn. Bloody influenza again. It's spreading like wildfire.'

'Oh.' Stephen came fully to himself, set down his glass, and pushed himself out of his chair. He picked up his coat. 'I should go. I'm sorry. I didn't mean to impose.'

'No, no, stay put.' Dunbar put a hand on his shoulder. 'It's only up the road. I won't be more than half an hour.'

'No, I should go. I've a long walk home.'

'Stay, please. I insist. Stay the night, if you like – I've got an empty flat downstairs, after all.' Dunbar gently pushed him down again. He knew the difference a few hours of warmth and comfort could make, and he was intrigued by the conversation they'd had. Could it be that he actually missed the army? It had been so long since he'd been able to talk to another soldier. 'Please, make yourself comfortable. I won't be long, and we can talk again when I come back.'

It was after midnight by the time Joe got back to his boarding house on Gardiner Street. Most landladies would have locked up by then, but Mrs Kelly knew what hours he kept and he let himself in with his own key.

He went up the stairs slowly, tired but in good humour. He could still smell her on himself, still feel her softness, taste her in his mouth. He'd brought Maggie to a pub when they got off the tram – partly to keep her sweet, but partly because he wanted to. He'd made an effort to be chatty – he really liked Maggie, but the business that had brought them together hung over them like a shadow, and if the talk dried up even for a few seconds, then it fell down between them. So he had talked to her about her landlady, her home, her family down in the country – anything but the orders he'd been sent to collect. And it had worked, too – it had worked so well that he managed to forget all about them, until they got ready to leave and Maggie had excused herself to the lavatory. When she came back she placed a thin wad of carbon paper on the table and slid it across to him. He picked it up and put it into his inside pocket without a word. That was the way she wanted it.

But once he had the orders, they became a problem. He was far more likely to be stopped and searched than she was, and he had to get rid of them as quickly as he could. Nevertheless, he walked her back to her lodgings – it wasn't far anyway.

'Well, I suppose you'll be off now that you've got what you want,' she said, when they stopped at the gate. He stood facing her with his hands thrust into his pockets.

'How do you know that's all I want?' he asked, with a grin. Then she put her hands on his shoulders, pulled him closer, and reached up to kiss him, her tongue worming into his mouth so that he could feel the heat of it and taste the gin. When she pulled away she left her hands on his chest and smiled at him.

'That's more like it,' he told her, his grin even broader.

'Go on, you rogue.' She gently pushed him away. 'You'd best be getting home before the coppers catch you.'

But he'd stood his ground and watched her go inside, waving to her when she turned on the doorstep. When he set off, he moved quickly, taking side streets and lanes where he could, keeping one eye out for police or soldiers. At last, he stopped outside a nondescript house in Drumcondra and took the carbon papers from his pocket. He looked up at the windows – all dark, showing no signs of life. All the times he'd been here he'd never seen anybody come or go, never a face, never a light in a window. That was probably how they wanted it, he thought, and opened the gate, went in and slipped the papers through the letterbox.

Twenty minutes later he let himself into his boarding house, and now he was on the landing, listening in the dark and watching the thin sliver of light at the bottom of the door. He knew he'd be listening, so he crept up to the door as quietly as he could, then burst in all of a sudden. Garvey looked up sharply. He was sitting on one of the beds with a paraffin lamp on the table beside him and a rag spread over his lap. Half a dozen bullets lay in the hollow of the rag and there was a small silver gun in his hand.

'I thought I told you about that thing,' Joe said sharply, but Garvey deliberately pulled out the magazine and started pushing the bullets into it one by one.

'It's my gun, I can have it if I want,' he answered sullenly.

It was such a childish thing to say that Joe didn't reply at first. Small though it was, the gun was no toy; a .25 automatic – perhaps not powerful enough to kill a man except at very close range, but enough to get the holder locked up. Joe didn't know how Garvey had come by it, but he was very attached to it, and carried it everywhere he went.

'Not in here you can't. If the police catch you with that, they'll put the pair of us in jail.'

'Ah, don't be worrying about the police,' Garvey said complacently, pushing the magazine in and cocking the slide. 'It's them should be worrying about us.'

Joe sat on his bed and started to undress. He was wary of Garvey. He'd been wary of him two years ago, when he met him during that by-election, but those two years had not improved him. If anything, they had made him worse – more cocky, more excitable. And those were not good qualities for a man on the run. He'd had other lads through here – men who'd come to the notice of the police in their own towns or parishes, and had been sent to the city until the heat died down – but they'd all played it safe. They'd kept themselves to themselves, avoided trouble, and if anybody asked, they were cousins up from the country, looking for work. But not Garvey. Garvey carried his gun everywhere, and wasn't afraid to show it to anybody he liked.

He talked too much, and he followed Joe around like a stray dog. It had been all Joe could do to get him to stay in tonight with the excuse that he was expecting a message from headquarters. But the truth was he didn't like having him near Maggie. He didn't like the way he looked at her.

'And how was our dear Maggie, tonight?' Garvey asked, as Joe took off his tie. Joe gritted his teeth. There it was again – that familiarity, that false intimacy.

'She was fine,' he answered curtly.

'Aye, but did she give you anything?' Garvey asked, and cackled lewdly.

'You watch your mouth,' Joe warned, looking up from unlacing his boots, 'and turn off that light. I want to get some sleep.'

'All right, all right.' Garvey reached across and turned out the light, and Joe quickly finished undressing and rolled himself under the covers. He heard Garvey moving about behind him, getting undressed. He didn't like anybody to see his leg, so he always undressed in the dark. When he finally slipped himself into the other bed, there was a long pause, and then he spoke again.

'I forgot to tell you. Paddy Daly was here earlier.'

Joe frowned in the dark. The message from headquarters had been a lie – an excuse to keep Garvey in the house – but such messages weren't unheard of either. Then again, a visit in person from one of Collins's right-hand men was a rare event. It was just like Garvey to wait until he was in bed before telling him.

'What did he want?' Joe asked, trying not to sound interested.

'He wants to see the pair of us tomorrow night. He said we're to drop around to the engineer's place at half eight.'

'Did he say what it was about?'

'No.'

'Right. Well, goodnight, then.'

'Goodnight, Joe.'

Joe turned over and looked at the faint glow through the curtain for a few moments, waiting for sleep. He wondered what Maggie was doing, how she might be lying with her hair spread out across the pillow and her face relaxed and peaceful. He liked to think of her like that. She seemed pure then, so far away from what they were all doing.

IX

He could talk to Dunbar, and Dunbar could listen. Once Stephen got going, Dunbar almost never interrupted him, but he had some knack of conveying that he understood, and Stephen knew that his words made complete sense to him. He knew what it was like, he had lived through it himself. He had been *there*.

They were meeting a couple of times a week – always in Dunbar's house, and always in the big sitting room. Dunbar kept the fire lit and the port flowing and Stephen would have come for those two things alone – just for the chance to get out of his bloody awful flat. Dunbar never asked him to talk about the war, but he usually did. In a way, it was like falling asleep; it crept up on him, and he started to dream out loud. Only in this dream, he was in control. In this dream he knew what would happen. He knew what he had done . . .

The earth was wet and black and clung to their boots in thick, heavy clods. Still they moved quickly, spread out in a line across the field, the winter stubble crackling under their feet. It was still dark, though the sky was lightening and he could already make out the angular walls and roofs of the village. Just then, the rising sun slipped out from behind a bank of low cloud and painted the church steeple a deep blood-red. *Faster, faster*. He lengthened his stride and loped forward, feeling the men on either side doing the same. Grunting, panting, straining to close the distance before they were spotted. Not a word, and hardly a sound except for their thumping feet and the slap of a strap on a rifle as they ran.

Stirred by the sun, a cock crowed, only to be cut off in his first call by the crack of a rifle.

'Move! Move!' Stephen shouted, as a bullet whizzed past and thudded into the earth. Then he saw the ground falling away a few yards ahead – long grass fringing a narrow cleft that swirled with milky mist. The stream. He was nearly there, bounding, his breath burning in his throat, and then the machine gun opened fire.

He landed in a heap in the bottom, water up to his knees, crashing his shoulder against the far bank. Gulping for air, he inched up and peered over the bank towards the stone houses. He could feel the machine-gun bullets beating the earth just a few feet away, and had to shield himself from the spray of earth and stones they threw up. The gun was in a house not thirty yards away – he could see the barrel spitting from a downstairs window. But the Germans had waited too long before opening fire. They should never have let them get to the river.

'Stop that machine gun, sergeant,' he barked to Kinsella, and waded past him, shouting instructions, pointing and encouraging, heedless of the bullets that were hissing and thudding into the far bank of the stream. When he reached the end of his line, he could see the bridge, and Nightingale's men already flopping down and firing from the shallow ditch beside the road. Turning back, he saw two men with grenades slotted into the barrels of their rifles rise up and fire at the machine gun. He watched the apple-sized bombs wobbling through the air and saw one hit the wall and bounce off, exploding harmlessly a few yards away. The other crashed through the window and detonated with a bright orange flash that blew out glass and bits of timber. The machine gun fell silent.

'Come on, lads,' he bellowed, and they scrambled out of the stream and went haring towards the houses. Now it was different. He could feel the air rushing past as he ran and the exhilaration building in his chest until he thought it might burst. Hurdling a small fence he ran across ploughed earth strewn with cabbages, then felt the rough stone of a cottage wall as he threw himself against it. Crouching down, he popped his head around the corner and saw men in grey uniforms running in all directions. With hardly a thought he brought up the rifle and fired once, twice – and saw two of them falling down. A small knot of men ran past, firing as they charged into the village, and then he was up and running again. He saw Kinsella and two men kick in a door, lob bombs inside, and the blast whistled past him like hot breath. He ran on, finding cobbles underfoot, open doors and curtained windows.

In the village square, the Germans had made a makeshift barricade of farm carts and furniture, but there was nobody left to man it. He heard firing across the square, and out of the corner of his eye he saw more khaki figures darting down the road from the bridge. A man in grey burst out of a doorway and they fired again and sent him sprawling in the street. Stephen started to run across the square. Two men darted from behind a house and he fired from the hip. He heard the clatter of bootnails behind him, shouting, shooting, but he ran on. They had them now! He saw three men walk out from behind the church, hands held up high, helmets off. Another dragged out of a doorway by one of Nightingale's men. But his blood was still up, his heart pounding. Down the side of the church, and he saw he had run clear through the village. A narrow band of vegetable gardens, a small cemetery, and then the fields stretched away again, broken by the black grid of neat hedgerows. Even as he looked he saw Germans running through gardens, scrambling through ditches and fleeing across the fields.

Dropping to one knee he closed the bolt on his rifle, and took aim at the furthest one. He was already across the field, almost in the safety of the ditch. He squeezed the trigger and the man went down. With a smooth, easy action, he worked the bolt, felt the empty case whistling past his ear, and took aim on the next, following his bouncing progress across the heavy earth. His breathing was smooth, he held it, focused, and started to squeeze again. Then the rifle was pushed upwards, the force of it almost knocking him over.

'Cease firing, Stephen!'

It was Nightingale, panting for breath, bent almost double, and with his revolver dangling on the lanyard round his neck. 'What the hell are you doing? Cease firing. They're running – can't you see?'

But it was still boiling inside him, and he had to bite back an angry shout. They were getting away. He was the one who couldn't see. But Nightingale was looking at him strangely, gasping for breath and frowing.

'Stephen, are you wounded?'

'No,' Stephen answered first, then checked himself, running his hand across his body, as if to make sure everything was still there. 'No. I'm fine. Why?'

'You're covered in blood. Look. It's all over your face. Are you sure you're all right?'

Stephen wiped his fingers across his cheek and they came away red. When he looked down he saw the shoulder and breast of his tunic were soaked through. He checked again, but he was certain he wasn't wounded. Nevertheless, when he stood up he suddenly felt weak, dizzy and nauseous. He stumbled sideways, and Nightingale had to grab him by the arm to stop him falling over.

'Steady on, old man,' he said lightly. 'It's all right. I've got you.'

'You said that was the end of the war,' Dunbar said. 'But it went on a bit after that, didn't it?'

'Two or three days,' Stephen agreed, staring into the fire. It was a few weeks since Dunbar had first seen him, and the bruises had faded so that they were hardly noticeable. But they had been replaced by dark patches under the eyes, and by a weary pallor that Dunbar easily recognized. Insomnia. Stephen looked like he hadn't slept in days. 'But as far as I'm concerned, that was the end. That was the last fight we were in, and that was the last shot I fired. After it, we marched into a forest and dug in. I didn't even see another German until the armistice.'

He thought back again to that day. Under cover of darkness they'd moved to a wet ditch on the edge of the forest. It wasn't cold, but it was drizzling with rain. The men were in a curious state. The rumour of a ceasefire had not had much outward effect on any individual – they had all been disappointed before – and yet there was an air of hopeful expectation in the ditch. Stephen felt it too, although he had reason to believe it was more than a rumour this time. He'd had his orders from the colonel himself: sit tight and wait. Do not fire unless fired upon. Eleven o'clock was the time he'd been given, and as the morning wore on he found himself looking at his watch every few minutes. Kinsella was worse. Even though sentries had been posted, he stood in a half-crouch against the side of the ditch, never taking his eyes off the distant copse where the Germans were dug in. Then, with barely a minute to go, he looked down at Stephen, his face an almost ludicrous mask of suspicion and concern.

'Sir, I see 'em moving.'

Stephen had been crouched down so long his legs had gone to sleep but the threat brought him awkwardly to his feet. The other sentries had seen it too, and as they tensed and cocked their rifles, alarm rippled along the ditch.

'Where?'

'Just in front of them trees.' Kinsella jerked his chin towards the copse, and Stephen saw for himself a grey-clad figure dart forward and disappear, dropping into a trench. 'Should we stand to, sir?'

'No, sergeant, let's not be too—' He was cut off by a machine gun that opened fire from the German position. 'Christ!' He flinched, but saw that it was firing high. The tracer rounds sparkled in a bright arc far up in the grey sky. 'What the hell are they doing?'

The rest of the men were standing up now, watching, frowning – some of them laughing. Then the belt ran out and the last shot rang sharp through the damp air. A single German soldier stood up in front of the trees, swept off his helmet and bowed from the waist.

'Goodbye, gentlemen,' he called out, his voice echoing around the clearing, and then he turned and disappeared into the forest.

'Why did you shoot him?' Dunbar asked.

'Eh?' Stephen started out of his reverie. The heat and the port were making him drowsy again. 'I didn't shoot him.'

'But you just said you shot that man who was running away through the field. Why did you do that? He was hardly a threat.'

'Oh, I don't know.' Still flummoxed, Stephen had to think for a moment. 'The heat of battle, I suppose – or instinct. I was an excellent shot, you know,' he added uncertainly. It was like trying to remember another life. 'I once shot a man out of an observation balloon that was three-quarters of a mile away. I was the toast of the battalion.'

'That doesn't really answer my question,' Dunbar pointed out.

'But you must admit, it was quite a feat – and the other one, too. A running man at four hundred yards and I dropped him like a pheasant. Not many men could have done it.'

'But now it troubles you,' Dunbar tried. 'It's keeping you awake.'

'Not really.' Again Stephen sounded uncertain, frowning slightly as if he was trying to remember something. 'Not so much the shooting as the blood.'

'Ah yes, the blood,' Dunbar said, as if that were significant. But then he too frowned. 'If it wasn't yours, then where did it come from?'

'I have no idea. I've gone through that attack dozens of times in my head but I still don't know where it could have come from.'

'Were there casualties?'

'Yes. Three dead and five wounded on our side. But none of them were near me when they copped it.'

'And now you have nightmares about blood. Is that it?'

'Not exactly.' Stephen's lips compressed in a grim smile. He'd endured enough nightmares to know that you needed to be asleep to suffer from them. But this . . . this *thing* was keeping him awake. For the last week he'd had it. How it had come about, or why at this particular time, he didn't know, but it was like a morbid fixation on blood. He could taste it in his food, smell it sometimes, and when he lay on his narrow bed he could feel it in the shadows, oozing from the walls. It followed him everywhere, and if he ever did start to drowse, he could feel it welling up, threatening to engulf him. He always woke up gasping for breath, as if he were drowning.

Although he didn't realize it, he was drifting again. Dunbar watched him closely, saw the nodding head and the drooping eyelids. He was clearly exhausted – maybe it would be better to let him sleep, if he could. Perhaps even a sleeping pill would be in order. But then Stephen caught himself; his head came up and he blinked.

'Sorry. Where were we?'

'You were telling me why you shot that man who was running away.'

'Was I?' Stephen blinked. 'Well, I think I said it was the heat of battle – instinct, I suppose.'

Dunbar's mouth twisted into a thin smile. He shook his head and opened the cigarette box beside his chair, took out a cigarette and lit it with a spill of paper from the fire.

'Balls,' he said, through a cloud of smoke. 'Instinct my arse. That's what's really keeping you awake, isn't it? You might be seeing blood, but it's him you're thinking about.'

'No,' Stephen said flatly, but he knew that Dunbar was on to something. He'd seen blood before, copious amounts of it. Why, then, did he always go back to that attack, to that one part of the attack? The rest was a blur, frenetic, unclear, but he could remember every second of that shot. He could feel the pressure of the trigger under his finger, the rough stone of the church wall as he steadied himself against it, the smooth wood of the rifle against his cheek. He could clearly see the little black figure running for the ditch, staggering across the rough earth, and the round bead of the sight sweeping over him like the finger of death. His finger, pressing down on the trigger, smooth and steady like he'd been taught . . .

He was sitting frozen in his chair, that last denial still on his lips. Dunbar knew what had happened. After everything he had been through, everything he had endured, guilt was catching up with Stephen. He felt a pang of unease. Perhaps he shouldn't have pushed him so hard – he certainly shouldn't have been so glib about it. But at least he'd dragged it out in the open. The wound was exposed, and it was better that way. Left to fester, that sort of guilt would be corrosive.

'You're not a murderer,' he said. 'That man could have turned around and shot you. He could have had a machine gun in the ditch; he could have come back with the rest of his battalion. You know damn well there was any number of things that could have happened. But they didn't, because you were a soldier and you did your job. You killed the enemy who would have killed you, given half a chance. Now you should get on with your life and stop beating yourself up over it.'

But Stephen's face was stony. The running man had been merely the last. What about all the others? What about the legions of dead, friend and enemy alike? Men he had known, men he had liked – they were all just as dead as that man. But not him. Why not? What had he done to escape?

'What if I can't get on with my life?' he asked, with a bitter smile. 'What if *that's* my life? What if that's all I'm good for? What if I did it because I *liked* it?'

Joe watched the tram coming down the Rathmines Road. It was late this morning, and there were more people waiting than he would have liked. He slyly scanned their faces for any that looked out of the ordinary. A glance here, a look there – it was hard to do without drawing attention to himself. But if things didn't work out as planned, then the fewer people who remembered him getting on the tram, the better.

His eyes briefly met Garvey's and then darted away again. He hadn't wanted him here, but Paddy Daly had insisted on it, and Paddy Daly was the boss. He'd called them both to the Engineer's Hall the night before, but invited Joe into the office on his own.

'Do you know this fella?' he'd asked, sliding an index card across the table. Joe was surprised by the name at the top, but even more by the amount of information written in a neat hand below it. It was mostly mundane stuff – places, dates, a few other names underlined in red – but it was very fresh, and it was clear that they'd been watching him for a while.

'Yeah, sort of. I've met him once or twice. He's really a friend of—'

'Does he know you?' Daly took the card back and slipped it into an envelope.

'He knows who I am.'

'Right. Then here's the way it is.' Daly's voice was hard and clipped, the way it always was when he talked business – which wasn't surprising, considering the business he was in. 'He's working for the Castle – looking into some things that could cause us problems. And I mean big problems. When the Chief found out what he was up to, he said straight away that he wanted him dead – but some of the other boys spoke up for him. Seems he might be a supporter of ours, which means he could be useful.'

'So you want me to have a word with him,' Joe said, relieved.

'I want you to frighten the bejesus out of him,' Daly answered, without smiling. 'You go and talk to him and make it clear that we're not messing around. But you bring Garvey with you, and if your man won't play ball, then Garvey can plug him.'

'Garvey,' Joe started to protest, but Daly just shook his head.

'That's the order, Joe,' he said. 'I won't lie to you. If it comes to it, we think you might have a problem shooting this fella, seeing as you know him. That's why Garvey is going with you. He won't.'

Daly stood up and put on his coat. Once an order was given, he never waited around.

'Do it tomorrow,' he said curtly. 'He'll be on the half eight tram from Rathmines. Ned Kelliher will give you the guns tonight.'

The gun he'd been given hung heavily in the pocket of Joe's overcoat. It wasn't as if he hadn't used one before, but still, it felt ominous. The tram came clanging to a halt and he let himself be jostled on to the back platform with all the others. As they jerked into motion again, he hung on to the bar and tried to get his bearings. He knew Garvey was standing somewhere behind him, but he didn't look in that direction. The tram was crowded, but there were a few seats to be had. He saw a black homburg above sloping black-coated shoulders and thought he recognized the shape of the head. There was an empty seat a couple of rows behind, but he waited until the conductor came thumping down the stairs, and paid for his ticket with the tuppence in his fist. They were always told to be careful about things like that. No point in drawing attention to yourself – just play by the rules and be as normal as possible. Slipping the ticket into his pocket, Joe made his way forward and sat down.

As the tram crept up over the hump of the canal bridge, Joe felt the weight of the gun again, gently knocking against his thigh with the motion. He shoved his newspaper into his pocket to stop it and again scanned those faces he could see, trying to spot any sign of trouble. He felt time pressing. Another two stops was all they had. After that they'd be in town – crowded streets, policemen. It'd be too busy to get him off then.

But the next stop was popular and nearly half the passengers got off all at once. Suddenly, the tram felt empty, and Joe saw his chance and took it. He got up and moved forward, slipping into the empty seat and pulling the gun from his pocket in the same movement. He laid his newspaper on top of it for cover.

'Good morning to you, Billy,' he said quietly, and when Billy turned towards him, smiling, he prodded him in the ribs with the gun. 'Don't say a word,' he warned, staring straight ahead. They'd be at the next stop in under a minute.

'But . . .' Billy stammered, looking down at the gun, now out from under the newspaper. Joe knew it wasn't cocked, but Billy would never know the difference.

'We're getting off at the next stop. I'll get up and ring the bell and you get off in front of me. Don't try anything, I'm warning you. I don't want to shoot you, but I will if I have to.'

He could see the stop in the distance, and the lane across the road. He and Garvey had scouted it early that morning, before walking up to wait for the tram. He stood up and rang the bell and his eyes met Billy's for a moment as he stood up, but he looked away. He'd seen that look before – enough times to know that Billy understood what was happening. His face was pale, his movements unsteady as he hauled himself out of his seat and made his way back down the tram.

Garvey was still on the back platform, holding a copy of the *Daily Sketch* up in front of his face, but with his eyes darting all over the place. When they came up beside him, he took the paper down and leaned close to Billy.

'Try anything, and I'll put a bullet into you.'

'Why?' Billy began, in a high-pitched, querulous voice, and Joe prodded him in the back with the newspaper.

'Just keep quiet and do what we tell you.'

The tram rumbled to a halt and the three of them stepped down.

'Wait here until it goes,' Joe murmured, and when the road was clear he could see straight into the lane on the other side. He looked up and down the road, but it was empty. Everything was going according to plan.

'Come on, now,' he said, and they walked across the street. In a few seconds they were in the lane, Billy walking in front,

Joe and Garvey behind. Joe cast his eyes left and right, looking up to the back windows of the houses – looking for a face, a witness. A few yards in, the laneway turned and took on a rustic character – blackberry bushes and nettles curving up to screen them even from the highest windows. Just as they reached the turn, he looked at Garvey.

'Wait here,' he said, and glanced at the gun in Garvey's hand. 'Put that away and keep your eye out for the coppers. Whistle if you see anything.'

Garvey nodded and slipped his gun into his pocket, but he looked sullen. Joe knew damn well what he wanted, but he was determined not to give it to him. Billy had stopped and started to turn around, but Joe gave him a push and followed him down the lane.

It was very quiet down there. Soon he could hear only the crunch of their shoes and some birds twittering in the hedges. But after a few more paces, Billy found his tongue again.

'Where are we going?' he demanded, and his voice was lower, steadier than it had been on the tram.

'Just keep walking,' Joe said through gritted teeth.

'Are you going to kill me?'

'Shut up.'

Billy's mind was racing. He knew that the further he went from the street, the more danger he was in, and with every step his legs felt more leaden and his heart thumped harder. He tried to think of other things – the way the backs of the houses seemed to teeter over him as the lane got narrower, the smell of the bushes and the shiny newness of their leaves. But he couldn't keep it up for long. The desperate danger, the thought of that ugly snubby little gun in his back, kept pressing in on him. Soon he could think of nothing else, he became lost in it, and when

Joe stopped he walked on another two paces before he realized this was the place. He was afraid to turn round.

'Why are you doing this?' he managed to ask.

'Why are you working for Military Intelligence?'

'I'm not working for Military Intelligence. I work for a man called Frank Mercer.'

'Frank Mercer is a ranking member of Lord French's Secret Intelligence Committee.'

Billy didn't answer. His shoulders slumped. The further he'd gone into this business, the more he'd suspected that Mercer was a bit more than the ordinary civil servant he pretended to be.

'He has you investigating Sinn Fein money, doesn't he? Loans, bank accounts, all that stuff.'

'Yes,' Billy admitted bleakly.

'How much did you find out?'

'Quite a bit,' Billy said defiantly. If this was to be the end, then at least he wanted them to know that it was he who had beaten them in some way. But then he began to wonder at all the questions. Surely they already knew what he was doing, and if they'd decided to kill him, they wouldn't be standing here trying to justify it. 'Quite a bit more than I've let on. I've given them a few bits and pieces, but I haven't made my full report yet.'

Silence. Somehow, Billy found the courage to turn round and he saw Joe standing three feet away with the gun levelled at him. His feet were slightly apart, his hand steady. He had the look of a man who'd done this sort of thing before – and yet he was smiling.

'We want to see that report before Frank Mercer does,' Joe said, and relief flooded through Billy. He gave a silent sigh and closed his eyes for a moment, feeling his legs start to go weak at last.

'Of course,' he agreed. 'I would have offered anyway, but then I didn't know whom to trust.'

'You trust me, and nobody else,' Joe told him, and Billy started when the gun clicked loudly in his hand. But then he relaxed again as Joe slid it into his pocket. 'You tell me everything and give me everything – keep nothing back. Because, make no mistake, you were a marked man today. That fella up the lane would have shot you already, only they sent me to try and talk sense into you first. We're at war here, Billy – if you cross us, you'll be killed. Do you understand that?'

'Yes,' Billy said, without the slightest hesitation.

'Grand.' Joe nodded and wiped his hand across his lips – the first sign of nervousness Billy had seen. 'Tell nobody about this – and I mean nobody, not even my brother.' He nodded down the lane. 'Keep going that way. Go back to your work and wait for me to get in touch with you.'

Without another word, Joe turned on his heel and started back up the lane. Billy waited until he was out of sight, then he let out a loud gasp as all the strength went out of him. Suddenly everything felt heavy – his coat, his briefcase, even the hat pressing down on his head. He felt nauseous, and tears pricked his eyes. But after a minute he became aware of himself, standing slumped and alone in some anonymous back lane, with the birds singing in the bushes and the breeze twisting down a spill of chimney smoke. He straightened himself, turned on his heel, and set off quickly in the other direction.

'Well?' Garvey demanded, when Joe came back up the lane. He was still standing where Joe had left him, with his hands thrust deep in his pockets, looking shifty.

'He's our man,' Joe told him, walking past without a pause. He was pleased it had turned out as he had hoped, and he didn't want to listen to Garvey's carping.

'We should've plugged him,' Garvey said, hurrying after him and making heavy weather with his gammy leg. 'I don't like the look of him, Joe. He's not to be trusted. We should have put a bullet in him, and be done with it.'

Joe turned round so sharply that Garvey nearly ran into him.

'That's your answer to everything, isn't it?' he demanded, feeling suddenly very savage. 'What sort of a country do you think we'll have if we can get it only by murder, eh? You answer me that.'

But Garvey had no answer. He dropped his eyes and mumbled something into his collar. Joe turned and looked out into the street. It looked different, now that the tension was gone – the picture of a clear winter's morning in the city; two women walked down the other side, pushing a pram, and a motorcar puttered past.

'We'd better split up,' he said. 'I'll see you later.' And before Garvey could say anything else, he was out and walking, with only the weight of the gun in his pocket to remind him of what had just happened.

X

Head down, hurrying, he ran up the stairs three at a time. The strain of it sent stabs of pain up his leg, but he ignored them. The knee had been at him all week – it always hurt when the weather turned cold – but that wasn't what had kept him late.

He reached the top landing and looked at the door to the lecture hall. It would probably be simpler if he didn't go in at all, but it would be warmer in there than in his freezing little flat. So he steeled himself and pulled open the door. With the flu going around, Professor Barrett was taking the class himself, and Stephen saw him on the dais, looking small and bent in the distance. The hall was almost empty – it seemed the flu was cutting down students and staff alike – and his entry was more obvious than he would have liked. Heads turned, and there was a momentary pause in Professor Barrett's speech as he peered sharply over the top of his spectacles.

'Discontinuous functions,' he began again in his reedy voice, watching Stephen slide into a seat. More than anything else, he hated lateness. 'Discontinuous functions are therefore very useful to us in cases where . . .'

Stephen heard little else. He was tired and his head hurt. He was still chasing sleep, and even though it came more regularly now, it never seemed quite enough and it was usually troubled.

Last night he'd stayed up late working on a paper – a wasted effort, nothing had come to him – and when he went to bed he had dreamed that ghosts surrounded his bed. But they weren't ghosts in the usual sense – they weren't dead people. Instead, they were the relatives of the dead, the mothers and fathers and brothers and sisters and children who had been left behind. They had packed his tiny bedroom and stood all around his bed, looking down at him with silent, accusing eyes.

He tried once more to focus on the blackboard, scratching his chin, which was itchy with stubble. There was a sour taste in his mouth from the whiskey. He'd finished the bottle last night, and still it hadn't kept those flaming ghosts away. Christ, he was a wreck. If it wasn't the ghosts, it was the blood, or the bodies in the canal. Was there no escape? Was he going mad? No, it was worse than that – at least a madman might be secure in his delusion, but not him – he couldn't think, could hardly sleep. No money either. What he had saved from his army pay was almost gone and the pension he got for his wounded leg was hardly worth the cost of the weekly envelope. Shivering in the dark last night, under a threadbare blanket and his greatcoat, and waiting for whatever horror sleep might bring, he'd felt despair welling up from deep inside him. The dead were lucky, he realized now. At least they'd seen the end of it.

There was a snap and a thump as Professor Barrett put down his cane and slammed shut the book on his desk. Stephen started in his seat. Was it over already? He must have dozed off. The scattered students stood up to leave and he wearily rose to follow them, but Barrett's head came up sharply.

'Mr Ryan, would you please stay behind? I wish to speak to you.'

Stephen turned round and went down the steps, standing aside as the last few students passed him by. Most of them wouldn't even meet his eye, but he could hardly blame them for that. It wasn't that he was different, that he was older, that he had been in the war, or even that he had a *reputation*. It was that he was doomed. Failure was written all over him, and they would not look at that. There but for the grace of God, was the common thought he could see in each averted face.

Barrett came round from behind his desk.

'Late again, Mr Ryan,' he said, and although he looked tired and worn, there was fire in his eyes. 'Do you think you are above the normal rules of attendance?'

Mr Ryan. The formality wasn't lost on Stephen, and he knew he'd reached the end of whatever privileges he'd once enjoyed. He bowed his head.

'No, sir.'

'No, sir? Is that all you have to say to me? No, sir?'

'I'm sorry, sir. It won't happen again.' He was mumbling, but he could feel resentment building inside his chest. He wasn't going to bend down and beg forgiveness. He'd walk out before he'd do that.

Barrett grimaced, looking at his downcast face, his dishevelled clothes. He was angry with him, but even more disappointed. Where was the boy he had known before the war? The one who had solved the most arcane problems as easy as breathing. The one who had stood up here year after year and fairly dazzled his classmates, who'd given most of them their one and only glimpse of real genius. Where had that boy gone? No doubt he'd had a hard time of it in the war, but that didn't mean he could just throw it all away. He had survived, he had come home. He had been given something that many had not – the chance to start again; a clean slate, a future. And what was he doing with it? Nothing.

'Are you sick? Have you got the flu?'

Stephen shook his head. 'No, sir.'

'Then for God's sake get a grip on yourself, man. Look at the state of you. You come in here dressed like a scarecrow and stinking, stinking of drink and God knows what. Late and half asleep or hungover, and all you can say is it won't happen again. Well, I don't believe you. Where is the paper you were to have for me last week? The one on complex numbers.'

'I'll have it today,' Stephen muttered, his heart sinking when he thought of the ragged pages stuffed in his haversack.

Barrett glared at him. 'Today is late. If you were any other student, I'd throw you out of this class. Are you listening to me? Good God, man, what's the matter with you?'

Stephen finally raised his head. His eyes were sunken and blood-shot and he had the face of one who was past caring.

'I'm just a bit tired, professor. I'll be all right later on.'

Barrett quivered with rage but bit his tongue. The things he wanted to say didn't bear saying. He'd had such high hopes for this young man – he had come to respect him and even to admire him – but he knew he was within an inch of losing him entirely. He could feel it – he could see it in the way he hung his head. He was angry and sullen and barely a hair's breadth from doing something they might both regret. It took a great effort, but Barrett clamped his teeth shut and stiffly picked up his books, then took his stick from where it stood against the leg of the desk.

'I want that paper today, Mr Ryan,' he said, in a much quieter voice. 'There is a limit to my patience and I have many other students to consider. Have it on my desk by the end of the day or by God you'll have plenty of time for sleeping.'

The crowds were thinning out on Henry Street. The working day had ended; shops were closing and people were going home. Joe turned towards a shop window and pretended to look at his watch. The reflection in the window, showed him the entrance to the café. He only had to turn his head to see Byrne lounging in a doorway a few yards down the street, and he knew Garvey and Kelliher were in similar positions on the other side of the street. He knew if he turned around he'd be able to pick them out in a second, and that wasn't good. They'd been here too long already, and if they didn't get it done soon, they'd start to stand out. People would take note of them, and that would be that.

He decided to allow five more minutes. Five more minutes, and after that they'd have to go back to the depot. He decided to go for another walk, and pulled his cap down lower over his eyes as he strolled down the street past Byrne, their eyes meeting for only a second, then turned and crossed the street, passing Kelliher, and crossing again after he had walked past Garvey.

He was halfway across the street when he heard Garvey's whistle behind him. He had to run to get out of the way of a brewer's cart, but when he turned around again he saw a couple in the door of the café. The woman was fixing her hat and the man was waiting for her, his hands in his pockets and a smile on his face. Joe stared at him for a few seconds; a tall man with sallow skin and pockmarked cheeks. He wore a greasy-looking bowler hat and a grey overcoat down to his knees. Joe turned his head and looked directly at Kelliher. He knew the man, had been questioned by him – and beaten. Kelliher nodded and started walking towards the couple. Another cart came by, this one laden with furniture, and blocked Joe's view for a few seconds. By the time it passed the couple had moved out of the restaurant and were walking down the street with their arms linked, moving out of range. But Kelliher was coming up fast behind them, his face set, one hand in his pocket. Joe stepped up on the kerb and put his hand in his own pocket, feeling the cold weight of the gun. He looked up and down the street: no uniforms, no helmets. It was all clear. His eye found Kelliher again, almost on top of them.

'Detective Inspector Doyle,' Kelliher called out, and as the man turned in answer to his name, Kelliher pulled the gun from his pocket and shot him twice in the chest. Joe saw him fall down, and the woman's hands fly to her mouth as she started to scream.

Kelliher was already walking away. He was moving smoothly down the street, his hands thrust in his pockets, staring straight ahead. Joe stood his ground, waiting for the others to get clear before he followed them. It was all as they had planned. Kelliher was nearly out of sight and Byrne was moving after him. The woman had backed away, screaming, and was leaning against the wall with her hands over her mouth, giving out muffled sobs and groans. There was a crowd gathering, shocked murmurs, the shrill of a whistle from further down the street. Another few seconds and he could go. But here was Garvey coming back up the street, limping steadily towards where the policeman was lying on the pavement. What the hell was he doing? Joe's hand tightened on his gun, his head darting up and down the street. He had the strong urge to shout at him, to tell him he was going the wrong way. But Garvey knew damn well what he was doing. Five paces from the woman he pulled out his gun and shot her once. The woman screamed, slumped, and started to slide down the wall and Garvey shot her again. The screaming stopped, but there was an angry yell from the crowd as it closed in around Garvey. He fired again, into the air, and the crowd parted enough for Garvey to dart out and bolt down the street, moving as quickly as his bad leg would allow.

'Christ almighty!' Joe whispered to himself, and he heard the whistles shrilling closer and saw helmets bobbing through the crowd. The police were almost here. He put one hand in his pocket to steady the weight of the revolver and turned up his collar with the other one. Then he stepped back on the pavement and walked steadily away, never looking back.

> Trinity College,
> Cambridge
> 12 December 1919

Dear Ms Bryce,

Thank you for your letter. I assure you that the pleasure of having both you and Mr Ryan come to Trinity would be ours entirely. Your transcendental method is still much talked about in our mathematical common room, and the chance of having its authors come and speak to our students is one of which we would be only to happy to avail ourselves.

To this end, I would propose a short seminar, to last at least one week but no more than two, which will be attended by our mathematical fellows and some of our brighter undergraduates. Now that we have finally thrown off the shadow of that dreadful war, I am sure this would be the simplest thing to arrange for the springtime. Shall we say next April? I shall leave the finer points to your own discretion, as I am sure you will need to make the necessary arrangements with your own college. I look forward to hearing your answer in due course.

Yours sincerely,

> *Prof. J. E. Littlewood*

Night was coming on by the time Lillian found him. He was in the library, which was all but empty at that hour, with the bays between the tall shelves falling deeper into shadow. She shivered as she walked through, pulling her coat tighter under her chin, feeling uneasy at the echo of her own footsteps. She gave herself quite a start when she finally found him in the most remote corner, slumped over a desk piled with books, head on his arms, fast asleep.

'Stephen?' she said softly, but he didn't stir. She cast a quick glance up and down the long hall, wondering if anybody else had seen him like this. For that matter, how long had he been here? She stepped closer, watching him. Even when he was asleep, his face seemed contorted, somehow suffused with a bad colour, as if he was ill. Was he ill? she wondered. Three of her students had fallen sick that week alone. The flu came on so quickly. In the morning they'd seemed perfectly fine, but by lunchtime they were sweating and unsteady on their feet, so she'd sent them home, fearful herself. It seemed two of them would recover, but one had died and the funeral would be next week. How suddenly it could happen – a life snuffed out in just a couple of days. And it seemed to afflict the young so badly, too. The healthiest, the fittest. It knocked them down first.

'Stephen?' she whispered again, but he still didn't move. She reached out to shake him, but stopped herself. Suddenly she felt like a stranger, and she was afraid to touch him. How long since she had seen him? Two weeks? Three? She knew he'd been avoiding her, but that wasn't what stayed her hand. He seemed so fragile, lying like that – like a broken doll. He'd lost all his strength. Somehow, he'd seemed tougher when he was in the army. She'd still been afraid for him – terrified she'd lose him when he went back to France – but he'd seemed more able to deal with the dangers; harder and stronger – even after he was wounded. His uniform had been like a suit of armour in some ways. But when she looked at the shabby greatcoat hung on the back of the chair, with the frayed threads where he'd cut off the epaulettes, she saw through her illusion. God love him, it would hardly even keep out the cold.

'Stephen, wake up,' she whispered, and when her hand touched his shoulder, she could feel the bone underneath. She started to shake him gently but he flew awake with such a start that she jumped backwards. Before she knew what was happening, he was half out of the chair, eyes wild, arms flailing. The look on his face was shocking – it wasn't him! But then he seemed to come to his senses and stopped himself, looked at her, and gradually subsided into the chair, blinking.

'I'm sorry, Stephen, I didn't mean to startle you,' she said, pulling out a chair and sitting down opposite him. He wiped a hand across his face.

'Sorry about that, I must have nodded off,' he explained, waving his hand at the books and papers that covered the desk – even though he'd read neither since he'd got there. 'Complex numbers always bored me. I have to get a paper in to Professor Barrett today or I'm in trouble.'

'Oh? Do you need a hand?' she asked, and was dismayed at the guarded look he gave her. Did he suspect what had happened? Did he know that Professor Barrett had all but sent her here – had called her aside in the staffroom and told her what would happen if he didn't sort himself out?

The first thing she'd felt, after Barrett had explained the situation, was guilt. She'd already suspected something was wrong, but she'd been afraid to confront Stephen about it – though, to be fair, she hadn't had much opportunity. She saw him so rarely these days and on the few occasions they did meet, he seemed so cold towards her – almost hostile – that she could hardly talk to him. But she'd tried to console herself that things could hardly be that bad. This was the great Stephen Ryan, who Professor

Barrett freely admitted was the most gifted student he'd ever had, and who was the man she knew, the man who had survived the worst the war could throw at him. And yet . . . looking at him across the table, she felt like she hardly knew him at all. His face was grey and he looked ill. He was thin, drawn, and it looked like he could hardly bring himself to write a simple paper on complex numbers – something he could have done in his sleep before.

'No, no, it's done. I just stopped for a rest.' He picked up his pen and leafed through a few pages. One glance and Lillian knew it wasn't done at all. She didn't like the look of it. There was a lot of blotting and crossing out, three or four crumpled pages in a heap on one side. The Stephen she knew had never turned in work like that. He'd always been neat and careful, no mistakes, no rewriting. Perfect first time, every time.

He wouldn't meet her eyes. He shuffled the pages, looked at one, shuffled them again. She knew he was waiting for her to leave but she wouldn't let him push her away like that. She sat watching him steadily.

'What time is it?' he asked.

'It's just after five o'clock,' she answered.

'I'm cutting it a bit fine, I suppose,' he said, shuffling through the pages. 'I'd better check it before I hand it in.'

'I'll check it for you, if you like.'

'Oh, no, no. I won't trouble you.'

She felt the smile die on her face.

'It's no trouble, honestly.'

'No, no. It's all right. Sure it's dark out. You should be getting home.'

Lillian frowned. This wasn't the man she knew. The old Stephen would have insisted on walking her home. Was he really sending her away? Just then, she felt a stabbing pain in her temples and the room seemed to fade away for a moment. She gripped the edge of the table to steady herself.

'Not at all, Stephen,' she said, clearing her throat. 'Why don't I check it and then we can go for some tea on the way home? It's ages since I've seen you, and—'

'I've been busy,' he cut across, but he still wouldn't look at her. He was holding the pages up, close to his chest. Was he trying to hide behind them? Or was he trying to hide them from her?

'So have I, Stephen,' she said slowly. 'But I wanted to talk to you about something as well. I got a letter from Professor Littlewood, in Cambridge.'

'Oh?' He carefully put down the pages – face down, she noticed – and clasped his hands together. 'What is it about?'

She had the letter in her pocket but she didn't take it out. Something in his manner told her he knew what she was talking about, although the fact was, he hadn't opened a letter in weeks – unless it was one of the little brown envelopes from the army.

'Didn't you get one too?'

'I don't think so,' he said evasively. 'I don't remember seeing anything.'

'Well, he's invited us to Cambridge next spring. He wants us to give a seminar on our transcendental method.'

'In the spring? I'm not sure. I'll have my exams then, don't forget.'

The guarded look was there again. Lillian could hardly believe it. Suddenly, she no longer felt sorry for him, but angry.

'Really, Stephen, you remember who Professor Littlewood is, don't you? He's professor of mathematics at Trinity College, Cambridge. Trinity, Stephen – remember how we used to talk about it?'

'Of course I remember.' His voice was sullen, but there was an edge to it.

'Well, we could go after your exams. I thought we might make a holiday out of it.'

'A holiday, yes of course.' His voice was distant. 'I'll have to think about it. I have so much to do in the meantime, you know how it is.'

'Very well, I'll leave you to think,' Lillian said sharply, standing up and pushing her chair back under the table with very deliberate care. As she did this, the room went dim again and she swayed on her feet. She had to hold on to the back of the chair to keep from falling over, but Stephen seemed not to notice.

'Stephen, what have I ever done to you?' she asked. She felt light-headed and the words came out without her bidding, as if they'd taken on a life of their own. He was in the middle of picking up his pages again, and he looked up at her with a blank frown.

'What do you mean?'

'Why are you treating me so coldly? Have I done something to you, have I offended you in some way?'

He let out half a breath. She could tell he was feigning surprise; he'd never been good at it.

'I don't know what you're talking about.'

'No, Stephen, you know exactly what I'm talking about and you should at least have the decency to admit it. What's the matter with you? Giving a seminar in Cambridge could be the making of both of us – and you, most of all. If you do well in your exams you'll be up for a studentship, and with that sort of feather in your cap it will be guaranteed. But all you can say is that you'll think about it?'

He didn't answer, but looked down and started to shuffle the pages again. He was like some poor creature who had lost his wits, repeating the same feeble motions over and over again. It was too much.

'Oh, for goodness' sake, Stephen!' she cried, and snatched the pages out of his hands. She scarcely realized what she'd done before he lunged violently across the table and snatched them back. Startled, she backed away as he subsided into his chair, his cheeks flaring an angry red.

'It's not for you to look at,' he mumbled.

'Well.' She stood up straight and held her head erect, even though she felt weak. 'I thought we were friends. I see I was mistaken.'

Stephen looked down at the pages in his hand, at the mess of inkblots and scrawled lines. It wasn't that he was afraid she would look at them – he was ashamed of them. Slowly, and without looking at her, he started to rip them into shreds.

'Stephen, what are you doing?'

'Go away,' he said, shaking his head, and then, in a louder voice, 'go away. Just leave me alone.'

'Very well,' Lillian said, turning away. There was a tightness in her chest, and she could hardly find the breath to go on. 'I can see there's no point in talking to you when you're like this. Perhaps when you're in a more reasonable frame of mind, we can talk about it like adults.' And, letting go of the back of the chair, she walked away through the library as fast as she could go.

Lillian was scarcely outside the college gate before she started to feel light-headed again. She got off her bicycle and pushed it along the pavement, but she still felt dizzy; the bicycle was heavy and unruly in her hand, her legs like lead. There was a painful constriction in her throat and she felt close to tears. She shuddered to remember the scene that had just passed. It was wrong of her to leave him like that, in that . . . state. She should have gone back and pleaded with him – but pleaded for what? He'd made his feelings abundantly clear and, besides, she didn't think she had the energy to get back up the steps, never mind to face him again. She felt so tired, so utterly wrung out, that all she wanted was her bed. And yet, she couldn't get it out of her head. If only . . .

She was so lost in thought that she almost bumped into the soldier. He loomed up in front of her, a tall figure in a khaki overcoat, and for one brief, hopeful moment she thought it was Stephen. But this young man wore a helmet and held his rifle slung over his shoulder. His face was serious.

'I beg your pardon, miss, but may I ask where you're going?'

'What?' She frowned and looked across the gloomy street. There were soldiers over there as well, three of them. 'Oh, I'm going home. I live in Percy Place, just over the canal. Why? Is something wrong?'

'Yes miss. A policeman was murdered over on Henry Street. We have orders to stop and search everybody, I'm afraid. May I ask where it is you're coming from, miss?'

'Trinity College.' She gestured over her shoulder and this small movement almost unbalanced her. She swayed on her feet, holding the bicycle tight with both hands. A sort of hot shiver started at the top of her head and dropped in a wave down the full length of her body. The soldier said something else, but she could hardly hear it.

'I beg your pardon?' she whispered.

'I said would you mind if I looked in your bag?'

She frowned at the bag – inside, a few books, papers, and other odds and ends – lying in the basket on the handlebars.

'No, not at all.'

He pulled open the bag and gave it a cursory look. Then he frowned.

'Are you all right, miss? You look like you might be taking a bit poorly.'

'Yes, I'm, well . . . I'm just a bit tired, I think. It's been a long day.'

'Well, then, you'd best be getting home.' The soldier's face cracked into a smile. 'I won't keep you any longer.'

She walked on, feeling the darkness closing in around her. The short dusk had faded and the gaslights hardly seemed to penetrate the gloom. She started to drift, her mind suddenly filled with all sorts of images. She saw Stephen before the war, terribly young and terribly nervous of people, but almost glowing with an inner confidence. Then she saw faces she had only seen in photographs. Littlewood and Hardy and . . . a brown face with dark eyes and very dark hair. She had to struggle to remember the name, but it came to her at last – Ramanujan, Hardy's wondrous Indian. Professor Barrett had once compared Stephen to Ramanujan. He had discerned the same sort of insight, the same feeling for mathematics that had to be innate, that could never be taught. But the Indian had not thrived – even though they had brought him to Cambridge and appointed him to a fellowship. She had heard he was very ill, that he seemed to be wasting away. Was that the way they went? Was that the price to be paid for such a gift?

The din of plunging water brought her back to herself. She was on the canal bridge and the jet of water into the lock was a white blur in the gloom below. She was nearly home now, but she felt as if she was at the end of her strength. Everything looked blurred, slightly out of shape, as if she was looking at it through thick glass. She felt cold, too. Freezing cold, shivering as she walked. Her hand was clammy and stuck to the handlebars of her bicycle, and she could feel icy spasms rippling up and down her spine.

Her one thought was to get home. She could see the house as she turned off the bridge – the iron gate and the chestnut tree in the garden. Her father had planted that tree and she had helped him when she was only a little girl. She remembered the shock and surprise she felt when she came home after two years away in England and found it had grown – it had grown so tall that she hardly recognized it. Now it looked sinister; a bare, leafless skeleton that made spidery shadows in the gaslight. But it was fading in and out of sight. The whole house was, everything was. Now it was near, now it was far away. Her feet were dragging on the ground, and as she crossed the road she stumbled on the kerb and almost fell on top of the bicycle. She knew she was sick, but Sheila would be home. Sheila was a nurse – was still a nurse, even now there was so little nursing to be done with the war over – and she would know what to do. She would make it better.

The garden gate had a sticky catch, needed a trick to lift the latch, a push at just the right moment. She could do it with her eyes closed, she knew that gate so well, but now it rebelled against her. She fumbled at it, pushed, pulled, tugged and twisted until she was on the verge of tears. Why wouldn't it open? She felt like a little girl again, her eyes burning. Why, why, why? At last something clicked and the gate swung open. She wheeled the bicycle up the path, feeling tired, oh so tired, she thought she might fall asleep right where she stood. The steps loomed up in front of her. Five granite slabs leading up to the front door. She would never get the bicycle up there. Best leave it here until later. She pushed it towards the railing, thinking to stand it up, but when she let it go it fell over with a crash. She hadn't the strength to pick it up, but she bent down anyway, and the whole world seemed to go dark. She straightened again, hurriedly, and swayed on her feet. Thirsty, she was thirsty, too. Must be the fever. Because she was sick. She knew she was sick.

She heard the front door open, saw a dim figure standing on

the doorstep. She heard a voice but she didn't recognize it. Too far away. Must have heard the bicycle falling over. She was coming, she was coming, she breathed, and put her hand on the railing to pull herself up. She raised one foot to climb up the steps, but the effort was too great and, with darkness rising up to swallow her, she fell headlong into the garden.

XI

From Henry Street to Moreland's carpentry shop was a distance of only a few hundred yards, but two hours had passed before Joe let himself in through the wicket gate. He stepped into the darkness, aromatic of wood shavings and glue, and leaned back against the door for a few moments to collect himself.

It had been a long walk, but worth the trouble since he hadn't been arrested, and he was completely certain that nobody had followed him. He'd gone against the gathering crowds in Henry Street, across Capel Street and then through the fruit and vegetable market. He'd walked quickly, but not so fast that anybody would think he was in a hurry. An army lorry had passed him on Capel Street and he'd let it go by, feeling the weight of the gun in his pocket, but sure, from the blank looks of the soldiers jolting in the back, that they didn't even know what had happened yet. Still, he was happier when he got to the fruit market and found the door of the costermonger's shed. A quick glance to make sure nobody was watching, and he shoved the gun under the door as he'd been told. Feeling much lighter in mind and body, he pressed on through the cold air that stank of rotten vegetables and horse manure.

When he reached the Four Courts, he turned towards the river. There was a pub on the corner, and he had almost passed it by before a blast of warm air and the scent of stale beer and cigarettes stopped him in his tracks. He knew it would be no harm for him to be seen this far away from the scene of the crime, so he stepped inside and pushed his way to the middle of the bar. The place was bubbling with life – an odd mixture of carters and fruit sellers and clerks from the law courts. They were all talking loudly about the weather and the football and the price of oranges, all blithely unaware of what had happened not half a mile away. He knew he was safe now, that he should be able to relax, but he couldn't. He was on edge as he sat in their midst, listening and waiting, and his hand shook when he held up a cigarette and asked the man beside him for a light. All he could see was that woman, and the look on her face when Garvey shot her. Even with his eyes closed, he could see her hand coming up, and the fear in her eyes. He quickly finished his pint and threw back his chaser, and in five minutes he was out again and on his way.

He hadn't gone a hundred yards before he ran into a foot patrol. Four soldiers and a copper. They didn't like the dark and were more nervous than he was, but he played it genial and bade them good evening, and asked what was going on before he let them search him. Even as they went about their business he kept up the chat and, once they found nothing to say he wasn't a solicitor's clerk on his way home for the evening, they let him go.

Inside the carpenter's shop it took a moment for his eyes to become accustomed to the dark. A half-finished sideboard loomed in the middle of the floor, and he could see the darker mass of the workbench standing against the wall. He walked over to the bench and picked a small mallet from among the tools hanging on pegs above. Then he looked at the band of light filtering under the door at the back. There was a little canteen out there, a small room with a table and a few benches, and he knew they were already in there. A thump, a clap of hands, and muffled laughter drifted out to him. It stopped short as he pushed open the door and stepped inside, holding the mallet hidden in his pocket. They were all in there; Kelliher and Byrne facing him from the far side of the rickety card table, and Paddy Daly leaning against the wall with his arms folded across his chest. There was a bottle of whiskey open on the table, a few greasy cards scattered around it. Garvey was grinning up at him, his face flushed and his eyes like pinpricks.

'There you are, Joe,' he exclaimed. 'By Jesus, what kept you? We thought you'd been picked up. You look a bit shook. Will you not have a drink?'

He was reaching for the bottle when Joe pulled the mallet from his pocket and clubbed him on the side of his face. He put all his strength into the blow and Garvey sprawled across the table, knocking over the bottle and sending the others leaping back for safety. Grabbing him by the hair, he rolled him over and pressed the shaft of the mallet down across his throat.

'You fucking bastard!' he hissed, in an angry whisper. 'What the fuck did you do the woman for?'

Garvey's answer came out in a strangled whine. 'She saw me, Joe, honest. She was looking straight at me when Kelliher shot the inspector. I had to shoot her, Joe, or she'd have picked me out if I was caught.'

'You're fucking lying. I saw her clear as day. She never saw you at all. Our orders were to shoot the copper – not the woman, not anybody else.' He glanced up at Daly, who was looking on impassively. Then he pressed even harder on Garvey's throat. He started to choke, coughing and spitting. 'We're not fucking murderers, do you hear me? If you ever do anything like that again, I'll kill you myself. I'll shoot you like a fucking dog, right?'

Garvey nodded as vigorously as he could, even though his eyes were rolling in their sockets and his lips were turning blue. For the first time, Joe felt his slight body threshing feebly under him. He could sense how weak he was, how vulnerable – and how easy to kill. Another few seconds and it would all be over.

'That's enough, now, Joe,' Daly said quietly, and his words brought Joe back from the brink. He pushed himself up and threw the mallet into the corner, standing back as Garvey slid off the table, without even the strength to stop himself. Daly's face was impassive, but his eyes were fixed on Joe's. When he spoke, it was in a sharp, commanding tone.

'It's time you boys were going home,' he said. 'You've all done your job, now go home and wait for orders.' He looked at Garvey, who was trying to pull himself up on the table. 'You can go with Ned for the time being.'

Kelliher and Byrne took an arm each and half carried Garvey out into the workshop. Joe didn't move until Daly sat down and scooped up the scattered playing cards. Then he sank on to a bench and watched him turning the greasy deck between his fingers and halving it, rifling the two halves together, then halving it again. He kept at it, over and over, until he heard the outside door close.

'You shouldn't have done that, Joe,' he said softly. 'That was a mistake.'

'A mistake? It was a mistake letting that fucking lunatic out on a job,' Joe answered, reaching for the upturned bottle and slopping the dregs of the whiskey into an enamel mug. 'He's not right in the head. There was no need to shoot that woman – no need at all.'

'Maybe she did see him,' Daly said, looking up for the first time.

'Balls, she saw him. He only did it out of badness. She was looking at her husband when he was shot, and if she saw anybody, she saw Kelliher. He could have plugged her but he didn't. He knows better than that. Besides, I saw the look on Garvey's face when he did it. He was enjoying himself.'

'That's as maybe,' Daly said, shifting uncomfortably. 'But you should know better than whipping him like that in front of the other lads. He'll resent you for it.'

'I don't give a shite if he resents me,' Joe said sullenly. 'And he needn't think he's coming back to the boarding house with me, either. He can stay with Ned, or he can find his own fucking place. I'm not minding him any more.'

'Be careful, Joe – that's all I'm saying.' Daly had spread the deck across the table and was absently turning over cards. 'No matter where he lives, you'll still have to work with him – and the last thing you need in this job is an enemy at your back.'

Joe didn't answer, but looked into the amber whiskey as he swirled it around the mug. Much as he hated to hear it, he knew Daly was right. There were only a handful of men in this squad and what they did was so dangerous that they had to trust each other with their lives. How could he possibly trust Garvey now? He hadn't much liked him before, but now the man had reason to wish him harm.

'Now don't get me wrong, I don't like Garvey either,' Daly went on. 'And I've heard stories . . .'

Joe's head came up.

'What stories?'

'About how he came to be up here, how he ended up on the run.' Daly swept the cards up with both hands and shuffled them nimbly. 'Did he ever tell you himself?'

'No,' Joe shook his head, 'all he ever said was that the coppers were after him.'

'Well, we can all say that, can't we?' A rare grin lit Daly's face, but he suddenly stopped shuffling the cards and set them lightly on the table. 'The way I heard it, himself and a few of the boys down there went raiding for guns one night. Nothing very spectacular – just knocking up a few small farms and getting them to hand over their shotguns. But one of these farms belonged to an old pair called Clancy, who recognized Garvey even with a mask on and started abusing him for terrorizing innocent people. Once they knew the cat was out of the bag, the other lads all ran for it, but the story goes that Garvey stayed behind. Nobody knows exactly what happened after that, but the neighbours found the Clancy's cottage burned down with the pair of them inside it.'

Joe was staring at him, dumbfounded. Daly stood up from the table, folded his coat over his arm and put his cap on the back of his head.

'He's not the sort of fella you want for an enemy,' he warned, patting Joe on the shoulder. 'He's a dangerous little bastard and he'll have you some day, when you're not expecting it. So, if I were you, I'd make friends with him because, otherwise, you'll need eyes in the back of your head.' Daly stopped with his hand on the door, looking as if he might say something else, but he just grinned again. 'Goodnight to you, now, Joe – and don't forget to lock up when you leave, will you?'

He couldn't remember going home. In fact, he couldn't remember leaving the library, or picking up his books, or anything after she walked away. His next clear memory was of leaning back against the door of his flat, his whole body racked with dry, anguished sobs. He slid down the door, feeling as if he were slipping into the depths of misery, and started to cry. Rage and self-pity welled up inside him, each feeding off the other, and he beat himself with his fists, writhed, twisted and kicked in his impotent fury. Then he felt something underneath him and his hand found an envelope on the floor – the army pension, shoved under the door. He smiled bitterly when he saw it was addressed to *Captain* S. Ryan. Five shillings and sixpence for the week – all he got for four years of his life and a permanent limp. He flung it across the room with a shout and buried his face in his hands.

Eventually, he could cry no more. He pushed himself up and looked around the dingy flat. Damp walls and a yellowing ceiling and the few rickety bits of furniture lit by the gaslight filtering through a grimy window. But it didn't oppress him as it once had. He realized, as he stood there wiping his eyes, that there was nothing to keep him there any more. He had cut himself off from everything else, so why not this miserable hole? From a small flicker of an idea, the urge to flee grew quickly. He could get out and go . . . anywhere, anywhere at all – the mere thought of it made him giddy. The sense of freedom was overpowering.

Suddenly, he couldn't move fast enough. He found a match and lit the lamp. Then he strode over to the bed and pulled out his kitbag. He stuffed it quickly – shirts, shoes, books, everything went in until it bulged with hard bumps and corners. He hurried around the flat, collecting the last few tins from the kitchen, then to the tiny desk. More books. He weighed them in his hands. What bloody use were they any more? He put them down and pulled open the drawer. There was a jumble of bronze and silver and pawn tickets that suddenly stopped his rush. He sat down and pulled out a fistful: the lapel pins and shoulder flashes from his tunic, his Military Cross on its purple and white ribbon, and a bronze oak leaf for his mention in dispatches. Closing his fingers, he squeezed and squeezed, feeling the edges and corners cutting into his palms. Was that it? Was that all there was? He opened his hand and let everything drop, then pulled the drawer out all the way and lifted out the bulky object wrapped in a chamois cloth. He laid it on the desk and opened the bow in the twine so that the cloth fell away. Then he picked up his service revolver and felt its familiar heft. He had kept it well, and it gleamed darkly in the lamplight. Almost without a thought, he reached back into the drawer and took out the canvas bag that held the reloader, cleaning kit, and a dozen or so shells. He pulled out one shell, and held it up to the light so that the brass glistened under its thin film of grease. A deadly little thing, though it looked so small and simple, like a sweet or a bauble. He cracked open the revolver and pushed the shell into one of the chambers, closed it, and spun the barrel, turning the gun over in his hands until he found himself looking straight into the barrel. What was he looking at? Was it an empty chamber, or the dull lead point of the bullet? He hooked his thumb against the trigger and started to push it back.

There was a knock at the door. A gentle knock, almost timid, and certainly not the peremptory hammering that Mrs O'Brien usually gave when she was looking for the rent. His heart leapt. It was a woman's knock. When he looked at the gun again, it was with a kind of horror, and he gingerly put it down on the desk and went into the gloomy hall. There was frosted glass in the door and he could see the shape of his visitor in the gloom outside. It was a woman, but he knew it wasn't Lillian. His heart sank, and he opened the door with an angry jerk. A young woman was standing outside, half turned away and looking up into the scrubby garden. Not Lillian, but her sister, Sheila. She turned towards him, her face anxious and pale.

'Sheila,' he began, frowning, 'what are you doing . . .'

'Oh, thank God you're here, Stephen. You must come quick. Lillie's sick with the flu. She's very bad.'

Flu. The word hit him like a slap in the face. He knew there was another epidemic – he'd heard Dunbar talking about it and he'd even seen people collapsing with it out on the street; blue in the face and gasping for breath. But, somehow, it had never seemed like a threat. With everything else that troubled him, he'd never thought it could touch him.

'Where is she?' he asked, turning back into the hall. He'd need money for a cab. What had he done with that envelope? 'Come in, come in,' he beckoned. 'Did she go to the hospital?'

'No, she's at home. Mam put her to bed and I went to fetch a doctor. I went to the hospital, but they were too . . .' Her face screwed up and she started to cry, but she wiped her eyes impatiently with the back of her hand and went on. 'They're just too busy. They know me and all, Stephen, but there's just too many people coming in. Doctor McCluskey said he'd look in on her when his shift was over, but . . . I tried my best, Stephen, I really did . . .'

This was too much for her, and her words disintegrated into incoherence. Stephen watched her starting to bawl with a mounting sense of dread. Although she was only twenty-two, Sheila had been a nurse during the war and had seen enough death and suffering that she wouldn't cry too easily. Awkwardly, he put his arms around her and pulled her close.

'Hush, hush now. Don't be blaming yourself. It's not your fault, you did everything you could.'

'But she's very bad, Stephen. She's terrible sick. I've seen them like that at the hospital. They always die.'

'Now, she won't die. She's very strong, isn't she? Is she not the strongest girl you ever knew?' He had his hands on her shoulders, looking into her red-rimmed eyes, and he was trying to make her believe him, really trying, though he knew he was really trying to convince himself.

'I'll come with you right this minute,' he told her. 'Did you come in a cab?'

'No, I came on my bicycle.'

'That's even better. It'll be faster than trying to find a cab around here. Well, here's what to do . . .' He was leading her to the door with his arm around her shoulders, but stopped and dashed back to the desk, where he hastily scribbled a note. 'Do you know Doctor Dunbar on Northumberland Road?' She shook her head, so he racked his brain for the number, then scribbled it on the back of the note. 'He's a good doctor – a friend of mine from the army. He's not far from your house. Tell him I sent you and give him this note. He'll go with you directly, I promise. Now, do you think you can do that?'

Sheila nodded, her face brightening.

'Good girl. Now go as fast as you can. I'll go straight over in a cab.'

Sheila dashed for the door, and then changed her mind and ran back, reaching up to kiss him on the cheek.

'Thank you, Stephen,' she whispered. 'I knew we could rely on you.'

When the taxi stopped he stepped out, paid the driver and then stood for a few moments in the street, feeling the cold breeze tugging at his coat and breathing in the watery stink of the canal. A barge chugged past in the dark, its chimney puffing a stream of cinders into the night air and mixing smoke and burned wood with the canal smell. He looked up at the bedroom window, with just a chink of light showing between the curtains. How long since he'd last been here? He couldn't remember, and the thought made him apprehensive. They would not have called him unless it was serious. Was he too late already? After what had happened between them, he didn't think he could bear that.

Steeling himself, he walked into the garden and climbed the familiar granite steps. His hand had barely reached the knocker when the door opened and Sheila darted out, grabbing him by the arm and dragging him into the hall.

'The doctor is with her now,' she whispered excitedly. 'He came straight away, just like you said. The minute he read your note he put on his coat and came with me. Now come into the kitchen and have a cup of tea with us until he's finished.'

The last thing he wanted was a cup of tea – still less with Lillian's mother, who must be beside herself. But Sheila towed him down the hallway to the kitchen, where her mother was sitting calmly sipping tea from a china cup. He knew by the look of her that she had placed all her faith in Dunbar, and he hoped to God it wasn't misplaced. Her face brightened when she saw him come in.

'How nice of you to come, Stephen,' she whispered, sitting him down and pouring a cup of tea from the kettle on the stove. It was the first time he'd ever heard her use his Christian name. She was the widow of a sea officer, and she had always referred to him as *captain*, with an unmistakable note of pride. He thanked her for the tea, but could think of nothing else to say, so they all sat in silence sipping from their cups and looking to the ceiling every now and then. Then they heard the bedroom door opening.

'You go up, dear,' Mrs Bryce told him in a gentle voice. 'Tell the doctor to come and have some tea before he goes.'

With a sudden bite of anxiety, Stephen set his cup down, clattering it awkwardly on the saucer and nervously straightening his tie. After peering fearfully up the stairs, he went up slowly, and saw Dunbar in the bathroom, washing his hands.

'Well, well,' he said in a loud voice, looking at Stephen in the mirror. 'I thought it might be you.'

He turned, dried his hands, and started rolling down his sleeves. Despite his cheery voice, his face looked pinched and drawn and his eyes lowered when they saw the questioning look on Stephen's face.

'You did right to send for me,' he said, and then added apologetically, 'I came as quickly as I could.'

'How is she?'

'She's got the flu,' Dunbar said, and shrugged. 'What else can I say? This is the third outbreak I've seen in two years, and every time it comes back it seems to get worse. I'd like to tell you that she's young and strong and that she's got every chance, but if I had a ha'penny for every young and strong patient I've seen this bugger carry off, well . . .' He spread his arms and shrugged again.

Stephen leaned on the banister and let his head sink onto his arms. He looked as if he was at the end of his tether, and Dunbar regretted his harsh words. All these weeks, he'd hoped to see an improvement, some sign that Stephen was finding his feet again, but now he looked even worse – tired, haggard, worn out. He realized there was more than one life hanging in the balance here.

'I've done everything I can,' Dunbar said softly, putting a hand on Stephen's shoulder. 'I've given her fluids and a mild sedative to help her sleep. The next few hours will be critical. If she makes it to the morning, then there's every reason to hope she'll be all right. But I won't lie to you. It's going to be a bloody long night.'

'Can I sit with her?'

'You can, but try not to wake her.' Dunbar leaned down to his medical bag and pulled out a cotton mask. 'And you should wear this, and wash your hands afterwards.'

Stephen looked at the mask. It seemed so impersonal – the very height of detachment. He shook his head.

'Put it on, Stephen,' Dunbar warned. 'She's highly infectious, and there's no guarantee that whatever you had in France will give you any immunity.'

'No, thanks, I'd rather take my chances.' Stephen stood up and held out his hand. 'Thank you for coming. I appreciate it.'

'Well, it's your bloody funeral,' Dunbar muttered under his breath, but he shook Stephen's hand before he bent down and picked up his medical bag. 'I'm going home now, but I'll be back first thing in the morning. If anything happens before then – anything at all – you know where to find me.'

Stephen watched him go downstairs, then turned and put his hand on the bedroom door. Now that the moment had come, he was not afraid. He went inside and gently closed the door behind him. The room was dark, except for the low fire glowing in the grate, and it took a few moments for his eyes to adjust to the gloom. The air was heavy and warm and the only sound was Lillian's breathing, which was harsh and laboured. This cut him to his heart, because it brought him back to his childhood. He remembered when he'd gone into his mother's room one night, as she lay dying of consumption, and he'd stood near the door, listening in the dark, afraid to go any closer. Even though he'd only been seven years old, he was sure he had heard death in the rattling of her breath.

Slowly, the room emerged from the darkness. He'd never been in here before, but it seemed somehow familiar, as if she'd left signs of herself all over. His hand brushed the ghostly white shape of a nightdress hanging on the door and, when he turned, he saw the image of himself in the mirror on the dressing table. A couple of steps and he was standing over the bed, and as he looked down he thought his heart might break. She was lying on her side, half curled under the covers, with her hair spread across the pillow. She was very tall for a woman – almost six foot – and yet she seemed to have shrunk. How small she looked – how fragile. Her arm, lying over the covers, seemed thin and bony. There was no sign of the energy he had always felt within her, the dignified vitality that powered her every step. She looked frail.

He got down beside the bed, kneeling like a supplicant, but he was afraid to touch her – as if he might hurt her with his clumsy hands. Perhaps sensing he was there, she groaned and took a deep, dragging breath. Then she turned towards him and let out her breath in a long whisper. His name. He heard his name, and his heart was wrung. He reached across, and as he took her hot hand in his, he felt tears streaming down his cheeks.

'Here I am, sweetheart,' he murmured, and he leaned over and kissed her gently on the lips.

XII

I, Major-General G. F. Boyd, C.B., C.M.G., D.S.O., D.C.M., Competent Military Authority, in exercise of the powers conferred on me by Regulation No. 13 of the Defence of the Realm Regulations, and of all other powers me thereunto enabling, do hereby order and require every person within the Dublin Metropolitan Police District to remain within doors between the hours of 12 o'clock midnight and 5 o'clock a.m., unless provided with a permit, in writing, from the Competent Military Authority, or some person duly authorized by him.

    This Order shall come into force at 12 o'clock midnight on the 23rd day of February, 1920.

G. F. BOYD,
Major-General, Competent Military Authority

Something had disturbed the people in the street. It was Saturday afternoon, a fine spring day, and the street was crowded with shoppers. Yet they were darting around like startled fish; heads down, shoulders hunched. Then there was a low rumbling that slowly grew into a roar. The windows rattled and the murmur of conversation died away all along the bar. A monstrous shape crept into view, sinister even in the sunlight, and rolled slowly past like some ancient, lumbering beast. It was an armoured car, with a stony-faced soldier sitting on top and rifles sticking from the slits like antennae. When it was gone, Billy turned back to his friend.

'It's a pretty pass we've come to,' he remarked wistfully, and Stephen nodded. They had both been stopped and searched, both scrutinized, questioned. They had both heard shots in the street and, one morning as he walked up from his tram, Billy had seen blood staining the pavement. Stephen, however, felt that the scrutiny was a little less intense where he was concerned. All of these new policemen, these Black and Tans, as people called them, were ex-soldiers, and he thought they recognized a kindred spirit.

'We're at war again,' he said, taking a mouthful from his glass of stout.

'Indeed we are.' Billy cocked a grin at him. 'And will you be joining in this time?'

'Certainly not,' Stephen said flatly, for he was acutely aware of his own good fortune, and even more conscious of the kindness of others. Lillian had lived, and Dunbar had insisted that Stephen move into his basement flat so he could be closer to her. The flat was dry, comfortable, and a million miles from Mrs O'Brien's damp hovel – and he had fallen into the routine of breakfasting with Dunbar before he went to college, and then taking tea with Lillian every evening. He had put on weight, he felt fit and well, and he was sleeping easily most nights. He had the overwhelming sense that his war, at long last, was over.

'And what about your brother?' Billy asked, and although his tone was light his intention was serious. He had a feeling that he knew much more than Stephen did about his brother and his part in this war, but this knowledge, gained through regular clandestine meetings, whispered conversations in public places and short, cryptic notes, was wearing him out. Billy still worked in Dublin Castle, he still passed the sentries every day, and met

Frank Mercer once a week, but it was all a lie. Mercer was pleased with the progress he was making, but lamented the fact that they seemed unable to strike a decisive blow. This was exactly as Billy had planned – a few hundred pounds here, a few hundred there. The big money always eluded them because Billy made sure it did, and he didn't know how long he could keep it up. To make matters worse, Joe kept asking for more information – nothing major, just the names of men at meetings, or the comings and goings of various assistant secretaries – and Billy was becoming more and more convinced that he would be found out, that some little look or omission would give him away. The tension of it was unbearable, and he longed to unburden himself to someone he could trust. If Stephen would just give him some little sign, some hint that he was involved, that he already had an *idea*, then he would tell him everything. But Stephen shook his head.

'My brother is his own man,' he said. 'He can do as he sees fit. He already tried to recruit me for something, but I wasn't having any of it.'

'Oh?' Billy couldn't mask his curiosity. 'Recruit you for what?'

'Training. They run night classes to teach their men drill and basic musketry. But I told him I have enough teaching to be going on with.' He patted the small stack of books he had placed on the bar when he came in. He'd just spent the morning with an anxious young man, helping him cram for the civil service examinations. It wasn't exactly higher mathematics, but the money was decent.

'Well, each to his own,' Billy said disconsolately and, fearing that he might blurt something out, he deliberately changed the subject. 'And what about Lillian? How is she? Getting better, I hope.'

'Much better, thanks,' Stephen told him, and he glanced up at the clock behind the bar and drained his glass. 'As a matter of fact, she's expecting me, so I'm afraid I'll have to leave you.'

'She's expecting you?' Billy grinned knowingly. 'Keeping you on a tight leash, is she?'

'She's giving me a maths lesson,' Stephen told him, popping on his cap and picking up his books.

'She's giving a maths lesson to the great Stephen Ryan?' Billy's surprise was only partly feigned. 'Surely there's nothing she can teach you.'

'Well, it's more of an interrogation,' Stephen admitted, thinking that if the weather stayed fine he might bring her out to sit on a bench by the canal while they went on with their lesson. She was still pitifully weak, even after all these weeks, but she enjoyed the air and the bursting greenery along the canal. And her mind was every bit as sharp as it had been. Billy was right; there was not much she could teach him, but she did have the capacity to question him, and she was just as keen to keep herself in practice as she was to hone his ability with these daily *viva voce* sessions.

Just as Stephen stood up, the door burst open and three men walked in. One a regular RIC constable, the others dressed in a combination of khaki trousers and black police tunics. Holsters on their hips and a belligerent look in their eyes. One of the Black and Tans put his hands on his hips and looked up and down the bar. Stephen subsided back into his chair and Billy watched them with a sinking feeling in his heart.

'Looks like you might be getting more of an interrogation than you bargained for,' Billy murmured.

'Good afternoon, gentlemen,' the first Black and Tan called out in a sergeant major's voice. 'We are conducting a search of these premises. Everybody keep your hands where we can see them and don't move until we tell you. Anybody who refuses to cooperate or tries to leave without submitting to a search will be arrested under the Defence of the Realm Act and may be detained indefinitely.' He jerked his head at the other two. 'Right, lads, get on with it.'

Joe had been crouching down for so long that the backs of his knees were burning and one of his feet was going numb. He shifted his weight and wiggled his toes. The urge to stand up was powerful, but he forced himself to stay down. Any minute now, he told himself. They'd see the lights, and then he'd have other things to worry about.

His breath was steaming on the chilly air and he could see the broad swatch of stars arcing over his head until they disappeared into the tallest trees in the Phoenix Park. Summer was coming, but it wasn't here yet and he was starting to feel the cold. How long had they been out here? He'd lost track of the time, but he was starting to think they'd have to call it a night. The whole job had been cursed from the start. First, they'd got the train times mixed up and had to stay in the pub a bit longer than was right for a gang of men who were trying not to attract attention. Then word had come that the job was off – he wasn't coming at all, had decided to stay in Roscommon. With a face like thunder, Paddy Daly had gone off to make a telephone call, and had come back saying that he would be on the next train, after all. Joe was having his doubts. This wasn't any old civil servant. It was Viscount French they were after – the Lord Lieutenant of Ireland. The head-buck cat, Collins had called him, and they'd all laughed – though not for very long. They'd tried to get him more than once before, and failed every time. For all his public appearances and high profile, French was a hard man to pin down, and he never went anywhere without a military escort. They were banking on lighter security tonight, since it was only a five-minute drive from the train station to his residence in the park, but Joe had a bad feeling. They'd been out here too long already, and in another few minutes they'd have to call it off. Part of him wished they would.

He shifted his weight again and looked up and down the ditch. There wasn't much of a moon, but he could make out the black shapes sitting and crouching to his right and left. The nearest one on the left was Garvey. He was easy enough to spot because he couldn't kneel down with his gammy leg, and had to sit down flat with his legs straight out in front of him. This was the first time he'd seen him since that job on Henry Street, but it was still too soon as far as Joe was concerned. They hadn't said two words to each other all evening, but he'd caught Garvey staring at him once, when he turned his head quickly.

There was the flash of a light from up the road, and then the distant sound of an engine. His heart started racing and he dived one hand into his pocket for the revolver, the other for the bomb.

'Get ready, lads,' a voice called softly, and he heard the clicks as rifles and pistols were cocked all along the ditch.

The headlights swept spidery shadows through the air as they turned and then the rumble of engines grew louder. Out of the corner of his eye he saw Garvey awkwardly getting to his feet and he straightened himself a bit so that he could see over the ditch. How many cars? Was it only two? There were supposed to be three. He cast an anxious look along the length of the ditch, hoping for a wave, a signal. What if it wasn't the convoy? Three cars was what they'd been told; an escort in front and back and Lord French in the middle. If there were only two, then the whole thing was knocked into a cocked hat. Once again he looked up and down the ditch, but he saw no sign from the others. They were all up now, pressing close against the ditch, ready to pounce. Joe took out the revolver and cocked it. Two cars or three, they were going to take it either way. He took the bomb from his other pocket and slipped the ring over his finger.

When the cars were less than fifty feet away he stood up to his full height. The glare of the lights dazzled him. Two cars, all right, and they'd have to take them both. Joe looked down the road to the gates of the Phoenix Park, only a couple of hundred yards away. He didn't like the look of this. They didn't even have the road blocked, and if they couldn't stop the first car in its tracks then all they'd get is one volley, and maybe a good raking from the escort in return. He made up his mind to take the first car. If he could stop it, they'd have him. With one sharp tug the pin came ringing out of the bomb and he tossed it between the beams of the headlights.

But even as it left his hand he knew he'd been spotted. The first car gunned its engine and shot forward. The bomb rattled across the bonnet and dropped into the far ditch. Something whistled past his ear as he brought the gun up, and then there was a hard thump and a flash as the grenade went off and the car bucked and slewed across the road. The second car was screeching to a halt, the headlights doused and yellow sparks of gunfire coming from the windows. Joe squeezed the trigger and the gun bucked in his hand, but the first car was moving again, gears grinding and something thumping underneath, it was bumping forward. Then there was the stuttering rattle of a machine gun from the second car and the double thump of a shotgun. They were coming out fighting, all right. He could smell it in the air now: burning rubber and gun smoke. There was a lot of shouting going on, but still he had his eye on the first car. It was getting away, and he took careful aim at the back window and squeezed the trigger. The glass fell in, but the car kept moving. The engine roared and the car picked up speed. Gripping the revolver with both hands, Joe planted his feet firmly and took aim again. He was squeezing the trigger when, out of the corner of his eye, he saw a flash from somewhere low down in the ditch. Something kicked him high in the chest and he staggered backwards, slipped, and then felt the cold grass and his head hitting the earth with a thump. It knocked all the wind out of him and he gasped painfully. There was more shooting now, bullets whizzing and spitting through the hedgerow, but he managed to roll on to his front, get to his knees, get up. His legs felt weak, his arm dead.

'Jesus,' he breathed to himself, as he staggered to his feet. More lights; there was a third car coming down the road. No; something heavier. A truck, or a Crossley tender. There were muzzle flashes coming from it as it drove.

'Run for it, lads!' somebody shouted, but Joe hardly had the strength to stay standing. He saw shadows flitting from the hedgerow and running for safety across the field. He looked at them, knowing he'd never be able to follow. His gun, he needed his gun. He'd dropped it somewhere, and in shuffling through the grass his feet found it. He bent down to pick it up and felt his head spinning as he did. The shooting had stopped and suddenly he could hear everything; brakes squealing, men shouting. Boot nails crunched and rang as they jumped down from the tender. Joe stuffed the revolver in his pocket and staggered down the ditch, breathing hard and feeling shards of pain through his chest every time he did.

It took all his concentration just to stay on his feet. No time to look back and see if they were coming after him, no time to worry about a shot ringing out behind him. He focused his eyes on the black line of the hedge that ran out across the field. If he could get through that then at least he'd have some cover. Close up, he found that it was sparse and broken and he could just walk through a gap, stumbling in the ditch and feeling cold water slop into his boots. Now he could see the wall of the park in front of him, smooth and straight in the moonlight. He hurried towards it as quickly as his legs would carry him, holding one hand to his shoulder. The pain was dull but constant now, and his breathing had steadied so it no longer stabbed at him. But every step jarred him, and he could feel blood trickling down his ribs.

The noises behind him grew fainter, but his back was tingling. They'd be on the hunt now. Coming down the ditch, beating it like they were trying to rouse pheasants. He kept going, panting and lurching towards the wall, but only when he was right up against it did he realize how high it was. He could hear the breeze in the tall trees inside, but he knew there was no way he'd get over that. Turning, he headed back to the road. Find the gate, he told himself. You're in no state to be climbing walls. Find the road, the road has a gate. Get inside the park.

The hedge along the roadway nearly defeated him, but by walking back a few yards he found a gap he could crawl through. Scraped by thorns and with his shoulder throbbing unmercifully, he crept out on all fours and felt the solid surface of the road under his hands. It took all his strength to get back on his feet, but then he saw the lights flickering across the gate pillars and when he looked over his shoulder he saw a car coming. He darted through the gate, throwing himself in behind the wall just as the car rounded a shallow corner and rumbled past. He watched until the tail lights dipped out of sight and lay still a few moments, listening as the noise faded away. All clear. He pushed himself up once again and stumbled along the road.

Later on, he couldn't remember how long it took him to cross the park. He'd gone about a quarter of a mile along the road before it occurred to him that it wasn't safe, that he should go across country. He stumbled into the darkness and soon became lost between the looming trunks of huge trees. He felt like he was in a maze, and he could have been going around in circles, for all he knew. He was feeling the cold, too. He shivered as he walked, wrapping his overcoat tightly around himself and hugging his bad arm to his chest with his good. After a while, he felt the first shiver of panic, and he knew he had to find a way out. Big though it was, this park was a trap, walled in and with a barracks in the middle of it. Any light, any human sign at all was a danger to him. That car would have made it back by now, shot up and maybe full of wounded men. They'd have every man out searching and if they found him they'd soon know what he'd been up to. Even if he threw away the revolver, they'd see the hole in him in no time.

He felt himself slowing down, tiring, his legs no longer responding and the pain taking over, sapping his strength. Then he saw a solid dark shape through the trees, rising up tall and straight – too tall and too straight to be a tree. He stopped and squinted up at it. He knew it – the Wellington monument! Jesus Christ, he must have wandered right across the park. And better yet, he knew his way out from here. Feeling new strength in his legs, he hurried on towards the monument.

A few minutes later he stumbled across a road which he knew led down towards the gate. Five minutes and he'd be in Parkgate Street. No, no, no. He stopped himself and turned around. Parkgate Street was always full of soldiers, even when it was quiet, and they'd surely stirred up a hornet's nest by now. Back the other way, towards Islandbridge. He walked as straight as he could, the road glowing faintly white in front of him. His shoulder was aching, and he felt a terrible thirst deep down in his throat.

At last the road curved down, and he knew he'd soon come to the gate. Would it be open, though? He didn't think he'd have the strength to climb, but as he stopped and looked down past the gatekeeper's house, he felt a gush of relief when he saw the iron wicket across the footpath. He slipped through with barely a squeak of the hinges, and emerged from the park, blinking. It was like walking into another world. There were houses out here; gas lamps glowing and windows yellow and green behind curtains. But still not another sinner to be seen. He stopped for a minute and leaned his back against the wall of the park, trying to get his bearings. The Liffey was on the other side of the road, Islandbridge to his right. He turned and walked in that direction; he needed to stay in the dark, and he needed to find a car or a cart or some way of getting away from here. Two lights pierced the darkness in front of him and he stepped back into shadow. Of course, any car coming this way might be full of soldiers. He squinted into the lights as they came closer. It wasn't a car; it was bigger than a car. But it wasn't a lorry either, or a tender. He saw some writing on the side, and knew he had to move quickly. Launching himself away from the wall, he staggered across the road. The asthmatic horn blared weakly as he stumbled into the lights, and he heard the squeal of brakes and a few shouted words, mistaking him for a drunk. When the vehicle stopped he darted from the lights and around to the driver's door, pulling the gun out of his pocket with his good hand. He found himself pointing it at a middle-aged man with grey whiskers, his indignant face now starting to melt into fear.

'I don't mean you any harm,' Joe said, and that was all he could get out before he had to catch his breath. He'd not said a word since he'd been shot, and it caused a stabbing pain that went right through his chest. He doubled over with the pain, clutching his chest, and felt everything start to spin in the darkness. He dimly heard the door opening, footsteps, and then strong hands take him around the shoulders, walking him to the other side of the van. He started to cough uncontrollably, tasting blood in his mouth, but he managed to get hold of the handle and open the door. Feeling his legs go weak, he was barely able to clamber in, before the whiskered man shoved the door shut behind him and then climbed back behind the steering wheel. He stared at Joe for a few moments; slumped in his seat, still weakly clutching the revolver.

'There's no fucking need for that thing,' he said, and before Joe could move, he reached across, snatched the gun, and flung it over the ditch, 'I'll take you to the hospital. Just sit easy for a few minutes.'

They drove back towards the city. Joe was too weak to talk but he kept his eyes on the road ahead, afraid of a roadblock. Not that there was anything he could do if they were stopped; he had no gun now, and he was in no state to run for it. He closed his eyes for a moment, and when he opened them again they were outside Parkgate Street Barracks. He saw the gate and the barrier and the sentry standing outside. The driver gave no sign he had even seen it. He just looked straight ahead, his two hands clamped on the wheel. Joe looked down as they passed under a gaslight, and saw the ragged hole in his overcoat, and the broad patch of blood that was soaking out around it.

'No hospital,' he said, but he hardly had the breath to get the words out.

'What?' The driver shot him a worried look.

'Not the hospital,' he whispered, 'I don't want to go to the hospital.' His head was spinning now, and he knew it was from the blood he'd lost. His stomach was churning, too. He had to clamp his mouth tight shut to keep from being sick.

'Then where do you want to go? I can't just leave you at the side of the road, not in the state you're in.'

'Northumberland Road,' Joe whispered, and the driver opened his mouth as if to say something else, but thought better of it when he saw the look on Joe's face. 'Take me to Northumberland Road, please.'

'Right you are, so. Northumberland Road it is.'

Now that Stephen was alone again, he was restless. He'd walked home with every intention of studying some more, but since coming in he hadn't opened a book. He'd made himself a cup of tea, then left it untouched on the table as he paced around the flat. But it wasn't anxiety that had him going, it was more like anticipation – the sense that his time had almost come. He was outwardly restless, but inside he was calm. He had worked hard these last few weeks. He had done everything he could, and he was not afraid of what was to come. A few more hours and it would all be over, he told himself. There was no point in fretting over it now.

He walked over to the sofa and flopped down. The cushions were still rumpled where Lillian had been sitting and he ran his hand over them, trying to feel the shape of her again. He hadn't done much studying when she was here, either, and the thought of it made him smile. She'd tried to coax him, but he'd been too much taken with the warmth of her sitting beside him, too easily distracted by the shape of her ear, or by the fine hairs on the nape of her neck as she bent over a book. He loved the way she curled against him, the living touch of her flesh under his hands, the way he could *feel* her breathing. The intimacy between them was so deep and so easy that it seemed as if it had always been there, and yet the joy of it was that it was so new.

Three footsteps on the gravel and then there was a pounding on the door. Stephen sat up, frowning. He wasn't expecting any visitors, and he hadn't heard Dunbar moving about since he got back. Two more thumps, not so loud, and he heard the dragging of gravel, harsh breathing and a groan. He stood up and looked

236

at the door of the bedroom. His service revolver was in there, lying in its box under the bed. But then he heard some muttered curses, and his own name in a weak whisper.

'Stephen?'

He walked into the tiny hallway and peered out through the glass, but it was too dark to see anything. He listened for a moment and then opened the door a crack and saw a figure slumped outside, facing away. A dirty overcoat and a cap pushed to one side. Only when the figure turned awkwardly to face him did he recognize his own brother, pale as ever he'd seen him, his face grey and pinched with pain and exhaustion.

'Joe? What on earth—' he began, but then he had to run to catch him as his brother staggered and all but fell in the door.

'I had nowhere else to go,' Joe gasped, wincing as he spoke. 'I'm after getting hurt.'

'Come in and sit down.' Stephen helped him inside, and closed the door with his foot. Then across the living room. Stephen felt his brother's laboured breathing hot on his cheek and he eased him down into an armchair. Automatically, he started to unbutton his brother's overcoat. Just as he saw the crimson patch staining the front of his shirt, he smelled it, and the shock of it made him retch.

'Jesus.' Joe's face was drenched with sweat, but he managed a bleak grin. 'After everything you've seen, I didn't think you'd be squeamish.'

'Don't worry about me,' Stephen said, but he had to bite down on what was squirming up his throat. He managed to get the overcoat off, dragging it gently down the injured arm, and opened his brother's shirt, soaked red all down one side of his chest. There was a small hole in the fabric a few inches above the heart, ragged and ringed with deep crimson. He'd seen enough gunshot wounds in his time to know what it was.

'What the hell happened?' he asked, tugging gently at the shirt, but Joe flinched and grabbed his wrist.

'For fuck's sake, Stephen, will you stop pulling out of me. I'll be fine. I just need to rest and have a drink. Have you got any whiskey at all?'

Stephen shook his head. Ever since moving in here he'd drunk nothing stronger than the odd bottle of stout with Billy. He'd not owned so much as a bottle of sherry this last three months.

'I've nothing at all, Joe. Now lean forward a bit, I need to see your back.'

His brother leaned forward obediently, though he shuddered with pain as he did so, and Stephen pulled up his shirt and examined the skin below his shoulder. It was badly bruised, but there was no blood. That meant the bullet was still in there, and it would have to come out.

'There's a doctor upstairs,' he said, standing up. 'I'd better get him to have a look at that.'

Joe's head shot up, his face hardening.

'No. No doctor. I just need to rest a bit and stop the bleeding. Have you got an old bed sheet, or something we can use for a bandage?'

But he knew that wouldn't do, and Stephen knew it too.

'Don't be so bloody stupid. There's a bullet inside you, and you've already lost a lot of blood. The doctor's not just my landlord, he's a friend and he can be trusted.'

Joe didn't say anything, just gritted his teeth against a fresh stab of pain, and Stephen left him and went up the narrow staircase to Dunbar's house. The sound of music drifted out of the living room, and when he walked in he caught the last few bars of one of the *Brandenburg Concertos*, and found Dunbar sprawled in an armchair with his head thrown back, snoring steadily. Stephen touched his shoulder and he came awake with a start.

'Eh? What?' he grunted, blinking and screwing up his eyes at Stephen. 'Oh, it's you. What's the matter? Was I snoring again? Not that loud, surely? I wasn't disturbing your study, was I?'

'My brother's downstairs. He's been hurt,' Stephen told him. 'Can you come and have a look?'

'Hurt? How?' Dunbar was on his feet, yawning and scratching his head.

'He's been shot,' Stephen said, and looked steadily at Dunbar, who did a decent job of masking his surprise.

'All right, then. I'd best fetch my bag.'

By the time he came downstairs, Stephen had helped his brother on to the sofa, fetched a blanket and draped it over him. Dunbar was all business. First, he picked up a wrist and felt for a pulse, then he lifted the blanket and examined the wound, palpating gently with his fingers.

'Bullet still in?' he asked Stephen.

'Yes, I think so.'

'Looks like the collarbone stopped it – though the impact caused a fracture. Still, it will have to come out.' He fixed his eyes on Joe's and spoke in loud, certain tones. 'Now then, young man. We shall have to take that bullet out, and to do that I shall have to give you an anaesthetic . . .'

'No,' Joe protested weakly. 'No anaesthetic. Don't knock me out – I can't stay here.' His eyes darted from Dunbar to Stephen. 'It's not safe for any of us.'

'Well, we'll see.' Dunbar stepped back and looked at Stephen. 'Get his shirt off. I need to get some things from upstairs.'

'What the hell do you mean, it's not safe?' Stephen asked, as he gently disentangled the shirt and slid it away from the wounded shoulder. In doing so, he saw the older scars – the dimpled circles that were souvenirs of his brother's last brush with the British Army. 'What have you done?'

'I don't think you want to know,' Joe said grimly, but seeing the look on his brother's face and feeling he at least owed him an explanation, he told him briefly about the ambush, and how it had unfolded. Stephen listened carefully, nodding from time to time, but otherwise showing no emotion.

'So, do you think you were set up?' he asked.

'I'm not sure. It could have been a coincidence, that lorry coming along when it did. There's a depot in the park, after all.'

'And how did you come to get shot by one of your own men?'

'I didn't say he was one of my own,' Joe said sharply. 'I said I thought it came from that side of the ditch. It could have been a ricochet, or maybe one of the soldiers jumped out of the car and crawled through the hedge.'

Stephen could tell by the way Joe said it that he didn't really believe that either, but he knew his brother was in no state to argue.

'Well, either way, you should get out of town for a while,' he said. 'You ambushed the Lord Lieutenant, for Christ's sake. They'll turn the place upside down for whoever did that, and if they catch you with a bullet hole in you, they'll string you up.'

'I'll be grand.' Joe waved his good hand, and winced at the effort.

'You should go,' Stephen insisted. 'Go away, go down to the country. You could stay with Granda for a couple of weeks, down in Mayo.'

Joe snorted. 'Go on out of that, Stephen. I haven't been down there since I was nine – and even then the old fella tanned the arse off me for robbing apples from his lordship's orchard.'

'All the more reason to go,' Stephen began, but then he heard Dunbar coming down the stairs.

'Are you sure you can trust him?' Joe whispered, watching Dunbar cross the room with a kidney dish of instruments and a surgeon's apron draped over his shoulder.

'With my life.'

It was after midnight before they finished. Dunbar had injected novocaine into the wound, but it couldn't quite numb all the pain and Joe had writhed and groaned as he dug into his shoulder with the forceps, trying to get a grip on the bullet. Stephen had looked on and swabbed and held things as best he could. His initial nausea had passed and he found he could stand there quite dispassionately, as if he were looking at a picture instead of his own brother's blood streaming down his chest.

'Got you, you little bastard,' Dunbar grunted, and the bullet came out in the jaws of the forceps, gleaming dully under the blood. He wiped off the worst of the gore and examined it carefully. 'Well, it's a bit small, but it looks intact. What do you think?'

He dropped the bullet in Stephen's palm and he felt the jagged tip, where it had flattened against the bone. But Dunbar was right; it did look intact, if very small.

'That didn't come from an army weapon,' he said. 'It's more like a twenty-two calibre, or maybe a twenty-five.'

'Fuck,' his brother said, but he gritted his teeth and hissed out a painful breath as Dunbar started to sew the wound shut.

A few minutes later, it was all done. The wound was dressed and bandaged, and Joe's arm put in a sling. Dunbar wiped his hands on a towel, looking pleased with himself.

'Well, I haven't done that in a while,' he said. 'Bit of a change from the usual sniffles and hernias – and not a bad job, if I do say so myself.'

'Thanks, doctor,' Joe muttered, looking pale but relieved.

'Don't mention it,' Dunbar said and, with a significant look at

Stephen, 'perhaps we'll leave you to rest for a bit. Your brother can help me put everything away.'

Stephen carried up the kidney dish, now swishing with blood and cluttered with soaked cotton swabs and bloody instruments. Dunbar didn't say a word until everything was washed and put away in his surgery. Then he nodded towards the living room.

'What about a snifter of port?' he asked. Stephen just nodded and followed him down the hallway.

'I'm sorry about all this,' he said, as Dunbar busied himself at the drinks cabinet. 'I . . . well, he's my brother. What else could I do?'

'You are aware, of course, that this isn't the first time he's been shot,' Dunbar said, businesslike, thrusting a glass into his hand.

'Yes, I'm aware. He picked up the first one in the Easter Rebellion. It was a damn sight more serious, too.'

'The Easter Rebellion?' Dunbar chuckled. 'While you were gallivanting around on the King's business? There's a curious tale to be told there, I'll bet.'

'That's one way to describe it,' Stephen admitted, but he was in no humour to tell it. The nervous excitement was wearing off and he suddenly felt very sleepy, his eyelids gummed and closing under their own weight. He yawned.

'I suppose you'd better get some bloody sleep,' Dunbar told him. 'You've got an exam in the morning. See if your brother will sleep in your bed, and you can take the spare one up here.'

Stephen yawned again, but before he could take another step, there was a loud hammering at the front door.

'What the bloody hell is it now?' Dunbar muttered, pushing past him and walking down the hall. He hadn't gone halfway before there was a loud crash and the door flew open under the force of a dozen soldiers in steel helmets, with their rifles at the ready. They swarmed along the hallway, one of them pinning

Dunbar to the wall, and another levelling his rifle at Stephen, who slowly set down his glass and raised his hands.

'What the fuck do you think you're doing?' Dunbar demanded hotly. 'This is a private house. You have no right.'

A lieutenant came in through the gaping door – a small, round-headed man in cavalry breeches and with a swagger stick tucked under his arm.

'I'm afraid we have every right, under the Defence of the Realm regulations,' he said in a clipped, superior voice. 'We're looking for Joseph Ryan in connection with an incident that took place earlier this evening. We believe he may have made contact with his brother, one Stephen Ryan.'

'I'm Stephen Ryan,' Stephen said, looking straight at the lieutenant, who turned his head and glared at him.

'Of course you are. Where is your brother, Mr Ryan?'

'He's not bloody here,' Dunbar shouted, before Stephen could open his mouth. '*Captain* Ryan was with me all evening.'

Dunbar's use of his rank was deliberate, and it had the desired effect. The man pinning him to the wall loosened his grip and the young lieutenant's face took on a guarded look, his eyes narrowing.

'Captain Ryan?' he said, half to himself. Then he turned to Dunbar. 'And who might you be?'

'Colonel James Dunbar, Royal Army Medical Corps,' Dunbar barked. This was too much for the soldier pinning him to the wall, who backed away as if he'd just sprouted horns and a tail. Free to move at last, Dunbar rounded furiously on the lieutenant. 'You ignorant little shit. How dare you come barging into my house in the middle of the night? I don't care about your fucking regulations, I'll have you broke for this! What's your name?'

It was a creditable performance, but the lieutenant's was just as good. He swallowed and looked uneasy, but he stood his ground.

'My name is Fanshawe, sir,' he said stiffly. 'I apologize for the inconvenience, but I have orders to search this house. If you and the captain will make yourselves comfortable, I'll try to be as quick as possible.'

He stood with his arm out, pointing Dunbar to the living room. Dunbar scowled, but held his peace as Fanshawe barked out orders to his men. Three of them ran upstairs and three more bolted down the narrow stairs to the basement. That was all Stephen saw before Fanshawe shut the door and gestured to the Chesterfield sofa.

'Please, sit down, gentlemen. This won't take long.' He watched them sit side by side but stayed standing in the middle of the floor, gently flexing his swagger stick behind his back. Nobody spoke, but Stephen shot a look at Dunbar and rolled his eyes. In return, Dunbar grinned and gave him a barely perceptible shrug.

They sat like that for five minutes by the mantel clock. The only sounds were the muffled footfalls coming from above and below and the ticking of the clock. Stephen dreaded the shout, the scuffle – perhaps even the noise of a shot. He started when there was a polite knock on the door and one of the soldiers came in, tipping a quick salute to Fanshawe. The lieutenant turned to face him, and Stephen saw his knuckles were white on the swagger stick.

'Well, corporal?'

'We've searched the house, sir. Top to bottom – attic and all.'

'And?'

'It's empty, sir. There's nobody else here.'

Part Three

Fire

XIII

The unseasonable heat had burned all the colour out of the country. Green fields had been scorched to pale yellow by the sun and they stretched away under the hazy sky, divided by dusty-brown hedgerows and dry ditches. The horizon was nothing but a long blur along the edge of the land, and even that was smudged here and there by the smoke of furze fires rising up from the bog.

The train ran west, bumping and rattling gently along the raised embankment that cut straight and true across the flat expanse of

247

turf. Stephen drowsed in the heat, nodding softly with the motion of the carriage. He was aware of Lillian sitting beside him, her arm gently bumping his as she turned the pages of her book, but his mind was elsewhere. He remembered this journey – had made it many times before. He had always dreamed of making it with Lillian, but not under these circumstances. Not when he knew that this would probably be the last time. Not after that telegram had arrived.

It had been delivered to him in the mathematics common room, where Lillian had been helping him to prepare for the new term. Professor Barrett having been as good as his word, Stephen had been awarded a studentship, which meant he was expected to lecture part-time as he worked towards a fellowship. This was a considerable step up from giving maths crams for the civil service exams, and the prospect made him nervous. Mathematics was one thing but teaching quite another, and he envied Lillian's easy familiarity with it. There also appeared to be more to it than he had imagined, and they had already spent the entire morning working through a short series of lectures on algebra when there was a knock on the door and a porter came in, doffing his cap.

'Telegram for you, sir,' he had said, holding out the envelope. Stephen took it with a sense of foreboding and knew even as he opened it that it was bad news:

TO: CAPTAIN S. RYAN – TRINITY COLLEGE, DUBLIN
SAD TO REPORT DEATH OF YR GRANDFATHER. UNUSUAL CIRCS. FUNERAL TOMORROW. PLS REPLY WITH YR WISHES FOR PROPERTY. BOURKE.

'Stephen? What is it?' Lillian had asked, looking at him with concern. He had felt the blood draining from his face and tears pricking the corners of his eyes. He might have known there

248

would be a crash. He had been happy – too happy. He had enjoyed the summer, he had been to Cambridge with Lillian and had come home to a good job with the prospect of a fellowship. His life was almost complete, and now . . .

'Oh Stephen, I'm so sorry.' Lillian had come around and read the telegram. She put her arms around him and pulled him close, cradling his head in the warm hollow below her shoulder. He closed his eyes for a moment, feeling the softness, breathing the scent – but then a thought struck him.

'Unusual circumstances?' he asked, pulling away and looking up at her. 'What docs that mcan?'

His first thought was that his brother was involved. He'd not seen him since that night in Dunbar's house, but about a week afterwards he'd received a postcard in his brother's handwriting. The card simply said 'keeping well' but it was postmarked West-port, which was the nearest town to their grandfather's place. So he had gone after all. But that was four months ago. Surely he couldn't . . .

'And who is this Bourke?' Lillian asked, pointing to the name at the end of the telegram. 'Is he a neighbour or a friend? Do you know him?'

Stephen shook his head. Bourke? The name wasn't familiar. And who would address him as captain? It wasn't likely that the neighbours he remembered from before the war – who had welcomed him every summer since he was a boy – would be so formal. But then it came to him. Bourke, of course!

'It's the Viscount of Mayo,' he said, and when Lillian gave him a disbelieving look, he explained, 'my grandfather worked for them all his life – he had his cottage from them as an estate worker. Bourke is their family name.'

'Well, perhaps you can write and ask him to explain.'

'I'll do better than that.' Stephen stood up and folded the

telegram into his pocket. I'll go down there and find out for myself.'

The plan was already forming in his mind: today was Friday. If he caught the afternoon train he could make the funeral tomorrow and come home on Sunday – in plenty of time to give his first lecture on Monday morning.

'Would you like me to come with you?'

The offer was made without any hesitation on Lillian's part, but Stephen wavered. More than anything, he *did* want her to come with him, but he wondered if that would be too presumptuous after what had passed between them in Cambridge. He didn't want to make things any more awkward than they already were, but then, he didn't want to face whatever might have to be faced alone.

'Yes, please.'

Sitting on the train, he turned his head away from the window and watched her for a few moments. She was deeply absorbed in her book, sitting perfectly still in her summer dress and old-fashioned lace gloves. And yet there was nothing else old-fashioned about her. There was certainly nothing old-fashioned about the way she had gone home, packed a bag and announced that she was going away to Mayo for the weekend with a young man. But then, he had already had a foretaste of this when they had set off to Cambridge a few weeks before.

'My mother knows I won't do anything foolish.' She had told him, when he had asked her how her family felt about it. 'I'm a grown woman, after all. And besides, she's spent half her life fighting for women's rights – which includes the right to go where we please, when we please.'

In fact, Stephen hadn't been worried so much about what people might say as he had been about her health. Even though Professor Littlewood had been perfectly happy to postpone their seminar until she had fully recuperated, Stephen still had qualms about it. Was she really well enough to travel? Would it cause a relapse? But he needn't have worried. Far from finding the journey a strain, she had enjoyed it, and was fairly bubbling with excitement by the time they arrived in Cambridge.

Their visit had turned out to be everything they had hoped it would. Professor Littlewood himself had met them at the train station, and he was only the first of a series of eminent men who were anxious to hear what they had to say. This being the last week of the summer vacation there were no undergraduates, so the men whom Littlewood had gathered together were either professors or fellows – some of them famous, all of them very serious mathematicians. These were men who lived and breathed mathematics, who would give no quarter in an argument, and Stephen suddenly became very conscious that the ink was barely dry on his undergraduate degree. And as for Lillian . . . well, once again, he had no need to worry about her. Once their seminar started, the days were long and intense; the debate over abstruse mathematical points often running through mealtimes and frequently lasting from one day to the next. Stephen had found it exhilarating, but tiring. Lillian had bloomed.

She had done so well, in fact, that it took him a few days to notice the constraint that these men had when they were around her. Intellectually, she was every bit their equal, but it slowly dawned on Stephen that they didn't know what to make of her. They had not seen her like before. Although women were allowed to study at Cambridge, they were not permitted to take degrees, still less to teach. Nor were they allowed to stay overnight within the colleges and so, while Stephen had been given rooms overlooking the Great Court, she had been billeted outside, with one of the junior fellows and his young wife.

At the same time he realized that there was a certain amount of speculation as to the nature of their relationship. Everybody was far too polite to say anything directly, but he could tell from the looks and from the indulgent smiles of the men – and from the asperity of some of the senior fellows' wives – that it was much talked about. Only once did it come anywhere near the surface, when a nervous young man from Christ Church approached him after one of the talks had ended.

'Mr Ryan, I wonder if you and your . . . ahem, your, er . . .' He looked uncertainly towards Lillian. 'If you and your colleague would care to join us for tea tomorrow afternoon?'

Stephen knew that she was as keenly aware of it as he was, but he did not say anything. This was her triumph as much as his and she was more than capable of proving herself to these hidebound old men without having to lean on him. And yet the thought grew on him that he should do something. He knew little enough about the social niceties, but he was aware that if a man and woman had known each other as long as they had, if they went away together like this and, above all, if they felt about each other as they did . . . or, at least, as *he* did, then there was an expectation that their relationship should be formalized.

He had not quite made up his mind about this by the time their two weeks were up. On the last night they were invited to dine at high table as guests of Professor Littlewood. Afterwards, Stephen walked her back to her lodgings on Bridge Street and, as they crossed the Great Court together, he felt sublimely happy. The night was warm and the moon was out and even though they were going home the next day, he felt as if the world was at his feet. He knew Lillian felt the same. He could feel happiness radiating from her, through her hand as he held it in his, in the brush of her hair as she leaned her head on his shoulder.

They were walking slowly towards the Great Gate, and he could see the lantern there, and the shadow of the porter waiting to let them out. On an impulse he steered Lillian off the sandstone flags and brought her crunching through the gravel margin to the octagonal fountain that stood in the centre of the court. When they stopped, he could hear the bubbling of the water in the fountain, and his nose was filled with the sweet scent of the flowers that surrounded it.

'Stephen, what are you doing?' Lillian asked, giggling.

Stephen had drunk his fair share of wine and port over dinner, and it was with a certain flourish that he swept off his academic gown and laid it on the steps of the fountain.

'Will you sit down for a minute? I want to ask you something.'

'Sit down?' Lillian looked first at the gown, like an inky pool in the moonlight, and then at Stephen. 'Very well,' she said, sweeping her skirt against her legs and sitting down on the step. 'What is it you wish to ask me, Mr Ryan?'

He sat down beside her and took her hand in both his.

'Miss Bryce,' he said, echoing the formal way they had once addressed each other, 'will you do me the honour of marrying me?'

'Oh.' Her eyes widened, gleaming white, and she leaned across and kissed him gently on the cheek. But he felt her hand clench under his, and he braced himself when she looked away and then smiled. 'Well,' she said, 'I shall certainly think about it.'

Later, after he had left her at her lodgings and made his way back to the college, he asked himself what else he had expected. She was intelligent and strong-willed and he loved her for it. She was certainly not the sort of woman to fling herself into his arms and start blubbing yes, yes, yes. But still, he was disappointed. He knew he shouldn't have asked, or he should have hinted first. He'd mucked it up, and he wished he'd kept his mouth shut.

But, on the surface at least, it was as if nothing had happened. When he called at her lodgings in the taxi she had kissed him and held his hand all the way to the station. The journey home was every bit as pleasant and relaxed as the journey out, but still he knew it was there. The question had been asked, and it hung over him like a cloud. With every hour that passed, he wished more and more that he could un-ask it.

And yet, this last week they had slipped easily back into their old routine. They had been friends before and now they were colleagues, too, so they spent most of the day together and at night they went out to the theatre or to the cinema. But still he could feel it, like a tiny splinter in his flesh. The urge to say something was very strong. He wanted to tell her that she was under no obligation – that he hoped he hadn't been too forward. This trip to Mayo was, he realized, an opportunity to do exactly that. But still . . .

Lillian closed her book with a snap and Stephen started and straightened in his seat. He'd been so lost in thought that he hadn't noticed the train had crossed the Shannon and now the landscape was changing. They were running fast across flat, rocky terrain, chequered by dry-stone walls and dotted with white thatched cottages. He was surprised to see that the compartment was empty, though he couldn't even remember who had been sitting across from him.

'Stephen, dear,' Lillian said. 'We need to talk about this marriage business.'

'Yes, of course,' he said, though his voice was stronger than he felt. He was suddenly, unaccountably nervous as Lillian reached across, took his hand, and set it firmly in her lap.

'First of all, I'm flattered and I'm honoured that you asked me – and I'm sorry I wasn't able to answer you straight away. But there are a few things that we need to think about first.'

If anything, Stephen's nervousness increased, and he found himself smiling and frowning at the same time.

'Such as?' he asked.

'Well, such as religion.'

This was not what he had been expecting.

'Religion?' As his frown deepened, his smile faded. 'What's that got to do with anything?'

'Well, quite a lot, as I understand it,' Lillian said. 'You are a Roman Catholic, Stephen, and I am not. Surely you can see the problem.'

'Oh, is that all?' he exclaimed and, seeing that this was not what *she* had been expecting, he hurried to explain. 'I mean, I'm not exactly a Catholic, or at least not a very good one. I haven't been to Mass in years.' He paused to consider for a moment. 'I was thinking we could be married in a registry office, but if you want to be married in a church, then I'll convert, if that's what it takes.'

'No, Stephen, that's the last thing I want you to do. I don't want you to change just because you feel you have to – and certainly not just for the sake of *form*. Which brings me on to the other thing. It's all very well you being willing to give up your religion if it means nothing to you, but have you thought what I would have to give up if we were married? I won't just lose my name, I'll lose my job. I'll lose everything I've been working for these last seven years. It's a light enough thing for a man to get married, but it's much more serious for a woman.'

She spoke in a low, grave tone – but her words were clear, even over the squeal of brakes as the train started to slow down. Stephen's mouth tightened. She was quite right, of course, but he thought she was missing something.

'It's no light thing for me,' he said thickly. 'I love you. That's why I . . .' He stumbled over the words. He'd had no notion that marriage could be anything other than an expression of love, a commitment they would make to one another. It had not occurred to him that it might *harm* her.

'And I love you too, Stephen, with all my heart.' She reached across and kissed him hastily. A promise, a smile. 'And the answer is yes. I will marry you, but not just now. We've both of us just got our lives back and this is a new world we're living in. Let's enjoy it for a little while before we go changing it again.'

Stephen's heart was bounding in his chest as the train shuddered to a halt in a burst of steam. He could see people milling around on the platform outside, a mass of bodies and cases and bags, hats bobbing. He heard doors slamming open, and footsteps in the corridor as more passengers got on.

'So, are we engaged?' he asked keenly, knowing they'd be interrupted any moment.

'Yes,' she laughed. 'If you want to be old-fashioned about it, we are engaged to be married.'

Billy's flat was on the top floor of a small but comfortable house near Rathmines village, not far from the tram. He walked into the garden and closed the gate behind him, feeling the iron cool under his hand and pausing for a moment to inhale the fresh scent of the roses that bordered the path. The night was so warm that he had taken off his jacket and carried it slung over his shoulder, with his hat pushed far back on his head.

As he turned, he looked up at the curtained windows with something like dismay. It was Friday night in an Indian summer and what had he to look forward to? A book, a glass of wine, and then a night spent tossing and turning in the heat. But it wasn't the heat that was the problem – it was the loneliness, the isolation. He wished he'd gone to his club – at least he might have snagged some other lonely soul to talk to over a gin and tonic. But then he rarely went there any more for fear somebody might ask him about his work and he'd grown tired of the deliberately vague answers.

Not that he needed to be so deliberately vague any more. The truth was, his job had become bland, boring and pointless. It seemed that the Castle had given up hope of strangling Sinn Fein with their own purse strings – though he was partly to blame for that, since he'd made sure they could never quite get enough of a grip on them. But there was more to it than that. There was a different climate abroad in the Castle, and it felt like the military men had the upper hand with their police reserves and this new auxiliary force. Brute force was the order of the day, and Frank Mercer, when he wasn't obviously avoiding Billy, had the look of a man who knew his days were numbered. Billy supposed that that meant his were too, but he was not much bothered. It was about time he got a job where he could safely socialize with his colleagues. Lies and deception were bad enough, but now that boredom had been added into the mix . . . His face brightened as an idea came to him. He would take a stroll down to the law library on Monday and see if he could spot any faces. The place would be crawling with juniors preparing cases for the Michaelmas term, and he could pick up some juicy gossip without giving himself away too much.

This thought put a spring in his step, and he bounded up to the front door, pulling the key from his pocket.

'Good evening to you, Billy,' a voice said from the deep shadow in the corner of the porch – it was so close to his elbow that he jumped in fright and dropped the key.

'For God's sake, Joe,' he panted, leaning against the door. 'You frightened the life out of me.'

'Well, it's been a while,' Joe said, and his teeth flashed in the shadow. 'I thought I'd stop by for a chat.'

'It *has* been a while,' Billy said, bending down to pick up his key. 'Where have you been?'

He asked this question knowing full well that he probably wouldn't get an answer. He had his own idea, anyway. He'd seen for himself the furore that had followed the ambush on Viscount French – extra detectives drafted in, soldiers milling around, and some very serious-looking men brought over from England. He hadn't heard from Joe since, and he assumed he'd been mixed up in it somehow. The surprising thing was how much he had missed their contacts. Passing secrets to Joe – not to say actively conspiring with him to keep Sinn Fein money in Sinn Fein hands – had been dangerous and stressful, but it had at least been exciting. Meeting him again, like this, in the dark, set his heart racing.

'I was down the country. I had to get away for a while,' Joe said, though he didn't mention that he'd meant to stay away for a while longer, until a bad feeling had brought him home. Two letters to Maggie, and neither of them answered. He'd used a false name, of course, but she was a clever girl – she would have recognized his writing. She would have known it was him. He gave her a week after the second one, and then made up his mind to come back to Dublin.

'I'm sure that was nice,' Billy said, and with a twist and a push the door opened on to a darkened hallway. The couple in the downstairs flat had gone away for the week, and he had the house to himself. 'Would you like to come in? I'm afraid I don't have anything . . .'

'All right.' Joe followed him into the hallway, feeling as if he was committing himself. He wasn't sure if he could trust Billy, but he didn't have much choice. Who else could he rely on? The city felt more dangerous now than when he'd left. Perhaps he'd been away too long, but it felt like every time he turned a corner

he ran into a patrol of police or soldiers, or these new Auxiliaries. The boarding house he was staying in didn't feel as safe
as it used to, and he was now absolutely certain that something
bad had happened to Maggie Clancy. He'd gone straight to her
lodgings from the train station, and her landlady had told him
a story that he found hard to believe. She'd not seen Maggie for
weeks – she'd been called away home because her father was
taken poorly. Maggie's cousin had explained it all to her when
he came to collect all her clothes and her mail. A nice young
man, though he had a very bad leg . . .

'I need somewhere to stay,' Joe blurted out, as he followed
Billy up the stairs. 'Just for a couple of days, like, until I get
myself sorted.'

Billy turned on the landing light and looked at Joe as he opened
the door to his flat. His face was pinched and pale, and he carried his arm strangely. He had the hunted look of a wounded
animal, and Billy thought it might be a while before he got himself sorted.

'All right,' he said. 'But you'll have to sleep on the sofa.'

Joe just nodded and followed him inside. He stood in the
middle of the room as Billy hung up his coat and then filled the
kettle and lit the gas stove.

'Sit down.' He gestured to the armchair. 'Make yourself at home.'

'I need a favour, as well,' Joe said without moving. 'It's a bit
out of your usual area.'

'What is it?'

'I need you to ask around the detective division in the Castle
– discreetly, like – see if they've got anything on a missing girl.
Maggie is her name, Maggie Clancy.'

Billy stopped moving and stood with the coffee can in his
hands. Curiouser and curiouser.

'What do you mean "missing"?'

'She hasn't been seen in a few weeks.'

'Well, neither have you,' Billy said, though he instantly regretted the lightness of his tone. There was something about the way Joe stood there, with his head hanging and his shoulders hunched, that made him look hurt, battered almost. 'Are you sure she hasn't just moved away?'

'No,' Joe said, and there was desolation in that one syllable. He sat down heavily on the armchair and stared across the room. 'No. I'm pretty sure she's dead.'

Dusk was coming on by the time the train rolled into Westport, and Stephen realized that they would have to stay in the town. In other years his grandfather had met him from the train, and the crowning of the journey had always been the ten-mile ride through the silky dark, feeling the mountains rising up steeply over him as the cart rattled along the rocky road to the tiny village of Kilbarry. But now there was no telling what waited out there, at the end of that road, and little hope of finding someone to take them there.

'We shall have to find a hotel,' he murmured to Lillian, but as they walked out of the station, his heart sank. Even though it was late enough for the first stars to be showing, the street was swarming with people and the humid air was heavy with the smell of livestock.

'It's market day tomorrow,' the stationmaster said, coming up beside them and surveying the scene with his thumbs hooked into his waistcoat. He sucked his teeth uncertainly. 'You'll be hard-pressed to find a room in this town tonight.'

But with night coming on, they had little choice except to try. 'I wish he wouldn't look so pleased with himself,' Lillian remarked a few minutes later, as they passed him again, having found the Station Hotel full to the rafters.

'There are plenty of guest houses along the mall,' Stephen assured her, but after they had been turned away from the third of these, he started to worry. Though the atmosphere in the town was festive, with lamps blazing and every pub overflowing, the heat and the people and the gathering dark weighed on him. He suddenly felt the smallness of the place, and cursed himself for not planning ahead. It wasn't that he minded so much for himself, but he felt responsible for Lillian.

'Which way are the quays?' Lillian asked. Despite Stephen's misgivings, she seemed quite amused at the prospect of having nowhere to sleep. Nevertheless, she had pressed the last landlord for a suggestion as to where else they might try.

'That way.' Stephen jerked his chin across the river, and in the same motion looked up into the sky, where thick black clouds were crowding across the velvet purple. There was an electric crackle in the air, and the heavy feel of imminent rain. 'It's about a mile.'

'Then we'd better be going,' she said, glancing into the sky and taking his arm again.

They had not gone far before they heard the blare of a motor horn, and then a gunshot rang out. Stephen automatically pressed himself against the wall, pulling Lillian close behind him. His eyes darted up and down Bridge Street, and then he saw the car, a Crossley tender, nosing its way past the crowds that spilled out of the pubs. A knot of men stood in the back, all wearing tam-o'-shanters and one of them brandishing a rifle. As the tender came closer, he worked the bolt, and Stephen saw the empty casing glittering in the light from a window before the man pointed the rifle into the sky and fired again.

'Get out of the fucking road!' he roared, and the other men all laughed. Then one of them spotted Lillian and gave an ear-splitting whistle.

'All right, darling? Where are you going tonight?'

'Yeah, why don't you come with us? We'll show you a good time!'

Another burst of ribald laughter and then a blare of the horn as the tender revved its engine and bolted down the crowded street, sending people darting out of its path.

'Sorry about that,' Stephen apologized.

'My father was a sailor, dear.' Lillian grinned. 'I believe I could do better myself.'

They walked on, and Stephen couldn't resist looking over his shoulder as they passed from the hubbub of the busy town to the quiet country lane that led out towards the quays. Those men had been soldiers, of a sort – and officers too. He had recognized the uniforms they wore with those tam-o'-shanters, although they had seemed an odd mixture of different styles and insignia. But officers did not go around together like that, and nor did they behave like that – at least not the ones he had known. Or was he being too prim? This was a different time, after all. Times had changed.

The weather was a more immediate concern. The breeze was picking up, and it blew through the tall trees that lined the road in a dark rustling of leaves. It had already blown away the heat of the day and the threat of rain was even stronger than before. Without speaking, they both lengthened their stride and hurried along the road. Now and again, Stephen saw the sheen of the sea ahead and a little to the right. They were almost on the bay.

Rounding a bend, they saw a large white house standing out on a spit of land at the end of a long drive. There were lights glowing in the windows, and in the gathering darkness, with the gleam of the sea stretching out behind, it looked like it was floating on the water.

'That's the place,' he said, for it matched exactly the description they had been given. But the moment he spoke he felt the first heavy drops of rain. There was a flash and, a few moments later, the rumble of thunder from behind them.

'Oh Lord!' Lillian said, but she was laughing as they hurried up the drive, with the big drops patting into the gravel all around them. Halfway to the hotel there was another flash, an instant crash, and the skies opened.

'Run!' Stephen shouted, but they had no chance against the sudden downpour. By the time they reached the shelter of the porch they were both soaked and giggling together as they shook out their hats and wiped the rain from their faces. When they had made themselves look as respectable as they could, they went inside and walked down a gloomy hallway that smelled of soup and was lit by a single flickering oil lamp. At the far end, there was an open hatch, where a small, wizened old man appeared and peered at them over an enormous ledger.

'Good evening and welcome to you,' he said, looking them up and down and noting their dripping clothes. 'The rain caught you, I see. Is it a room you're looking for?'

'Yes, please,' they answered together.

He ran a crooked finger down the ledger.

'It's market day tomorrow,' he remarked, without looking up at them. 'But you're in luck. We have one room left. Only a single bed, though. Will that do you?'

'That will do fine,' Lillian said, and when Stephen opened his mouth to say something, she kicked his ankle.

'Right you are.' The old man picked up a pen and frowned at them over the top of his spectacles. 'You are married, aren't you?'

'Of course we are,' she answered sweetly, with a sly glance at Stephen. 'This is our honeymoon. Ryan is the name. Mr and Mrs Ryan.'

The old man didn't blink, but studied them both for a few

moments. 'Well, I wish you had better weather for it,' he said at last, and handed her a key. 'Go all the way up the stairs. Yours is the second door on the right. The bathroom's at the end.'

The stairs went up and up, until they ended under the apex of the roof. Pausing only to light a candle on the second landing, they climbed up in silence and let themselves into their room. The door was so low that they had to bow their heads to get in, and they found that the ceiling was not much higher, though the room was broad and had a window looking out over the sea. There was a washstand, a wardrobe and a narrow bed, and a fire already set in the grate. It was basic, but with the rain lashing the window and drumming loudly on the roof over their heads, they were both glad of it. The storm was right on top of them now. There was a crack and peal of thunder that seemed to shake the floorboards, and an electric blue flash lit up the whole room. Stephen suddenly felt his clothes wet and clammy against his skin, and looked to Lillian. The thick tweed of his jacket had taken the brunt of the downpour and left him at least partially dry underneath, but her light summer dress was soaked through, and she was shivering.

'You should change out of those things,' he told her. 'You'll catch your death.'

Lillian's brush with influenza had made him highly sensitive to her health, which, in turn, made her highly sensitive to his fussing over her. Over the last few months, she had pointed out several times that he wasn't her mother, but on this occasion she just nodded, and went down to the bathroom at the end of the landing. While she was gone, Stephen took off his wet jacket and knelt to the fire. It had been laid since the spring, and the sticks and papers were so dry that they soon crackled into life. He hung his jacket nearby to dry, and he was unpacking his bag when Lillian came back, barefoot and wearing her nightdress.

She stood and warmed herself for a few moments and he turned and put his arms around her, feeling the cold still in her hands and her hair damp against his cheek.

'Go to bed,' he whispered. 'I'll sleep on the floor.'

'No,' she said and, twisting around in his arms, she kissed him. Then she led him across to the bed and sat on the edge. 'You'll do no such thing. We are equals, Stephen, and when we are married it will be a marriage of equals. Do you understand me, sweetheart?' She kissed him again, feeling his hands firm on her waist, pulling her body closer to his. Then she put her arms around him, feeling his breath, his warmth, his heart – and willing him to feel hers. 'Equals, Stephen,' she whispered fiercely into his ear, feeeling his hands, his lips. 'Equal in everything. I will love you and be your wife, but I won't be owned by any man.'

The village church was even smaller than Stephen remembered. In his mind it had been a very gloomy place, full of shadows and smelling of candle wax. But that morning it was filled with light. The storm had passed, and in passing it had washed the air clear and left the sky a deep and spotless blue. As the old priest finally finished the slow and solemn rites of the funeral, the pungent clouds of incense swirled and drifted through the broad shafts of sunlight that streamed in through the high windows.

When it was over, Stephen stood up and took his place beside the coffin. Three youngish men joined him – brown, weathered faces he vaguely remembered from years before, although he couldn't recall their names. There had been no time for introductions when he and Lillian arrived at the church, as every soul in the village was already starting to crowd inside. Somebody had recognized him, however, and a whisper had passed forward, clearing a path to the front pew. It was only as he sat down, folding his cap in his hands, that he saw the coffin, and the sight of it jarred him. It had been such a perfect morning, so warm and bright and pleasant, and he'd been so happy to be with Lillian, to feel her close and remember the intimacy of the night before. He had all but forgotten the reason for the journey, and yet there it was, right in front of him. The memory of that kind old man came back to him so suddenly that he dropped his head and felt tears pricking at the corners of his eyes.

By now he had gathered himself, and the four of them lifted the coffin together and began the slow walk down the aisle. They emerged into the warm sunlight, with the funeral bell tolling above, and climbed the few stone steps to the little cemetery that adjoined the church. The grave had already been dug and Stephen felt the shadow of an old fear passing over him when he saw the hole and the black spill of earth. But, again, he steadied himself. There was work to be done, and he followed the others as they set down the coffin and busied themselves with the ropes while the rest of the congregation gathered around the grave.

The priest came out of the church, clutching stole and Bible, but as he mounted the steps there was a rumbling sound from down the lane, and all heads turned towards it. Stephen saw a lorry bumping slowly towards them, with men sitting in the back. He recognized the Crossley tender from the night before, but he wasn't expecting the ripple of fear that spread through the mourners when they saw it. There was an audible gasp, and a noticeable change came over the crowd as they closed ranks and watched uncertainly as the lorry squealed to a halt just outside the cemetery gate.

Stephen wasn't sure what was happening, but he instinctively put his arm around Lillian and drew her closer. The tender stood there for a full minute with its engine ticking over before a voice finally broke from the crowd of mourners.

'Murderers!'

There was a murmur of assent from the others, but no reaction from the men in the tender. Eventually, one of them stood up, lifted his hat, and made an elaborate, smirking bow. Then he sat down again and the lorry ground on up the valley.

Even after it was gone, the tender cast a shadow over the funeral. The coffin was lowered, the priest hurried through the final rites, and the congregation began to break up, some of them looking fearfully up the valley road before hurrying away. A few came and hastily shook hands with Stephen, offering their condolences, but little else by way of an explanation. It was as if they feared to speak of what had happened, and by the time everybody had left, Stephen knew little more about his grandfather's death than when he had arrived. All that he had been able to glean from them was that his grandfather had been attacked two nights ago, and that those men in the tender had had something to do with it. It appeared that his brother also had something to do with it, but exactly what was unclear, because he had gone back to Dublin a few days before.

'I think I'll go out to the cottage,' Stephen said. His grandfather's cottage lay a mile up the valley – in the same direction that the tender had gone. He had also thought of asking Lillian to stay in the village, but, knowing what answer he'd get, he kept that thought to himself.

'I'd really like to see it,' Lillian said, taking his hand. He had told her all about the cottage last night, as they lay together in the narrow bed, with the firelight flickering on their faces. He had talked and talked and talked; about his grandfather, about the summers he had spent here, and about the cottage by the lake. After so many years away he thought he would only dimly remember it, but it had come back to him so vividly that when he drifted off to sleep, he dreamed about the place.

It came back to him again as they walked along the road. Not just the familiar houses and hills they passed, but the road itself seemed to be just as he remembered it. The loose gravel and the leafy hedges, the ripe fruit on the blackberry bushes and the shocking purple splash of a patch of foxgloves. It was like one long memory unfolding itself in front of him, becoming more and more familiar with every step, until at last he saw the stand of tall ash trees and then the black sheen of the lake behind.

'That's it,' he told Lillian, almost excited, but as they left the road and walked down towards the trees, his heart grew cold. He smelled it first; the bitter, acrid stink of smoke. Then he saw the cottage and he stopped in his tracks. The thatched roof was gone and only a few charred beams remained between the scorched and smoke-blackened walls. The windows were all burned and broken and gaped at him like dead eyes.

'Oh my God,' Lillian said, her hand to her mouth.

Just then, Stephen heard the low hum of an engine and he turned to look back towards the road. There were precious few cars around here, and he was sure it could only be the tender coming back. But the sound seemed to be coming up the road, from the direction of the village, and when the car finally came into view he saw it was smaller and sleeker than the tender – a gleaming black Rolls-Royce. It stopped without a squeak and a uniformed chauffeur got out and held the back door open while a small, portly man in tweeds and a red waistcoat climbed out.

'Good morning!' he called out, raising his cap. Stephen and Lillian looked at each other uncertainly as the portly man walked down towards them.

'Captain Ryan, I presume?' he asked, and when Stephen nodded slowly, he thrust out his hand. 'My name is Bourke, Richard Bourke. I'm the chap who sent the telegram.'

'Pleased to meet you, your lordship,' Stephen said, shaking his pudgy hand. 'May I introduce my fiancée, Lillian Bryce?'

'Delighted to meet you, ma'am,' Bourke said, and as he shook her hand, Stephen studied his florid face. He had a vague memory of being presented at the big house when he was very young. The old lord had been rather frightening to a seven-year-old boy – bent and wizened and tucked into a bath chair with a plaid blanket over his knees. But he also remembered his son, a dashing black-haired man in tennis whites who had bounded around the gloomy house and had seemed to laugh a lot. Could this really be him?

'Well, I'm very glad I caught you. They told me in the village that you'd come out this way. I only wish we were meeting under happier circumstances.' Bourke gestured at the cottage. 'First the funeral, and now to see this.' He shook his head. 'It's sad. Very sad.'

'Was he . . .' Stephen began, and looked uncertainly at Lillian. 'Was he burned to death?'

'Oh, no. No, thank God.' Bourke frowned. 'But haven't you been told what happened? Didn't they tell you at the funeral?'

'Not in any detail,' Stephen answered. 'The Auxiliaries put in an appearance, and I think they frightened everybody off.'

'Ah, yes, so I heard.' Bourke's face darkened. 'Well, even if nobody told you, I'm sure you've already worked out that it was those beggars who did this.' Bourke threw out an angry gesture at the burned shell of the cottage. 'Unfortunately, nobody saw them, or if they did, they're too terrified to say so. I'm the resident magistrate here, you see, and I've been gathering information with a view to pressing criminal charges. Why I wasn't at the funeral, you see – I was in Westport, on the blasted telephone to Dublin. And a right old waste of a morning it was, too.'

'What happened?' Stephen asked, thrusting his hands into his pockets and setting his feet apart, as if to brace himself.

'Well, those Auxiliaries showed up about a week ago,' Bourke said, and he went on to explain that they had given precious little warning to the police superintendent there – just a telegram instructing him to organize a billet for twelve men, and a few hours later they arrived in their lorry. A rough bunch, armed to the teeth and, appropriately enough, under the command of a Captain Wilde.

'It seems they were searching for somebody,' Bourke said, his face troubled, his eyes darting from Lillian to Stephen. 'Not to put too fine a point on it, they were looking for your brother, I'm afraid.'

'Go on,' Stephen said.

Their methods had not been subtle. They had been tipped off that Joe was in the area, but they had nothing else to go on. Their solution was to pick up three or four young men at a time, take them back to the old grain merchant's where they were billeted, and interrogate them.

'I mean torture them, of course,' Bourke added, with an apologetic look at Lillian. 'I've seen some of the results for myself, and it doesn't bear thinking about. Bruises, burns, teeth, fingernails. Really, they are the most appalling savages I've ever seen. And to think they call themselves policemen!'

'So, they found out eventually,' Stephen said grimly, gazing around the familiar yard, which was full of warm air and sunlight dappled by the shivering shadows of the ash trees. With his back to the ruined cottage it looked just as he had remembered it – as if nothing had happened.

'Yes, they did. Of course, you can't really blame the poor lad who told them, especially as he knew your brother had already moved on. Well, to cut a long story short, they came out here two nights ago and presumably were not pleased when they found they'd missed their man. From what I can gather, they dragged your grandfather out here and tried to beat a location out of him, but if he did know, he wouldn't tell them.' Bourke scuffed his toe uncomfortably in the dust of the yard. 'According to the doctor, they beat him with their rifles. They beat him very badly indeed.'

'An old man!' Lillian exclaimed, her face pale with anger, and she groped for Stephen's hand and held it tight. Stephen closed his eyes for a moment. He could imagine the scene, and it made his blood boil.

'And then they burned the cottage and left him for dead,' he said.

'Yes, precisely. The nearest cottage is nearly a quarter of a mile away, but when they saw the fire they came running. They found your grandfather here, unconscious but still breathing. They brought him to their home in a cart and summoned the doctor, but I'm sorry to say he didn't last the night.'

Stephen turned away and slowly let his eyes take in the scene. They ran down the rocky hump of one mountain to the tail of the lake, then along the broad swathe of heather that made a desolate sweep out to the sea, before rising up again to the pointed peak on the far side of the valley, the quartz cone glittering like silver. How many mornings had he stood here and bathed in the warming sun? How many tranquil evenings had he sat down by the lake, feeling the gentle dusk rising like smoke from the water? But now it was defiled. These so-called policemen, these auxiliaries, had committed murder in this place, and then come back to mock the living.

'And yet you tell me there will be no criminal charges brought,' he said bitterly.

'I doubt it,' Bourke answered candidly. 'I've gathered what evidence I can, but there is no way I could charge them with anything. Even if the local constables weren't as terrified of them as everybody else, they are under the protection of Dublin Castle. There is a policy of official reprisals, which unfortunately means they can literally get away with murder. They are, I'm sorry to say, a law unto themselves.'

XIV

Gravesend
15 September 1920

Dear Stephen,

*Good news! I'm coming to Ireland at last. It's about time,
I know – to think I spent three years in an Irish regiment
and never even set foot in the place!*

*Well, what brings me there is this job I've landed, and
about time, too, because I've been having the devil of a time
finding work. You would think that, as a former officer with
a good service record, I wouldn't have any trouble picking
up a job, but the fact is the place is simply awash with ex-
soldiers, and some of them are very much on their uppers.*

*Luckily, the Government is running this scheme to recruit
ex-soldiers to work in the Irish police. They placed an
advertisement in the newspapers here, looking for ex-officers
with war experience and a clean service record. The pay they
were offering was even better than what we got in the army,
so naturally I decided to throw my hat in the ring and, what
do you know? I've got the job. I am now officially a cadet
with the Auxiliary Division of the Royal Irish Constabulary
and I'll be starting training in Dublin next week.*

I'm told it could be quite rough work. Looking at the newspapers, I see you're still having a lot of trouble with those Sinn Fein fellows that started the Easter Rebellion, but I'm sure if we get a few chaps of our own who know a thing or two about fighting, we'll soon show them who's better at it! As I say, the pay is rather good and I reckon a year will see me clear of debt and put enough in my pocket to get me to Canada.

Anyway, I shall certainly look you up when I arrive next week. Are you still going out with that girl who used to send you presents at the front, and who used to write you all those letters? Good for you, if you are. Perhaps I can meet her in the flesh when I get to Dublin, and the pair of you can show me around the place in return for a slap-up dinner out of my first week's wages.

I look forward to seeing you soon.

Best wishes,

Edmund Nightingale

They were halfway there before Joe worked up the courage to speak again. He drew a breath, but then he lost his nerve. A few moments passed, and the only sound was the click and scrape of their boots as they walked along together. Then it seemed to come out by itself.

'So, you went to the funeral, then,' he said.

'I did.' Stephen looked at him sideways. They were walking down a darkened street, and seemed to be heading for Ranelagh, though he couldn't be certain. Joe hadn't said where they were going – he hadn't said much at all since he'd knocked on the door of his flat ten minutes ago. Not a word of apology or explanation, not a question or an answer. He'd just nodded and jerked his head up the street.

'Have you got a few minutes? A few friends of mine want to have a word with you.'

'What friends?' Stephen had asked, suspiciously. It was a week since he'd got home from Mayo and even though he knew his brother was back in town, he hadn't expected to see him so soon.

'They're on the headquarters staff,' Joe said, and Stephen frowned. He'd always known the Irish Volunteers were organized along military lines, but now that they'd started calling themselves the Irish Republican Army, they seemed to be going all the way. He knew they had a chief of staff, an intelligence department, and even a minister of defence in the Dáil that they were all answerable to. What he didn't know was how his brother fit into all this, but that wasn't what was bothering him.

'It's important,' Joe added. 'Come on, it won't take long.'

Stephen put on his coat and followed him up the street. All the way home from Mayo, he'd thought about Joe's part in what had happened there. Was it his fault? No more than it was his own fault, he'd decided. After all, he was the one who'd sent his brother there in the first place. And yet he couldn't help feeling angry with him. A week had gone by, a whole week, and nothing, not a word from him – until this. And now he was walking fast, with his head down and his shoulders hunched, as if to deflect any accusation.

'Did you hear about what happened?' Stephen asked.

'I heard.'

'You heard they were looking for you.' It was meant to be a question, but it came out flat – more like an accusation.

'I heard that as well.' Joe looked at him as they passed under a street lamp. His face was hard and the flaring light cast deep shadows in his cheeks and eye sockets.

'And?'

'And what?' Joe stopped suddenly and turned on his brother.

'What the fuck do you want me to say? I'm sorry? All right. I'm sorry. I didn't want that to happen, but innocent people get hurt sometimes.'

'Innocent people?' Stephen felt anger flaring red in his cheeks. 'He wasn't just innocent people, for God's sake. He was our grandfather, and they beat him to death.'

Joe flinched when he said it, and just for a second his mask slipped. His face seemed to shrivel in the harsh light, but then he mastered it and the stony look returned, though his eyes were burning.

'Come on, we'll be late.'

He started walking again. Stephen hesitated, but then followed him.

'Who are we going to see?' he asked in an angry tone. He was starting to lose his patience.

'Dick Mulcahy and Liam Tobin.'

'Yes, but who are they?'

'Mulcahy is the army Chief of Staff and Tobin is the Assistant Director of Intelligence.'

Impressive titles, but what did they mean? Apart from his brother, all he'd ever seen of the IRA was what he'd read in the newspapers – a skirmish here, a raid there. Now and again they pulled off something spectacular, but he still had the impression that there couldn't be many of them. Perhaps only a few thousand altogether, he thought, but he had to admit they were effective. They were effective enough to make the Government deploy the Auxiliaries – to make them terrorize the whole country.

He was surprised when they stopped outside a large, prosperous-looking house. There was a motor car in the drive and lights glowing through the curtains in the bay windows. It didn't look like the sort of place he might find desperate men with pistols and bombs, but Joe lifted the latch on the gate and led him through the garden. A small, well-dressed woman answered the doorbell and ushered them into the living room without a word. Joe sat in an armchair without any preamble, and Stephen lowered himself on to the sofa, wondering at the signs of ordinary domestic life. There was a newspaper folded on the arm of the sofa, a toy bear sitting beside it, and a few toys scattered near the fireplace.

They sat in silence until the door opened abruptly and two men marched in. Both lean and serious-looking, one a little taller than the other. Joe got to his feet. Stephen looked them up and down, but didn't move.

'Joe, thanks for coming over.' They both shook his hand, then looked at Stephen. The short one grinned.

'You must be this fella's brother. Stephen, isn't it? Thanks for coming to see us.'

Stephen stood up, shook their hands in turn, and listened to their introductions. The short one was Tobin, the taller one Mulcahy. They were both older than he was, but still much younger than he would have expected. He sat down again and Mulcahy folded himself into a worn-looking armchair beside the fireplace, while Tobin pulled a chair from the dining table that stood over near the bay window.

'First of all,' Mulcahy said in a steady, sonorous voice. 'We want to express our condolences on the death of your grandfather.' These words were clearly meant for both of them, but Mulcahy didn't take his eyes off Stephen as he spoke. 'It was a terrible thing to happen to anybody, least of all to an old man.'

'Thank you,' Stephen answered, with a nod.

'We'll come back to that in a minute,' Mulcahy went on, looking down and absently plucking an invisible speck from the seam of his trousers. 'Before we do that, we want to ask you about a meeting you had two days ago, in Robert's Café on Grafton Street.'

Stephen stiffened. He'd suspected it at the time, but now he knew for sure. Somebody had been watching them.

'What about it?'

'The man you met is of interest to us,' Tobin said, leaning back against his chair and crossing his legs at the ankles. 'He's of interest to us because we believe he's an Auxiliary. We don't know his name yet, but we understand he came over with the last draft from England, and he's training in the depot in the Phoenix Park.'

'That's right,' Stephen agreed. 'His name is Nightingale, Edmund Nightingale. We served together in the army.'

Mulcahy and Tobin exchanged looks, and Stephen was aware that his brother was openly staring at him, but he kept his face blank.

'But he's an Auxiliary now. And you're aware it was the Auxiliaries who killed your grandfather?'

'I am.'

'So you were just catching up on old times?' Mulcahy asked with a faintly amused look. 'Two old comrades sharing war stories?'

'Not quite,' Stephen answered. He remembered the white, appalled look that came over Nightingale's face when he told him what had happened to his grandfather. He hadn't spared him any of the details. It was easier to get what he wanted that way. 'I asked him to get me some information about the men who killed my grandfather.'

'What information was that?' Tobin cut in, leaning forward, his face keen.

'I wanted to know who sent them, and how they knew where to go.'

'You think there was an informer?'

Stephen turned his gaze on Tobin. Still mild, but a little incredulous.

'Dublin Castle sent a squad of men all the way across the country to find *him*.' He nodded in the direction of his brother, who was starting to look agitated. 'They didn't just stick a pin in the map. They knew where to look. Somebody sent them.'

Another look passed between Mulcahy and Tobin, and Mulcahy glanced at Joe before he took up the thread.

'Did he give you a name?' he asked, his voice hardening. Stephen felt the name come to the tip of his tongue but held it a moment. Nightingale had been far from certain – he was, after all, still training, and not privy to any intelligence more rarefied than which pubs were safe to drink in. But the name he'd come up with had rung so true that Stephen was sure it was right.

'The man who sent them is called Captain Maunsell,' he said, and he saw a smile play at the corners of his brother's mouth. 'He works for Colonel Winter's intelligence operation in Dublin Castle.'

'That fits. Maunsell is known to us, as is Winter,' Tobin said.

'And what about the informer?' Mulcahy asked, all business.

'He didn't give me a name.'

'So there's no informer?'

'I didn't say that. Nightingale didn't give me a name because he wasn't able to find it out. But he believes there is an informer. The rumour is that Joe's capture was meant to be some sort of payment for this informer tipping Maunsell off about the ambush on Viscount French. It seems this informer doesn't want him around the place.'

Stephen spoke deliberately, slowly, watching his brother all the while. Joe sat hunched forward, his face as hard as stone. When Stephen had finished speaking, there was a tense silence. He could hear the clock ticking on the mantel before Mulcahy sighed.

'Well, that's just a rumour, as you said. And that ambush was a bad job from the start. Too many men involved for it ever to work. Maybe they were tipped off, but it could have been anybody.'

'It was fucking Garvey!' Joe burst out. 'It was him and you know it. The dirty little bastard is a tout!'

'Where's your proof, Joe?' Tobin asked, turning in his chair. 'What have you got on him? Only the word of an Auxie, and he couldn't even get a name.'

'I've got proof enough to kill the bastard,' Joe muttered darkly. 'He's a tout. You know what we do to touts.'

'You'll do no such thing, lieutenant,' Mulcahy barked. 'He's still one of our men and he's entitled to a court martial.' He turned on Stephen. 'And as for you, Mr Ryan, I hope you won't take matters into your own hands, as you did in Mayo.'

Stephen kept his mild face. He'd been wondering when they would come back to that.

'I don't know what you mean,' he said. But Tobin laughed out loud.

'Oh don't you, now? You don't know anything about an ambush on an Auxiliary lorry near Westport the morning after your grandfather's funeral?'

Stephen remembered leaving the hotel in the very early morning, slipping gently out of bed so as not to wake Lillian. He'd dressed in the dark and taken the rifle, case and all. His grandfather's rifle, presented to him by Lord Mayo after he'd invited them back to Kilbarry House for afternoon tea.

'I understand you are something of a marksman,' Bourke had said. The case was charred and scorched on the outside, but the thick leather and its hiding place under his grandfather's bed had saved the contents. The plush velvet lining was untouched, and the rifle itself gleamed dull blue in the afternoon sun. 'Your grandfather was very proud of that. He taught you to shoot, did he not? I'm afraid he tried the same with me, but without much success.'

The rifle had been a gift to his grandfather from the sixth earl. It was a severely beautiful Rigby, with an octagonal barrel and a smooth, heavy action. His grandfather had shot with it at Wimbledon, and had allowed Stephen to fire it as a special treat when he was younger. Taking it out of the case and feeling the heft of it in his hand, he realized that this was all that was left of the old man. A widower for most of his life, he'd never been much for ornament, had lived simply, and the few letters and photographs he might have treasured had been lost in the fire. This was all that remained.

When he got back to the hotel his trousers were wet with dew and the only thing left of the rifle was the faint whiff of powder from his clothes. Taking off his boots, he carried them silently up the stairs – but still, Lillian was awake. She knew. She was sitting in the armchair with her legs pulled up under her and a blanket around her shoulders. Her bright eyes met his as he came in the door.

'What did you do?' she asked, and he told her. He told her everything.

'I don't know anything about that,' Stephen told Tobin, but he could feel his brother's stare on him.

'Come off it, Mr Ryan,' Mulcahy said, leaning back in his chair and giving him a knowing grin. 'We don't know much about what happened that morning, but we know it wasn't us. Our boys down there are good lads, but ten of them together couldn't have shot the driver of a moving lorry, then picked off three more men when it crashed into the ditch and they all jumped out the back.' Mulcahy raised a bony hand and snapped his fingers. 'Bang, bang, bang. Just like that. Three Auxies killed, and another will never walk again. And nobody saw a thing.'

Out of the corner of his eye, Stephen could see his brother's stare had turned to open disbelief. He shrugged.

'Well, I won't be shedding any tears for them.'

'Nor will we, Mr Ryan, but we could use a man with skills like that.'

Stephen looked at Mulcahy for a moment, trying to remember what he had felt that morning. Nothing at all while he was shooting. He'd steeled himself to do it and he had done it calmly and coldly, without a qualm or a quiver. By the time the remaining Auxies got into the cover of the ditch he was gone, falling back behind a copse of stunted trees and hiking away while they loosed off a few panicked, wild shots. It was only after a few minutes had passed that he felt any sort of emotion, and it was not the one he had been expecting. It was neither triumph nor shame, but a sort of emptiness – as if he had lost a part of himself.

Once he crested the hill, his path took him down to a small mountain lake, gleaming like a black mirror in the early light. When he reached the shore he unslung the rifle and held it in his hands for a moment, feeling the warmth in the wood and thinking back to the many mornings just like this one when he'd gone hunting with his grandfather. Then he changed his grip, holding the gun by the barrel, and flung it as far as he could into the lake.

'I'm sure you could use a man like that,' Stephen told Mulcahy. 'But I'm not that man. I already fought in one war, and I've no intention of getting into another one.'

Mulcahy gave him a grim smile.

'So you're definitely not that man,' he said. 'Well, I'm glad to hear it. Because if you were that man, I'd have to tell you that, by way of a reprisal, the surviving Auxies burned four farms that night – one for each of their men that were shot. Two innocent people were killed. So, that man – whoever he is – is already in this war, whether he likes it or not. He's in it right up to his neck.'

There was still a light showing on the top floor of the boarding house. They watched it together in silence, Stephen feeling that some sort of test had been sprung on him and not sure if he resented it. A few hours ago he'd been giving a tutorial on geometrical sequences, now he was in a damp alleyway off Gardiner Street with his service revolver hanging in a holster under his overcoat.

The light winked out and Joe leaned away from the wall, looking up at the house that was now in total darkness. He dropped the butt of his cigarette and ground it under his heel.

'Where is the bastard?' he asked impatiently, and leaned further out to look down the street. Stephen sneaked a glance at his wristwatch. Less than an hour until the curfew – if he didn't show up in the next few minutes, then they'd have to leave, or risk being stopped by an army patrol.

Joe was fishing in his pocket for another cigarette when Stephen gripped his arm and nodded up the street. They listened as faint footsteps grew louder, and Joe quickly recognized that uneven scraping tread. A small dark figure appeared around the corner, climbed the steps to the boarding house, and let himself in by the front door.

'That's him,' Joe whispered, but still they waited. His room was at the back of the house, on the top floor, and Joe wanted to give him time to get up there and settled in before they made their move. He waited, waited – then he made up his mind.

'Right, come on,' he said, and they crossed the empty street together. Joe had a key, and he let them in through the front door, closing it softly behind them. He knew this house – had lived here himself for a few months – and knew the floorboards in the hall went like a drum even under the little feet of the land-lady's daughter. They stood still for a few moments, listening to the darkened hallway. The air was cool and damp and smelled of boiled food and musty carpets.

'You go up the front stairs,' he told his brother, whispering now. 'There's a back stairs that goes directly to his room – I'll go up that way. If he runs, you stop him.'

'All right.' Stephen pulled the revolver from under his coat and cocked it. Joe stopped him with a hand on his arm.

'Don't use that unless you have to,' he added. 'He has to get a trial.'

Stephen didn't answer. He just nodded and set off up the stairs, climbing slowly, feeling the floorboards bend and creak under his weight and brushing one hand lightly against the thick, patterned wallpaper. He reached the first landing and saw a thin crack of light seeping out under a door at the far end. He watched it for a few moments, listening intently, but when he heard no sound he turned the corner and climbed on again. When he reached the top floor he looked down the hallway. No sound, no lights either. He stood in the darkness for a moment and listened. Somebody, somewhere, was humming a tune to themselves. He stepped back around the corner, down one step of the stairs, and uncocked his revolver, holding it pressed against his thigh, waiting.

After a few moments he heard a door opening and closing with a bang, then the murmur of voices, growing louder. Suddenly there was a crash, a door burst open and footsteps came thundering down the landing towards him. A strange, uneven tread: *Da-dum, da-dum, da-dum* . . . He waited, waited, and then turned as the footsteps finally reached him, and swung the heavy revolver at the dimly seen head. It connected with a crunch and the man went sprawling backwards.

'Ah, Jesus, me eye!' Garvey screeched, clutching his face as he writhed on the carpet. Stephen reached around and flicked on the light as Joe came striding along the landing, holding a gun in one hand and with the other to his cheek. There was blood seeping between his fingers.

'Stop your fucking racket, Garvey!' he hissed and swung a kick at his head. 'Shut your fucking gob or I'll shut it for you.'

'What's all that noise?' a voice called up from the landing below.

'It's only an old cat, missus,' Joe called down, without taking his gun off Garvey. 'I don't know how he got in, but I've got him now. Don't you worry about it.'

'There's no pets allowed in here!' the voice called up again.

'Ah, don't you worry about me, missus. I'll be away in a minute.'

'On your feet,' Stephen told Garvey, gesturing with his gun.

'Fuck off.'

Stephen cocked the revolver and pointed it at Garvey's head. 'Get up, or I'll shoot you lying down.'

'Fuck off, the pair of you. I'll have you for this.'

'You'll have us, will you?' Joe asked, reaching down and hauling Garvey up by a handful of his hair. Garvey yelped and whimpered, but quickly scrambled to his feet. Joe shoved his face into the wall and screwed the barrel of his gun into his cheek. 'Why? What are you going to do? Rat on us to your pal Maunsell?'

'I never heard of him,' Garvey gasped, but he was laughing, and even with the side of his face pushed hard against the wall, he looked Stephen up and down. 'You're his brother, aren't you?'

'Shut up,' Joe hissed.

'So he has you running around after him now as well, does he?' Garvey gasped as Joe punched him in the ribs. 'Just like that little bitch he used to have. Well, she was a tasty little one, I can tell you.'

'You shut your fucking mouth,' Joe whispered in his ear, his voice ragged with fury. 'You shut your filthy fucking gob. You'll get a bullet for what you did to her.'

Garvey laughed again, a mad cackle that sent blood and spittle dribbling over his lips.

'You don't know what I did to her,' he leered at Joe. 'She was lovely, she was. Real soft. Bit of fight in her, too, but I soon knocked that out of her.'

'Shut up!' Joe shouted, and with a quick jerk he cocked the snub-nosed pistol he had pressed to Garvey's head. 'Shut up or I'll fucking do you now.'

Stephen could see the dangerous look in his brother's eye, and his finger tensing on the trigger. But Garvey's eyes were wild, and he licked his bloody lips as he laughed. He'd found Joe's nerve, and he was twisting it.

'Go on, then. Shoot me. It'll be worth it. Lovely, she was, sweet as a peach . . .'

'Joe.' Stephen's hand shot out and pushed the gun up as his brother's face went white with fury. 'Don't. You said he had to get a trial.'

'Trial my arse,' Joe said, but the fire was going out of him. He still had Garvey pinned to the wall by the scruff of his neck, but he uncocked the pistol and released his grip so the gun twisted around his trigger finger and into the palm of his hand. He let out a long breath through his nose. 'He'll get a trial all right, but it'll be more than he deserves.' And he brought the gun down with such force that it crunched against Garvey's skull and splashed blood along the wall.

The lecture hall emptied quickly, and Stephen turned and started to pack his notes into his briefcase. Complex numbers again – not his favourite subject, though he thought he had managed well enough, even if his mind had not been entirely focused. A few of the students' questions had foxed him, and he'd had to ask for them to be repeated before answering slowly, deliberately – almost as if he was trying to convince himself. Part of him was still thinking about his brother and about what he'd heard that night in the boarding house. He wondered about this girl whom Garvey had mentioned – and shuddered to think what might have happened to her. But as the two of them had manhandled Garvey's limp body down the stairs and along the passage to the back door, he hadn't thought it right to ask him about her. When the motor car came and they shoved Garvey across the back seat, Joe had offered Stephen a lift, but he knew from the closed look on his face that he didn't want him to take it. He shook his head and watched the car drive off before walking home.

As he walked, he realized how little he knew about his own brother. Apart from the few he'd met thus far, he knew nothing about his comrades, and he'd had no idea about this unfortunate girl, whoever she was. What he did know was that Joe was taking a chance, not only with his own life but also with those of his friends – himself included. Stephen didn't mind that so much for his own part, but he had to wonder if it was right to follow his brother down this path he was on. There were other things to think of – not least of which was Lillian. Was it fair to ask her to stand by him if he ran the risk of imprisonment or even death? He had risked death before, but this was different and, from what he had just heard, it seemed to him that it could easily be *her* death he was risking. This was a very different game he was getting into, and the rules were far from clear. All pieces were in play.

Closing his briefcase, he was startled by the sound of clapping coming from the back of the hall. He half turned to see a man rising from a seat and clapping slowly as he made his way into the aisle.

'Bravo, professor,' he said, coming down the steps. 'A most stimulating lecture. I can't say I understood a word of it, but the delivery was most entertaining.'

Stephen studied him carefully as he came closer; a small man, perhaps forty years old, and very well dressed. He wore a fashionable grey suit with a white carnation in his buttonhole, and carried a top hat and a long black cane. He had flat, intelligent features, a broad forehead, and he was smiling as he came down the steps.

'I'm not a professor,' Stephen answered, and the man made a disappointed face as he set his top hat and cane on the desk.

'But you will be one day, I'm sure of it. I have a nose for these things.' His hand shot out quite suddenly – a small hand, brown and well manicured. The man smiled. 'Cope's the name, by the way. Alfred Cope, but people call me Andy.'

'What can I do for you, Mr Cope?'

'Please, call me Andy.' Cope's eyes roved around the room for a few moments, and then settled on the blackboard, covered with lines and lines of equations on complex numbers. He seemed to study it for a while, and then he went on, 'What can I call you, then, if it's not professor?'

'Mr Ryan is what my students call me.'

'Oh, it's Mister Ryan, is it?' Cope nodded. 'You don't prefer Captain Ryan, then?'

With hardly a blink, Stephen picked up his briefcase and pulled his overcoat from the back of his chair, making as if to leave. But Cope didn't budge and Stephen stopped to face him with his legs well apart and his free hand shoved in his trouser pocket.

'Who are you, and what do you want?'

'I'm an assistant to the Chief Secretary of Ireland, and I want to talk, Mister Ryan,' Cope said, his voice hardening, but then he relaxed, shrugged and smiled. 'That's all. Just a little chat.'

'What do you want to talk to me for?'

'Well, I hope you won't be offended, but I don't want to talk *to* you as much as I want to talk *through* you. I would like you to relay a message to a man I believe is, if not a friend, at least an acquaintance of yours. A Mr Michael Collins.'

There was still a touch of humour in Cope's voice, but his eyes were no longer smiling. Stephen shrugged.

'I'm sorry, but I don't know anybody by that name.'

'Oh, come on, Mr Ryan. Don't you read the newspapers? From what I hear, everybody knows Michael Collins. He's quite the celebrity in this town.'

'I've never met him,' Stephen told him, looking straight into his eyes. It was no lie. He'd never met Collins, and didn't expect he ever would.

'I'm sure you haven't. But I'm equally sure you know some people who have – your brother, for instance. I'm sure he's met him several times.'

Stephen was instantly on his guard. He felt the hairs bristle on the back of his neck and his legs stiffened. Cope kept looking at him coolly, a faint smile playing around his lips, but not his eyes.

'Since you seem to know so much about Mr Collins, it shouldn't be very difficult for you to arrange a meeting yourself,' Stephen suggested.

'Oh, how I wish that were true.' Cope's smile brightened a little as he picked up his hat and cane from the table. 'Unfortunately, he and I move in very different circles and, just as it wouldn't be safe for him to walk into Dublin Castle to see me, it would be very rash of me to go and beard the lion in his den, as it were. No, this is a situation that calls for neutral ground. And what could be more neutral than this?' Cope spread his arms to indicate the gloomy space of the lecture theatre. 'It's as safe a place as any in this city for a gentleman like me, but also one where Mr Collins and his associates can move freely if they so wish. A convenient meeting place for both parties, I would think. So, I would regard it as a favour if you could pass a message to Mr Collins that I will be here on this day next week. Tell him I shall sit outside the chapel in my lunch hour, and if he would like to communicate with me, I am prepared to listen to what he has to say.'

Stephen thrust his hands in his pockets and looked Cope up and down, hardly believing what he had said, but curiously engaged by the man.

'You know he could send a gunman, or somebody to take you as a hostage. You might be worth more to him that way.'

'So I might,' Cope admitted, placing his top hat on his head and flourishing his cane as he turned to go back up the steps, 'but I understand Mr Collins is an intelligent man. He knows very well I'll be more trouble than I'm worth as a hostage. More to the point, he knows that he'll have to talk to somebody sooner or later, and the cleverest men always do it sooner rather than later.'

'But he's winning the war,' Stephen called after him, a slight hint of triumph in his voice. 'Why would he want to talk if he's winning?'

'Why?' Cope stopped on the bottom step, turned around and leaned on his cane. 'Because nobody wins a war, Mr Ryan. You should know that better than anybody. Peace is always restored eventually, and then it's just a question of who paid the highest price for it.'

He reached up to tip his hat, but frowned at the blackboard again.

'This business about the square root of minus one,' he said, nodding at the figures scrawled in chalk.

Stephen looked over his shoulder.

'What about it?'

'Well, I can't pretend to be an educated man, but my old master always led me to believe that there's no such thing. Minus one doesn't have a square root.'

'Of course it does,' Stephen answered, looking at him with some amusement. 'It must. Just because we can't calculate it doesn't mean it can't exist.'

Cope nodded, a broad grin spreading across his face.

'Well, there you have it, Mr Ryan. There you have it precisely. Good day to you, sir. I thank you for your time.'

XV

Joe fiddled with the sleeve of his gown, trying to tug it across his broad shoulders and instead managing to chafe his neck.

'Do I have to wear this fecking thing?'

Stephen looked at him and realized that the academic gown was probably wasted on his brother. He knew Joe could blend in very easily on the streets, in spite of his bulk, but the ancient confines of the college had seemed to bring out the ape in him. He had walked across the front square with a bowed, almost deferential gait, and when a gaggle of freshmen had passed them by, babbling and laughing to each other, he had dropped his eyes and thrust his hands into his pockets – managing to look shifty when there was nothing to be shifty about. The fact was, he looked nothing like a student, and Stephen knew there would probably be trouble if one of the porters spotted him going around in academicals. But still, he could well remember the first day he'd brought his gown home from college, and the unmerciful ragging his brother had given him about it. Do him good to wear one himself for a while, he thought, and looked back across the front square.

'Here he comes,' he said, nodding towards the front gate, which Cope had just strode through, swinging his cane and tipping his hat to the porter. He felt Joe push close behind him, straining for a look.

'Well, he didn't come on his own,' Joe said, seeing the two men who came through the gate after Cope. Plainclothes policemen, if ever he saw them. They walked together but didn't speak to each other and, without so much as a look between them, they split apart, one sitting on a bench near the gate, the other strolling slowly around the square.

'If you were him, would you come alone?'

'No chance.'

They both peered around the corner of the library wall as Cope stopped at the bench outside the chapel, took out his handkerchief, and carefully dusted it off before hitching up his trousers and sitting down. He opened his newspaper and started to read, looking exactly like any other civil servant on his lunch hour.

Joe squared his shoulders against the wall and produced a pack of cigarettes and a box of matches. Stephen stood away from the wall and thrust his hands in his pockets, watching him light a cigarette.

'What do you want me to do?'

'Go and talk to him. You know what to say.'

'All right.' Stephen stepped out from cover and pulled his academic gown tighter around him. The weather had turned bitter and it didn't offer him much protection. He walked across the square, nodding to a couple of students he happened to know, and carefully studied Cope as he approached. As far as he could tell, he was who he'd said he was. He'd asked Billy Standing to make a few discreet enquiries, and had been encouraged by the report he'd got back one evening in Davy Byrne's pub.

'Andy Cope is a rather odd fish,' Billy had told him, inching forward on his stool and leaning closer, so that they could talk in whispers. 'Officially, he is what he told you he is – an assistant undersecretary. But the fact is, he's one of a handful of top men drafted in by Sir Warren Fisher to straighten out the Castle Administration. The strange thing is, he's left very much to his own devices. He keeps to himself, takes little part in the day-to-day work, and often disappears for long spells without telling anybody where he's going. Given the way things stand at the moment, you can be sure that's got a good few people talking.'

'What does the Chief Secretary have to say about it?' Stephen asked.

'Nothing at all – which is why his behaviour is tolerated. Cope himself is rather a remarkable creature. He started out as a runner in Customs and Excise, and has since climbed very high up the ladder. Last year, he was put in charge of the Ministry of Pensions, and basically managed to sort the place out before it collapsed – which people in the know tell me was nothing short of a miracle. As for his current position, the feeling in the Castle is that he answers to a power even higher than the Chief Secretary, if you know what I mean.' Billy tapped the side of his nose significantly. 'And the fact that he seems to brook no interference from either Colonel Winter's intelligence department, or even General Macready's army staff, rather smacks of his being an emissary of some sort. He is most definitely what the novelists would call a man of mystery.'

Stephen reached the bench and sat down. Cope made no acknowledgement of his presence, and didn't look up from his newspaper.

'Good afternoon, Mr Cope,' Stephen said, and Cope grinned as he folded his newspaper.

'Good afternoon, Mr Ryan. We meet again, it seems.'

'So it seems.'

'I don't wish to sound rude, but I had been hoping to be met by somebody else.'

'I've been asked to offer Mr Collins's apologies. He's otherwise engaged. I can speak for him in a very limited fashion. I've been told to hear what you have to say and arrange another meeting where we can exchange answers to any questions that might arise today.'

Stephen felt as if he was speaking from a script, and the tone was not lost on Cope. Nevertheless, he folded his newspaper and turned a little towards him. 'Very well. Are there any preliminary questions that our elusive friend asked you to put to me?'

'In the first place, he wants to know whom you speak for.'

'I speak for the Prime Minister,' Cope said, matter-of-factly. 'I speak for him directly and without any obstruction and, of course, completely unofficially. Should any newspaper reports attempt to link me or my activities with Mr Lloyd George, they will be denied. Of course, should you wish to see some bona fides, I can produce a letter—'

'I'm sure a man of your talents could produce a forged letter more easily than you could produce those two plainclothes men you brought with you,' Stephen observed. 'I think I'll take those at face value and we'll proceed for the time being.'

Cope looked at him, grinned, and then shrugged.

'I tip my hat to you, Mr Ryan. I believe you're not the mindless intermediary you make yourself out to be. Any other questions?'

'He also wants to know exactly what it is you want.'

'Ah, now here's where the questions get harder to answer.' Cope grinned again, then paused to gather his thoughts. 'In simple terms, I want to put a stop to this dirty little war we're in the middle of.'

'A war? I didn't think the Prime Minister was prepared to dignify it by calling it a war.'

'The Prime Minister says what he has to say, and to whom he must say it in order to keep the ship of state afloat. I, on the other hand, am at liberty to speak as I please, and I firmly believe in calling a spade a spade. People are being shot every other day, there are houses burned, beatings, kidnappings, and the capital city of this country is being kept under martial law. We are at war, Mr Ryan, and since you've already been through one war, I'm sure you're as keen as I am to stop this one before it gets out of hand.'

'And how do you propose to stop it?'

'A truce, an armistice. Call it what you want. We'll agree to stop shooting if you will.'

'Just like that?' Stephen gave him a disbelieving look. 'It took you four years to stop shooting the last time.'

'Yes, and I think we've all learned our lesson from that,' Cope responded, grimacing. 'But we both know that the real problem with war is that it's self-sustaining. The more men killed, the more reasons for not giving in. The trick is to get people to stop fighting without looking like they've surrendered.'

'You're assuming, of course, that the other side wants to stop fighting. What if they don't?'

'Of course they do. They've been wanting to stop ever since they started. Only fools and lunatics are glad to go to war. The whole point was to drag us to the negotiating table, and here we are. Not there just yet, but getting closer.'

'Fools and lunatics?' Stephen muttered. 'I was glad to go to war once. Which do you think I am?'

Cope laughed, folded his newspaper, and stood up.

'Until next week, then, Mr Ryan. Shall we say the same time and place?'

Stephen agreed, shook his hand, and watched Cope walk

towards the gate, waving his plainclothes companions to follow him. Then he got up and walked back around the corner of the library to where his brother waited.

'He wants to talk peace,' he said, in answer to a questioning look.

'I bet he does.'

Stephen glanced back across the square just in time to see Cope disappear under the gloomy arch of the front gate.

'You don't think he's genuine?'

'No, he's genuine, all right. But he's only the carrot. They have bigger sticks, and more of them. The Auxies are only one. That fella Winter above in the Castle is another. He runs a gang of intelligence men brought in special from London. He's not here to talk peace.'

'So which do you think it will be?'

Joe shrugged and shook his head. It was always more questions with his brother. What made him think he had any of the answers?

'I don't know. I suppose it'll be the carrot eventually – but we'll have to break the sticks first.'

Joe could hear somebody moving about inside; the scrape of an ash-pan in the grate, soft footfalls. The house was just waking. One look at Kelliher, a nod, and he reached up and rapped lightly on the door. No answer, no sign of a change. He looked up and down the empty street. Byrne stood at one end, his brother at the other – both of them pressed tight into doorways so you'd have to look hard to see them. Joe knocked again and there was a clank and then the whisper of bare feet coming to the door.

'Good morning to you, love,' he said into the crack that opened, revealing a bleary young face, hair straggling from under a nightcap, and a hand clutching a shawl under her throat. The door started to close, but he got his foot in and pushed into the hallway.

'We're here for Captain Bagely,' he said in a half-whisper. 'You've nothing to worry about. Now go down to the kitchen and stay there until we're gone.'

Out on Pembroke Street, Stephen stood in his doorway and kept his hands thrust into the pockets of his greatcoat. It was a sharp, clear winter's morning, barely bright, and the air was cold. He could see his own breath misting on it, feel it pinching his ears. He looked up and down the street but saw nothing. Sunday morning in the city, and all was quiet.

But he didn't feel quiet in his mind. Joe had sprung this on him very suddenly, hammering on his door at seven o'clock that morning.

'I told you I didn't want to get involved,' he had said, after Joe had explained what he wanted him for.

'Well, you didn't mind getting involved when we went to pick up Garvey.'

'That was different.'

'And what about what you did over in Mayo? Was that different too?'

'You know bloody well it was,' Stephen had said, lowering himself into an armchair. He was still in his pyjamas, barefoot and cold. 'Everything's changed. I met Cope again the other day. You saw that – you watched me talk to him. And now you want me to go off and help you shoot somebody?'

'You don't have to shoot anybody,' Joe had said. 'Just keep watch, like I said. Come on, Stephen, it won't take long, and I need somebody I can trust.'

Stephen shivered and turned up the collar of his greatcoat. Bloody stupid, he thought, blowing on his hands and then thrusting them back into his pockets, where he could feel the hard shape of the revolver on his hip. He had thought twice about bringing it with him, but he was glad he had. He'd had a bad feeling about this from the moment he'd opened the door to his brother, but it had worsened as they turned off Leeson Street, and he had thought to ask his brother who the target was.

'We're going after Winter's mob,' Joe had explained. 'Intelligence men sent over from London – ex-army, most of them. We call them the Cairo gang.'

'How many of them are there?'

'About fifteen.'

'Jesus Christ!'

Joe had laughed. 'Don't worry, Stephen – they're not all in the one place. They're in hotels and boarding houses all over town.' He grinned at his brother. 'They don't know it yet, but a few of our lads will be joining them for breakfast this morning.'

Breakfast. Joe remembered his words as the maid went scampering down to the kitchen and the smell of sausages came wafting out to him. He shouldn't have been so flip about it, he thought, feeling the knot in his stomach and swallowing the nausea that the smell brought on. Kelliher was beside him, pulling the gun from his pocket – all business, as usual. But then, he didn't know what Joe knew; that Dick McKee and Peadar Clancy had been picked up by the Auxiliaries the night before. The two top men in the Dublin Brigade, who had planned this operation between them and knew every part of it by heart. He'd heard nothing more except that they'd been taken to the Castle – and he knew very well what waited for them there. If they had talked, then God only knew what was waiting for them at the top of the stairs.

'Are you right, Joe?' Kelliher whispered, nodding up towards the gloomy landing. Joe pulled the gun from his pocket, cocked it, and set off up the stairs. He told himself that he knew exactly what was up there. The picture had been put together from a dozen different sources. Captain Bagely would be in the back bedroom. He would be in there with his wife. They normally rose at nine on a Sunday, had breakfast, and went to Sunday Service at the Peppercanister Church. All very normal, all very proper. But Joe also knew that Captain Bagely had his hands dirty. Murder, torture . . . he mightn't be too surprised to see them, after all. His wife, on the other hand . . .

Joe stepped up on the landing and, as he did so, the floor creaked loudly under him. He stopped and listened. He could hear two voices; one a woman's, laughing, the other deeper, sonorous. There was the door; pale cream, and gleaming in the light that streamed in through the landing window. Gently, quietly, he shifted his weight and walked softly towards it. Then he waited until Kelliher was ready on the other side. His heart was thumping, his mouth was dry, but he was reaching for the handle. A twist, a kick, and they were in. The wife was sitting in bed and Bagely was at the washstand, shaving. Joe saw his eyes widening in the mirror, then heard the razor clatter into the basin.

'Captain . . .' he began, but Bagely was already spinning round to face him, low and dangerous. Joe pulled the trigger and the bang of the gun seemed to shatter the air in the room. Bagely stumbled back against the washstand, his mouth gaping, and a revolver fell from his hand. Joe fired again and the wife screamed, her shriek piercing the echo of the second shot.

'Shut up!' he shouted, turning on her. She was slumped sideways in the bed, both hands over her mouth, sobbing as she stared wildly at her husband lying dead against the washstand. She screamed again and curled up in a frightened ball, trying to wriggle away from the gun he was pointing at her. He dropped his arm. He could feel his hand shaking already. 'I . . .' he began, looking at the pathetic figure in the bed; terror, hatred, God knows what on her face. 'I'm sorry, missus.'

'Come on, Joe.' Kelliher touched his arm. 'Let's get out of here.'

Outside, Stephen scraped the sole of his shoe on the iron boot-scraper, clenched his fists, yawned, and looked into the sky. He was getting nervous. It felt like they'd been inside for hours, and he could hear signs of life behind the door he was standing against. What would happen if the door opened behind him? How would he explain himself to the startled maid? He watched a white cloud scudding by, floating over the curving walls of the houses. This was not war. Neat brickwork and high roofs, windows gazing down on an empty street. A milk cart clopped down the next street, the churns ringing like bells in the still air. Where was the noise of battle? Where were the trenches and the wire, the stink of gas and death and fear? This was not the sort of battlefield he was used to.

Thump. A door closed down the street. He saw Joe and the other man coming down the steps. Stephen straightened, frowned at them. They were coming towards him but he hadn't heard anything: no shots, no screams, nothing out of the way. What had happened?

'Is it done?' he asked, coming down the steps to meet them.

Joe didn't answer. He looked away, and Stephen could see his face was white and his breathing quick and shallow. He stumbled a little, his boot nails scraping on the flags.

'It's done, all right,' the other man said, supporting his brother by the arm. 'Give us a hand here, will you? I'd say he's not the better of it yet.'

It was starting to get dark by the time Nightingale came out of the barracks and looked down the length of the Castle yard. The crowds had gone, but there were still a few stragglers standing around, some of them looking hopefully in his direction, all of them looking lost.

The mess hall door opened and Hitchins came out with his hands in his pockets, whistling a tune. Nightingale had glimpsed him when the lorry rolled in the gate, bringing the men back from the football match, his face flushed as he laughed with the others riding in the back. He knew that look from the war. It was the look of a man who'd had his first brush with action and survived. He also knew how quickly it faded, and he could tell that Hitchins's euphoria had already turned to melancholy, and he was only whistling to stave it off. Even a good dinner had not brightened him up, and he slunk across the yard with his head bowed, a slovenly looking creature.

'They're all gone, then,' he said to Nightingale. 'Or most of them, at any rate.'

'Most of them,' Nightingale agreed, staring at a bulky man in a long overcoat, who appeared to be rooted to the spot in a corner of the yard. What was his story? he wondered. Though he had wondered that a lot when he saw them streaming in that morning, arriving in a long queue of cars and taxicabs that blocked the gate. Men, women and children had all come crowding in together, most of them with bags, cases, even bits of furniture.

'Fucking parasites,' Hitchins remarked, hawking up a gobbet of phlegm and spitting on the cobbles. 'The Micks kill a few of Winter's mob and look what happens. Every rat in the city comes running in here for shelter.'

Nightingale didn't reply. Even if what Hitchins had said was true, he couldn't reconcile it with the little girl he'd seen, sitting on a trunk in her blue pinafore and straw hat, clutching a doll to her chest. It was a tangled bloody web they had woven.

'What happened at the match?' he asked, for he could feel that Hitchins wanted to talk about it, and he was curious.

'We bagged a few Micks.' Hitchins grinned, and he was about to say more when a voice cracked like a whip across the yard.

'You men! What the fuck do you think you're doing there?'

It was Captain King, and they both instantly straightened, Hitchins surreptitiously trying to fasten his tunic. The captain came bearing down on them with his face like thunder and his compact, hard body bouncing furiously over the cobbles. Despite his ferocity, Nightingale liked King. He was a hard man but he was a good soldier. He'd met a few tough characters here, but he reckoned half of them were shams. They drank too much, talked too much, and had the nervous excitability of raw recruits. Hitchins was one of these. God knew how he had survived the war, but it hadn't been by fighting. King was different. King had wound stripes and medals, and he wore both with pride, but never bragged about them. Nightingale thought that if the day ever came when he got into a real killing fight with the IRA, then King was the man he'd want to have at his back. He was the real thing.

For his part, King recognized another man who'd seen real fighting, and the fire and fury he breathed was directed not at Nightingale, but at Hitchins, whom he despised.

''Itchins,' he murmured, in a deadly undertone, his basilisk's eye glaring at the unfortunate Hitchins, who had managed to fasten three buttons of his tunic through the wrong holes. 'You 'orrible little sack of shit. You get into that fucking barracks and don't come out again until you look like a proper fucking soldier!'

They were none of them proper soldiers, Nightingale reflected, but he knew Hitchins wasn't going to argue the point.

'Y-yes, sir!' he exclaimed, saluted, and set off at a run. When he was gone, King's expression softened as much as it ever did. He jerked his head towards the guardroom and dropped his voice to a hoarse, conspiratorial whisper.

'Got a little job for you, Mr Nightingale. You'd better come with me.'

Nightingale followed him diagonally down the yard towards the guardroom. He wasn't expecting any conversation, but King suddenly spoke.

'Fourteen all.'

Nightingale frowned. King was moving at his usual furious pace, and he wasn't sure if he'd heard him correctly.

'I beg your pardon?'

'I said, fourteen all. The Micks got fourteen of ours this morning,' King explained, a note of grudging admiration in his voice. 'And we got fourteen of theirs at that Mick football match. But now we're gonna score the winning goal. Just you wait and see!'

King burst into the guardroom without so much as a knock, and Nightingale followed him in. The room was badly lit, but the smell that assailed him was all too familiar; the stench of stale sweat and blood and fear. There was a man lounging on a chair by the door with a rifle across his knees, and he jumped up sharply as they entered. But that wasn't what caught Nightingale's eye. Against the far wall there was a wooden bench, and three men were slumped on it, their heads bowed as if they were asleep.

'McKee!' King barked, and the middle one looked up. His face was grey and shrunken, but otherwise unmarked. But his shirt was bloodstained and open to the waist, and underneath Nightingale could see the mottling of bruises all over his chest. His eyes met Nightingale's and he mumbled something, but too low to be audible.

'Don't you start talking your fucking Hottentot again!' King told him in a loud voice, and then he explained to Nightingale.

'They always talk fucking Irish like they think it's gonna save them. But it's not today, is it, boys? No, no, no. You and your mates have been very naughty, and somebody has to pay for all the damage.'

'Who are they?' Nightingale asked in a whisper, feeling all their eyes turned upon him now. They had all been badly beaten, and they were all looking at him like wounded animals; fearful, horrified, but also pleading.

'This one's McKee and this one's Clancy, and the one on the end there is Clune,' King said, stirring each one with his foot. 'Big men, they are, aren't you, boys? Big men in the IRA, but you ain't so big now, are you, eh?' He bent down and grabbed the middle one by the chin, twisting his face upwards. 'Or would you it prefer if I called you Brigadier McKee? Eh?'

'I'm only a printer,' the man mumbled, gasping and fumbling over each word.

'Bollocks,' King spat, and pushed his face away with a savage twist. 'You're a brigadier, and this one here's a colonel.' Again, he turned to Nightingale. 'These two were behind this morning's little operation. Clune was in it as well, somehow.'

'Did they confess?' Nightingale asked, but he had a sinking feeling that he already knew what King's answer was going to be.

'Fuck, no. They're tough buggers, these boys. Wouldn't give us anything more than a name and fucking address. But we know it was them, sure as eggs is eggs. And now they're gonna pay the fucking price, make no mistake. You.' King jerked his head at the man sitting by the door. 'Get outside that door and don't let nobody in, no matter what fucking happens.'

King unholstered his service revolver and handed it to Nightingale without looking at him. Nightingale took it in a clammy, shaking hand. He was used to combat – he was even used to killing – but this? King never even noticed. Quickly taking off his tunic and draping it over the empty chair, he went to the rack of rifles chained against the wall and twisted the bayonet off the barrel of one.

'Now, my beauties,' he said, coming back with a vicious gleam in his eye, 'which one of you wants to talk first?'

XVI

A week went by and Cope failed to appear at his usual time. Stephen was disappointed, but not surprised. As he pieced together what had happened, he had scarcely been able to reconcile the momentous events of that Sunday with the few minutes he'd spent skulking in a doorway. Even the newspapers hadn't quite done it justice. They had given all the details; lurid accounts of men storming into houses, of the horror that had followed at Croke Park. But they had not captured the sense of shock that had settled over the city in the days that followed. People went about their business quietly and meekly and the police and the Auxiliaries kept mostly to themselves. But beneath this peaceful façade there was a dreadful tension. It seemed as if the city was ready to explode, and the smallest thing might set it off. Stephen knew that this was no time for doves, and Cope had had his wings clipped.

Another week passed before Joe called at the flat. He made no mention of what had happened that day, or what had come after-wards, but he brought news of Garvey.

'They banished him,' he said.

'Banished him? What the hell does that mean?'

'It means they sent him to England,' Joe answered tiredly. 'It's a suspended death sentence. If he sets foot back in Ireland he'll be killed.'

'That's it? That's all? I thought they *were* going to kill him. I thought that's what they did to informers.'

'They couldn't prove he was a tout. He wouldn't admit to it, and they had no witnesses.'

Stephen shook his head. If ever he wanted proof that this secret government with its secret army was trying to act legitimately, here it was. Proof, sentences, trials. There was some sort of legal machinery there, but it was infuriating.

'Then what did they banish him for?' he demanded.

'For murder,' Joe answered, and he looked his brother directly in the eye, daring him to push it. Stephen just shook his head.

As Christmas came closer, life seemed to return to normal, but it was still far from normal. The city itself was quiet, but news filtered in of new attacks and atrocities all over the country. The war was intensifying, and although there were no single incidents on the scale of that day in November, it felt like the violence was building up to an even higher pitch. Some Auxiliaries were killed in an ambush and the entire city of Cork was burned as a reprisal. Then there were more ambushes and skirmishes, and more men killed; three here, six there. Houses were burned and whole villages terrorized.

Soon, it seemed like hardly a day went by without another murder, but Stephen felt as if he was remote from it. His days were filled with lectures and seminars, with research and the abstract beauty of mathematics. In the evenings, there was Lillian. Sometimes they went out to the theatre or the cinema, sometimes she came to the flat and they spent a few hours in Stephen's narrow bed. One night, as they lay together, he feeling her heart beating next to his, he realized that it had finally arrived – that *this*, this was happiness. This moment of bliss, and the next one, and the long hours of anticipation that might lie in between, it was all he had ever dreamed of.

But still, he watched for Cope. As he crossed the front square every morning he looked towards the bench where they had met, half expecting to see him there, in his stylish suit with a carnation in his buttonhole. Sometimes, if he had a few minutes to spare, he took a turn around the square – even when the snow lay thick over the cobbles he crunched through it, brushed it from the slats of the bench and sat down for a few minutes – but Cope failed to appear.

Then, one evening towards the end of January, he saw a familiar figure standing near the front gate of the college. It wasn't Cope, but Stephen would have recognized that gangly shape anywhere. And yet, his first impulse was to run, to turn off into the library or find some convenient door he could bolt into. He might have done, too, had not the figure spotted him, and waved.

'Well, Stephen,' Nightingale said, shaking his hand. 'This is where you work, is it?' He looked around the square as if seeing it for the first time. 'Good for you. I always knew you had brains to burn. Do you like it here?'

Stephen shook his hand warily. Nightingale was dressed in civilian clothes, but he was wearing heavy boots and his army greatcoat over his suit. Stephen had worn one of those once but, somehow, it hadn't made him look so much like an Auxiliary.

'What are you doing here?' Stephen asked, looking around in case somebody was watching. He found it hard to meet his friend's eyes, but when he did, he was shocked at what he saw. Nightingale was unshaven, his eyes sunken and his cheeks hollow. His hands were shaking and he had to swallow hard before he could speak again.

'I need to talk to you, Stephen,' he said. 'I need your help.'

I need your help. Those words stayed with Stephen all evening. Lillian came around to the flat, and he managed to push them to the back of his mind, but as the night wore on, the thought of Nightingale weighed on him more and more.

'What's the matter, Stephen?' Lillian asked, after she had propped herself up on one elbow and studied him for a few moments.

'Nothing,' he murmured sleepily. It was late, and he knew she'd have to go home soon, but for now he was happy to let the time drag by as he lay there with her in the bed beside him, feeling the warmth of her body next to his.

'It's not nothing,' she said. 'Something's troubling you, I can tell.'

'I met an old friend tonight,' he said, and told her how Nightingale had been waiting for him at the college gate. He had told her about Nightingale before, and she knew very well who he was and, more to the point, *what* he was.

'What did he want?' she asked, frowning.

'I'm not sure. Absolution, I suppose. He's done some things . . .' Stephen rolled over and traced the curve of her neck with his fingers, feeling the soft brush of her hair, and the warmth of the skin on her naked shoulder. He often wondered how much he should tell her. She was strong, and not in the least bit squeamish, but there was something else about her, a sort of purity that might be sullied by the gory details. 'He's done some things he isn't happy about, and he doesn't want to be an Auxiliary any more. He says it's worse than thuggery. He's probably right.'

'Then why doesn't he resign?'

'He needs the money. He's planning to move to Canada and he needs to stay in until he's made enough. Besides, his contract still has another six months to run.'

'Well, there's not much you can do about that, is there?'

'No, I know. But . . .' Stephen rolled over again, and fixed his eyes on the ceiling. 'That's not what's bothering me. It's the way I treated him. He came to me for help – even if it was just a shoulder to cry on – and I could barely even stand to give him the time of day. I told him he'd made his bed, he'd just have to bloody well lie in it.'

Lillian rolled over and kissed him. He brought his hand up to brush her hair away from her face, and she smiled at him.

'You have a good heart, Stephen Ryan,' she said. 'He was your friend before. You can't help what he's become now.'

'I would have walked through fire for him before,' Stephen said unhappily. 'What's happened to us? How on earth did it ever come to this?'

As winter turned to spring, Stephen managed to forget all about Cope. He was a busy man; his teaching duties had increased, and he found himself sufficiently confident to start working on a new paper. It would be a solo effort this time, and nowhere near as ambitious as the one on the transcendental method, but for the first time in his life he realized that there was no rush. He was twenty-five years old. He had plenty of time.

Then, one bright May day, when the summer exams were looming, and the trees in the square were full of leaf and blossom, Cope reappeared. Stephen was walking out to lunch with Lillian when, out of the corner of his eye, he saw somebody reading a newspaper on that very bench. The newspaper came down, and there was the carnation, and an elegant hat shading his eyes. Stephen stopped so suddenly that Lillian, with her arm linked through his, was pulled up short.

'Stephen? What's the matter?' she asked.

'Wait here a minute,' he told her, and walked over to the bench. Cope looked up as he approached and grinned.

'Well, well. Professor Ryan, how do you do?'

'I'm sorry to say, I'm still not a professor.'

'Oh? A man of your talents?' Cope looked downcast for a moment but then his face brightened. 'Still, it will happen one of these days. I'm sure these things take time. All good things take time.'

'They certainly do.' Stephen stood before him, his hands thrust in his pockets, waiting.

'Won't you sit down?' Cope gestured to the other end of the bench. 'It's so long since we last spoke, I'm sure we have such a lot to talk about.'

'I can't stop, I'm afraid.' Stephen glanced over his shoulder. 'I was just on my way out to lunch with my fiancée.'

'Ah yes, the charming Miss Bryce.' Cope tipped his hat and smiled at Lillian. 'Why don't you ask her to join us?'

'I'd rather not. She's not involved in any of this.'

'Well, then, what can I say? I'm sure you know why I'm here.'

Stephen shrugged. 'To tell you the truth, I'm not certain. You've been gone such a long time I hadn't expected to see you again. After what happened, I was sure you'd been recalled.'

'I *was* recalled.' Cope shrugged. 'Officially, I went home for Christmas but, not to put too fine a point on it, I was summoned home to help put out the fires that had broken out. Very angry fires, I might add, that took a great deal of putting out. However, I believe the worst is past, and while I was there I spoke to my friend Mr Lloyd George. He was very interested to hear about our little chats.'

'I'm sure he was,' Stephen said, and added with a smile, 'it seems he thought he had murder by the throat, but then he lost his grip.'

'Quite.' Cope's lips twitched into an involuntary smile, but his eyes hardened. 'I'm sure he'll learn his lesson about making rash statements, just as we all must. But you should appreciate that, compared to some of the talk I heard around Whitehall, his words sound like the very soul of reason.'

Stephen nodded. He had no great love for Lloyd George, but he knew that the Prime Minister was quite moderate compared to some of the men who stalked the corridors of power. According to Billy, a few were already in Dublin Castle, but there were many more hotheads only too anxious to get in.

'What sort of talk?'

'Well, let's just say that for some, the answer to the Irish question starts with more troops – and I mean whole divisions – and ends with concentration camps.'

'Concentration camps?'

Cope gave him a surprised look that turned into a sour smile. 'Come come, professor. I would have thought a logical mind like yours would appreciate the argument. Concentration camps worked for us in South Africa, why would they not work here?'

'There would be outright war,' Stephen told him.

Cope shrugged.

'That's the beauty of it, you see. We could win an outright war – that's exactly what the proponents of this course are hoping for – but we'll never win this endless tit-for-tat business. Mr Collins and his men will never beat us by themselves, but with the press and public opinion on their side, they can certainly make a fair show of it. All they have to do to win is stay standing, and there is a certain school of thought that says we must knock them down, whatever it takes.'

Cope glanced up at the clock and started to fold his newspaper. Stephen took the opportunity to study him more closely. There was more grey in his hair, he thought, and his face, though still smooth and handsome, looked more haggard than it had before.

'And are you in agreement with this school of thought?' he asked.

'No. My position is as it was before. Sooner or later we will have to talk, and sooner is always better than later.'

The bells of Christchurch started to tell the hour, the sound carrying down faintly on the breeze and Stephen looked once more at Lillian. She stood waiting patiently where he'd left her.

'Best not to keep her waiting,' Cope advised, standing up and folding his newspaper under one arm, then draping his overcoat over the other. But Stephen stood his ground.

'Where do we go from here?'

'Where?' Cope shook his head. 'God knows. But it seems to me that we must learn to trust one another before we go anywhere.'

'And how do we do that?'

'To be honest, I'm not sure. Perhaps we *can't* trust each other.' Cope shook his head again, but then took a deep breath and seemed to consider a moment. When he spoke again his voice was low and urgent, almost a whisper. 'Please remember that what I'm about to tell you could cost me my job, and perhaps even my life, if the wrong people find out about it. I'm sure it's no secret that the authorities know more about the movements of the IRA than the IRA would like. I'll not explain how this comes to be, but I dare say you can guess. In any event, the military commanders in Dublin Castle are aware of an operation that is being planned, and which they believe will take place within the next week. They don't know where it will take place, or exactly when, but they do know it will consist of a massed attack by IRA soldiers on a prominent government building. Needless to say, the Administration is prepared for this, and means to turn it to their advantage by either capturing or killing as many of the IRA's men as they can.'

Stephen gave him a piercing look. 'Why are you telling me

this? Do you want me to have it called off? Surely it's to your advantage to just let them—'

'It's a token of trust,' Cope said, with an edge in his voice. 'Yes, of course it would be to our advantage to let this attack proceed – but only in the short term. In the long term the advantage will lie with the IRA. Their organization thrives on martyrs – as we have already learned the hard way – and even if the attack were defeated it would be an embarrassment to the Administration and to the Empire.'

'You defeat your own argument, Mr Cope,' Stephen warned, with a grim smile. 'If I pass on your warning and the attack is cancelled, then the greater gains are on your side, are they not?'

'You were a soldier once, professor.' Cope looked at him candidly. 'You know better than I do that the IRA has neither the men nor the equipment to carry out massed attacks – and certainly not against a superior force that knows they are coming. Yes, in the short term, it will be a victory for us, and in the long term perhaps a greater victory for the IRA – but at what cost? Men will be killed, others will go to jail, and this blasted war will continue until doomsday. I told you it was a question of trust, and I need you to trust me when I tell you that I offer this information, not in the interests of saving the blushes of my government, but of stopping the war. I want to stop the war, Mr Ryan, that is all.'

Stephen could feel the intensity of his gaze, and he knew that, whatever greater game was going on around him, Cope was sincere in what he said.

'I will pass your message on,' he said after a few moments. 'I can't guarantee that it will get through and, even if it does, you understand it might not be heeded.'

'Of course.' Cope nodded, smiling. He seemed relieved. 'But you will try?'

'I'll try.' Stephen held out his hand, and Cope shook it.

'Well, then, that's good enough for me.'

Joe followed Kelliher up the stairs. The petrol tin was heavy and sloshed noisily as he climbed. Kelliher was going fast, taking the steps two at a time, his coat tails flying until he reached the landing and burst out into a long corridor. Joe came out after him, changing hands on the tin and wiping his palm on his coat. The top must have been leaking, because he could smell the stuff and his hands were all wet.

Kelliher walked over to the window and looked out. From where he stood, Joe could see only some buildings on the opposite quay and, further up the river, the iron lattice of the loop line bridge. But Kelliher looked down into the street below.

'All clear,' he said, and they both looked up and down the corridor. Door after door stretched away into the distance, and the polished floor gleamed in the sunlight that poured in through the windows. Not a soul stirred from one end of the building to the other, and it seemed eerily quiet after all the running and shouting downstairs.

'Where do we start?' Joe asked.

'It's the middle office,' Kelliher said. 'That's where all the papers are.'

Off he went again, his coat tails flying, only now he had his pistol out, holding it down towards the floor as he went. Joe lumbered after him with the petrol tin. He knew he should have been off on his own, but they'd deliberately put him with Kelliher. They trusted Kelliher; he was reliable, but Joe had too many things hanging over him. The way he'd folded after he shot Bagely on Mount Street had got back to Paddy Daly, who hadn't been pleased about him bringing his brother in on a job without telling anybody. Then there was all that business with

Garvey. Even though he'd done no wrong, Joe hadn't come out of it well. They all knew Garvey was dirty and, even if they couldn't prove it, most of them believed he was an informer – but Joe was so tightly wrapped up in the whole thing that some of Garvey's dirt had rubbed off on him, and he knew he was no longer trusted. He'd known that even before he brought the warning from his brother, so he was hardly surprised at the reception it got. Still, he'd promised to pass it on, and he'd passed it on. And now here they were.

A door squeaked open somewhere, and the clacking of a typewriter echoed down the corridor. Joe looked over his shoulder, but he could see nothing. Kelliher reached the middle door and barged in without knocking. Joe followed him in. It was a large office, filled with wooden cabinets and shelves and shelves of files, but there were only two people inside. A round bald-headed little man sat at the desk, staring at them through his wire spectacles. Across from him, a woman sat with a notepad on her knee and a pencil at the ready. She gaped at Joe, then at the petrol can.

'What is the meaning of this?' the little man yelped, half-standing out of his chair.

'Youse need to leave,' Kelliher said, jerking his thumb over his shoulder. 'Go on, skedaddle.'

'But . . . but who are you? You can't simply order us to leave.'

'Yes I can.' Kelliher showed him the gun, and the little man's face blanched. 'Now, you better get downstairs, unless the pair of you want to be burned alive.'

They didn't need to be told twice, and Joe tipped his hat to them as they ran out the door. Then he put the petrol tin on the floor and helped Kelliher pile ledgers and files on the desk. Tax records, letters, bills. The musty smell of ink and old paper didn't last long once Joe opened the tin and drenched it all with petrol.

'That'll make a nice little blaze,' Kelliher remarked, when the tin was empty and they stood back to admire their handiwork. Joe didn't have time to answer before they heard the crack of gunfire from outside.

'Sounds like our friends are here.' Kelliher grinned, and they ran back into the corridor and looked out the nearest window. Down below, Joe could see a policeman running down Custom House Quay. He stopped, fired off two shots, and then darted into the shadow of the Loop Line Bridge. There were more of them there, and he saw the flash of gunfire from underneath the bridge. Faint screams rose up from the civilians scattering across Beresford Place.

'Give us a hand, Joe,' Kelliher said, and between them they lifted the heavy sash of the window. Kelliher rested his arms on the sill and started to fire, slowly, deliberately, towards the bridge. Joe took the revolver from his pocket, cocked it, but hesitated. What was the point? The police were already here, and there would be more on the way. They'd have the place surrounded in no time. Then what were they supposed to do? They'd be hemmed in against the river, stuck in a burning building with no means of escape. Stephen had been right. They had no advantage here. They'd be slaughtered.

'What are you waiting for, Joe?' Kelliher demanded, as he fired off his last shot and then tipped the empty shells from his revolver. He fished in his pocket for some more ammunition and started to reload. Even as he did that, he was grinning, panting, his face ecstatic. Joe didn't feel like that. He just felt tired – sick and tired. The smell of the petrol was making him nauseous.

'Go on, Joe, give them a few bangs,' Kelliher urged, but then they heard the shrill of a whistle from downstairs. Two long blasts, followed by shouts, and a renewed volley of gunfire.

'That's the signal,' Kelliher said. He jerked his head back towards the office. 'Burn it.'

Joe walked back into the office and tore a page out of one of the big ledgers. The petrol soaked his hands, and he felt slightly dizzy with the fumes as he balled it up and went back out into the corridor. Kelliher was still at the window, blazing away.

'Come on, you fuckers! Come out where I can see you!'

Joe stood with his back to the wall and watched him until he ran out of ammunition again. Then he took the matches from his pocket.

'Are you right, Ned?'

'Go on, Joe. Light it up.'

The petrol-soaked paper lit with a puff, and Joe had to throw it quickly to avoid burning his fingers. *Woof*. The room went up so quick he felt it through the wall. Then smoke and flame poured out through the door, and the still air in the corridor started to dance with the heat.

The street was full of smoke. It swirled and curled on an eddy of the breeze, dipping now and then to brush his face and make his eyes water as he stumbled along. Sometimes big friable sheets of smouldering ash drifted through it, and he had to dodge them, swatting them away with one hand as the other held a handkerchief over his mouth.

He had smelled the smoke first. It had come drifting in through the window of the common room and he knew in an instant what it meant. He went outside and saw the thin grey spindle twisting up into the clear sky. But where was it coming from? Was it across the river? Then a porter came running to say it was the Custom House. The Custom House was on fire, and there was shooting down there as well. Stephen knew he'd failed. He knew they'd gone ahead anyway.

Joe had been surprised by what he told him, but he didn't seem dismayed.

'Dev wants an open fight,' he said, shrugging. 'There'd be no fight if the other side didn't show up.'

'Remember the last time you had an open fight? Remember what happened? They'll crush you.'

But he knew from the look on his brother's face that he wasn't listening. He was resigned.

'They'll crush you,' he said again. 'They'll bring the army, the police, the Auxiliaries. The minute you come out in the open, they'll be down on you like a ton of bricks.'

'But we have to prove we can take them on,' Joe burst out. 'We have to show them we can take over something bigger than a police barracks. We have to show them that we're an army, and not just a bunch of fellas with pistols.'

Something about this didn't ring true. It wasn't his brother talking. His brother would have said it with conviction, with fire in his eyes. But then Stephen realized that he hadn't seen *that* in his brother for a long time. Not since . . . well, he couldn't remember. Something had killed his conviction, but he couldn't be sure what it was. Guilt, perhaps, over the death of his grandfather – but then, they'd never been that close. Or else this business with Garvey. Whatever had gone on there had cut him deep, but they had never spoken about the girl, or about what had happened to her. All he knew was that his brother was drifting, he had lost his belief, and now he was only going through the motions.

'I'll pass on what you told me,' Joe said. 'But it won't make any difference. The job will go ahead.'

'Where?' Stephen asked, but his brother shook his head.

'I don't know yet. But it'll be in all the newspapers – you can bet on that. We may die famous.'

'You're mad,' Stephen said, and his brother just gave him a smile and walked away.

'You're mad,' Stephen said to himself, as he walked quickly

across O'Connell Bridge and turned down the quay towards the Custom House. The broad, handsome façade was now half obscured by a thick pall of smoke, the tall copper dome crumpling and collapsing as orange flames licked around it. People had come out of shops and offices to stand and gape and the lunchtime traffic had ground to a halt. But he heard a horn blaring, the revving of a heavy engine, and when he looked behind he saw three army lorries trying to push through the jam.

'You're bloody mad,' he muttered, as he turned into the alleyway and a blast of smoke hit him. He started to cough and fumbled for his handkerchief. What the hell did he think he was doing? He had no gun, and not much of a plan, either. Find his brother . . . and then what? Try to talk him out of it? It was a bit late for that. But, somehow, he knew he had to keep going. He had to be there because he was part of it – part of this whole sprawling mess. Whether he wanted to be or not, he was involved; he was tangled up in it just as much as anybody else. It was impossible for him not to be there. How could he just stand and look at the smoke? How could he stand by with all the others, and shake his head and then read about the outcome in the newspapers? He had to go. He had no choice.

He was nearly at the railway bridge. Something cracked through the smoke above his head and he ducked down automatically. Well, that was a familiar sound. He pressed himself closer to the wall and edged up to the corner. He was alone now, and this was the hard part. He could see clear across Beresford Place to the iron pillars of the railway bridge, and beyond that was the cobbled square around the Custom House, ringed with decorative stone bollards joined by chains. It was wide open, and under the pall of smoke he could see an army lorry and an armoured car, with plenty of men milling around on foot. As he watched, the lorry mounted the pavement and drove towards the knot of men standing near the side door of the Custom House. One of them darted towards it, and a few seconds later there was an explosion and the back of the lorry burst into flames. Two or three men jumped down, all of them on fire.

'Christ almighty!' Stephen whispered to himself, but he pressed on. He ran across Beresford Place and under the shadow of the railway bridge. He was close enough to hear the fire now, the flames crackling out the windows, and the low roar of it coming from inside the huge building. There was a loud clang above his head and he looked up. Ding! It went again, and he realized it was the sound of bullets hitting the bridge. There were soldiers out in the square, crouching down and darting for the meagre cover of a few ornamental bollards as more bullets cracked and spat off the cobbles. Just his bloody luck, he thought. If the soldiers didn't get him, then that bugger with the rifle surely would.

The thought of it made him hesitate. What was the bloody point? Even if he could get in, there was only a slim chance he might find Joe – and then what? What was he trying to do? He could hardly talk him into coming out, and even if he did, they were surrounded by soldiers, with plenty more on the way. But he knew it wasn't about that – he knew his brother would never come with him anyway. It was about doing something; a gesture, his duty – he didn't really know what to call it. The important thing was not to have done nothing. That was all.

But before he could think what to do next, things started happening out in the square. Part of the Custom House roof fell in, sending up a shower of livid orange sparks that glowed like stars even in the May sun. Then the armoured car growled into life. It inched its snout up on to the kerb and slowly ground down towards the main door of the Custom House, the turret on top rotating all the time. When it squealed to a halt, the machine gun fired a long burst right through the doors, the angry ripping noise of it echoing across the river. Finally, the two lorries he had seen on Eden Quay thundered across Beresford Place, ran right past him and screeched to a halt behind the armoured car. While they were still rocking on their springs, men started to jump down and scatter for cover along the quay. The net was closing. Almost without thinking, Stephen stepped out of cover and started to walk towards the side door of the Custom House.

'You there! Stop!' The voice was far away and he pretended not to hear it. He was focused on the doorway. He could feel the heat of the fire now, the warm kiss of it in a twist of the breeze. A rifle fired, and two bullets skipped off the cobbles just beside him. He couldn't ignore *that*, and dropped into a crouch, running for cover.

'Halt!' They were closer now, two of them running towards him. Out of the corner of his eye he saw tam-o'-shanters, bandoliers across their chests. They were Auxiliaries. 'Halt!' they both shouted hoarsely, and then one of them called his name, 'Stephen!'

He stumbled into the cover of a bollard, surprised, staring at the two Auxiliaries. The one on the left was Nightingale, sprinting towards him with his rifle held in one hand. The other was shorter, stouter, and already lagging behind.

'Stephen, what the bloody hell are you doing?' Nightingale panted. He dropped down behind the bollard, which hadn't even been big enough for one, never mind the two of them. Another shot cracked over their heads and they both flinched and then grinned at each other, old times remembered.

'I . . .' Stephen began, but his voice trailed off. He felt guilty. He'd used his friend for information and then shunned him for what he was, for what he'd become. He felt a deeper pang when he saw the insignia on his uniform. Nightingale had kept the old Dublin Fusiliers badges, the bronze bombs exploding on his lapels. He'd kept them because he was proud of them – just as Stephen had been proud of them once. And now, here they were, under fire together again.

'Where do you think you're going?' Nightingale asked. 'You can't go in there. The bloody place is burning.'

'My brother . . .' Stephen stumbled over the words again. He couldn't even explain it to himself, never mind anybody else.

'Get out of it.' Nightingale stood up, pulling him by the arm. 'Go back and take cover. This is no place for you.'

Stephen let him pull him up. He was right. He had tried. He had tried and failed. What more could he do?

'Go on, Stephen,' Nightingale said, pushing him gently. 'Go on, get back. This isn't your fight.'

Stephen nodded and reached out to shake his hand. He was right, of course. Then he heard the crack of the rifle and hot blood splashed his face. Nightingale's expression changed, his eyes widening in shock as he went down on his knees. Stephen had him by the arm, feeling his weight as he lowered him on to the cobbles.

'Oh Christ!' he gasped. There was blood pumping from Nightingale's throat, spraying and dribbling down his tunic. 'Jesus, no!' His hand darted to the wound, pressing his handkerchief to it, but it was soaked through in a second. Nightingale's hand had his sleeve in a tight grip, but he could feel it fading, slipping away. Another second and it was loose, the last breath sighing out of his body. Stephen stared at his blank face, tears pricking the corner of his eyes.

Still holding the lifeless arm, he heard boots running up and looked up, blinking away his tears. He saw an older man, his hard face florid and sweaty from running, his eyes bulging.

'He's dead,' Stephen said, and the man grunted and swung his rifle up and brought it crashing down on his head.

*

He could remember being on the lorry, but not how he got there. He was lying on the boards, feeling the vibration of the cobbles under him, feeling his body lolling and sagging as they turned corners. There was a splitting ache in his head and he could barely get his eyes open, but when he did he saw scuffed boots and puttees. He heard voices – English accents – and then it all faded again.

They manhandled him off the lorry and on to a stretcher. He remembered that much because they were none too gentle. He saw a blurry figure leaning over him, then winced, gasped and recoiled as unseen hands touched his head.

'Stay easy, now,' a gruff voice said, and the pain eased a little as something cold was poured on his wound. He felt a bandage being wrapped around his head, but still he couldn't open his eyes. After a few minutes he was on the move again. The pain in his head had eased, but it felt tender and, perhaps because he couldn't see, his hearing had become painfully acute. Every foot-fall, every scrape and thump pierced his ears like a nail. The rattle of keys in a lock and he winced as an iron door screeched open, then shuddered as it clanged shut behind them. More footsteps, the cold feel of stale air, and another door opening. Then he felt a bump and hands were lifting him, every nerve in his body screaming as it sagged and flopped down somewhere soft. Foot-steps, another screech and clang, and he was alone.

He didn't know how long he stayed like that. After a while he became more aware of his surroundings. The air was cool and damp and there was a strong stink of smoke. Eventually, he real-ized that the smell was coming off his clothes. He tried opening his eyes, and found he was looking at a rough stone wall. Just to make sure, he reached out and ran his fingers over it. It was real. He pushed himself up and looked around, blinking. He was in a small room, very gloomy, with a high window and an iron door. He was lying on a lumpy straw mattress with a single coarse blanket thrown over him. A prison cell.

After a while he turned and sat and listened. He could hear feet running, doors opening and closing, raised voices at a distance. They were busy. He stared at the door. There was a peephole in the centre, and sometimes he thought he heard whispering outside. Were they watching him?

Time passed. The meagre light from the high window gradually grew thinner and thinner, until the cell was in darkness and he could see a thin strip of light under the door. The noise outside grew less and less, and gradually he fell into a sort of trance. With his head leaning back against the wall, he stared at the door, imagining what he would see if he could look back out through the peephole. The world out there was mad, chaotic. It whirled around and flung things everywhere, heedless of what happened or where they fell. But in here it was quiet and calm. There was silence and stillness in the air. He closed his eyes for a few moments, and then opened them again when he heard the jangle of keys in the lock. The door swung open and a soldier walked in with an oil lamp. Without a word, he set it down in the middle of the floor and walked out again. Then Andy Cope came in.

'Well, professor,' he said, smiling his usual placid smile. 'It seems you've been in the wars again.'

Stephen didn't say anything at first. Cope, in his pale grey suit and spats, with his hat in his hand and his silver-topped cane, looked so incongruous that he thought he must be dreaming. But Cope chuckled and paced the short distance from door to wall.

'They really don't know what to make of you,' he said.

'Where am I?' Stephen asked.

'Richmond Barracks,' came the answer. 'And on the point of going before a military tribunal, I might add.'

'I haven't done anything. I wasn't even armed.'

'I know you weren't. But that doesn't explain what you were doing outside the Custom House.'

'Where's my brother?'

'He was inside the Custom House, it seems. He's now being detained in Kilmainham Jail. He *will* be going before a military tribunal, I'm afraid.'

Stephen looked out through the open door. It was quiet out there, too. No noise, no voices, no hurrying feet. Suddenly, he saw Nightingale again, felt the slackening grip on his arm. He swallowed.

'I tried to stop it,' he said, in an angry voice. 'But it can't be stopped.'

'Maybe it can't,' Cope agreed, walking back to the door. 'Maybe it's bigger than all of us. But then again, it will have to stop eventually, and we must keep trying until it does.'

'We?' Stephen shook his head, wincing as he did so. 'Why us? We've already failed.'

'Why us?' Cope smiled and put on his hat. 'Because there's nobody else, Mr Ryan. There is simply nobody else.'

He walked out into the corridor, turned and tipped his hat.

'You're free to go,' he said. 'I'll be in touch.'

And with that he was gone, and Stephen stared out through the open door, listening until the footsteps died away and the silence crowded in on him again. Then, with his joints creaking and his head throbbing, he slowly got to his feet and walked outside.